ONE:

ANGELS ARE HARD TO LOVE

ONE:
ANGELS ARE HARD TO LOVE

DARK CONTEMPORARY ROMANCE FOR STRONG WOMEN

AWAKENING MADNESS SERIES BOOK 1

BY KRISTIN KAY

Translated by: Dessi Nikko
Edited by: Benjamin Watts
Illustrated by: Mina Nacheva

ISBN Paperback:#978-1-3999-2211-1
ISBN Electronic:#978-1-3999-2212-8

Kristin Kay Ltd
AuthorKristinKay.com

DISCLAIMER
This book contains adult language, sexual and mature content, which may be offensive to some readers and is inappropriate for children. Reader discretion is advised. The thoughts, actions, and/or beliefs of characters in this book do not portray the thoughts, actions, and/or beliefs of the author.

Dedicated to
the misfits
who break the patterns
and make our reality extraordinary,
and to my parents, who taught me why to break them.

TABLE OF CONTENTS

vii

PLAYLIST

Do I wanna know - Arctic Monkeys
Layla - Eric Clapton
In A Manner Of Speaking - Nouvelle Vague
Bellyache – Billie Eilish
Englishman in New York - Sting
Burn for you – The Police
Feel Like I Am Drowning - Two Feet
Devil Eyes - Hippie sabotage
Happy Birthday Mr. President - Marilyn Monroe
Созвездие ангела (Cluster of the Angel Stars) - Jah Khalib
Babel - Gustavo Santaolalla
Game Of Thrones (Original Mix) - Mahmut Orhan

ONE:
ANGELS ARE HARD TO LOVE

BEFORE ONE

HER: *wondering who she was...*

It was over.

Another meaningless day was over. Relieved, I counted my 55 steps of something like joy, still bothered by the fact that there were 17 days left until the end of my internship. I didn't know what was coming next, and I had no clue how crazy the following weeks were going to be.

I stuffed my heels into my backpack, replacing them with my colourful trainers. A surge of people caught up with me as I leaned against one of the columns in the huge foyer. I hid behind it. I like hiding places. It's surprising how many dull spaces turn out to be great hiding places. My skin, for example.

He was walking among the crowd, eyes fixed straight ahead, as always. Or, should I say, as he had done the previous five times, I watched him from behind the column. An aura of superiority and a crown of people surrounded him.

I could detect a rhythm.

One of his suited, nervous followers was insistently trying to drag his attention to some documents. He shot a contemptuous glare at the man as if he was looking at a cockroach. I shrilled in annoyance as I recognised the folder I had copied earlier. The mistakes in the financial forecast were irritating, obvious, and there were dozens of them. Glowing. Burning my brain.

How could they abuse numbers like that? Damn it!

His arrogant gaze crossed mine. Or rather, his arrogant gaze sliced into mine. The rhythm of his steps changed. The rhythm of my breath changed as well.

A wave of shivers down my spine made me hide behind the column again.

HIM: *fighting with himself...*

Another idiot was shoving documents under my nose, struggling for my attention. I didn't remember his name. It didn't matter. They were all doing their best to be equally useless; it was difficult for me to tell one from the other.

They merged. They bored me. I despised them.

Their stupid mistakes were driving me crazy. I wondered if they made them on purpose, or whether I was supposed to accept that this was the limit of their pathetic minds.

Three years, five months, and thirteen days! I have another 1259 effing days left in this role I am playing. At least there's a specified end date...

On my way out, I tried my best not to think about the unbearable mediocrity that surrounded me. My brain cells were screaming, as if they were dying. A rage of intolerance crept up my bones. And then, suddenly, I was startled. My rhythm was interrupted.

A strange pair of eyes was peering at me from a distance. They slid down my bones, scratching and burning. I managed to pull myself together and continued coldly counting the remaining steps, my eyes fixed on the exit.

THEM: *not suspecting a thing...*

An incomprehensible vibration. You just know. No logic, no arguments. You are simply aware that something is about to happen. You are on fire. Goosebumps cover your skin. Intuitive sensations within you wave their red flags. Usually, people ignore it. Or maybe it's just twisted people, like those two, who tend to ignore it.

They didn't even suspect it was the beginning of a dark story. Madness. As with any other madness in the world, this one had its beginning, contained in that very second.

For no logical reason, the same echoed in their minds:

ONE!

ONE

The usual clacking of the train, over and over. Another morning on the metro, which smelled, looked, and sounded exactly like the morning before. The absolute lack of novelty raised questions of whether this day and the last were actually one and the same. I already suspected that this was the main purpose of life: similar days, repeated, so people wouldn't get too confused. Routine life carries the label of being "grey" for a reason. It is quite logical that it would be assigned a trivial colour with no vividness at all. Unremarkable, even.

I was counting: a knock to the left, two knocks to the right. The familiar rhythm of the wheels. Once again, I searched through the passengers for something new. But again, they merged into a dull, collective image, the same as yesterday, no different from the day before. The faceless view was making me sleepy, and the train showed no intention of surprising me with any unexpected bumps. All it would give me was its usual rhythm. I enjoyed creating a pattern of the sounds. My attention would drift away. The cacophony in my twisted mind would still for a while. The questions, the arguments, the debates—they would all stop. The entities in my head would keep silent. Even loquacious *Reason* swayed wordlessly to the rhythm.

My eyes squinted as I scanned the general reality around me. It was impossible for me to comprehend many of its details, and I often pondered on them. This morning as well, of course, since it was exactly like yesterday's morning. I was thinking:

Smooth, monotonous, uniform sounds. Same as people. People manage to be equally mundane, even if they ride on different trains in different directions, well aware of the purpose of routine life: all days must be the same. Maybe that's what happiness is. People wake up in the morning, start existing, and the most challenging sensation of the day is the flavour of their toothpaste. They probably even frown at it for being provocative. They have resigned themselves to doing exactly the same as yesterday, all the while dreaming of what they will not do tomorrow. This, I guess, is another paradox moulded into an acceptable fact via peoples' beloved phrase: "It's normal". They just love applying this label in the general reality. Or maybe it actually is normal, because such people, like me, have calculated the negligible probability of getting a chance for something more.

Somewhere in my brain, *Knowledge* coughed in his sophisticated manner. He is my favourite of the entities inhabiting my twisted mind, yet his voice is irritating. It reminds me of a squeaky cartoon character. In fact, they all resemble cartoon characters, but at least the voices of the others are more bearable.

Knowledge's dry fingers flipped through some pages, then he began to recite even though he didn't have the slightest idea of the true nature of routine life and normality:

According to the statistics, chances for something more are an exception here. The probability of an uneventful existence is calculated to be very high.

Reason, who is definitely not one of my favourites, broke into the conversation and the entities in my head began an early-morning dialogue:

Existence is a simple sequence. We are at the stage of studying and working, which is followed by family, children, working again, and, finally, a natural ending. But the sequence is not guaranteed. In our case, it is not guaranteed at all.

Knowledge took over:

I confirm! Exact term for existence here: predetermined. I accept another term as well: doomed.

The rhythm of the train was disturbed. The machine rushed into the part of the route that I despised the most: an old tunnel, a weird buzzing sound. The lamps flashed menacingly for twenty-two seconds. I experienced my every-morning encounter with *Fear*. Panic crept up my bones, ready to attack. My pulse quickened. Struggling to breathe evenly, I clenched my hands into fists. I began to silently recite numerical sequences. My phobias made everyone in my head hide in their corners. Only skinny *Confidence* kept whispering from somewhere:

It's just dark! It's just dark!

Squeezing my eyelids, I repeated silently after her.

'NIA! Hello!' Andre nudged me. 'You drifted away again! Come on, get back to reality and help me.'

'She drifts away all the time! Being in *our* reality is more of an exception to her.'

Maddie radiated sex appeal even this early in the morning. She pulled out her insolent smile, too. Her shiny hair resembled a stream of wet tar, and in the depths of her bright green eyes there was something that made me sick.

I stared at Andre's hands. My ordinary boyfriend had the habit of exercising his ordinary brain by engaging with the various numerical and logic-based puzzles in the newspaper. His ride was short. He usually got off on the fourth stop. Maddie on the sixth, and I on the ninth, which was downtown. After leaving the metro, each one of us headed towards our respective internship. The last torture before graduation.

'Fibonacci[1]. A sequence. Can't you see it? It's even more perfect in squares.' I said after throwing a glance at his newspaper. The lack of comprehension on his face bored me even more than usual, and the tone of his voice showed me that he had noticed.

'No, Nia, no! I cannot see it. Not everyone is so...' He was silent for a moment, trying to pick the right label. '...weird! Normal people don't

---

[1] *Leonardo Fibonacci – an Italian mathematician. In 1202, he published a sequence of numbers called The Fibonacci Numbers. He learned about it during his travels in Eastern countries. Each number is the sum of the two preceding ones, beginning from 0 and 1. The larger the numbers in the Fibonacci sequence, the closer the ratio of the last two numbers is to the "golden ratio". An infinite number of digits in the sequence are equal to the golden ratio, also known as the golden section, golden mean, or divine proportion – author's notes.*

see patterns, they don't count their footsteps, and they don't wrinkle their noses at even numbers.'

'They don't drift away, they communicate like proper human beings, and they try to act in acceptable ways, or they at least know what the social norms of behaviour are. And they don't get mental blocks, only you do!' Maddie made sure to emphasise every word sarcastically.

'Listen, sweetheart. You were lucky to get an internship at the president's office. The guys at the university must have worked hard to find a place for you. You can at least try to be like everyone else. Don't annoy people, blend in. If you act weird there as well, you're going to be fired! It doesn't matter if they want you to carry coffees around, or copy documents, this is a chance for you to have a job.'

Andre was mentoring me, driven by his ambitions of an orderly, meaningless, simple life. I found even the monotonous clatter of the train more fascinating than his voice. At the last moment, I had been refused the state scholarship for education in England, which was promised to me. Because I had missed some important deadlines, I ended up in the ridiculous Political Science programme. A whole portion of my life was thoroughly lost on studying political elites, families, ideas, and systems. The expectation was that all this crap was going to be useful. And now, apparently, I was also expected to express gratitude for the stupid internship. My boyfriend was somewhat right that I should become more socially acceptable, but I wasn't coping at all. In my mind, I was indignant.

And what exactly am I supposed to learn from this internship? The Art of Normality, Ten Proven Ways to Depersonalise Yourself, How to Effectively Turn Today into Yesterday? *Or maybe they offer some other priceless skills?'*

I sighed, taking my bored eyes off him.

'You'd better listen to Andre. The chances for people like us are scarce, but for people like you there are no chances at all, freak! You'd rather carry coffees around at the president's office than take endless shifts God knows where for a miserable salary, right? That's how things go in the real world, though I don't know what they look like in yours.' Maddie agreed with Andre's life philosophy as she sipped her coffee.

'Obviously, our notions of "a chance" are diametrically opposed. Maddie, your conclusion lacks arguments again. You lack arguments all the time. I can confirm that it is statistically possible that you both are right, but it's only a hypothesis. At this stage, I cannot calculate the exact probability. Plus, I do put effort into my work. I put in a lot of effort into striving for my brain cells not to die.' I replied, staring at her with my usual even voice, but it often sounded as if I was scolding.

'I don't get your bullshit, you know! And I'm telling you for the thousandth time: don't stare at me like that, you give me the creeps!' Maddie hissed with her eyes narrowed. I knew perfectly well how much she hated the provocation of my expressionless black eyes, and I enjoyed teasing her.

Maddie and Andre's talk gave me even more tension than the voices in my head. I was most annoyed whenever she spoke, even though we had been living together for almost a year already. This happened by chance, not by will, after my only girlfriend ran away. Sharing an apartment with Maddie was another one of the absurdities in my life. The only useful thing about her was her good knowledge about the general reality, but she bored me with her prosaic instructions and her relentless quest to fit into people's most faulty patterns. I didn't enjoy her insults either, but I had long since stopped taking offence.

Like you don't drift away to your own make-believe world. I know what the chance you crave for looks like: you put it between your legs, and it will sort out your every problem. You're even more warped and inane than everyone else! Contempt had woken up. He was secretly evaluating Maddie with his white eyes, and I smirked at his conclusion.

Unlike me, Maddie and Andre were comfortable with reality's distortions and banality. They never complained about our predetermined future. Andre was actually looking forward to it: he was graduating soon, and after the internship he was to do the same thing for 40 years, earning barely enough money to live. He would be carefully resigned, diligently dreaming of the things he was not to do tomorrow, absolutely precise in complying with the main purpose of a routine life. He was perfectly able to grind the days into a homogeneous mixture of time. Andre had even found a solution to the challenging toothpaste issue: he used a fruit-flavoured one to lessen the sensation. He and Maddie both shared the same enviable obedience to fate, possessing no desire for something more. They would grow old according to the most ordinary pattern, replacing real life with simple existence, and none of that terrified them. Moreover, it did not seem to terrify the people on the metro, in the streets, anywhere I observed. They acted as if they had numerous lives ahead and didn't care that time in this life was ticking away. Although I was disturbed by this insane fact, I had to admit that it was either normal, or it was some mass method for achieving happiness, or at least an imitation of it. I still had not finished analysing this irrational process.

Sometimes, Maddie took the wrong path. She didn't bother to conceal the hope that her beautiful face and flawless body would push her into the right rich arms. There, she expected to find something extraordinary, or rather something more than just an ordinary life. She still lacked arguments, of course, but then again, she was struggling with that in general. Although I was doing my best not to reproach or judge her, our disagreements about her maddening absence of logic were not rare. In our Eastern European country, after the fall of communism and the mafia thundering about for years, the rich-man-who-buys-a-beautiful-woman pattern was a common thing. I didn't know what the situation was in other countries, but such a disproportionate deal was a desired goal here, an aspiration for many girls. Young Eastern European women found that the chance for something more was limited to one of the following plans: to find a way out on their own, escape and find a rich guy, or escape after finding him.

The weather was not good for walking, so I reluctantly took the bus for two stops. It had been raining for weeks. The thick autumn fog reminded me of routine life's colour. It was meant to extinguish people's last sparkle of brightness. Once again, the repulsive, dirty, gloomy city tortured my mind. The normality of the world tied my throat into a knot, tighter and tighter, especially when I was alone. In fact, my being alone was relative, because most of the time—among people or not—the entities in my head kept me company. But at the end of it all, I still had no place to hide from the general reality. Its lack of logic was killing me; the irrationality of the masses tortured me. For my hyper-rational mind, people and their behaviour were an incomprehensible mixture of insanity and paradoxes. Without realising it, I was talking to myself again while I was watching traces of mud speeding down the reflection of my face.

What if they are right? Maybe I am not entitled to the chance for something more. Why would I be? A not-all-there girl at the bottom of the social ladder. Opportunities: none. Advantages: smart, but there is a probability that this won't come in handy in the general reality. Disadvantages: not smart enough to understand how to avoid the predetermined existence. What is my motivation for wanting this? Fear of normality? Definitely, it is on the list. New question: what is "normal"? I can't even understand how they decide where to put the labels of normality. Damn it! My goal is to escape from something, yet I can't even figure out exactly what that something is. What the...?!

Running my fingers over my temples, only the twitching of my lips showed the chaos of my thoughts. *Knowledge* initiated another one of his speeches. His squeaky voice gave me a start:

Exact term: paradox.

I jumped and looked around.

I drifted away! Again! Damn my twisted mind!

I didn't know what annoyed me more: missing my stop again, or the fact that it was pouring outside. I never checked the weather forecast because I did not want the expectation it would give me—the expectation of order in my day. I didn't like the order, not at all. However, my revolt against the umbrella was nothing but a provocation to my luck.

When I entered the president's office, I was wet, late, and freezing. Right from the start, Thursday promised not to bring me any success. A clap of thunder echoed in my mind:

ONE!

As always, I started walking with my right foot, tapping the fingers of my right hand. As I took my second step—annoying because of its even number—my boss informed me that I was to take up the duties of the chief coffee carrier for as long as necessary. At least she gave me a couple of minutes to squeeze the water out of my hair. Maddie always insisted that mascara was an absolute must for work and that I should wear some, so now dark, irregular-shaped streams were flowing down to the middle of my cheeks, resisting my attempts to erase them. I pulled some black particles off my lashes and I watched in the mirror how moisture gathered in my slanted eyes. *Knowledge* was quick to provide information:

Chemical substances are entering the mucous membrane. Saline is being released. Exact term: tears.

I snorted at his new burst of babbling:

Thank you for the useless information. It's like pouring rain, except there is no umbrella to wield against it!

Over the years, I had gotten used to the entities in my head, to their constant chattering, to communicating with them. I was not sure when or even if I had created them. Maybe they had been living there from the very beginning, or maybe I had forgotten how they had appeared. I liked *Knowledge's* chatter best, so my white teeth shone behind a smile.

Despite being a substitute in charge of the coffee and discreetly trembling, I was not spared from the endless copying and carrying of folders up and down the corridors. Already, I was convinced that this was the most sought-after duty of the administrative staff. They quickly learn that the higher the piles of paper you carry around, the less likely it is for someone to bother you with real work. They make sure to maintain a busy and overwhelmed air around them, and at some point, it remains stuck on their faces forever. *Curiosity* kept wondering how they could put so much effort into merging into one being; he couldn't figure out how they achieved it. Another thing that provoked his interest was the mass longing for Friday. Employees began dreaming out loud about it from Monday morning, and the whole process resembled some occult ritual. I was tormented by the question of how this behaviour had become normal. I observed with interest the older employees as they pretended to be busy. Now I could tell by their facial expressions that they were anxious. Behind the sticky expression, there was tension and nervousness about all that was new in the general reality.

I was a child when our country became democratic. Since then, until a few months ago, it was ruled by an undercover communist, who pretended to be a democrat. During the darkest years, he was even a distinguished mafia boss. A nasty man with an evil face. Everyone who had been in their twenties since 1990 had protested in the squares against him at some point. Rumour has it that many were beaten by the police, and they were proud of that. A similar story was happening again now.

I was twenty-three. For a brief moment, I had also experienced the chance to be rebellious. I guess my recent bouts of demonstrating at protests had also helped the coming to power of the new president. Sixteen years older than me, he was probably the youngest president in the world. He was one-third enigmatic and two-thirds peculiar, and he seemed to be determined to stop the decadence of the country. His face never showed any emotions, and yet he gained people's trust in some inexplicable way. Behind his back, there was an entire business empire, which was built on quite a lot of question marks. Among them, there was his first-class education, for which us mortals can only dream or sacrifice a kidney. His success was complemented by an enormous family heritage, about which almost nothing was known. Most likely, in addition to a business empire and money, his family had also secured him with membership in the club of the world's elite. It was clear that the newly elected president lived on top of a mountain of extreme privilege, and he did not care to hide it at all.

He came to the political scene unexpectedly and, to everyone's surprise, won the election in less than a year. He wiped out the eternal communist president with one wave of his hand, radiating raw composure in every appearance. He seemed to have drawn up his actions in a precise manner, step by step. His plan resembled an engineering project for a sophisticated bridge construction, and he had been following it with maniacal accuracy since day one. That was probably what had attracted the voters of our plundered country, where there were no prospects and no hope. In him, they anticipated someone who could defeat the chaos with sharpness and brutality; someone who could grab the chaos, bend its arms behind its back and extort discipline and prosperity out of it.

The state, which was already under Victor Kaov's control, was small, yet rather important. Left bloodless after the communists and the mafia, it was now rising again. As soon as he took office, the new president introduced his reasonable policies and began to sketch a horizon for decades to come. Apparently, the special university for privileged people like him taught its students how to rule the world with ease. Then, it sent them off with a Guide to Greatness under their arm.

In my pointless printing room, I was watching Kaov's short speech to the ministers on TV. I was arranging an odd number of piles of documents, with paper clips in alternating colours. In my struggle with boredom, I found all sorts of ways to create patterns, even if they were elementary. The president was brief, clear and categorical. I wonder how he managed to be that cool and restrained, showing no facial expressions, as if a statue was speaking in this reality, while the true him was in some other, very distant universe. I assumed that he was just meant to be special. There are beings who are destined to live an extraordinary life since birth. Fate gives them the chance of having something more. Confident, arrogant, and embarrassingly focused, Victor Kaov seemed to embody a triumphal march to the throne of the world. Symmetrical, tall, and sombre, he appeared to carry everything that people dream of, but are afraid to possess. His posture demanded worship, probably rightly so, because one could see his dominance, even on TV, after meeting his measured gaze.

I had peeked from behind the columns in the building several times as he had passed, surrounded by his team. Although he looked like a classic bastard, I noticed something peculiar about him. To me, his steps seemed too rhythmic, as if he was counting, and I never distinguished a single expression on his face. His superiority rose like an impregnable wall that could be sensed from a distance. I found this inappropriate for our century.

I was staring in his flat, blue eyes on the screen when *Reason* started chiding me:

You see? Now this is what a special person looks like! You've got to start from somewhere. How about from the chaos of your crazy mind? Learn how to communicate, how to understand people, the norms... After that, all you will need is a good idea to work on. And with a little luck, you'll get out of here! Are we supposed to rot in this hellhole? Is this all there is for us, Nia?

Reason—annoying, tall and square-headed— was waving his finger inside my brain. Immersed in the nonsense of my work, I was again analysing the likelihood of being given the chance for something more. Actually, the question was not if one is entitled to such a chance, but what one should be like in order to receive it. Born in the right country, in the right family, with the right education and environment? For some people these prerogatives are simply a gift from fate. Their destiny is predetermined in a different way: they automatically find themselves in the middle of the ladder, without even having to stick a single toe in the mud. This phenomenon was also labelled "normal", though I found it ill-grounded. *Confidence*, skinny and short, was once again trying to convince me that nothing was predetermined but I wasn't sure if that was practically true.

Although I belonged to the club of the unprivileged and insignificant, I had scrutinised myself with the utmost precision. I was gifted with a remarkable intellect, extraordinary mind, and useful intuition. Alas, this intuition often contradicted my hyper-rational thinking. I ignored it. My aspirations reached a level of being harmful, and my inclination to challenge myself was even dangerous. I was always tempted to prove myself, too, even though I had long known how pointless that was.

My madness was probably my most distinctive feature. I refracted the world through the prism of this madness, and it was why the world kept trying to refract me. I guess the same happened to everyone who wouldn't conform to the norms of society, who is unworthy of the "normal" label. I was always quick and explicit, noticing the faulty patterns, the distorted people, and the broken tiles in the general reality, and there were several things that caused me the mental blocks: *Fear*, normality, voluntary depersonalisation, even numbers. Another one of my many defects was the fact that I tended to drift away whenever I couldn't find any logic in what was going on around me. There was also a gift from birth that separated me from the world—the "barrier". I considered it valuable. It was my safest hiding place. An invisible, yet strong, barrier, behind which I could hide myself, and even an elephant if I so wished, leaving only my expressionless black eyes on the other side.

All the endless analyses, arguments, sometimes even clamorous fights between me and the entities in my head seemed to prove that my consciousness stood on the border between healthy and sick. However, I was used to it. I had accepted it all. As I observed normal people, I suspected that there were voices and entities in their heads, too, but I never spoke about this openly. The topic would only bring more critical looks in my direction.

In my reality, I was driven by a desire for a challenging life and a chance for something more. In the general reality though, I found myself with nothing but faint prospects, an annoying boyfriend, hateful accommodation, and constantly being labelled. I forced myself to reduce my desires to specific results, because they are more convenient in the general reality. They call them "goals" there. It is banal to stuff a whole life's worth of aspiration into a box—because that is what "goals" looked like in my head—but I was doing my best. I fit complete freedom into the image of a giant skyscraper in New York. I wished to escape there, to hide from what was predetermined, from prejudice; to do whatever I wanted, challenge myself and, most of all, to get rid of all the crap that restrained the scale of my mind and myself. I craved the indefinite everything of unlimited possibilities. I assumed that was what happiness looked like, or at least that I would be able to gather data on what happiness really is.

The problematic fact was that I wanted this everything at once, and I was endowed with zero patience. I often argued with ordinary beings who could not understand my hyper-rational mind—that was also an issue. Their weak brains strained me even more than their square perceptions and insults.

φ

My lack of patience, straightforwardness, and inability to communicate had a bad effect on the general reality. As I left the pointless room at the end of the workday, I hissed at my boss that she was killing my brain cells with stupid tasks. She snapped back:

'Don't push your luck, girl, or you'll be out of here in no time! Do you know how many others like you are waiting out there? Who do you think is going to put up with your impudent mouth?' She waved a menacing finger under my nose.

'The answer should be easy even for you. It's obvious. Someone who will appreciate what comes out of my mouth, or who will at least understand what I say.' I gave her a crooked smirk.

Mind your tone, Nia! The words are not OK, either!

Reason was angry with me for teasing people again.

'I'm sick of you! You're unbelievable! Get out of here and learn how to behave!' She exploded in a high pitch.

'Bring coffee and water for everyone, quick!' The chief advisor's secretary startled her. 'Come on, move! The meeting has begun!'

We looked at each other and my boss apparently decided to postpone firing me. She rejoiced serving coffee there, as if the temple of pleasure was hidden behind the boardroom door. With her feminine gait, she moved gracefully. She needed help, however, so she shoved a tray full of cups into my hands.

There was an absolute inverse relation between the dexterity of my body and that of my mind. I could prove this with thousands of examples and numerous scars, like the one on the tip of my eyebrow. Focusing on my breathing and clutching the tray, I followed my boss to the boardroom.

More than twenty advisors, ministers, and other important men were conversing around a giant table. A couple of female secretaries and assistants occupied distant chairs by the wall. My head was thundering:

Faulty pattern! Violation of balance! It should be male, female... male, female... male, female... Balance! The current pattern is wrong, it's ineffective.

Bright lines rushed through my mind as I evaluated the reality before me. Then, all of a sudden, I found a good alternating pattern of the men in the room: one had a blank gaze, the one next to him seemed distressed, then another blank gaze, and another face in distress next to it. I looked through them mockingly, my brain focusing on the perfect succession. As I handed my boss yet another cup of coffee, I finished tracing the sequence of gazes on the long side of the table. To my annoyance, the rhythm was then interrupted by the unreadable face of a statue. I decided to use it as a dividing line for my counting, but for some reason, I couldn't take my eyes off him. He was speaking in a quick, quiet manner. From this close, he was even more symmetrical with his sharp features, bright skin, and dark radiance. His black hair was carefully slicked back, slightly to the side. He clenched his jaw and I could see the clear outline of the muscles under his stubble beard. But still, even up close, I could not find any definite facial expression.

Why are we staring like this?

Curiosity's cute voice disturbed the silence in my head. Its crooked eyes were blinking rapidly behind its huge glasses. I shrugged. I did not bother to define the reason, but at least the question helped me to move my interest away.

I handed out the last cup of coffee and was ready to leave, when, all of a sudden, he looked up and pinned me with his sharp eyes. An unfamiliar neurological process dilated my pupils first, then opened my mouth and did not care to close it, so I simply stood there, stupefied and gaping. A stranger, who was shaking all over, burst into my head. Every pair of eyes around the table followed the invisible thread of attention that extended to me, but I still couldn't move. Only my boss's persistent pull managed to extract me from the awkward situation. Without permission, she grasped my elbow and let go only after we had walked far enough away from the boardroom.

'Don't drag me like that. You have absolutely no right to touch me.' I resisted her.

'And you have no right to stare brazenly like that! Don't you know who he is, you lunatic?' She put the menacing finger back into use.

'Certainly, I know. He was the one who was staring brazenly.' I walked irritated towards the printing room.

'Yeah, sure! The president would stare at you, of all people!' Her insults ricocheted off my back; they didn't penetrate as they meant nothing to me.

The minutes dragged on as my mind was tortured by mental replays of what had happened in the boardroom. The president's icy gaze was still there, before me. My boss's rude voice brought me out of my trance. She commanded me to gather the cups and whatever was left in the boardroom.

'They're finished? But we just served the coffee.' I replied dizzily.

'You want me to explain why they didn't drink it, or what? Go there right now, and you and I are having a serious talk tomorrow!' She ordered in her malevolent tone, angry as always at her own existence.

I got to the task reluctantly. At least I could think about the 55 steps of something like joy that were ahead. I was going to leave soon, to read on my way home in order to make it up for the lost brain cells. I couldn't wait to get stuck into some kind of calculation; numbers were my impregnable fortress, in which I could hide from all this crap and just relax. They were the only thing I got along with easily. They never made me tense.

'By the time I stop working here, I will probably be left without even one functioning brain cell. They all will be slaughtered! I will get dumb, I will keep dragging folders up and down corridors forever, like all the others, and every Monday I will start my occult rituals for summoning Friday. Damn! I've had enough of this wretched reality for today. And tomorrow will be the same, anyway!'

I was complaining aloud amidst the huge boardroom. I wanted to distract myself, so I turned my attention to the rhythm of the clock. I looked at the pile of cups and counted the first second:

'ONE'

I turned to carry the cups away, and then he made me jump. I somehow managed not to drop the whole tray, but one crystal cup flew to the ground, breaking at my feet.

'Shit!' I shrieked.

The president was standing behind my back, silent as a marble statue in his suit. I froze.

If that's the way I stare at Maddie, now I know why she gets the creeps!

He didn't even react to the breaking cup. He didn't blink before he spoke in his even voice:

'You are too loud.'

I was staring at him from less than half a metre away. Staring at the cold blue of his eyes. His haughty gaze was a perfect match for his grim air, and the black three-piece suit was a good final touch to his image of an ultimate jerk.

The stranger in my head was shaking again. He made me stop staring brazenly and say something instead, but it sounded rude, as usual:

'You scared me. I won't make any more noise, but you shouldn't sneak behind people like that.' I snapped, looking at the broken pieces on the floor. He stepped in front of me, his eyelids narrowed, and I didn't know where to turn.

'What is...?'

'Nia.'

I wondered if I was going to be unemployed tomorrow because of my attitude.

'Nia?' He repeated absentmindedly, seemingly looking through me.

'That's my name, yes. Isn't that what you asked?' Once again, I couldn't help sounding rude.

He focused on me and I shivered. I stepped back to collect the broken pieces. The president did not budge as he watched my actions from above. As I crouched, putting the pieces back on the tray, a shard of sharp crystal sank into my palm. Another loud curse escaped my throat. As I stood up, the blue irises pierced me reproachfully. The situation was getting even more awkward, but I took a breath, looked down, and then to the side, before heading for the door. He stopped me. Without saying a word, he placed the tray on the table, produced a handkerchief from his pocket, and took a hold of my wrist. I pulled myself away abruptly.

'I'd rather you didn't touch me!' I muttered, clutching the white cloth. He flinched for a moment, but there was still no expression on his face. I kept walking towards the door, carrying the tray. Before I left, his voice caught up with me:

'Who is killing your brain cells, Nia?'

'What do you care?'

I gave him a mean look and he raised his eyebrows in question. After a brief moment of awkward silence, there was reproach in his eyes again.

'I asked you something!' His voice was barely audible, and yet I was annoyed by his tone.

'Reality is killing them. The general reality. Have a nice evening.'

'Nia is an odd name.'

He meant no offence, but I shivered.

'Yes, it is quite odd. Suits me well.'

I guess I was misbehaving again because he slammed the door to his office without answering. I frowned both at his rude attitude and at my own inability to communicate properly.

My boss took her revenge by flooding me with other useless tasks, which involved cups, sheets of paper, and folders. She destroyed another hour of my existence before I was free to walk my 55 steps of something like joy. There was no one left in the corridors, so at least on my way out I could count aloud as much as I wished. As I headed for the metro station, I detected within myself a sense of relief. The darkness outside was even nastier than the rain. I put my earphones in, trying to distance myself from the reality around me. I walked, immersed in my thoughts. Whilst I was waiting to cross the wide boulevard, I was startled by three identical cars stopping directly in front of me. Six huge men came out of them. I gaped and froze as they surrounded me. The door of the jeep in front of me opened. Victor Kaov's icy-cold eyes stared at me and made me take my earphones out. His even, metallic voice slammed into my eardrums:

'It's raining.'

'For nineteen days now. Haven't you noticed?' I snorted with my eyebrows raised.

'You are not carrying an umbrella!'

'I don't like umbrellas, nor being startled!'

'Wear a raincoat then and stop being startled. I'll drive you home.' He snapped.

'You are being driven yourself, so it's incorrect to say that you will drive me. I always take the metro and I don't like raincoats either.'

'There is a station next to our building. Why didn't you take it from there, instead of walking in the dark, in the rain?'

'Because I want to take it for an odd number of stops.' I was confident in my answer, although he looked at me with suspicion.

'Get in!' He hissed through his teeth.

'No, there is no need.'

'It was not a question.' He narrowed his eyelids and I did the same, without moving. He pulled me abruptly inside in one motion, so I found myself on the seat next to him. The cut on my hand started bleeding again. I growled. When he noticed I was squeezing the handkerchief, he took hold of my wrist.

'Shit!' I groaned as he wrapped the cloth as a bandage.

'Stop swearing!'

I was surprised to see an expression similar to irritation on his face

'It hurts! And I can swear as much as I like because I'm not at work. Plus, I don't like being touched!' I frowned.

He tied the handkerchief and let go of my hand. Crossing my arms, I leaned my back against the door. He ordered me to tell my address to the driver, then we fell into awkward silence. More than awkward. The red-blue strobe on the dashboard was getting on my nerves and I started counting them. There was this odd sense of discomfort, as if I was on my way to the dentist, or something even more unpleasant. I kept shifting nervously in the seat, throwing hidden glances at him, but he didn't move his attention away from his phone. He didn't say a word. With every passing minute in the car, my lungs tightened even more, and I suspected my claustrophobia was going to attack any minute now. A few blocks before my apartment, I couldn't stand it anymore. I was short of breath. As soon as we stopped at a traffic light, I muttered something like a thank you for the ride and I escaped from the car beneath his arrogant gaze.

My hand was pulsating, but at least it had stopped bleeding. As I walked towards my apartment, I looked into the glassy blue eyes that lingered in my mind, unsure whether I was talking to them, or to myself:

How do you always achieve everything like that? Damn it! He has conquered the business world, he is free to do whatever he likes, he is reaching for the big-time world of politics. Is this all meant only for people like him? A cliché of a pattern, designed for a group of special privileged jerks but, of course, not for freaks like me. Some people are meant to live extraordinary lives to show ants that flying is possible. Surely this is normal in the general reality!

I entered my temporary home, wondering who the new intruder was that kept vibrating in my twisted mind. Maddie was on the couch watching some crappy reality show, boredom on her face, beer in her hand. As usual, I was annoyed that she hadn't switched on the lights. Whenever the hateful quarters looked too dark, I started seeing images, then hearing voices, and they were not the ones that normally lived in my head. I guess it was *Fear* who sent them, along with the panic down my spine.

'Why are you like this?' Maddie aimed the neck of the bottle at me.

'Good evening. Like what?' I snapped. It was rude of her not to even greet me.

'Even weirder than usual? Somewhat excited, I'd say, if that's even an option for an Egyptian mummy like yourself.' She was examining me shamelessly, becoming the first one to conclude that the strange intruder in my head was actually *Excitement*. I had not guessed that.

'I met the president.' I murmured and Maddie gaped at me in disbelief. 'Well, not really. I saw him when I was carrying the cups, and then I saw him again when I was taking them away. Obviously, I knew his name already, and now he knows mine as well, so...' *Excitement* introduced himself to my mind and an unnatural smile shone on my face. I decided to spare Maddie the awkward part about my ride home and Kaov's arrogant behaviour.

'Tell me everything!' She came to life and even turned off the TV.

'I already did.'

'What did he say to you? Is he as sexy as he looks on TV?'

'He asked me about my name and who was killing my brain cells. He also gave me a handkerchief, because I cut myself. That's all.' I shrugged in conclusion.

'Okay, okay, you can skip all that bull about brain cells and your ridiculous clumsiness. Does he look sexy? Describe him to me!'

'Maddie, you can at least try to express yourself properly. The word "sexy" does not relate to looks, it relates to perception. Thus, I cannot use it to describe anyone. I can confirm that he is symmetrical, his features are sharp and regular, he has a pronounced mandible. He is quite a lot taller than the average man and his muscles are well-developed, probably due to training. He carries the genetic mutation of blue eyes, but they are not like any other eyes I've seen before. Their colour is unique, they look like glass. He also likes to stare, but his gaze is arrogant, and it makes people nervous. His expression is that of a statue, not of a human. The usual facial expressions are not present, which is weird from a neurological point of view. Besides this, he seems to demonstrate his superiority all the time, which, in my opinion, is very rude. This is the most accurate description.'

I gave another shrug.

'For Christ's sake! It's impossible to talk to you without getting a headache. You could have simply said that he is blue-eyed, sexy, composed, and manly. Was he hitting on you?' My roommate was already burning with fantasies.

'Illogical question. Damn, you really must do something about your issue with arguments!' I wrinkled my nose at her assumption. 'It's not that hard. I've seen him on the news, you have as well. Do I resemble even slightly the women he appears with? How can you assume that he was hitting on me? Why would he?' My gaze, agitated by her lack of logic, pierced through her.

'You look nothing like them, for sure, but you must do your best. If he fucked you, even once, you might get a lot: money, gifts, an apartment, or maybe a car! Who knows? He seems generous to me. Then you will introduce me, and I'll make sure I look exactly the way I should. Or the way he wants me to! For this man, with his position and his money, I will cosplay, or go along with whatever his fetishes he has, if I have to.' Before my gaping face, she dived with enthusiasm into an ocean of longing.

'Maddie! Arguments! First of all, I am not qualified whatsoever. I have no interest, and no skills, in this type of activity.' I shivered at the thought that Andre and I had actually engaged in it, even if it was quite a rare occurrence. I can't stand being touched, and as it turns out, this is the main feature of sex. 'You are the master in this field, but you'd better think twice whether this type of self-destructive philosophy is useful. Second of all... cosplay? Come on! Even you can do better.'

She was angry, either with my tone, or with my words. In my communication, I never managed to choose either of them well.

'I can do better?' She grimaced in a way I didn't understand. 'I want a good life, Nia! I'm not a slut, don't look down on me as if I am a slut! Stop preaching morality and start taking advantage!'

'I don't know how one looks down on somebody as if they are a slut, and there is nothing to take advantage of. If you compare the two halves of such a deal, you will see that they're not equal. There is no balance. There is no solid ground. It's nothing more than a faulty pattern. End of conversation.'

'What's even right about balance? We're just about to graduate from some shitty state university. We live in a shithole, we have no money, no strings to pull, no nothing. I don't want to work as a donkey, barely able to make ends meet, Nia! All I want is a good life, and I don't care if it's right or wrong!'

There was terror in her eyes. I realised that she was also afraid of how difficult the concept of living is, though she was afraid in a different way, with some perverted notion of hope.

'What you are describing doesn't sound like "good life". Besides, it was your choice to just hang on to the shitty university and not do anything else. There are plenty of free online courses for people like us. See, I've already learned several languages, I'm constantly searching for information on potentially useful subjects, I make my own forecasts and calculations. One doesn't need any chances in order to make a logical decision. I even applied for a scholarship at the Columbia University in New York.' I tried to give real-life examples, but apparently, I still couldn't find the correct way of speaking to her. She was angry.

'You applied, and so what? Think they're waiting for you? Even if you ever get a scholarship, you won't be able to afford the ticket to get there! You gonna swim, or what?' She sneered. 'Oh, come on! Since we have no money, it's just not possible for us to jump off the bottom without help. Your high IQ doesn't matter, the fact that you can memorise three books in half a day doesn't matter, your smartness does not matter, because it makes you weird and it disengages you from reality! We don't stand a chance, you know that, and—yes!—if I could, I would take advantage of a rich man's money and I would build a better life for myself, far from this shithole!' She snarled at me.

'I doubt you will be able to. It would be a huge life compromise for both parties in the deal. You expect someone to pay thousands for your body, even if he wouldn't give a penny for its contents. There is no proportion, if...'

I was interrupted by the expression that exploded on Maddie's face. I already knew that it led to no good, and the best thing to do was to just disappear. Everything I said was frank; this was my usual way of communicating, though people defined it as "rude", sometimes even "cruel". I could never understand how truth, which is equal to reality, tends to be perceived as cruel, and why people constantly try to avoid it. But this was another common faulty pattern.

'And then again, you can do what you want with your life. I'm not going to preach, Maddie. I'm off to bed.' I forced a smile while shooting these sentences, hoping she wouldn't start shouting.

'Eff you, freak! Can't you stop being a sociopath for once and have a normal conversation?!' She yelled behind my back. I had no answer for her. Maddie constantly repeated the words "normal conversation" to me, but I couldn't get what the criteria were for such a thing. I didn't want to go into the usual explanation that "sociopath" was not the correct definition and it didn't correspond with the official medical opinion of me.

φ

In bed, I liked to read Jung's theories of general reality and humanity. I devoted myself to him at night, trying to understand people and, above all, to learn how to communicate with them. Reacting in a proper manner was also difficult for me, especially when it was necessary to mimic emotions. I was devoid of them, and since I didn't really know what they felt like, it was almost impossible for me to imitate them. At least I had learned how to recognise people's feelings by their facial expressions. I decided how to act on this basis.

All of a sudden, a pair of glassy blue irises appeared behind the letters of my book. They stared at me. *Excitement* engaged in a cheerful reggae dance and made me frown at the unfamiliar process.

Who does he think he is to just come here and dance? How long will we have to put up with this? Where the hell did he even come from?

Reason was justifiably displeased, but I couldn't give him an answer, not even a guess. New entities had not appeared in my head for a long time, so it was a surprise to me, too.

My eyelids squeezed shut, I kept pondering on Jung's profound insights, but they only hurled me into the spontaneous manifestations of the unconscious—Jung's definition of dreams. I was kicked out in the dark. Once again, darkness twisted into gracefully irregular shapes, in an insidious game of temptation.

You are mine!

Fear's ominous voice made me shiver in my sleep. I couldn't catch my breath and I shook, curled up in a ball. Night-time is a challenge for me. I guess my unconscious didn't like me too much because it appeared evil and sadistic.

A ringing phone made me jump from my sleep. Heart beating frantically, my body was snatched out of another nightmare. It was six in the morning! A female voice introduced herself as the president's secretary. She cheerfully informed me that I was expected there at seven. After I hung up, my sleepy eyes stared at the phone, wondering how normal people could be that fresh at this hour.

Damn! Why now? And why so early? Are they going to fire me because of yesterday?

Excitement was dancing to reggae again. I tried to seek help from someone else in my head, but at this time of the day, there was only snoring.

Brought up to be always on time, I entered the office hesitantly only seconds before seven. Men in suits were waiting around, their faces anxious, while the chief advisor was handing our assignments. He was giving his orders with an air of dissatisfaction. His facial expressions gave me the hint that something was bothering him. I was just about to ask what I could help with, when the wall creaked behind him. The president came out through something that looked like a hidden door. I defined the space as a great hiding place. His hair was freshly done, he seemed energetic and focused. He was followed by a perfect, almost divine woman, who looked exactly like the other women he was often photographed with. I gaped as another lady emerged after them.

'Unbalanced. It must be drawing a lot of energy.' My suspicions on the two-women-one-man pattern inappropriately broke the silence of the room.

I often babbled aloud, without noticing, and I definitely had to work on that defect. I pointed my nose at my shoes. My fingers started fiddling with the hem of the grey suit, which Maddie chose for me to wear every day, supposedly to blend in better. At least, in terms of colour, I blended in.

'Good morning, Nia. You are obviously equally as good with words, as you are with cups,' he stared at me impudently. Again, there was no facial expression.

What is this person doing to my brain?

I was silent. The strange vibration under my skin was irritating.

'You can leave.' He turned dryly to the women, and they walked to the door in unison. Then, he shot his metallic voice at the three men in the room. 'I am going to speak slowly, at the speed of your thoughts. You've received instructions already. I'm giving you 24 hours to do the job. One minute later, and you know what happens. Am I clear?' His words creaked, and the trio timidly replied with a simple "okay". 'Get out now.'

Well, that's weird. He definitely finds it hard to communicate, too. He may be a president, but he can't find the right tone, nor the right word. Just like me!

I analysed his disability with surprise. I had never expected that someone else—not a freak, like me—would have a hard time with these aspects of communication. Kaov treated people with rudeness and contempt, though, and when he turned his attention back to me, ice pendants pierced my body. His haughty gaze annoyed me, so I snapped first:

'Good morning to you, too. Excuse me for my inappropriate comment.'

'Inappropriate, indeed. You clearly start being rude from early in the morning!' He clenched his jaw. He seemed to be waiting for my reaction, but behind my barrier, all I did was blink. I began to count, touching the pad of my thumb to the rest of the fingers in a rhythm of odd taps. The president was looking at my hands. He seemed to have noticed the sequence. His eyelids narrowed as he continued:

'When you talk to yourself, aren't you supposed to be unheard by others?'

He followed the chief advisor's movement out of the room, then pinned his eyes on mine again.

'Oh!' His question caught me by surprise. 'Most of the time, I don't speak my thoughts out loud, but sometimes they just slip out without me noticing.'

'They just slip out on their own?' He raised his eyebrows at my nonsense. There was no way he could understand me.

'Yeah, I simply...' I stopped just before telling a stranger that my head was a place of chaos, inhabited by various entities.

All my life people had been showing me, again and again, by increasingly insulting words, that they did not relate to any of this, just as I did not fit into their reality. I took a breath to continue.

'Your secretary called me, but she didn't say what I could do for you? I guess it's not going to be a weather forecast.' I couldn't help but tease him a little. He smirked. I didn't like guys like him, I didn't appreciate their prerogatives, their arrogance, how highly they thought of themselves and how they looked down on everyone else. I couldn't find the balance in the fact that some people were given more than others for no logical reason.

'To begin with, you can stop jumping out of cars without warning the driver, because it's risky.' I was surprised by his request. He continued in an even voice: 'Nia, why are you here?'

'Because of a university programme for political science undergraduates. I am supposed to acquire useful practical skills which ostensibly help me find a job afterwards. My stupid specialty does not provide too many opportunities, though. To sum it up, I am here to suffer through an internship, in order to get a useless degree.'

The president tried to conceal a smile by putting the tips of his fingers to his lips. He was probably amused by my way of speaking.

'The only way this internship could possibly be useful to you is by helping you learn to communicate more skilfully.' He aimed a small smile at me.

'Not likely. There are no prerequisites here for me to improve my communication skills, because I don't find the people here interesting, and I generally avoid communication with uninteresting beings. It's a waste of time and it burdens my mind,' I stopped for a moment, looking to find some reaction, but I could not detect any. 'I should probably note that you are not completely uninteresting to me, because you are one of those...'

Shut up. Right now. Not a word anymore!

Reason was in rage, waving his hands all about. The president, gazing at the depths of my pupils, didn't seem to hear what I had said.

'It's a waste of time that you're even here! A huge waste!' He went silent for a moment. 'We will talk tonight, Nia. A driver will be picking you up at five o'clock,' he focused his questioning eyes on me, nervously touching his watch.

'I have to work until six, Mr. President. Up until that hour, I am supposed to be in no place other than here.' I watched him with suspicion.

'Victor!' He snapped and he seemed irritated. 'Use my given name, and don't talk to me in this rude manner!'

'I have to work until six, Victor. Up until that hour, I am not supposed to be anywhere else. Can't we talk here?'

'No, we cannot. Your working hours are my concern. What I am asking is if five is convenient for you.' His voice got even sharper.

'There is no logic in me deciding whether it's convenient. Those are my working hours, and my responsibilities are clear.' My expression was full of surprise.

'Okay then, I'll be even more specific!' Now he was talking rudely as well. 'What I am asking is if you would like to be picked up at five. I am not asking about your working hours, or about your responsibilities.' He wouldn't take his impudent irises off me. I found his explanation annoying.

That was not how he put it in the first place! He can't communicate properly, and he is inaccurate as well! Besides, how can I be sure if I want to go, given that I haven't been told what we are supposed to talk about! It would simply be a guess.

Victor stared at me as if he was eavesdropping on my conclusions. I decided to use *Curiosity* as motivation. *Curiosity* didn't object.

'All right. It's more likely that I want to go.' I shrugged at the most accurate wording possible.

'I will take this as a confirmative answer. Communicating with you will most certainly be a challenge!'

He didn't give any more details but headed towards the door at a confident pace.

Every fifteen minutes, my boss bothered to check how I was doing with my scanning, copying, and sorting of documents. I was doing as usual. After all, I made an effort to comply with the purpose of routine life, so I knew how to replicate my days quite well. When she came in for the tenth time, she poked her irritating, snub nose in front of my face.

'What's going on?' She seemed to be measuring me.

'With what?'

'You know perfectly well!'

'I don't know, neither perfectly, nor imperfectly well.' I stared at her in my particular manner—the stomach-twisting one—knowing it would work out.

Won't they ever get used to it?

In my mind, I giggled at the familiar reaction.

'Why did they call for you in the morning, and why are you leaving earlier today?'

'It's obvious. Even for you.'

Maybe she feels bad when I tease her. Maybe that's why she's always so mean!

Reason nodded with enthusiasm at my thoughts.

'Don't play innocent, girl! It's pretty clear what you are aiming for! I know young beauties like you.' She started speaking cynically. 'You smile with your juicy lips, you flutter the lashes of your wet eyes, then one wave of your tail, and you won't have to deal with any folders anymore!' She threw her mocking laugh at me. I gaped at her insane chain of thought.

'What are you talking about, ma'am? My smile is a muscles' reaction. My eyes are normally wet, this is their usual physiological condition. I don't have a tail, and I have no idea what the folders have to do with all this.' I headed for the door, clueless about what she meant.

'This country is full of gold diggers, and you all are getting more and more insolent! Don't you girls feel offended by being used as napkins? I guess that's all you can do anyway, and in fact you whores deserve just that!' She hissed behind my back. I froze for a second.

Yup! I'm definitely not going to tease her anymore. She's going crazy already and she's started to insult me too often, with words too incorrect.

I slipped out, without giving her a reply. I hid behind a column, waited for her to go out and did my best to avoid her for the rest of the day.

The driver who picked me up in the afternoon had no interest in speaking to me. *Curiosity's* questions flooded me, but they had to remain unanswered. The road climbed up high, squeezed between majestic pine trees on either side. It reached a massive wall with a beautiful wooden gate, hand-carved all over. The driver made me leave my coat and my bag in the car. He pointed to the entrance. I examined the exquisite wood carving on the door. Some unknown master had immortalised the magic of his hands there. I did not know that this magnificence disguised a whole new reality of ugliness and distortion.

In the middle of the lane, I was greeted by a misshapen, tallowy man. He looked so pleated with his layers of fat that I wondered how he could move. He stretched a toothy smile across his round face, then he started nudging me down the lane. While he was explaining how clean the air around his mansion was, I remembered why he looked so familiar. This fat guy was a well-known businessman, allegedly in control of part of the mafia, which was not supposed to be exactly a mafia anymore. Having thoroughly cleaned the suspicious stains off their businesses, people like him took offence whenever they were defined as mafiosi. Their faces appeared constantly in the news. He was most often there asserting the claims that he was an important *non-mafia* boss within the arms industry.

When I entered the house, I got my own confirmation of the fact that the manners of the supposedly new businessmen were no different from what urban legends say about the mafia period of the recent past. Overfed men lounged around; their fat was spilling over the edges of leather armchairs while cigars burned between their fingers. Beautiful women lurked in the smoke, their dresses even more expensive than they were, the air about them perfectly matching the surrounding distortion. I looked to all sides, studying the president's reality, and my head was ringing:

Faulty pattern!

As I critically examined my surroundings, I saw him sitting in a colossal armchair by the fireplace, alone with his gloominess. Kaov was immersed in his phone, wearing a white T-shirt and black cotton trousers. To my horror, the head of an elephant hung over him. Under his armchair, there was a polar bear who had lost its battle with distorted people's worst pattern. I got sick. *Justice* shook *Malice's* shoulders angrily, insisting that she should do something about all this. The chaos in my head was restrained behind the invisible barrier, which was of utmost importance in such situations. I froze, moving my stunned attention from the elephant to the bear, and back again. *Rage* turned my stomach into a walnut. An inner urge to leave made me turn to the exit, but the icy-cold voice from the morning changed my direction.

'Good evening, Nia. Wait for me in my study.' He sounded dry, but his curiosity was aroused for a second before he turned his gaze back to his phone.

The eyes of everybody present followed me like spotlights as a bodyguard escorted me. I found myself in a not-too-big room, made entirely of leather and wood. It didn't smell like anything familiar. My sense of smell is particularly sensitive; I can tell apart various fragrances without hesitation, but something here was unknown. I wondered what it might be.

While I was examining the paintings on the walls, he came in, walked over to me, and stopped closer to my face than appropriate. He didn't utter a word, and I frowned at the short distance between us. Kaov stared intently into the depths of my scattered mind which, for a brief moment, made me regret my decision to meet him. Trapped in his insistent gaze, I had nowhere to turn to, so I just grumbled:

'What do you wish to discuss with me in a place like this?'

He didn't reply. *Excitement* erupted and replaced the reggae with steppe. Each tap created a vibration that accelerated and resonated to the farthest corners of my body.

This is the anatomical reaction to the perception of "sexy"!

Excitement giggled before his pounding became unbearable. *Reason* hissed at him to spare us his nonsense. I swallowed dryly. There was something incomprehensible about this man, and it almost evoked a sensation of uneasiness within me. His stare made me nervous, he was exploring me like I was a piece in a museum. My pulse became unstable. Surrounded by his wall of superiority, he seemed even more arrogant, and yet I noticed something akin to surprise in his pupils.

'Why are there no colours in your eyes? They're pure black. Are you wearing lenses?' He was staring far beyond the colour of my eyes and his voice was devoid of any mood.

The question caught me off-guard, but I managed to reply that I didn't use lenses and that only 9% of the population carried the mutation of blue irises like his.

'They seem unreal.' He moved even closer, positioning himself in a space where I preferred no one to stand. He didn't hear my answer, or he didn't realise that the topic was inappropriate, or, most likely, he didn't care about my boundaries.

'I assure you that my eyes are perfectly real and right now they are helping me see that you are standing inappropriately close!' I snapped. My sharp voice made him narrow his eyelids. 'What do you want to talk about and why am I here?' I didn't manage to stare at him in my well-proven stomach-twisting way, so I just moved my gaze to the floor.

Startled by his touch on my wrist, I tried to pull away, but he was gripping tightly. I bristled, even though heat seeped through my skin. He carefully examined my cut before pinning his eyes back on me.

'Why are you worried about your brain cells?' He stepped back. His expression showed that he was deep in thought.

'Because they're all I have.' I shrugged. 'With this job, though, it's quite likely that I will lose them all. I make coffee, I copy documents, and nothing challenging...'

And I want so much more!

It sounded too demanding, so I decided to keep this sentence to myself.

'Can you do more?' He pierced me with his icy voice, and I hesitated.

Did I keep the last sentence to myself?

'Probably yes. But the truth is, I can only guess. I definitely have the potential, but I lack data to confirm or deny for sure. And though unsupported by facts, I really hope I can do more!'

'You are all mind, indeed.' He smiled peculiarly.

'I don't think I got that.'

'You rationalise everything, Nia. Your brilliant mind subordinates everything strictly to logic. That's the only method you have for perceiving people, the world, for drawing conclusions and making decisions. At least that's what the description of you from the university says. You need empirical data to judge whether you can do more, really?' He pursed his lips and lifted his eyebrows.

I was irritated by the fact that he had read the insultingly shallow student's character description that the university had drawn for me. It basically covered my inability to understand irrational and illogical things. It highlighted my lack of communication skills and my weak points, but it didn't say anything about the abilities of my brain. My annoyance was obvious, but it was quickly replaced by a logical question:

Why would he bother to dig up information about an insignificant person like me?

'Nia?'

His voice brought me back to reality.

'Any assessment without data is just speculation,' I said matter-of-factly. 'Most people do this, but you asked me an honest question and I am giving you my honest answer. That's it,' I was blinking rapidly.

'People make emotional assessments, too. And few are those who speak the truth.' He moved closer again. Only centimetres away, he sank into the voids of my pupils as if diving for some priceless treasure laying at the bottom of my eyes. I distinguished between different smells of musk and cedar, surrounded by the unfamiliar smell of the study, wine, and the distant scent of tobacco. My pulse was pounding, my throat went suddenly dry. This neurological process astounded me, as the president seemed to penetrate my brain.

'The first conclusion is not in the field of my knowledge, and the second one is logical. People like you rarely appreciate the truth, that's why those around them are afraid to speak it. *Fear* is a common occurrence.' I frowned, assuming he might find my statement offensive.

'Are you afraid of me, Nia?' he pronounced my name with curiosity.

My head exploded in a buzzing chaos. The timbre of his voice made me shiver. I even flinched and I hoped the inexplicable disturbances in my nervous system would remain safely hidden behind my barrier. He just stood there, expressionless and incomprehensible. His behaviour and the lack of distance paralysed me. Still, I managed to take a breath for a precise answer:

'There is no reason for *Fear*. Undoubtedly, there are many suspicious details about you, but none of them is on *Fear*'s list!' I did my best to pronounce the words clearly. Coming out of his stupor, *Reason* started counting mechanically:

On Fear's list, there are: darkness, water, failure, needles...

'You're so...' He stopped, probably because he didn't want some insulting words to spill out. I was used to insulting words, but I was somehow unenthused at the prospect of hearing another one of them now. I looked down, and suddenly he laughed. I was puzzled. The sound was pleasant to the ears and once again, I gaped at my body's reaction. 'How do you even survive in this insane world?'

'I write down my observations and conclusions about the general reality, but I can't define exactly how I survive yet.' My teeth shone behind a genuine smile.

Victor stepped back and moved away from me to the other end of the room. The disturbances disappeared, and yet I realised that his new position did not bring me more comfort. He sat down on the couch and asked me if I had noticed his interest in extraordinary, straight-talking, out-of-the-box people with beautiful minds. He was examining me in a manner which gave me the impression that he enjoyed my presence, and wouldn't put on me any of the insulting labels that others did.

Although totally different from me—successful and sane—he shared my lack of interest in the general reality. Again, there was no expression on his face, and yet I could clearly notice his boredom with normality. As we talked, I seemed to be finding the right words with him like never before—the right tone of voice as well. Our communication was devoid of my usual issues. All of a sudden, I found myself in the company of someone who could almost understand me, who seemed to even know me. He didn't stare at me in disbelief, pity, criticism, or in any other ways that I was used to. I couldn't tell what mood hid behind his blank expression, but he was definitely not looking down on me anymore. I could even assume that he was comfortable enough to communicate with unusual ease.

In the middle of my thoughts, he got up and came to me again. The wall of superiority rose for a moment and, through it, he stabbed me with his icy-cold eyes.

'You will work for me! That's why I called you here. Personally, for me, not as a president, but for my business,' I was following his words with suspicion. "Personally" means that you won't work for a company with bosses and working hours.' He paused, waiting for confirmation that I understood what he said, but I didn't reply. 'You will be given various tasks. Ones that you will complete on your own, at first, so you can get used to the environment and me. I read that you find it difficult to adapt. You will have assignments, which will challenge your mind, you will have a lot of work and no time for yourself. We will discuss all other details later.' He pinned his gaze on me. 'I expect a quick confirmation because I'm not going to accept anything else!'

For a moment, there seemed to be fire on his face, but then he went back to his usual statuesque composure.

'Was this even a question? It didn't sound like one.' My pupils dilated with surprise. As I was just about to direct another word to my open mouth, one of the bodyguards burst into the room. He reported that someone urgently needed to talk to the president, and Kaov hurried out.

I was left there alone, staring at one single point. I tried to assimilate the new information slowly, drop by drop, while dozens of questions were flying through my mind.

I cannot conclude anything. I am processing the data too slowly. Excitement is distracting me with all those dance moves and vibrations!

Reason propped the edge of his square head on his hands, puzzled as I was.

TWO

The same car took me back to my place. I sat on the stairs for nearly an hour, staring at the block of flats in front of me. Usually, I found the chaotic order of illuminated and unlit windows infuriating, but at that moment I badly needed to count, even an irregular sequence. *Reason* didn't have enough time to process the confusing information, and he snorted in frustration:

There is insufficient data available for a satisfactory assumption. I am trying to systemise. The cause of these neurological disturbances is also unclear!

The cold weather forced me inside. Buried deep in my thoughts, I walked up the stairs and unlocked the door on autopilot. Maddie was nervously circling the living room:

'You're not picking up your phone! What's going on? I was worried!'

'You, of all people? Good evening by the way!'

'Andre and I called you like a hundred times! You didn't warn anyone that you were going to be late. Look at the time! Were you held back at work?'

'Not that it's any of your business, but yeah. The president demanded to speak with me at some other place and the logistics took time. Anyway, why do I even have to warn the two of you?' I settled on the couch, unbothered by her reaction.

'What?! Speak with you about what?' Fascinated, she poured a glass of wine for me, too. 'Speak up!'

'He offered me a job.'

'To take coffees to *his* office?'

'No, to work personally for him.'

'Personally?' Her mouth twisted into a mocking smile. 'You were saying you're not that kind of a girl, right? And now look at the cheeky offer you've gotten!' She let out a loud laugh.

'Maddie! "Personally" means for his own business. I'll work for him, personally. No other bosses, no defined working hours. I'll have assignments that will challenge my mind, I'll have a lot of work to do and no time for myself,' I tried to quote Victor, but Maddie's laughter became even louder.

'Nia, for someone with such a genius mind, you are incredibly dumb. How is it possible that you always know so much, and yet you can never make accurate judgements of reality? There's nothing you can do for his business. The president is surrounded by dozens of smart men who make money for him out of thin air. Why would he want you? It's obvious that his offer is related to something else.'

'They might be smart, but they're quite ordinary. And I am not!' I snapped.

'No, wacko! That's just in your imagination. In reality, he is luring you to work for him in order to prevent a public scandal of him fucking some crazy trainee at the president's office,' she hissed viciously, certain about the truth of her words.

'Your issue with arguments is obvious again. First of all, there is no reason for him to have such intentions. I thought I made it clear to you last night. Second, such a relationship with an employee, even in his own business, would still create a scandal. Third, I already told you that I have no interest in practising sex!' My reaction was sharp, because her conclusions lacked logic once again.

'He owns companies. People like him do whatever they like, with whomever they like. You know it perfectly well. All he cares about is avoiding scandals! Nia, do you even have any doubts, or are you just willing to eff for this job?' Her narrowed eyes waited for my reply.

'Stop making things up, Maddie! Can't you just accept that this is a chance for something more? Much more than any other possible, or even make-believe, chance. If I am to decide against taking it, I will need solid arguments, not your absurd assumptions,' I was nervously unpacking my reasoning in front of her stupid face.

'This is not a chance for anything, Nia, you simply got lucky. I'll give you that! You keep moralising, but as it turns out, you are the real whore here, just a crazy and clever one. And he must be a pervert if he wants you,' her voice became spiteful. 'I should've ended up with that internship, damn it! How is this even possible? There is nothing feminine or passionate about you. You are a sociopath and a freak, who doesn't even feel normal human emotions. And you don't even try to be at least slightly normal!' She drank her wine in one gulp.

'I am not a sociopath. It doesn't matter what kind of a freak I am, because it's a job offer. What matters is my freaky intellect, which you do not have. Stop it!' I scolded her, sick of her insults.

'Yeah, it must've been your intellect that attracted him, because it's obvious you're nothing like those flawless beauties around him. He's probably going to have some perverted fun with you for a night or two, and then you will have to do some actual work. Just admit you are going to do this, Nia! You are going to surrender, he is going to eff you, even though I can't imagine how he will manage to do that, and that is how you plan to secure a better future for yourself. Everything else is bull!' She headed sulkily to her bedroom. 'Wake up, Nia! This is our goddamn reality, at least be honest enough to admit that you are exactly what I say.'

'Why are you always so vicious? Explain it to me, because there is no logic in what you say and I don't get it. Do you understand that?' I didn't like fighting with her, but it happened all the time.

'I understand, Nia! I understand perfectly! You say one thing, you play the innocent girl, you always know everything, you're always oh-so-smart, but in the end, you are an effing hypocrite. He has calculated your price and he is going to buy you. That's all. It's obvious even for me and the capacity of my brain. Stop pretending that you don't belong to the bunch of whores, just admit it!' She was red with rage.

'Magdalena!' I shouted. She kept on:

'I'm only curious whether he's going to make you more normal before he sleeps with you. Although, I doubt he can do that. Tons of cash won't be enough to fix the craziness in your eyes. Whenever you open your mouth, it becomes absolutely clear that you are a freak, too. Look at you! You can't even hold a decent conversation. You're no good for anything, neither to sleep with nor to talk to. I can't imagine why a man like him would want you, even for half a night. It must be some perverted thing for rich people. They get anything and anyone, then they get overly satisfied and go insane! Finally, they look for fun with freaks like you!' Every malicious word she spat ricocheted around the room.

I couldn't understand why she despised and insulted me so much. She slammed the door to her room. Behind my bulging eyes, *Reason* scratched his head:

Maddie has gone crazy again. Why is she behaving even more ridiculously than usual?

I shrugged silently. My body was tense as I finished my wine. Having a better understanding of general reality than me, my boss and Maddie had both defined me as a whore, and my roommate even suggested that I was useless. Over and over again, I dissected their sentences, trying to dig out their arguments and logic. After all, Maddie was not wrong in thinking that I was a freak, and Andre had obviously shared too much information about me and my defects. A volcano of insecurity had always bubbled inside of me, and Maddie's words had caused it to erupt. I was trying to calculate the probability of her being right about everything else, too, but the data was insufficient. Her claims simply could not be verified. Nevertheless, the mere fact that she understood people and reality much better provoked an irrational anxiety in me.

'Damn you, you absolutely crazy, wretched world! How is it possible that you exist thanks to precise laws, and yet not one of them is applicable to people?' A deep sigh escaped my murmuring lips as I poured myself more wine. 'How am I to tell who is right and who wants what, if there is no logic at all?'

The Monster, Fear's best friend, giggled. It stalked around my mind all the time, and now it was feasting on today's treats. It looked like a fat, nasty, grotesque monster, so that is what I called it, since I didn't know what exactly it was. It fed on insults, bitterness, and, of course, disappointment—its favourite delicacy. I stuffed all these things into its mouth; I was pleased to have somewhere to dispose of them. *The Monster* chewed like a famished predator and, with each bite, it seemed to grow even fatter, nastier, more grotesque. Oftentimes it would kick *Confidence* with its crooked leg. Poor *Confidence*! She would bump into a corner, whimper there for a couple of days, before eventually recovering. She was quite tough, I must give her that, but *the Monster* was stubborn, too. It was like a dangerous parasite: the bigger it got, the more food it required. The toxins it released poisoned me all the time, and it waited for even the tiniest crumb to help it remind me that I was good for nothing and no one. Not for people, not for the world. *The Monster* drowned my mind in sticky bitterness, and it needed only a second to turn me into the worst version of myself: one that despised everything and everyone, including myself, and didn't bother to hide it. *The Monster* also had the habit of waking *Malice* up. She lurked behind people and reality, particularly everything that was warped—on their patterns. She craved breaking the patterns, then fixing them again, usually by applying the most nefarious methods. It was hard for me to push her back before she would start dreaming of heavy or sharp objects.

Still munching on its food, *the Monster* began his all too familiar, horrible cackle:

Why all the effort? You're no good anyway! There's no chance for you. People are right to think that you're just unhinged. No one wants you and no one has any reason to want you, unless they are truly perverted or crazy.

Life must be easy for normal people who don't carry entities in their heads, nor monsters trying to convince them how useless and lacking they are. My dream was to grasp its throat and crush it. But it wasn't possible because *the Monster* had grown too big, and it never missed the chance to fatten up.

I'm not in the mood for you right now! I'm fed up with explaining to you that it is statistically impossible for her to be no good for anything and anyone. It's not going to work out for you today, so cut it out!

Reason shouted at him, waving threatening fists.

I've always been proven right! Your statistics suck, huh?

The Monster snickered, then decided to shut up.

φ

I was too overwhelmed and tired of information to torture myself with the incomprehensible, let alone to wrestle with *the Monster*. Finishing the bottle as quickly as I could, I collapsed on my bed. However, the chaos in my head swirled incessantly, unsure of the part of the day in which to bury itself. Even my headphones—volume up to the max—didn't help. *Reason* was tapping his foot, looking around, muttering:

Maddie can't handle logic, but she knows about general reality. Do not ignore the hypothesis that her suspicion is justified. Why would the president provide a real chance, just like that? He also experiences difficulties in communicating with people, he is probably not good at evaluating them either. It is possible that he has wrong expectations. He might be underestimating us!

Reason gave me a headache and I grunted at him to hush. I forced my eyelids closed. The night silenced my chaos. It didn't wake me up with its nightmares, which was not typical, but maybe it was just that the wine had sedated me hard enough. Everything was going fine, until the infuriating sound of my ringing phone woke me up.

Andre destroyed the pleasure of at least having some decent sleep on a Saturday, even though he knew perfectly well that it was all I wished for on the weekend. His voice resonated in a falsetto.

'Nia! When were you planning to tell me that the president wants to bang you?'

'Firstly, good morning. Secondly, I was not planning to tell you anything.'

'You weren't?' He shrieked in my ear.

'Of course not. Why would I tell you something untrue?'

'Oh, come on! Maddie told me everything. Is that what you want, Nia? I never thought that you were just one of those girls after money and power. Maddie even defined you as a whore,' he was hissing angrily.

'You were right not to think that. You, of all people, should know how I am and I really don't understand why you are saying all this,' I explained sleepily. 'I guess Maddie told you that I went somewhere with him, because he had a job offer for me. You know very well that he owns a huge business.'

'That's what you think!'

'I, and the president, which is quite enough. It's absurdly early, Andre. We'll meet and we'll analyse all the facts objectively. Maddie has been crazy these last few days and I have no idea why she's saying all this crap.'

'What facts? You are the crazy one here! It's more than obvious what a person like him would want with you. Bye!' He snapped angrily before he hung up.

I tucked myself back into bed. After a few seconds, the phone started clanging again. 'Oh, screw this! What is it this time, Andre?' I was just about to decline the call, when I realised that the number on the display was unknown.

'Yes!' I replied sulkily.

'The president will be expecting you in his office in half an hour, ma'am. I am sending you the address!' A hurried female voice recited in one breath.

'Good morning!' I shouted indignantly. *Why don't they greet politely, for Christ's sake, at least on a Saturday morning!* 'It's Saturday, ma'am, it's too early, I don't have such an appointment, and I can't make it that fast!'

'Just leave quickly then! Being late is unacceptable,' she hung up.

'What a shitty Saturday morning! These secretaries are like a bunch of alarms,' I roared as I hit the mattress.

Annoyed, I jumped out of bed, grabbing my jeans, a T-shirt, and a thick sweater. I put my hand-painted colourful trainers on, certain I would have to run. Tying my impractically long hair in a bun, I slapped my sleepy face twice to wake up and flew out, clutching my backpack and not greeting sour Maddie on the way.

Once I found myself on the pavement, I scanned both directions intently. Bright lines in my mind drew a diagram, estimating which stop was closer. Then suddenly, a man three heads taller than me appeared by my side. He stared at me with a question in his eyes.

'Nia?' He was examining my sleepy face and the messy bun on my head with curiosity. His timber woke me up completely. I looked at him sullenly from bottom to top.

'Yes?'

'I am supposed to drive you to the office.'

He was a giant, crooked in a somewhat cute way, and dressed all in black except a white T-shirt's hem which protruded from under his shirt. I noticed his enormous, rough shoes, their laces going through only two of the holes and tied in a bizarre sailor-textbook knot. Without saying anything else, he escorted me to a black, square jeep, before driving us off in perfect silence.

As we approached the address, the traffic stopped. Two idiots had bumped into each other, refusing to move their cars to make room. A couple of minutes late already, so, to the astonishment of the giant, I left the car.

It'd probably be useful if I did some sports other than yoga.

That was my only thought as I ran, following the direction of the secretary's index finger. I burst into the room without knocking, short of breath and thanking my trainers. The president's main company occupied an elegant baroque building in the centre of the city. The office, with its bright but cold colours, was full of order, which irritated my mind. But I was panting so hard that I didn't even react to that fact. My eyes ran up and down the scarce, exquisite furnishing, the straight lines, the lack of excess. There was not even the slightest of curves to balance things. I detected somewhat familiar irregular shapes in the dark, abstract paintings on the walls. Victor Kaov was leaning against the corner of his desk. Talking on the phone, he stood wearing jeans and a white shirt with rolled up sleeves. His hair, much messier than when it was the president's hair, triggered my curiosity. He stared at me questioningly, his attention freezing on my rapid breathing.

'It is impossible for you to just do what I say, isn't it?' He hissed in an icy voice before putting his mobile away. Then he pushed a button on the landline phone. A gentle female voice shrunk with two simple words:

'Yes, sir!'

'I want him out immediately, and I want five verified offers by Monday.'

The female voice tried to object, but he cut her off at the first sound.

'I was clear.' He hung up with the same button.

Though indifferent, the way he spoke still sounded arrogant and contemptuous. His face showed nothing but the impregnable haughty gleam of his cold eyes. No mood at all. Again, I ended up analysing the specifics of his inability to communicate. His conversation went well beyond being "inappropriate" and I suspected that it was even more difficult for him than me to find the right tone, the right words, let alone the right combination of both. I suddenly noticed one of the flawless women sitting on a leather armchair next to a low table. I hadn't met her before, though she looked almost the same as the two women who had emerged from the hidden room with him. She was drinking tea silently, not even caring to look up and say hi.

Damn! Where do they make them so perfect?

I caught myself pulling the hem of my sweater as I examined the curls of her blonde hair, her doll-like face, and the stylish garments on her killer body.

That's normal!

An echo in my head. A man like this was supposed to be with such a woman. A standard cliché of the current world.

That must be quite an expensive body. With some cheap intellect.

Contempt hissed while I threw secret glances at the woman. *Reason* scolded him:

Oh, come on! There is no data. We don't evaluate this way. It is not precise!

'Get out!' Victor's voice cooled the room down.

As I mechanically headed for the exit, I noticed the stunning long legs marching in the same direction. I turned to the president to meet a restrained smile, amused by my reaction.

'Good morning.' He said, staring at me again.

''Morning,' I muttered between two deep breaths, still under the influence of the running.

He came closer. In my trainers, I realised how small I was compared to him, not only because we inhabited two opposing steps of the social ladder. He was two heads above me, and his shoulders about a foot wider. The wall of superiority, thick and high, surrounded him. Powerful energy, visible behind his glassy eyes, looked like it could crush anyone on the other side.

'You are late. Have you been running?' He spoke quietly and I nodded. 'I sent a car. Why did you run?' A line appeared between his eyebrows.

'I am never late. It makes me tense. The street is blocked, and I was in a hurry!' My breath separated the words from one another. I started to suspect that my heart rate had quickened not only from running, but also because of the incomprehensible neurological processes. The president was silent for a moment, gazing closely at my open lips.

'You smell like candy,' the dreaminess in his voice surprised me, and his eyes seemed dreamy as well. He reached out to tuck a naughty lock of hair behind my ear. At that, even *Excitement* was startled. He started bouncing in my head, making my heart race faster than ever.

'Oh! I had my breakfast on the way. You want some?' I moved away from his hand and his irises focused on me again. I clumsily pulled a crushed pack of gummy bears out of my pocket. As they were my main source of food, I kept a good supply of them in my backpack. I shoved the pack under his nose.

'This is not breakfast,' there was irritation in his voice. 'You must stick to a healthier diet!'

'No, I certainly mustn't! These are like oranges, just without the annoying peel. Plus, they are much more compact to carry around,' I said confidently, my nod inviting him to try one.

'Now that is a wild conclusion!' he laughed. The sound warmed me. 'Sit here and drink some water, you are barely breathing.' He pressed his large hand to my back, pushing me toward the armchair. His touch stung me. I pulled away abruptly, causing him to immediately back up. He sat down on the couch opposite me. The pleasant sound of his laugh became an even voice once again.

'You will develop good work and personal habits once you align them with me and my schedule. It's busy, but you'll get used to it.'

'No, I certainly won't. My own habits are good!' I replied.

'Gummy bears for breakfast? Your breathing shows that you don't do much exercise. You seem tired. Your judgement on good habits is quite incorrect,' he shot this at me. I didn't like this patronising speech.

'No, it's certainly not. I'm tired because your secretary woke me up early. I am pretty active at night; mornings are just not my best time.'

'Active?' He repeated, raising his eyebrows. His surprise alerted me to the ambiguity of my words, and I was quick to clarify:

'Mentally active! At night, I calculate probabilities, I deal with numbers, read, study...' I swallowed dryly. 'Never mind. Candy carbs feed the brain, which is satisfactory for me. I don't do exercise because it takes time and it's boring. I am skinny nevertheless, which means I don't accumulate excess fat. I don't need more muscles, at least for now. Besides, I practice yoga. It's more than a sport, it just doesn't help with running,' I shrugged and he smiled with his pursed lips. I kept throwing inadvertent glances at them, but I managed to finish: 'My brain is in excellent shape, so is my body, so my habits are good. To conclude, my judgement is correct.' My explanations were getting slower and slower, as I realised that this time it was me staring in a completely inappropriate manner.

'I will have to put much effort into my communication with you. Do you argue all the time?' He pressed his fingers to his chin as I examined his face for any sign of expression.

'Certainly not! Only if I have solid arguments. Which is often enough, but not all the time,' I took a breath to help me focus on the topic of my conversation with Maddie. I went on in a more business-like fashion:

'Victor, we need to discuss your expectations for me because I don't want it to turn out that…' I cleared my throat to formulate the end of my sentence precisely. '…There are things beyond my capabilities. I would prefer to refuse your offer if there are such expectations.'

He paused, trying to read the expression on my face.

'I will definitely have to put in much effort,' he exhaled noisily through his gritted teeth. 'Nia, I will clarify my offer,' he stared impudently at me, and a spasm tightened my stomach. 'I thought you seemed uncertain when I offered you the job, and now my impression is confirmed. Obviously, you have to gather the empirical data you need first and get used to communicating. You seem to be even considering a refusal, though this is a chance for you to unleash your potential on a scale you have never imagined.'

'I'm considering this option in case…'

'I don't like to be interrupted, Nia!' His sharp tone startled me, but he continued in an even voice. 'I'm thinking of assigning you things that go beyond your comfort zone. I want a bigger office in a modern building and an apartment nearby. You will organise the whole process on your own, so that everything will be ready in a month. You will take personal responsibility for all the stages, including the finances. Several people from my team will assist you, so you can get used to them as well. You can talk to them on the phone, if it's easier for you,' he was explaining insistently. 'At this point you are not to communicate with the others, and not to come here. You are not to communicate with me, either, because that makes you nervous, even though it's reasonless. You will get used to the environment and to me. Once you finish successfully, you will feel calm enough to accept without hesitation. Your main problem is self-doubt. Then, we will discuss all other details regarding the job. The driver is outside, and he will take you to my people. Please keep in mind that your outfit is not suitable for work at all, even though the trainers are cute,' he was looking for a reaction, but I blinked foolishly.

Reason refused to speak. He was completely silent, that idiot! I was all alone in my head, not a sound was going in the direction of my throat, and this time I was not convinced that the barrier managed to hide my incomprehension.

The secretary burst in and announced that Victor was expected to attend a meeting. He gave no reply. Instead, he stared at me, waiting for my reaction. A quiet 'okay' rolled out of my mouth as I got up and was about to leave the room.

'Nia, the probability of you being able to do all this is high. You just don't know it yet because you haven't tried,' his voice caught up with me at the door, but I couldn't confirm his assumption.

It would have been more logical if he had given a smaller task to such a strange weirdo. Or even some calculations. He must have read what you can do. At least you are not going to be among people, but on the other hand, you are not qualified, you don't have the skills and the knowledge required! Yes, maybe finance and law, to a certain degree, and yet there are no arguments to justify his decision to assign this to you and assume you will be able to handle it. It's suspicious!

Reason was chatting on while I walked in astonishment towards the exit. All of a sudden, a ringing thought tore into my mind:

Maybe he's crazy, too!

I sensed someone's presence behind, then I heard his voice as if through a tunnel:

'Miss! Nia, the car is this way,' the same crooked giant led me outside.

A couple of hours later, I was still stunned, sitting at the table in my flat. I was examining a wad of cash, a credit card, and the business cards of the three men that I had briefly met that day. A lawyer, an accountant, and a financier. They invited me to a house outside the city, surrounded by dense wood, to inform me they were at my service. The financier seemed untrustworthy from the first instance. I guess it was my intuition, or that his facial expressions bothered me, perhaps. He handed me an envelope with a credit card with my name on it and the money, tied with an elastic band. He told me to use it for any expenses. Puzzled by what was happening, I basically did nothing other than nod.

On the way back, I muttered to the giant to drive me to the president. I needed answers to at least some of the urgent questions regarding his terms and conditions. It turned out that Victor had just gone abroad for a couple of days and I couldn't speak to him. The giant left me in front of my block. This is how I ended up baffled by my new reality and my chance for something more, staring into space.

My fingers took their time tapping the money in an irregular rhythm. Then I decided that every new beginning starts with a large cup of strong coffee. Maddie texted me that she was going to spend a few days at her parents'. I had no choice but to accept the intricate knots of events and disregard all dubious, unclear motives and details. Despite the chaos in my head, my body tensed in a way I enjoyed. I had always been looking for a way to challenge myself, but I had done this sluggishly due to the lack of actual challenges. I counted a sequence as I hesitated, deciding how to proceed. I came to the conclusion that there were no arguments for me to waste any of my short time, waiting for the president to come back. The competitor in me could not wait to take on the job and prove myself. *Reason* was pleased that we were at least about to gather indisputable evidence of whether I could handle such illogical matters on my own. I took a breath before counting:

ONE!

My unfailing brain focusing technique didn't work this time. The blue presidential irises staring in my mind didn't help, and the sensation of something squeezing my stomach was still there. Andre kept calling annoyingly often. After I listened to several of his excuses, I explained to him that I was tired and needed some rest.

Eventually, I somehow managed to focus and accelerate my mind in the mode of processing information painfully fast. Irregular squints of my eyes reflected that operation. I was speed reading the screen, studying the construction of deals like the ones I was expected to make—the stages and the sequence of necessary actions arranged in a mind map. I visited various buildings throughout the weekend but couldn't find what I was looking for. One question kept bugging me: why did I assume, with no arguments at all, what a person like him would want?

I couldn't sleep that night. It was too late to ride on the metro, so I took Maddie's disturbingly old car. Driving aimlessly around, the obsessive thought I would fail the president's ungrounded task maddened me. *The Monster*, utterly convinced of this outcome, kept repeating it. I guess it was the reason why I doubted myself so much. For all my life, it had been prowling behind me, and now it was hungrier than ever. I was always trying to compete—to prove my worth to others and myself, without success. I never succeeded. *The Monster* won every battle, usually at the very beginning, with its favourite statements: "this is not for you", "you are not good enough", "you cannot do it", "you do not deserve that". There was always a "not", it didn't even matter which exact words would follow.

This time, however, I was playing an imaginary game with the president. He unexpectedly raised the stakes with his illogical offer, and I was determined to reach even higher, because I needed to confirm that I truly deserved to be given a chance. Displeased with my failure so far, I drove on the deserted boulevards unreasonably fast for my skills until I found myself in the outskirts of the city. The foot of a magnificent mountain surrounded the entire area. I often looked at it when my mind got overwhelmed with its intolerance of normality.

All of a sudden, I saw an impudent towering building before me. It was made of metal and clad in glass. Symmetrical, expressionless, superior to everything around it.

'Did they design you based on his photograph?' I spoke to the colossus. It was built on the highest spot possible, countless lights would twinkle at the feet of anyone who could possess it. 'You're perfect!' I admired the curved reflection of the city displayed on the building's chest.

The Monster spat:

Unlike you!

Shut up, creep!

I was surprised that I had managed to chase the bastard back to its hole. I smiled smugly and hurried back to my flat.

I spent the remaining hours until sunrise digging out information on the building and the owner. My impatience made me turn up early on Monday at the seller's address. I took the president's remark into account and put on my suit for work.

One: inhale, take a step with the right foot; two: exhale, take a step with the left foot!

My brain was counting. This was my only technique for achieving focus and balance. My mind was searching for arguments to prove that I could handle the conversation and the task ahead.

Unlike ever before, I got lucky and I was invited to lunch with the owner. I had read that he was very involved with the previous president. My special barrier disguised my doubts and the seller mistakenly got the impression that I was a strong-minded person. Despite my difficulties in communicating, we went smoothly through all the details. I decided to tell him the truth and it triggered his interest. The glare in his eyes swirled in a whirlwind, betraying his determination to get close to the new people in power.

Confidence appeared five centimetres taller than ever before. She ironed the folds of my voice and composure. I was amazed by the fact that in reality someone, who had profited from the previous leader, could suddenly change his whole attitude. The enmity between the ex-president and the current one was a public secret. It was evident, however, that the seller would give anything to secure a deal with Victor. *Knowledge* explained:

Exact term: greed. It is not based on logic. It is widespread in general reality. It often becomes the ground for life compromises.

I was surprised, although I was long familiar with encountering faulty patterns that lacked logic, and irrational behaviour labelled as "normal". I was learning to accept the fact that people easily turn paradoxes into norms.

A few hours later, the guy called me to offer his assistance for me to buy a penthouse in the building next door, too.

I went to Victor's office to make an appointment. His secretary dryly informed me that he was back. She was expecting him soon, but she couldn't confirm whether he was going to speak to me, so I had to wait. I was sitting silently in her room in front of the office while the competitor in me was burning with impatience. Tapping my fingers, I was complacently convinced I would impress him with my quick results. I was disturbed, however, by the neurological process caused by the thought of our upcoming encounter. It brought an unfamiliar contraction to my stomach, and no one in my head could explain what it was.

Victor stormed in and a noisy group gathered around him. Everyone was speaking one after the other. He pinned his haughty, questioning eyes on me, and I shivered.

'Come in!' He opened the door to his office.

Everyone fell silent before turning to me. Fiddling with the sleeves of my blazer, I slipped inside, and he slammed the door.

'I didn't call for you! Why are you here?'

'Hello!' I muttered as *Confidence* shrank back to normal. 'I found what you want. I had a preliminary talk, too. That's why I came,' I explained to the back of his head while he was nervously pouring himself a drink.

'Interesting! And what is it that I want, Nia?' His voice sounded slightly mocking.

'I mean, according to your instructions about the real estate deal, which were quite scarce. Here is the information I gathered, and...'

He interrupted me as I put the sheets of paper on the table:

'We will discuss this after dinner,' he turned to face me. 'I want to introduce you to the rest of my team. This will be a formal dinner. Nia...' He came closer, examining me critically. He was silent for a second, as if he was trying to figure out how to continue. I assumed he was about to say something important, so I did my best to stay focused. 'The driver will take you to a place where your appearance will be taken care of. I expect you to be appropriate, and obviously you won't be able to pull this off by yourself, even though you were provided with everything necessary.'

I reddened as he spoke with the wrong voice and the wrong words: the usual rude combination that the president used whenever he experienced difficulties communicating with someone. The commanding notes vibrated like a badly tuned piano. On top of that, he looked down on me with disapproval. I often saw reproach in people, but it was the first time I had seen it in him and I was deeply annoyed. I tucked my messy hair behind my ears and smoothed my grey suit. *The Monster* swallowed the insult with appetite, and a bite of disappointment after that. Gritting my teeth, I shot my nastiest look so it would twist the president's stomach, but behind his wall of superiority, he didn't budge. *Pride* straightened her long spine and growled in my head. She was infuriated by Victor's lack of interest in my good results and by the judgement that there was something wrong with me again. Most of all, however, she was pissed because I was still expected to fit in with such standards. I tried to cool down, clenching my fists. He looked at my hands with his glassy eyes, then continued in an even more commanding tone:

'And one last thing: you applied for leave, but you are not an intern anymore. You will focus only on me and your job. You must get it done before the initial deadline.'

'I haven't accepted the offer,' I lowered my gaze. Again, there were no expressions on his face.

'You have no option but to accept. I want you to be available at any time. This means you shall not make appointments, especially for the evenings, because most of the time I'm only free then.'

'Excuse me, but...' I tried to snap at his arrogance, but he interrupted me.

'I was clear. You can leave now.' He hissed at my sulky face.

Before I could curse, his look stopped me. I left the office in a few quick steps. Perhaps Maddie had the same unpleasant experience every time I failed to choose my words and my tone well. At least I finally understood her remarks.

Screw *this unbelievable, rude attitude! There's nothing improper about my appearance! He has no right to judge me! What counts is my brain, and it doesn't have an appearance. It's just highly effective. Beyond highly effective! So damn highly effective that I lost my internship! I will probably lose that job as well. How am I going to get a degree without an internship? This unbearable, arrogant bastard is out of his mind. I won't be able to put up with him! I'll explode and insult him to his face, and I need his wretched money! I need a degree, too, to get out of here.*

I became increasingly desperate with every step down the corridor, but everyone in my head was silent. *The Monster*, on the other hand, was having a hard time trying to swallow all that it had just received. Its full mouth was assuring me that everything I thought was right:

How are your statistics? You've never been proper, why would you be now? Did you really believe in the chance for something more, freak?

The driver caught up with me as I growled. He threw me a glance of surprise, then insisted that we should go. After confirming the lack of alternatives, I reluctantly got in the car.

φ

We stopped in front of a shiny window. I was staggering towards the entrance while perfect, almost identical, women like the ones at Victor's streamed past me in both directions. The beauty with the curls came out of the door and waved energetically at the driver. I froze as she scornfully measured me from top to bottom with a sneer. She deliberately frowned. A clone of hers stood beside and even repeated her exact moves. The giant muttered something under his breath, pushing me in their direction, but I leaned stubbornly on his arm. I was moving my eyes from one perfect face to the other, in front of me and behind the window, when the mental block hit me. I was stunned.

Oh, God! That's where they make them!

The bright lines in my head shot chaotically. They flew in all directions, but couldn't gather into a shape, so I just blinked there rapidly, paralysed. Sometimes things in general reality had this effect on me. There was no logic and no arguments, and there was no chance for me to fix the faulty pattern, even in my head. Such irregularities made my hyper-rational mind stuck like an old computer that was unable to run new software. Some patterns were just deranged enough to evoke painful anarchy in my brain.

Symmetrical and depersonalised. With their consent. I thought that people only voluntarily depersonalised their existence. This woman was at the office, the one next to her looks exactly the same, the girls inside, too, and also the girls here. Damn, they are so many! What am I even doing here?

My eyes wouldn't stop moving. The giant pulled me out of the trance by clumsily pushing me towards the clones. I crossed my arms over my chest and clutched my shoulders.

'How could they possibly take care of me here? What do you think I am? Some... Damn, what does he expect me to do? He really is crazy! Yes, he is absolutely insane! You all are,' I shouted, pushing the giant's hand away. I ran down the street, shaking all over, and he followed.

'What's wrong with you? Are you OK?' He caught up with me and took hold of my elbow.

'Don't touch me! I don't like being touched. And stop walking after me with those big legs of yours. What's wrong? Can't you see?' I pointed nervously at the crazy place. His brown eyes bulged.

Continuing down the street, I looked over my shoulder at the warped reality that had crashed into my mind and driven it mad again. I sank into the metro entrance and got on a train. The rhythm swayed me, but it didn't make me drift away. My thoughts were running in different directions; nausea swept over me.

This one time, Maddie's logic will prove to be correct. It's all starting to look more like what she said than what I was deceiving myself to believe! I lost my internship, and now he's trying to make me normal, make me fit in! Maddie suggested this from the very beginning. I was supposed to unleash my potential, and look at what has happened now. For what exactly is this a chance? Is there even a chance, or... am I a girl for a night or two? Facts: he didn't care about what I had accomplished, meaning it doesn't matter. I need to look proper, too—proper for what? For a private time after dinner? Damn!'

My thoughts turned furious on my way to the flat.

φ

The data filled my mind as I tried to systemise it. Considering the money on the table and all the events, too, his motives were looking increasingly suspicious and insulting. Andre kept calling continuously again and eventually I answered. I had been using him to try to learn "normal" relationships, even though their ordinariness bored me. At this particular moment, however, I couldn't give him even a fraction of my attention. I did not want to see him, I did not want to listen to his assertions about the president's expectations, which were probably going to prove correct. There were two days left until the graduation exam and I used this as a perfect excuse for refusing to meet Andre. He was pissed, regardless.

I kept pacing up and down the living room, torturing my mind into making a decision. I could simply refuse the offer, not burden myself with the oddities of the new reality and bury myself in the everyday mud again. The risk of being left with no degree and no money, though, and the tiny possibility that the coveted chance might actually be so close, tightened my chest. I wanted this chance even more and, deep inside, I was convinced that it would be truly extraordinary. I even allowed myself to think that I might actually handle the whole task, despite *the Monster* insisting on the opposite. Besides, I urgently needed money to leave. At the same time, I couldn't reject the opinions of everybody around me. Kaov's actions were becoming suspicious, and following Maddie's logic. His inability to communicate, and his unbearable tone and attitude confused me even more. I had no data and no arguments to make a proper assessment of the situation. Alongside the mess in my head, there was also something that resembled anger at his judgement of me. This something didn't sink in *the Monster*'s greedy mouth, though. This something was drowning me. Victor underestimated me and my mind didn't like this at all.

Indeed, Maddie would provide some explanation. Damn! Why am I expected to look "proper", why dinner, and how can these depersonalised women possibly take care of me? Should I call her to ask, or maybe she'll start shouting again? God, what if Maddie is right? Can I do this to get a job? Am I really like that? What if I am a whore without even knowing it?

These questions wouldn't leave me alone as I paced in circles. Then, the bell shouted incessantly. I wrinkled my nose.

Andre! How annoying is that!

I opened the door, munching hungrily on some gummy bears. A bitten, green paw nearly fell out of my mouth as I saw Victor standing before me. The sulking giant was one step behind him, and the bodyguards were on the stairs. It seemed to me that hundreds of flames flashed in the blue irises before they made me freeze again. A statue in a suit, his appearance made my throat dry.

'I must admit that you surprised me, Nia. Was it the store that gave you the impression I was insane?'

'No, it certainly wasn't the store,' I cleared my throat after this reply slipped out. He clenched his jaw.

In one step, he came into the flat, slamming the door under the bodyguards' noses. I assumed he was angry because I had insulted him, though his timbre didn't betray anything.

'And so why did you do that? Why did you run away and how exactly did you come to the conclusion I was insane?' His eyes demanded answers, but I kept silent. 'Nia, Toma told me exactly what happened and I want to know the motives for your reaction.'

'Well, I left because of the pattern. This particular one drives me crazy,' I stammered as he hung on my every syllable. I looked down at my colourful socks. 'There was no logic in the expectation I could get any help at a place like that, and there was no logic in the expectation of me looking "proper". It was all very suspicious.'

'What exactly is suspicious?' He sounded annoyed and I looked up with surprise. He waited for my reply with squinted eyes.

'The motives! People around me shared the same suspicions. And then a whole bunch of facts supported the suspicions. All of a sudden, I ended up at the shop, expecting someone to take care of my appearance, so I could look proper for dinner. There is no logic in all this being related to my job. Besides, you had no interest in my work, and I started getting confused. You ended my internship, which Maddie had predicted, and your awful attitude doesn't...' I was gesticulating wildly as he evaluated every word.

'Nia!' I was startled by the raised voice. 'Stop it!' He took hold of my palm, but I pulled it abruptly to my chest. He sighed before going on: 'I'm not good at explaining, so let's try deduction, I guess it'd be easier,' I nodded. 'You are stunningly smart, but it's difficult and unusual communicating with you. I was going to introduce you to a part of my team today. I wanted you to feel comfortable and more relaxed. You've already gathered data confirming that you can handle all this, right? However, you will have to communicate with a lot of people, at many dinners, and the environment is different from the one you're familiar with. I want you to get used to it because people have identical mechanisms when communicating and they perceive strangers in a certain sequence of judgements.'

He spoke slowly, and I was examining the movement of his lips. *Reason* shouted:

Stop staring and listen! We are practising deduction. A conclusion will be needed after the facts. Focus!

A speech like a tape recording came out of my mouth. My mind sometimes did that: I would go into a trance-like state and my voice would simply announce the given information at a rapid pace.

'I can see the logic. One tenth of a second. That's how long it takes for people to get their first impression of a stranger. They subconsciously judge others by their outer appearance. They identify themselves! I need to look like the others. This is the rational approach, given my lack of socially acceptable communication skills. I cannot decide on my own what a "proper appearance" is because I am not familiar with the environment or the standards. I don't have the data,' I narrowed my eyes with every sentence flowing out of my mouth.

'Nia! Don't say it aloud! Try to synthesise this in your mind,' Victor was holding my gaze tight. 'My goal was to make it easier for you today. I don't know what you were thinking.'

He spoke in a new, soft timbre, but I snapped nevertheless:

'Why would you? You know that it's incorrect, don't you?' The faulty pattern kept spinning before my eyes.

'What's incorrect?'

'The judgement! If it's made that way, it's incorrect. It becomes a subject of stereotypes. The lack of arguments distorts the judgement. You know very well that it's likely that your team won't accept me. There's no way for me to fit, even if I adopt the proper appearance. The statistics confirm this! Besides, you're not supposed to treat me with condescension,' I spat out my conclusions, irritated.

'I'm not treating you with condescension, I'm just trying to create better conditions for you! You don't have to worry about my team. My people always understand and obey my decisions.'

'I'm not worried, I'm used to all that. People prefer to judge by the faults rather than by the merits. I'll just inform you, so you will know,' still in a trance, my mind rushed to a newly found faulty pattern. 'That if they always understand, it is impossible that they'll always obey. If they obey, however, we can be quite certain that...' The bright lines were speeding through my head and bumped into a figure. I stared into the blue eyes that followed the twists and curves of my chain of thought. 'If they always obey, then you can't trust them,' a loud "Oh!" came out of my throat. 'So that's how I'm going to be useful. I see the faulty patterns and I cannot obey them,' I smiled, nodding my head. I concluded he was aware of my personal qualities.

'The way you draw conclusions, it's really weird,' he sighed. He went silent for a while. 'Let's just assume that it can be explained this way. Naturally, I want to have someone who can give me an objective third-party opinion. It's evident that I will need time to learn how to communicate with you, though. Nia, what are you anxious about? What's bugging you? Explain it to me, so I can understand!'

'The logic of your motives. I couldn't see it. The people around me couldn't see it. They all keep repeating the same thing: that there's nothing I can be useful with. They insist that I'm a whore, too, although this definition is inapplicable to me. They confused me, and the facts were somehow arranged...'

'First of all,' he interrupted me with his eyes narrowed. 'Their claim has to do with people's ideas about me, not about you! Second, if it was up to me, I wouldn't allow them to insult you even in their minds. Third, there is no reason for you to allow them to insult you,' I detected facial expressions this time. I could tell that he was angry at this information.

'I know what they suggest is wrong! Unless I assume you are perverted, there are no grounds for it, but I lacked data.' His eyes opened wide for a moment. 'You're obviously interested in what's between my ears, and I don't get offended easily. I am used to labels and I don't usually let them get in my way. It was just that I had a hard time understanding the logic in your motives, but now it's all clear. My apologies for saying you were insane. I sometimes get a little weird. I'm sorry!'

He was silent, his jaw clenched. Maybe angry again, but I could only guess, because there were no expressions. In a short moment, he spoke quietly:

'There's nothing to be sorry about! You must understand, though, that with me, it will be difficult for you to find logic. At least the logic that your beautiful, rational mind can understand. It would be easier if you could simply accept my decisions.'

'I don't have the ability to simply accept decisions, and logic is logic, it's universal,' I caught myself staring at him as he crossed my gaze.

'It is not! You need to quickly understand this and learn,' the unpleasant voice was back.

The Monster whinnied with laughter that echoed through my head. Being its best friend, *Fear* supported it by clapping his hands and making me shake. I was stunned and choked by the disgusting voice:

Yeah, it's just that you can't understand, and you can't learn! Did you notice the way he's speaking to you now? He's already pissed with your crazy behaviour! It will only take him a couple of days to realise how screwed up you are, and then your chance will be gone in no time. You are not able to understand, to be proper, let alone to fit in with his pattern. Failure, freak! That's what you'll get!

Perhaps my lips trembled and I squeezed my eyes as *the Monster* spewed its bile. I was startled by Victor's hand gripping my shoulder. Sharp arrows shot out of his fingers and pierced my stomach. He pulled me out of my trance, his glassy gaze made *the Monster* evaporate. There was silence, but I couldn't stop shaking.

'Nia? Are you OK?'

'Yes. I was just thinking.' I muttered as I took a step to the side.

With a discreet smile, he stared at me. I was focused on him, too. His face relaxed, even the wall of superiority was gone.

'Trust my judgement and forget about logic. Logic is too ordinary for you. And stop being rude!' He came closer and ran the tip of his finger down the edge of my face. His touch was like thorns. Something like an electric shock disrupted the rhythm of my breathing, and the muscles of my entire body tightened in pain.

'No!' I jumped. Everyone in my head was amazed at the short circuit. I narrowed my eyes.

'Excuse me! I know you don't like to be touched!' He stepped away abruptly, without taking his icy irises off me.

'That's true, but what you said about logic is not. Logic is never ordinary, it's either valid, or not!' I hissed, running my fingers over the spot he had touched.

Victor exhaled loudly, and his face became metallic again. He walked away, changing the conversation.

'You were right about the estates. They are exactly what I want and you must finish as soon as possible. Prepare and check the details with the financier tomorrow, the lawyer will help you take care of the deal.'

He headed to the door before I could answer. Pausing, he addressed me with his soft voice again:

'Nia, everything you need is within you, along with your endless doubts and insecurities. Your communication skills are poor, but you will learn. You'll get used to me and to the environment. I hope that all that bothered you is now clear. Take some rest, we'll leave meeting the team for tomorrow evening. You can decide for yourself how to prepare. Just, to be precise, "proper" means an elegant dress, high heels, and usually hair is not supposed to be quite so messy,' my ears bristled at his deep timbre. He slammed the door before I managed to reply.

As I poured wine for myself, *the Monster* threw at me the fact that Victor was right. My communication skills were more than poor: they revealed my defects, and the worst thing was that I had no idea how to fix them. I urgently needed to skill up, start comprehending people and reality, and learn how to handle my crazy reactions. I needed to ignore the doubts and the suspicions that tortured me, so I could fully focus on my job. In order to cope, it was necessary for me to communicate in a more normal manner, which obviously didn't include being rude, nor all the other methods I was familiar with. While I was arranging my conclusions, strange vibrations ran down my body.

Damn! Why are people so much more complicated than numbers?

Maddie stormed in visibly excited. Her eyes ran across the living room before she spoke:

'I saw the motorcade! Was he here?' She hurled herself at me, went red in a second and squeaked in falsetto: 'And all this money? Nia?' The bundle on the table arrested her attention and she arched her arrogant eyebrows. 'So you are a whore after all, aren't you? If I was doing the job, I'd get much more! Did he even fuck you, or he only wanted something little and perverted from a freak like you? Aren't you a hypocritical moralist!' She waved the money as her mouth vomited the words.

'Magdalena! Stop with the "whore" thing! You have no grounds to call me that. Victor confirmed it, too. You don't get to insult me!'

'Did he shag you doggie style or in the mouth while he was confirming? Why did he give you this money? Huh? Because you're smart?' She laughed nastily.

'Stop insulting me! I am more than smart and it's not my fault that you have only three brain cells chasing each other around your head. A man from his team gave me the money. We already clarified how I can be useful to him. Your accusations are absurd. They managed to confuse me, but now the motives are clear. End of conversation!'

For the first time ever, holding each other's hands, *Pride* and *Confidence* shouted in a thunderous duet. I would often get mad and explode from the inside, but I would still speak in an even voice. Shouting or being shouted at could numb me, I even started hiccoughing sometimes, so I avoided such situations. Maddie was startled by my new tone and she probably gaped at my back as I entered my room. I turned at the door, throwing my stomach-twisting gaze at her.

'And, Maddie, don't talk to Andre about me anymore! All you say is nasty bullshit, and you're confusing him as well. Am I clear?' *Confidence* showed her teeth, and *Pride* nodded, before I slammed the door.

THREE

I woke up at dawn, fully motivated to focus on my job and get it done before the deadline. Victor had approved my choice. My new goal was to keep up the pace he expected from me. I badly needed to start refining myself—most importantly my inability to understand his reality—and to communicate with him and everyone else properly.

I had a long phone conversation with the lawyer, and the financier was nervously prompting him. Their stammering and unwillingness to give clear and precise answers pissed me off. At one point, the tone of the discussion became heated. They were underestimating me. Nevertheless, I expressed my opinion in line with the seller's requirements. I was relaxed, knowing I had analysed every detail with the utmost attention and everything suggested was logical and well-considered. They were both irritated with my insistence that I should be provided with documents and information about the transaction, the money, and its movement. I suppose they were frustrated by the prospect of spending time collecting all the data in the systemised table that I made. However, Victor had put me in charge of the whole process, and I kept pushing until they confirmed my demands would be met. Numbers were my superpower. My skills in them could also help me build my own wall of superiority. If the *Monster* would just leave me alone, that was.

In the afternoon, I was still waiting for the figures, when the lawyer called me. Insolently pleased with himself, he informed me that they had sealed the deal after a private conversation with the seller. The transaction was already finalised, and the financier was going to provide copies of the documents later on, because he was very busy. I didn't like that. They had rudely ignored me, but the office and the penthouse were bought, so it was time to quickly get to work on the next phase. The seller kept calling me, insisting he should talk to the president in private. I promised to set up a meeting, surprised that a person like me could be so slippery with commitments. I was suddenly dealing with communication much better, at least when it came to phone conversations, and new qualities seemed to emerge. My focus remained solely on the job. If someone in my head dared to speak, it was only to help me with useful conclusions and information. The entities didn't confuse me anymore.

Dinner was approaching. There were new bursts of doubts of whether I was going to be fine with the standards, the manner of communication, my appearance, and the possibility of fitting in. *The Monster* kept saying I was not what they needed, and although I pretended not to hear its voice, it made me insecure. It really did. Nevertheless, the competitor in me was bursting with enthusiasm, craving success, although my lack of arguments for high self-esteem didn't help much.

Still, audacity prevailed. My brain didn't like to be neglected; it was pushing me to approach the situation more vigorously, despite what *The Monster* was saying. I possessed one formal black dress with thin straps, tight-fitting, but with a decent neckline and length. I had worn it to my prom, but back then, I at least expressed my disapproval of such events: combining the dress with military boots and dye, which had turned my hair bright blue for a couple of days. My grandad's bath as well. Now I combined it with my only pair of heels—the ones I used for work. I fixed some sort of a messy bun on my head, put on light makeup, then looked at the mirror. I wondered if I could possibly blend in with the general reality and, more importantly, whether I even wanted to fit in its distortions. This doubt was to stand on a shelf in my head, next to all the other ambiguities.

I put on a daring red lipstick able to turn a grey city pigeon into a sparkling flamingo. Maddie had smeared it on my lips once, declaring red lipsticks made men turn after me. I thought it was actually my gaze that caught their attention: the absence of any expression. My black, cold, mad eyes. The fact that I looked at men with contempt contributed as well. My opinion that they were all the same, uninteresting beings was getting stronger with time. The more I evaluated them, the more I disliked them. They all possessed something equally distorted, leaving me with the impression they were subject to simple, identical impulses, and I attributed this to their elementary biochemistry. I enjoyed torturing them with my stomach-twisting gaze. I provoked feelings of uneasiness and observed the reactions, which I eventually summed up in a repeating pattern. Sometimes, I caught myself experiencing a kind of sadistic pleasure from embarrassing men. I definitely liked it, even though I didn't know why. The most frequent victim of my experiments was Andre.

Confidence kept tiptoeing all the way to the dinner as I attempted to convince myself I could play at being normal. The main entrance led me to a pompous, crowded hall. The guests were talking in pairs or in bigger groups. There was not a single person I recognised and, for a brief moment, I hesitated, deciding if I should walk any further. Eyes like bullets, coming from all sides, made me freeze on the spot. Then I marched without direction. I passed by a band of musicians, but couldn't hear what they were playing because of the rumble in my head. It seemed there was only dead silence and only the sound of my heels on the marble floor was echoing all around. Then I focused the blue gaze at the far end of the hall, staring at me in his blood-chilling manner, measuring each one of my steps. He was probably evaluating my appearance, and I realised that I was walking with my nose down. *Confidence* came to my rescue, lifting my chin up. Grabbing a glass of champagne from a nearby waiter, I headed straight to Victor and gave him the inappropriate stare, clearly out of my control. I was becoming increasingly irritated by my own illogical behaviour.

'Good evening!' An unfamiliar undertone to my voice arose, as the financier interjected.

'Nia, you look lovely! Happy to see you. Everything went according to plan today. I hope our too-quick deal seal won't bring any unexpected problems.' he grinned slyly.

'Why would you? Hoping equals assuming. There should be no grounds for any problems if you have analysed every detail carefully. You sealed the deal without me, so I can't confirm that. I will give you a more accurate assessment after you provide me with the documents. I am good at calculating probabilities so I can calculate the probability of there being potential problems if you want.'

I was confident that I had picked the right voice and the right words but, unexpectedly, he turned a nasty shade of green. Victor shook his head, covering his lips with his fingers, and I frowned.

'We will discuss everything. As you said, you are planning to go through all the documents, aren't you? Have a nice evening!' The financier turned on his heels and stormed off to another group of people. My palms were sweaty as a result of my effort to communicate properly.

Now it was Victor and I, and a perfect blonde clone by his left arm. She was even more stunning than those girls at the store. I was by his right arm, amidst a small group of strangers. Victor's wall of superiority was thicker than ever, his face showing no expression at all. An elegant man approached us. He shook hands with the president, greeting him in French. Victor replied and the vibration of the exquisite language slid down my spine. The clone nodded silently. In my mind, I mocked her for not knowing French. Then the stranger stared at me. Before I knew what was going on, he held my hand to his lips. I greeted and introduced myself in French. He gave me a charming smile, not letting go of my hand.

'Your accent is gorgeous! Have you lived in France, madame? Or maybe it's mademoiselle?'

Before I could reply, I heard Victor's metallic voice:

'She lives here, and she works for me! Like most people on my team, she fluently speaks several languages,' he threw a haughty look at me, and I clenched my jaw at the contemptuous comment. The clone gazed at me from above, holding on to Victor's elbow, and I guess it was her turn to mock me in her mind.

'That's correct. I live here, for now, and I speak five languages fluently. Just five!' I narrowed my eyes. The man nodded with respect, then he left.

There was irritation all over Victor's face, probably because I had snapped back at him again. He moved closer to me, but then someone else got his attention. They walked to the side, and I was left in the middle of an awkward silence. The others were reluctant to talk to me, though they kept examining me curiously. I could see it perfectly: I didn't fit, not at all, despite my efforts and intentions. They could see it, too. They were probably wondering what I was even doing there, and their interest in me was discouraging. I caught myself staring at the woman with Victor. The clone looked depersonalised, and yet so perfect. I couldn't understand how both conditions could exist simultaneously.

Every woman around Victor was like a sex dream: only centimetres shorter than him, their legs reaching up to my fifth rib. All blonde, with doll-like faces, elegantly dressed, it seemed none of them had ever even sniffed a carbohydrate. I followed her smooth moves, her exquisite manners. She resembled a well-trained shadow, programmed to stand precisely twenty centimetres away from him. She greeted politely, providing one-word replies, a perfect accompaniment to his flawless appearance. The depersonalised lady was absolutely appropriate for his superiority, she even complemented it. This conclusion made me suddenly annoyed, and I frowned as I rubbed my palms against my dress.

Only men surrounded me. They were chatting freely, and I just stood there like a guard or something. I was thankful that Victor had explained his arguments to me: at least my outfit blended in well. Had I appeared in sneakers and jeans, I would have looked like a shaggy patch on an ethereal dress. I mean, I was still a little shaggy, but not that much.

The minister of transport, a short and disgusting man, was standing two people away from me. He looked at me from top to bottom, a greasy smirk on his face. Apparently, his jacket was custom-tailored to hide his curves. I tried to respond with my trained expressionless eyes but the whole situation distracted me. Anxiety overwhelmed me entirely, and I tapped my fingers nervously. Though he was in the middle of a conversation, Victor noticed the movements of my hands. Aware of my discomfort, he approached me.

'Gentlemen, this is Nia!' He spoke in his inappropriate voice.

'Hello!' I greeted and followed every nod in response.

'She will be working for me. Nia, meet everyone! You can use whichever of the five languages you prefer, just avoid the rude one, if you please. We will discuss your behaviour later!' The last was hissed in my ear and I shivered.

A young man's head protruded from the far end of the group. He was properly dressed, like everyone else, and yet the crazy look of his eyes set him apart. Besides, he was much younger than the others, maybe a couple of years older than me. Tattoos were visible under his white shirt, extending over his collar.

Some official guests entered the hall. The president and his shadow headed to greet them. They exchanged polite remarks, then retired to a separate room. I was left behind with the strangers, not daring to move, and the repulsive gaze of the minister lingered on me, making me nervous.

Say something, come on, talk to them! Try!

I was struggling to motivate myself when a male voice interrupted my thoughts.

'That's odd! He usually works with supermodels. What are you?' The young guy with the crazy eyes measured me mockingly. He had the blond, shaggy hairstyle of a rebel, but he was dressed stylishly and in line with the current trends.

'I can't confirm whether or not your conclusion is correct,' I twisted him with my nastiest look. 'I don't know the people he works with; I have no data. I am smart, though, which means that he works with those too. What are you then? Would you say you are smart, or are a supermodel?'

'Hm,' he murmured under his nose.

After a complete minute of silence, I decided to get away.

'Have a nice evening,' I turned abruptly, taking a breath.

Damn! I need a guide to meaningless conversations. There must be some pattern to the proper topics, duration, and answers. I need to come up with one!

'Chris!' He said. I turned back at him to see something that resembled a smile. 'That's my name.'

'Nia! That's mine, but you already knew that.'

'You are the intern in charge of the new office, right?'

'Right, but I am not an intern anymore.'

'There are no other women on the team. I'm sorry if I insulted you with my comment!' He knitted his eyebrows and, once again, I was sorry for not having a guide. I took a deep breath and put in all my possible effort.

'No problem! I don't get offended if the comments are unfounded. I don't know you and your conclusions mean nothing to me. Therefore, you don't have to apologise. Goodbye!'

This was a precise answer. Damn, it's not easy, but I guess that was good communication after all.

I turned to go.

'Goodbye, Nia! Hope to see you soon,' Chris said behind my back while I was trying to concentrate on leaving the hall.

ONE!

The counting in my head began. Loud and clear. As always, I took the first step with my right foot, tapping the fingers of my right hand. I drifted through the huge hall towards the exit, my mind focused on the sound of my heels. My psyche and its defects had their positive side. I counted things all the time: tiles, stairs, steps, five with my left foot, five with the right. I had created my escape rhythm to flee from reality, normality, and awkward situations. The situation that evening was like an endless day in tight shoes. Counting was great for motivation, drifting away, and hyper-concentration too, but today it was just an escape. I put in a lot of effort, I seemed to be making some progress, and yet the results were unsatisfactory. *The Monster* went as far as to call them 'the complete failure you deserve'. I really tried to be self-confident, to cope in the new environment, but, instead, I was more like spat-out chewing gum. I found it hard to systemise my mistakes and *Fear* didn't miss the opportunity to make me shake.

My head was a buzzing beehive again. I decided to call Andre because some wine and a voice different from the ones in my mind seemed like a good way to spend the night. Andre knew a lot of clichés about communication, he was good at it, and my plan was to squeeze information about the possible patterns for meaningless conversations.

Maddie was still out, probably wandering about in her anger. Andre was waiting for me in front of the flat, the wet look of a loving pet on his face. He was the kind of guy who would endow his partner with kindness and no expectations, even after a semi-fight and days of ignoring him. 'Yes, sweetheart': he said it so often that I already despised those two words, together or separately. He was a good guy of my age. Undistinguishable in a crowd, he dreamed of peace and the opportunity to plan his entire ordinary life. Or rather existence, I'd say. If he could draw it all on a table, it would be ideal for him. He longed for family comfort. He could see himself having two kids, a white cloth on the dinner table and a plan for a summer vacation by February. Life without any challenges would gift him with pure happiness. He would also summon Friday eagerly from every Monday morning. Our relationship was boring, but he was fine with the fact that I could not experience normal emotions. I even think it even comforted him. We maintained a symbiosis of a mutual lack of expectations. Andre was just as passionate as a medium-sized Ficus plant, which suited me perfectly because I generally avoided sexual intercourse. Whenever we did have sex, he was eager to please me. My satisfaction was like a personal obsession for him; he had been trying to achieve it as diligently as an alpinist trying to conquer a precipitous mountain.

Sitting on the couch, I drifted away listening to him, like any other evening. I poured myself more wine, absolutely not interested in the story about his internship in the bank. I kept silent and with no intention of putting up with hints about the president and how obvious the situation was with him. I was not even motivated to argue that the facts had been clarified and all suspicions proved ungrounded. Maddie had obviously complied with my insistence that she should stop talking to Andre about me. She hadn't even told him that it is all clear now, and he kept repeating her previous nonsense. However, despite all this boredom, my body couldn't stop vibrating. Desperate to shut Andre up, and to the surprise of us both, I stared at him, offering sex right there and then. He nearly choked on the sip of wine in his mouth.

I had never learned to like sex. Maybe it was my fault, or possibly Andre's; we hadn't managed to turn it into something intriguing. The touch itself appeared to be severely problematic for me. Plus, only a person as twisted as me could know how annoying it was to count erratic sex rhythms. Andre and I had tried eight times altogether, and, as my one and only sexual partner, he never managed to convince me there was something meaningful in this activity. Andre had asked me numerous times what I liked—how I wanted him to do it. But I never gave him a proper answer, simply because I did not know. He wanted to kiss and touch; he offered gentle sex, hard sex, any type of sex he could think of. He was desperate to find the path to my pleasure, or at least that was what he claimed. My orgasm was his ultimate goal. He had tried to explain how essential orgasms were, and that they would fix my "twisted head". However, this complicated biochemical process remained utterly abstract to my body and neurons. I couldn't stand Andre's touch or him being inside me; I managed to live through his kisses, but only if they were not too slimy.

Eventually, I found out that sex was almost bearable if I was on top, keeping his hands away from my body. I moved slowly because, although tiny, his penis gave me pain. In this way, I created a harmonious rhythm suitable for counting. Whenever this happened, I liked to stare into Andre's eyes and deliberately slow down even more, just when he was about to cum. I kept him on the edge until every muscle of his body painfully tensed, not being able to hold it even for a second more. I tortured him some more and, in the end, watched his reactions closely as he finished. His heart rate quickened, his muscles contracted, some whimpering escaped from his throat, and the hair on his body stood up—not necessarily in this order. I observed the consequences of my actions and I liked them: under my control and on my count, I could create a pattern. I wondered if this was some sort of a particular turn-on for weirdos like me. *Curiosity*, though, was eager to find out what the sensation of an orgasm was like. After all, normal women experience it, but I had no grounds to assume that the complicated neurological process could run in my own body.

That night, after the first intercourse, we repeated the act. The second round was usually one minute longer and lasted for four minutes in total. Just before the end, a new image broke into my head. *Desire* took over my mind with brutal force. He dropped Victor's face on the bed under me. A severe shock and a deep breath later, I was already shaking, my heart racing. A whisper echoed through my mind:

That's what you want!

An unfamiliar female voice moaned in a dark corner. A wave rose from the tips of my toes, rushed through my body and electrified my hair. I shivered, closing my eyes to get rid of Victor, but he became even more real. The side of my face warmed: the exact spot where the president had touched me. The heat spread through my skin and my neck twisted back. My head exploded. All I could hear was a loud buzzing. A sigh crept from my mouth, and I stuck my nails into Andre's wrists. My rhythm was disrupted. My movements became sharp and uneven, and he came a moment later, whimpering. I jumped out of the bed. *The Monster's* disgusting neigh sounded from its hole:

You can't even think about this man! Why would he want you, you freak?

Andre's questioning eyes followed me along with his irritating voice:

'Did you like it?'

'Certainly! That's why we do it every few months,' I didn't even try to hide my sarcasm. In front of the mirror, I carefully inspected my pupils. Was I drunk? Is the wine responsible for my hallucinations? As I wondered, *The Monster's* mocking was exploding unbearably.

'Why the hell are you doing this, Nia? Why are you even with me?' Andre started dressing in a rush.

'Fair question,' I peered through the bathroom door. 'The first reason is that without a boyfriend, people keep mentoring all the time. So, I assumed that having one would be less annoying. Besides, you yourself said that no one else would be able to stand me. That's a reasonable assumption of yours. Plus, I'm still learning how to communicate, and you are quite skilled.'

'You know what? You indeed are a sociopath, and the fact you can't feel anything is the least of your problems! You're just insane,' he stormed into the living room.

Stop being honest with people, Nia! We already know they don't like it!

Reason was buzzing in my head again. I needed to find a way to reconcile with the new level of chaos in my mind. Insisting that I had a lot of work, and that I had to prepare for my exam, I asked Andre to leave quite impolitely.

I was struggling to ignore the image of the blue irises in my head, but the hallucination wouldn't go away. Moreover, vibrations were still walking up and down my body, evoking heat and muscle spasms on their way. I hid under the blanket in my bed as if to bury my insane thoughts. My mind sank into calculating probabilities; that was its relaxation exercise. It quickly estimated that apart from being insane, my thoughts related to impossible results, too. I was staring blankly at a point when my phone vibrated with a message on *Telegram*[2]. At first, I thought, enthusiastically, that it was my friend, Wildling but the number was unknown:

> *You gave up way too quickly today.*
> *You left without my permission.*
> *I will not accept disobedience!*
> *V.*

My mouth dried up. I started tapping the screen, blushing because of the hallucination that had attacked me and, simultaneously, annoyed by his message:

> *Putting in more effort was reasonless.*
> *Me staying longer wouldn't change the result.*
> *Nor your permission or my obedience.*
> *I will work on my mistakes.*

I stared at the typing indicator:

> *The problem with the world is*
> *that intelligent people are full of doubts,*

---

[2] *Encrypted messaging application – author's notes.*

while the stupid ones are full of confidence.[3]
You will never be stupid,
so work on your doubts.

Surprised that he had quoted one of my favourite authors, I smiled. Before I could realise what I was doing, I wrote:

I adore Bukowski.

I wrinkled my nose as my message appeared in the chat, followed by three smiley faces. My fingers were being honest, but not in the right place. Nor with the right person. I scolded myself, but then received a reply without any criticism:

Don't give up, despite all the doubts!
Are you active tonight?
PS: We both adore Bukowski.

My hips twisted, I blinked at the screen. Before I could figure out the ambiguity in his question, another message appeared:

If so, I have a challenging forecast for you to make.
You will have to make up for my disappointment with your
behaviour by using your skills.
I don't work with quitters.

My thoughts weren't about numbers. Not at all. The new, crazy neurological processes in my body flustered me, and yet my irritation at his assessment prevailed. I sat up in bed, struggling to ignore my physical reactions:

As I already said, at night I do calculations!
And they are never disappointing!!!

I frowned at my fingers, which produced so many exclamation marks. A minute later, he sent me a picture of a financial forecast. Only numbers,

---

[3] *A quote by Charles Bukowski – author's notes.*

no information on what it was about, but I noticed right away that it was incorrect. He asked if I could see the mistakes.

I certainly do! I'll fix this.

He immediately replied:

Tonight, you will be active with my numbers then.
As I already said, you should be available at any time,
mostly at night.

I made a face at the suggestion that I needed the whole night for a task that simple:

No, I certainly won't.
I will fix it in 30 minutes.
Only a quantum algorithm would take a whole night,
but I guess you're not interested in that.

He didn't reply and I got down to the forecast. Minutes before my own deadline, I sent three possible options. He responded in an hour:

You really do have a beautiful mind!
It'd be my pleasure to play chess with you some time.
Good night, Nia.

I didn't text back. I adored the game but had long decided to stay away from chess boards. My defects again. My brain always became overwhelmed with the countless patterns and possible moves, and I would get paralysed in my hyper-concentration. Occasionally, it would take a while to recover. Once I got stuck at the board at home for days and my grandad had to throw it away. He explained that I was to restrain myself from playing chess because it could devour me. Now I hoped the president would forget about his proposal; otherwise, I would be forced to conceal my freakiness by lying that I didn't know how to play. Though a sense of pleasure in impressing someone as special as him emerged within me, but somehow, I didn't like that I only impressed him with my brain. I disliked, even more, the fact I had taken the winding path of proving myself. My illogical thoughts kept flying around, so I decided to put myself to sleep. Both my body and mind needed to be cleansed from the weird processes taking place. *Fear* kept whispering in my ear throughout the night. Though shaking, I pretended not to hear his voice.

φ

As soon as I got up, I focused all my energy on the job. Fortunately, the hallucination had disappeared, but I still suspected that such realistic visions were a symptom of true madness. The new intruders in my head bothered me, although they were gone for now. I woke up long before the alarm went off, and a giant cup of coffee worked well for me. The flat I lived in and despised had one joyful advantage: it was in an old building's top floor, and the balcony revealed the golden-dome splendour of the city churches. Before the sun came up, I drank my coffee in the company of this spectacular view. My mind, unusually relaxed, enjoyed the morning despite the grey weather. Suddenly, the blue irises emerged again in my mind, staring arrogantly at me.

Reason was awake.

Where are these hallucinations coming from? Why are we seeing things? What is going on, Nia? Who are the newcomers? Are we going insane?! Focus! He already explained: you are going to unleash your potential. Possibly, you can even earn enough money to get us out of here. We must concentrate! We must not get distracted, we must not go crazy, and we must definitely not miss our chance for something more!

He hissed the last words and I looked down in embarrassment. He was absolutely right; I just had no idea what was wrong with me.

Motivated by the undeniable facts, I took the metro insanely early. Upon arriving at the empty office, I got to organising everything needed for the next stage. I came up with a pattern and a schedule. I forced my mind to work in fast rhythm with a distinct "One". This was my way to start every new endeavour with ease and to count the different stages as well.

For no reason, I couldn't get along with the woman sent to do the interior design. She arrived at 9 a.m. and started walking around arrogantly, a tablet in her hands. As instructed, I had to be in charge of everything, so I explained to her to simply develop visualisations under my direction. Then she left, offended. She said that she wasn't my assistant, but I didn't have time to pay much attention or analyse the grounds of her attitude. Vanilla, Minty, or Candy—whatever her nickname was, it irritated me as much as her resemblance to Victor's shadows. I didn't object when she slammed the door behind her back. I just picked up the plaster that fell to the floor, called some people I knew from the university, and they sent me a friendly, ambitious architecture student. He took interior designing and even some other activities in stride. He was craving a chance, too, and proved to be extremely useful.

As I circled the room, I thought exactly how appropriate Victor's idea was to assign this particular task to me. Indeed, it was outside my comfort zone, yet I was doing it on my own; I didn't have to communicate excessively, which allowed me to apply my entire focus. At the same time, I was getting used to managing my own work, and I had become relaxed with my newly-found skills. I grinned at the realisation that he actually understood my true essence.

I got stuck in planning the security systems. I had no clue. Where were the bodyguards supposed to be? Whether the windows were supposed to be tinted, nor who was supposed to take care of all this. Dissatisfied with my ignorance in the subject, I was speaking questions aloud to myself when the architecture student suddenly interrupted me: 'Toma knows about security, right? Why don't you ask him?'

'Who?' I looked up absent-mindedly beneath my eyebrows.

'The big guy dressed in black and hanging outside, Nia. I met him when I went for a smoke. He was complaining to someone on the phone and he wasn't pleased at all. I'll quote what I heard: "I am military! I specialise in security, damn it! I've spent my whole life with Victor, and now I'm supposed to babysit some crazy girl and take care of an office!" Then he said "damn it" one more time. Isn't he also on the team? And who's Victor?' The student was embarrassed to repeat all this and made sure to emphasise the fact that he only quoted what he heard.

Awkwardly, I haven't remembered Toma's name, and even more awkwardly, his conclusion was quite logical: my behaviour indeed gave him reasons to call me crazy.

φ

The workers placed a plastic table and a few battered chairs in front of the entrance. Nevertheless, Toma remained standing, his gaze focused on a point in space. The white T-shirt's hem peeked out beneath his black clothes, and so did the goodness in his eyes. I examined his shoelaces again. The knots were even more complicated than before.

'Hello!'

'Hello!'

'Usually, I am not that rude. You are fair to assume that I'm crazy, but if your approach is unbiased, you will find out that my craziness is highly efficient. I am learning how to communicate properly, and if my behaviour so far was improper, it wasn't on purpose. I am trying, and I have achieved certain results. By all this, I mean that I apologise! I heard that you were qualified. Would you like to help me with the security plans?' He gaped at me, blinking wildly. His face was crooked, and he was too tall and too large, but his brown eyes were warm. 'I can't handle this on my own, I don't have the relevant knowledge, and it would take time for me to understand it. All I know is that security is a priority here. Would you like me to fix you a coffee? As a sign that I mean well and am willing to communicate with you? The tradition of exchanging drinks comes from ancient times. In the past, that was a way for people to show they were not poisoning each other. I mean the same thing, though metaphorically. Do I make sense?' Toma was rough and good-natured at the same time. Later on, he would show me the meaning of care and loyalty.

'No milk, no sugar, strong. That's how I drink my coffee, miss!' He looked at me with suspicion. 'They've never had security systems here, I already checked. We're going to set everything up properly, starting from scratch. Just make sure you provide rooms for the boys: bathrooms, a bedroom and a kitchen,' he seemed relaxed, although surprised.

'Thanks!' I gave him a warm smile. I did that instinctively only for the people I truly liked. By that time, they were two: my grandad and my friend. Wildling was just as weird as me, though she was a true outlandish dreamer in the most fascinating way. That's why I called her Wildling, and in return, she called me Oddling. Much braver than me, she ran away from our predetermined future, went hitchhiking and, only God knows how, ended up somewhere at the end of the world rescuing elephants while I was left behind with Maddie. 'Oh, please, call me Nia. "Miss" doesn't go well with my trainers, and I don't like it. So, I'll call you Toma, unless you prefer something else.'

Something akin smile shone on his face.

'It's fine, Nia! I have one condition, though: don't make me search for you. From now on, you will always stay close to me. I don't want to have to give any more explanations. OK?'

'Why should you search for me, and why should you explain?' I shot a curious look at him.

'If you want us to get along well, you must accept that, first, I don't like talking, and second, I hate explaining. Deal? You're not going to make me do any of these things?' He snorted at me. Apparently, he didn't like talking or explaining, or faced difficulties with both.

'Deal! I also find it hard to communicate, so we'll be fine,' I held out my small hand, and he squeezed it in his giant paw.

'You are crazy, aren't you?' His brown eyes gazed at me, but they didn't mean to insult me, and neither did his words. He spoke in a soft, warm voice, there was even a playful undertone, which surprised me.

'Toma, your assumption is undoubtedly correct! I confirm. I'm crazy.'

We both laughed as we went inside.

The day raced by. Toma drove me to my flat late that night, and I was utterly exhausted. Maddie was asleep; my eyes insisted I should immediately go to bed too. The work had drained me. There were only hours left until my final graduation exam. The thought of failure and *the Monster*'s talents on such occasions worked for me like an energy drink taken intravenously. However, neither the tiredness, nor studying were strong enough to ease my irritation with the lack of new communication with Victor. The mere presence of this irritation made me even more tense, torturing my mind with its lack of logic. My task was detailed, work on it was going smoothly. There was nothing to discuss with him at that point. And still, some unknown force made me check my *Telegram* ridiculously often. *Reason* was strained by this circumstance and by the hallucinations, even if they were gone for now. He kept complaining about what was going on in my twisted head.

Focus was unreachable. Eventually, I gave up wasting energy on textbook scanning. Earlier that day, I had read that the president was giving an official event. Like never before, *Curiosity* implored me to turn on the TV and switch to the news. I carefully followed his comments on economic issues. He spoke in his even, sharp voice, with no facial expressions again. I wondered how he could control his nervous system so well: after all, facial expressions are a natural neurological process that takes place unconsciously. I considered the possibility of him being devoid of emotions, just like me, but it was almost impossible to be that successful and that crazy at the same time. I watched the report from the event as well. The wall of his superiority was so thick that it looked like frost. A glorious shadow in a dazzling dress to the ground shone by his left arm. They danced and I swayed like a drunk penguin as well, staring at the screen for a closer shot. As I was chewing a pink bear, the camera closed in on his hand on the naked back of the shadow. I growled when my hand switched off the TV. This involuntary action startled me. A quarrel broke out in my head, and *Desire*, the intruder, screamed madly:

That's where you want to be! In his arms!

The mad voice and its nonsense made me jump. Furious *Reason* tried to slap him.

Get out! This head is full of freaks already. Nia, do something about it! They are taking over.

Reason waved his bony finger. I kept blinking, stunned by the events in my own mind, while *the Monster's* mocking squeals sounded in the background.

FOUR

I couldn't sleep that night. The good thing about hearing voices, however, is that if you get along with them, they are a great help in complicated situations and exams. They are like a talking Google, always available, except for early in the morning. Thanks to the voices and my photographic memory, I passed the exam and achieved a satisfactory result, given the weird events of the previous days. I was one of the first to go in, so when I exited the building, it was still the perfect time for a strong coffee. Andre stood there, neat, an umbrella and a colourful bunch of flowers in his hands. He seemed uncomfortable, though. Seeing him provoked a whole new level of intolerance in me.

'You got a high grade, didn't you?' He handed me the flowers, then kissed me gently on the cheek.

'It's proportionate to my effort...' I gave him a crooked smile. I might have gritted my teeth at him, but I was not sure.

'I called you a lot, but you didn't pick up. Are you angry at me?'

'I was busy, besides I had to study for the exam,' It wasn't a lie, but the exact truth was that I had been deliberately avoiding him.

'Nia, would you please tell me what's going on. You've been even weirder than usual. It's impossible to speak to you! Let's talk about what's happening, the job offer, and us. Please, talk to me and explain!' His eyes were full of hope and sincerity, which surprised me.

Annoyingly decent, even likeable, he was wearing his tweed jacket, an ironed white shirt, and impeccably polished shoes. Andre was the perfect ordinary guy for a perfectly ordinary girl. What I liked about him was that he accepted me, or at least he didn't demand anything. I took advantage of the fact that I didn't have to fit into expectations. I didn't know how to explain my attitude, though. How do you tell someone that they are too ordinary or that you are too crazy? What did I even want from him? He represented what most women search for, or at least those women who prefer their partner to own a penis. He tolerated me, too, and *the Monster* had long convinced me there were not many candidates. I was staring at him, despite being aware that my eyes embarrassed him. He kept telling me there was a wall between us that he never managed to see through. He couldn't comprehend my birth gift, my special skill—my barrier, nor did he grasp my fear of normality. There was not a damn millimetre of me he could ever understand.

Staring at him, I listed his good qualities. At that particular moment, however, I couldn't stand him. The sensation was getting stronger than ever, and I suspected that this one time, the problem was not even him. As a matter of fact, I assumed it had never been him. My attempt to convince myself how good he was made me sick, both of him and of me. The faulty pattern in my own behaviour drew bright lines behind my eyelids. We, as a couple, were nothing more than an insanely horrific life compromise for both parties. *The Monster* erupted loudly and clearly:

See what you are now? You are the misfit! You don't fit anywhere!

Andre leaned to kiss me with all the passion he was capable of. I didn't budge. It was repulsive and slimy. *The Monster* filled my mouth and my mind with its sticky bitterness. It woke up *Malice*, too, with her controversial methods. Then *the Monster* collected phlegm in its greasy mouth, spat it down my throat to push me to the verge of puking. *Contempt* also stood up: for everything and everyone, including me. *Malice* lit her pyres, determined to burn this whole warped world down to ashes. My rapid breathing helped them blaze. Everyone in my head sheltered, and there was silence as *Rage* engulfed me. Andre spoke even more unbearably:

'C'mon, sweetheart, there's a nice café just around the corner. We'll drink a cappuccino or two, and we'll talk. It's cold here. We need to discuss that offer, too. It really is inappropriate for you! You won't deal with a person like him,' he smiled and hugged me cautiously with one arm.

'Inappropriate?' I laughed with my mouth shut. 'So now you know what I can deal with? Think you can make a proper judgement of me?' I looked at him with contempt. 'Is there the slightest idea how superior my brain is to yours? Do you truly believe you can mentor me?'

'But sweetheart, what's wrong?' He gaped at me.

'I don't want you to "sweetheart", kiss, or speak to me anymore. I don't want to hear your whimpering! I can't stand you for even a minute longer!' Without realising what I was doing, I started shouting in a manner that made passers-by stop in the rain. Hearing my cries as if from outside myself, I wondered who exactly was storming through my mouth.

The last thing I saw was the horror on his face. My feet flew at an unexpected speed. Only Andre's shrieks managed to reach me: "You really are insane". Running down the sidewalk, I pushed people out of my way, and *Reason* was confused:

When did we estimate what we don't want and can't stand? This is new, I need to analyse the data. The process is not familiar!

I hissed at him to shut up. I didn't know what was happening to me and why I exploded aloud. It was the first time I had done that in front of someone other than my grandad. I was free to rage in his presence, I often hit the walls when I was a kid.

Shut the hell up! I'm sick of your wretched data! When you shout under the rain, you should at least know why! What's wrong with me?

The Monster was chuckling beyond control:

That's who you are. There is no data, you freak! That's you! You're sick! Insane! A wacko! A freak! You can't do anything human!

I needed silence. My feet took me to my special place in the heart of the city. The long-forgotten home of a beloved poet. There, he used to weave harmony from letters. Although he had given grace to the world, the world apparently fancied other things now, and his tiny house was in ruins. Through an almost imperceivable door, I broke into the abandoned yard. Weeds and thorns had taken over. I fitted perfectly in the middle of this chaos and sat on the broken bench under the rain. Hundreds of thoughts sped through my mind like racing cars, painfully roaring, squeezing my eyes.

'Stop it! Just stop! All I want is a moment of silence! Stop it! Screw you! Stop!' I kept shouting the same thing over and over again, pressing my palms to my ears. My own shouts made me hiccough.

'Get up. You're gonna catch a cold,' his voice sounded distant, but his touch on my shoulder worked like a slap to bring me to my senses. I always needed a touch to get me out of my outbursts.

Toma was the most pragmatic person I had ever met. Pragmatic to the point of absurdity, sometimes. Whenever I was to encounter terrifying experiences, both for a normal person and for one with a broken mind like me, he was to remind me that a bowl of warm soup could cure anything. He frankly believed that. In previous years, he had served in the French Legion[4]; survival was all he was ever trained for. Up to him—water, shelter, and dinner were all one needed. Everything else was a whim. His mind was quite ordinary, and yet his qualities were beyond extraordinary.

I gaped at him in bewilderment. Me—in the middle of a fundamental personal crisis, and all he worried about was the prospect of me catching a cold. We inhabited distant realities indeed, but it seemed that the vast distance was precisely what brought us closer together. Giant Toma invaded without invitation the narrow space that I kept aside solely for grandad and Wildling.

'What's with your priorities? Is it really the cold that's bothering you right now?' I laughed out loud.

Me, my crisis, and two-metre-tall Toma, whose hands made the umbrella look like a paper hat, started giggling together.

'Something's wrong with me, Toma, and I don't even know what it is. I'm going crazy!'

'C'mon, Nia, get up! Look, don't be mad at me, but you really are nuts, and that is a fact. You know you talk to yourself, don't you?' He gave me a friendly look, and I laughed even louder.

'I must inform you this is the least of my concerns. Now I have hallucinations as well.'

He curved his mouth, not comprehending.

'You must change your clothes. You are soaking wet, and you really will catch a cold. Many tasks are waiting for you at the office. So, let's go,

---

[4] The French Foreign Legion *(French: Légion étrangère) is a military body of the French Army, composed mainly of foreigners. Training in the Legion is known to be a physical and mental challenge. About 8,000 people from 136 countries serve in the Legion's 11 regiments – author's notes.*

weirdo,' he held out his hand. There was no reproach, nor mockery, not even pity in his eyes.

Toma fully accepted me the way I was. There was no necessity to change to fit in his giant heart; there was enough space for me and all my edges. He held my hand tight and continued in a fatherly voice:

'Nia, I think you're just scared because your life's changing. You look like a wet, frightened, stray kitten to me. You will work for a very influential person, not to mention how difficult he is. You'll probably get everything you ever wanted. I've noticed that people go nuts whenever this happens. I guess you are the same. You seem unsure, but you must focus hard on your work. I hope you're well aware and ready for this!'

He said that in a caring yet firm voice. That was his typical communication manner: rough, frank, not sparing a thing. It was part of his un-ordinarity, which I gradually discovered. A painfully honest friend that one could only appreciate. He held nothing back, and his words sometimes punched one in the nose. I assumed he was right. There were grounds for me to think that *Fear* was conquering me; failure was on his list, but there was still no explanation for my illogical thoughts or for the irrational processes in my body.

Maddie was stalking me viciously in the apartment. She followed me all over the flat, producing sounds to hint that my presence was unpleasant. They were not even hints; this time she openly demonstrated how much she loathed me. My trainers were perfect for work, so I quickly changed them for my military boots. I opted for my thickest sweater, as the rain and the cold were still scratching deep on my bones.

I left the flat and jumped in the car, pinning a playful smile on Toma.

'I know this place where they make pancakes... No. The outstanding pancakes place!' A question was peeking in his eyes as he nervously pointed at his wrist. There was a watch on it. 'I want to take you there, come on, we won't be more than 15 minutes! Let's feast on the sweetness of life.'

'Nia, we don't have...'

'Toma, let's be honest! Is there anything in this world that is simpler and yet more perfect than pancakes?' I goggled foolishly at him, and Toma laughed as he started the car.

We walked down the sidewalk, and people were staring at us: a weird misfit with messy hair, randomly hand-painted trainers, holding the hand of a crooked giant in black clothes with a protruding white hem. We headed to my favourite place downtown. *Dream Factory* was a small restaurant for hipsters with a flair for food and a good atmosphere. I used to visit it whenever I could afford the bill. There, I would always meet someone as weird as me to make me blend in. On my way in, I read the familiar words on the entrance:

> *Logic will get you from A to B.*
> *Dreams will take you everywhere.*

The reworking of Einstein's[5] words evoked broad smiles on the visitors' lips. Toma smiled too, and so did I, which surprised me because of the indisputable arguments against this claim.

Logic is too ordinary for you.

Victor's voice boomed somewhere in the depths of my mind. It warmed me all over.

I had spent all my money and reluctantly took some from the financier's wad. I wanted to treat Toma. My intention was to give the money back after I got my first paycheck, so I shoved a note in the wad, saying how much I had taken and for what it was used. Thanks to Toma, the sensation of living in my own skin was better now, and I wanted to return the favour somehow. Pancakes and plain strong Ethiopian organic coffee in a French press seemed perfect for the occasion. While eating, I decided to follow *Curiosity*'s push and asked Toma why he was assigned to take care of me, given that he had been with the president for a long time and he was obviously well-qualified for more important things. He avoided my question.

'Nia, Kaov is strict, meticulous, and he doesn't compromise on security. His work and his life are under his full control. Surrounded by people with dubious intentions, right now he's keeping an eye on his subordinates. He asked me to be with you all the time. There's nothing more to explain, and I already told you that I don't like explaining.'

'All right, I won't push it. We have a deal. It's just that I can't get what he thinks of me and, as it turns out, this makes me tense. After our last meeting,

---

[5] *Albert Einstein: "Logic will get you from A to B. Imagination will take you everywhere." – author's notes.*

he was sharp to rebuke me, and now I don't know if I meet his expectations. And, Toma, better use the word "employees" instead of "subordinates". It's not considered appropriate anymore,' I winked as I said the last sentence, meaning to help him overcome his difficulties in explaining. His laughter thundered.

'Your generation is weird indeed. You're too sensitive to words! Nia, I'm absolutely sure that he explained to you what he wants. Knowing him, most clearly so,' he sighed with annoyance. 'Just do it, and everything will be fine. If Victor has taken this decision, then you meet his expectations. He is never wrong! You've been given a huge chance to move forward, do your best and try to do it perfectly. And one more thing...' He leaned over my face to whisper: 'You didn't have a meeting with him! You were present at a meeting. Don't confuse the words!'

'That's what I meant! Strange, I expressed myself incorrectly,' I grumped. After a brief pause, I continued: 'I'm trying to be perfect, but it hasn't worked out so far, and my communication is a tremendous failure. Besides, certain things lack logic and my focus shifts away! I lack logic and it's baffling. Whatever!' I rolled my eyes, thinking about my hallucinations. Toma examined me with suspicion.

'Kaov isn't logical. Sometimes his moves and decisions don't make sense, at least not to anyone around him,' he sighed heavily but finished with a smile: 'He can do anything, though, and working for him is a once-in-a-lifetime chance. I think you deserve it. All you need to do is focus entirely on your job. Nothing more! That's my advice. Let's go, look how late it is,' he jumped.

Time was more than a value for Toma. He was going to manage mine as well, without me even noticing. He wore an expensive watch, a gift from the president and the same as his, and he checked it every fifteen minutes. He was constantly chasing seconds, and he became annoyed whenever we deviated even for a moment. Sometimes he was far from understanding me, yet he could easily swallow my weirdness as if he was used to it.

I kept throwing glances at him while he was driving, smiling with the corner of my mouth.

Did you see that, creep? What can you say about statistics now? Here, I'm good enough for someone, and I don't even have to bend, break or fit. Just me being me. Who would have guessed that general reality offers such opportunities?

For the first time, I managed to squeeze *the Monster*'s throat. It squealed. *Reason* with his square head was jumping around, and I thought I even saw him repeating *Excitement*'s reggae moves.

Toma was right; there were a whole lot of tasks waiting for me at the office. I was dealing with a group of workers when a stranger arrived. He handed me a pot with a tiny but very prickly cactus. A small, blue flower had blossomed on the top. I opened the attached note with interest. One of its sides informed me about the cactus's Latin name and gave me some brief information that it was one of the most delicate plants. I was surprised by the lack of consistency between its appearance and its true nature. On the other side, a beautiful, visibly masculine handwriting said:

Congratulations on your graduation!
PS: Don't get fooled by its prickly appearance.
It's gentle and requires care.
If you provide this, the thorns will fall off.
However, be careful if you want to touch it.
It doesn't like being touched!
V.

The unexpected attention to my little, meaningless success surprised me. I found it positive that he was interested in his employees, even the new ones. In fact, I shuddered at the contact with Victor, albeit indirect. I was flattered by his attention to an insignificant being like me. The competitor in me was jumping because of the praise. Still, I was a little concerned because I wasn't skilled in maintaining the life of a single plant, let alone such a complex specimen. Toma threw a suspicious glance at the cactus. When I boasted that Kaov congratulated me on my graduation, he didn't reply. His facial expressions showed irritation, though, and I didn't know how to consider the reaction.

φ

Despite being tired, I finished pretty quickly. I distributed the tasks and hired a second team of workers to speed up the whole process. The renovation was in full swing. Ready with my calculations, I sent everything to the financier, but I was still concerned about the money. The transactions were massive, and he had not yet provided me with all the documents needed, even though I was in charge of verifying and confirming everything in the end. He gave me insufficient details of the deal and the payments, full of errors and omissions. Every time I spoke to him, the red flags in my mind flashed insistently. I was wary not to trust him.

Getting up early and my outburst in the morning had given me a headache. I found a good place for the cactus, and soon afternoon, I asked Toma to drive me home. His playlist was fantastic. Dancing was my way to soothe my body, and music soothed my mind. It was one of my favourite hiding places. Something similar to a sanctuary. Toma had hearing problems, so he didn't mind turning the volume to the max. *Do I Wanna Know*[6] was thundering in my ears, and the rhythm relaxed me. I was swaying to it when, out of nowhere, the glassy blue irises hit my brain. Something compressed my chest, and my breath whistled as if an arrow had pierced my navel. My mouth gaped open. One hand clung to the seat; the other clutched the door handle. Toma threw a questioning look at me, but I didn't say anything. Once again, the hallucination and the intrusive processes in my body astounded me.

Damn, I'm really going insane! Insane indeed.

As soon as we arrived, I got out of the car, puzzled, and hurried to the flat. It was Maddie's day off, and I was really hoping she would be out, busy with her favourite entertainment: wandering the malls. I was not in the mood to listen to another portion of her grumbling. The door was locked, which pleased me at first, but as I entered, surprise opened my mouth wide:

'Seriously, guys?' I shouted. The situation struck me as funny, but I covered my smile with my hand. 'Couldn't you come up with something better?' *Contempt* was bursting with laughter. Andre was struggling to pull his boxers on, and Maddie stood brazenly frozen on her elbows and knees, her ass up in the air.

'Like you would come up with something better! You, Nia! The woman lacking anything worthy to give to a man,' Maddie hissed in her impudent manner, putting Andre's T-shirt on.

'But why?' I looked at her with incomprehension.

'Sex, Nia! People like having it,' Andre tried to defend himself.

'No! Maddie, what I'm asking is, why would you have sex with him? I've tried, and I just can't understand your motives. You are not his girlfriend, you don't have to,' My frank question drove her mad.

'I'm not giving you any explanations! Sex is for normal people, not for freaks. We just do it without reason. We kiss, touch, lick each other, fuck,

---

[6] *Do I Wanna Know - Arctic Monkeys – author's notes.*

cum, and enjoy it. As for me, I don't understand what men would want with a freak like you, but I'm not demanding your explanations,' she hissed as I frowned, thinking of all the actions she mentioned.

'Maddie, stop!' Andre was ashamed. He clutched her raging hand, convulsing next to her ear, but he couldn't shut her raging mouth.

'Today, you shouted hysterically at Andre, you've insulted him. You've gone completely mad, haven't you? I told him a million times you're gonna go completely mad someday,' she raised her eyebrows, and so did I, because there was something right about the suggestion that I had gone crazy. 'Mad, but well-motivated indeed, if perverted Mr. President fucks you, or whatever he does to you. He's obviously into both supermodels and freaks!' Spite swished in her mouth. Her face twisted into a new, evil expression, which suited her perfectly.

'I assume your statements are to excuse your own actions. You seek reciprocity—I know this pattern—but there's no reciprocity here,' I pointed at them.

Reason was watching, clicking his tongue. He concluded that an ugly betrayal was taking place and it should not be tolerated under any circumstances. *Justice* stood right next to him, her image half black and half white. My weakest point. She was about to take over in her typical style: absolute rage. *Reason*, however, looked at her. Honest as always, he sighed:

We don't actually care one bit!

I nodded sulkily, slightly disappointed, realising he was right. I couldn't even get mad at Maddie and Andre to add a little amusement, emotion, or normality to my total indifference. Maddie was right as well: I was a freak in this regard. Now it was again only the faulty pattern that irritated me.

'I'm packing my stuff and leaving you alone, guys! I'll be quick. Just as quick as Andre,' I sighed, rolling my eyes.

There were not too many valuable possessions in my room, so I stuffed the main things into my small suitcase. I decided to deal with the rest some other time. I threw a glum glance at my only invaluable treasure: the piles of books that I hoped I'd manage to come and get soon. Each one of them had contributed to me eating fewer gummy bears, and each one of them was more precious to me than anything else. Less than ten minutes later, I left under Andre's guilty gaze and Maddie's smug grin.

As I hopped out of the building, the pouring rain hit me in the face, rudely reminding me of the lack of an umbrella. I sheltered my head with my hands, deciding which way to go. Perhaps my grandad's, where I would have to give an account of all recent events, or maybe I could use Victor's money for a hotel. While I was analysing the options, a hand pulling at my suitcase startled me.

'You are really determined to catch a cold today, aren't you!' Toma snorted as he walked to the car. He tossed the suitcase to the back seat, and I followed him.

'Why are you here?' I sat in the car, staring wearily but with gratitude.

'Just in case. If some work pops up. You came home early, so...' he murmured under his nose. 'I'm going to call Victor and ask where to drive you to.'

'Why ask him? I'm going to my grandad's or a hotel. I'm still considering,' he dialled before I could finish my sentence.

'Hello! Nia is in front of her flat, with a suitcase, and she isn't going back. What should...'

The weapons at the legion had damaged Toma's hearing, and people had to speak loudly to him. The volume of his phone was to the max, so I heard Victor interrupting him with the words: "Get her here. She caught them."

'OK, we're on our way,' Toma hung up as I gaped at him.

'How does he know? How does he know what I caught?' I stammered, and he froze.

He kept silent while I was pushing his elbow.

'Spit it out, damn it!' I hissed at his face.

'Andre shags Maddie. Clearly, you saw that,' he peered guiltily from under his eyebrows.

'Don't tell me what I saw! Tell me how he knows what I saw! How come both Victor and you know about that? No! How come you knew before me? And how do you know their names, damn it! Explain!' I shouted and he turned red. 'If you don't care about me, you must at least care about yourself! Tell me, or I'm going to ask someone else! This is a threat. I am going to take advantage of information obtained because of your deafness,' he remained silent as I shook my finger menacingly. 'All right then, I'm getting out and I'll ask my questions directly to Kaov!'

He pressed a button to lock the doors, then gazed at me in horror.

'Please don't, you're gonna get me in trouble,' his face flashed with a whole new level of distress before he took my hands.

'Toma!' I invaded the space right in front of his nose. 'You need to tell me everything!' *Confidence* jumped on the tip of my index finger. Behind my barrier, I shivered. It was the first time I had ever threatened someone.

'OK, fine. Calm down, please! You freaked me out at the store that day, so I don't want that again. I don't wanna see you like that ever again. And let's be clear: I care about you, crazy girl,' he went silent for a moment. 'Victor knows what you saw because there are cameras and mics in your flat. He has also made full inquiries about you and the people around you. I give him all the information about what you do the rest of the time. He told me about Andre the other day. That's all!'

'That's all? He knows my every single minute? He even knows before me that my boyfriend bangs my stupid roommate,' I nailed my stomach-twisting gaze into his warm, brown eyes, managing to embarrass him.

'Everything, Nia! What kind of gummy bears you have for breakfast, what kind of wine you drink, what time you go to bed, what time you get up...'

'And "that's all", is that what you say? God, you really are crazy! All of you! What's wrong with you people?' I was already twisting him in the worst way possible.

'Please, don't make me feel bad. Don't stare at me like that! You are like a nasty goblin, for Christ's sake,' Toma shook his head.

'I want you to explain slowly and consistently. How crazy is that? Even I know these things are not normal,' I looked down taking a deep breath. I didn't want to make him feel bad, and he was right; I acted like a nasty goblin sometimes. 'What do you mean by saying that he knows everything? And moreover, why the hell?'

'Nia, you work for a very powerful man, and you work for him, personally. You're handling sensitive business information. What did you expect? You're not forgetting who he is, are you? Besides, he is a control freak, he keeps everything under control, he must make sure that...' Toma was mumbling and I interrupted him.

'Make sure what? That I don't choke on a gummy bear, poison myself with Chinese food, or drink poor wine? Come on, this is absurd and has nothing to do with security. What were you doing? Watching me in my underwear, or naked, and then what? Exact term: "voyeurism"!' I caught myself shouting while *Rage* was at his peak again.

'It's not like that! I didn't watch. I've never seen you naked. Victor wouldn't ever allow that. Stop shouting, please!'

I pressed my hand to my mouth. The minutes were ticking away in complete silence.

'Damn it! He saw me having sex with Andre?' I lifted my eyebrows to my scalp. Toma was fully embarrassed now.

'Well, how do I know? I am the outside camera,' his red face frowned. His candour made me laugh. He had already said too much, and he went silent in distress.

'Toma, you are aware that all this is not OK, nor acceptable, aren't you? It's insane! I mean, truly insane, even according to my standards!'

'I know it's not, but not according to his standards. Now listen to me carefully, calm down and stop swearing like that!' He continued, clasping my hands: 'Some of his people—those who work for him personally—live on his estate. Victor is always busy, and since he is also a president now, he doesn't have a spare second. He works 24/7. Often people need to be close and available in the middle of the night or early morning. Now he expects me to take you there. OK? He would've demanded you to move there soon, anyway. Please, don't tell him anything. You must agree because I will be the victim of the situation, and he's not always reasonable, even when it comes to me. Please! Besides, it's positive you found out about those two.'

'There is some logic, but still, it's fucking insane! I won't say anything, don't worry about that! I wasn't going to ask him anyway, even if you had refused to answer my questions,' my menacing index finger went up again. 'Toma, my boundaries between right and wrong are very distinct, and I'm not a traitor. In my head, *Justice* is black and white, and everything else in my mind is black and white, too. I threatened you only to provoke you! And I care about you, too! I think you're even kind of a friend to me!' I scolded, but he only nodded without answering.

As we drove, *Excitement* went wild behind the explosion of questions and thoughts. This time, it held *Desire* into a raging tango, while I was raging in my mind. The closer we got, the more mesmerising their dance became, and I wondered if it was a good idea to go there. Propping his head on his hands, *Reason* was murmuring:

People are cheating on us, stalking us, lying to us, we are having outbursts, we are going crazy... Some freaks are dancing around. What's going on? Two steps forward, one back, and so on to madness. How do you expect me to deal with this chaos? Compose yourself, or we'll end up with vestibular-motor hallucinations as well!

He was right, but chaos was taking over me once again. Stronger than me, all I could do was shrug grimly.

φ

Situated only minutes away from the city, the estate was huge and set up in large separate buildings with a lot of smaller houses. Everything was surrounded by a high wall with barbed peaks and security equipment. The first checkpoint was at the entrance. The guards were supposed to look under the cars, open the trunks, search the passengers, rummage through their belongings, even. They were obviously instructed not to open Toma's car, because all they did was run their device under the chassis. They didn't even notice me sitting behind the tinted windows at the back, where Toma forced me to move without explanations. A long street inside took us to a lane leading to the main staff building. After a second and a third checkpoint, Toma drove down another inside street and showed me the president's house. Just opposite it, separated by a strip of glass, there were six equally nice two-storey houses. We stopped in front of the first one.

'This one's for you,' he said.

'For me only?' I stared in disbelief.

'Yup.'

'These are the houses of "his people"?' I smiled under my breath.

'Yup.'

'Where do you live?'

'In the last one,' he pointed at the distance.

'So you are in the group?'

'All my life and till my last breath!' he replied with a warm smile showing his respect for Victor.

'Can I stay with you? I'd rather not be alone, especially during the night, and I guess I'm staying here, at least for tonight.'

'Goblin, I don't mind, but it's not up to me,' he grabbed the suitcase and we headed for the door. 'It's really nice, see? There's an office, a large bedroom as well, and on the other side, there's only grass between this house and Victor's. We can drink coffee together, if you'd like that. I can keep you company if something bothers you' his friendly patter made me stagger.

There was a phone ring and he pointed at something resembling a landline. Before picking up, he explained that it was an internal connection.

'OK, got it!' He nodded at the voice on the other end.

'What's going on?'

'There's a meeting tonight, and I have to drive you there. The secretary repeated three times it was an official dinner; she insisted you know why.'

'Oh! Problematic insistence!' My frown puzzled Toma.

'Why?'

'Because I didn't put the "proper" stuff in the suitcase. Shit! We need to go back downtown. I know a place for shoes. Do you happen to know a place for dresses? Not the one with the clones, though, or I'll go crazy again.'

'Not the one with what?' He gaped.

'Where you took me the other day.'

'They don't sell clones there. It's just clothes and beauty-something.'

'Toma, are you crazy? They don't sell them, of course, they make them!'

Two hours later, I was back in the house, staring at the mirror, combing my hair. When freed from a hairband, it reached down to my waist. It was usually messy, deciding on its own how to look, and only a bun would tame it. This time, however, it presented me with a pretty curl on the left of my face. In its remaining part, it looked as it usually did, but that was its unique disobedient charm. A young, fashion-enthusiast man had slipped a black, clinging dress over my body. I was suspicious. The décolleté somehow managed to be high and tight and at the same time reveal a thin strip of skin between the breasts, to the point where the ribs form a tiny dip. The fashion enthusiast had perched me on insanely high but exquisite heels. Even though I didn't have a clue about trends, I would sometimes look through pictures of such shoes on the internet. I even had my favourites. Their harmonious lines deserved admiration, and so did their creator. An assumption slipped through my mouth:

'Do shoes fascinate crazy girls only, or are most girls crazy enough to be fascinated by shoes? Two equally plausible hypotheses,' I giggled, gazing at my feet.

I didn't know anything different from my usual make-up, but I put on the red lipstick that turned grey pigeons into sparkling flamingos. I was gaping and grinning at my new appearance in the mirror when *Confidence* made me laugh by emerging taller, slimmer and dazzling out of a triple pirouette, like a ballerina with freckles and a ginger bun on the top of her head. She had that ability—shrinking and enlarging suddenly, and her transformations often surprised me.

Well, well, well... Everybody looks fancy today! Only I stay the same. Of course, I am the one who has to handle those dancing monkeys. They are raging like lunatics, and all you do is gaze at your feet while we are going insane!

Reason was grumbling and pulling at his suspenders, but he couldn't kill my mood. The insanely high heels were torturous, yet they managed to stretch my posture. I walked to the car, focused on my efforts not to fall down. Toma helped me in. As soon as we drove off, he scolded me:

'You're not on a date. You're attending a meeting! I already told you that, but now you look as if you're ready for a date.'

'Toma. You're multiplying the nuances that I don't comprehend. I'm supposed to look appropriate, isn't that right? The other night I saw women dressed just like this. The shop consultant seemed to know his shit and I trust his choice! Don't I look more appropriate in this outfit? For their standards, at least?' I snapped at him sulkily.

'If we're talking about the same human being, you look more than gorgeous, not just appropriate! I'm not sure what your weird head assumes, but you are a beautiful, young lady. Apparently a short-sighted, beautiful, young lady,' he seemed serious. 'You need to work on your self-esteem! Maybe communication is not your strong side, but you have a number of qualities to be proud of, and it doesn't matter if you are wearing a shaggy sweater, or a sexy evening dress.'

I gaped at him. Silently, I was trying to figure out why he was talking to me like that.

'"Thanks", Nia! When someone says sincere, kind words to you, or even if they're not sincere, it is a complement, and you say "thanks". You don't gape!'

'Fine, fine! Thanks, Toma! Your assumptions caught me by surprise. Our evaluations differ. Probably because of the points of view and partly because of the gender differences. In fact, you evaluate me under the influence of biochemical...'

His laughter interrupted me.

'Just "thanks"! Saying "thanks" and giving a smile is enough. You can also complement the person in reply.'

'Ugh. Well! Thank you, Toma! Your subjective opinion is weird but kind. I find your black shirt boring and appropriate at the same time,' I faked a smile. 'Was it good?'

'Almost, but we'll keep practicing,' he was laughing at my puzzled face. 'You will learn!'

'If you say so!' I rolled my eyes.

'Are you always this sulky, goblin? You're snapping at people all the time,' he shook his head and I shrugged with a snort. 'To be honest, when you are angry, you speak more normally. You can examine the process and do it more often,' his new assumption surprised me and made me wonder whether it was correct. 'Do you want to talk about Andre?'

'What's there to say about him?'

'Like if whether all right. It's been a difficult day!' He touched my elbow and I pulled myself away.

'I'm perfectly fine! I thought we had a deal about explanations, and now you're pushing me. Leave me alone, there's nothing to discuss here!'

'Here goes the goblin, sulking again... Fine, but if you eventually change your mind, I'll be right here.'

He turned up the volume of the music and I sighed with relief.

We were driving to a mountain-top restaurant, like a private club for the elite. The architecture student called to inform me that there was a serious accident at the office and he needed help. I asked Toma to check what was wrong, but he refused. Missing the meeting was not an option for any of us. I got off in front of the restaurant and he sulkily made his way back.

I entered, balancing on my heels. A waiter led me to a table where ten people were having dinner. Victor had taken the central seat at the far end, the annoying interior designer from the office was sitting on his left. She was a beauty and perfectly fitted the standard: tall, blonde, stunningly sexy, dressed in a bright red dress. She measured me with narrowed eyes and I did the same. The president sipped his whisky with a blank expression on his face, judging my appearance. He squeezed the glass tightly, but I couldn't tell if he considered it appropriate or not. Not taking his eyes off me, he introduced me by my first name, and it seemed to me that flames swayed in the blue. He was evaluating me sternly, his jaw glued together, but as usual, there was no facial expression. A couple of seconds later he pulled his attention back to the person he was having a conversation with. Sitting two chairs away from me, the repulsive minister of transport greeted me with a greasy smile. He was sweaty and slightly drunk. Every now and then I kept bumping into Kaov's gaze, though he managed to sleekly shift it away. The designer threw glances at me, as if she wanted to evaporate me. I engaged in small talk and I was pleased with myself. I drew a clear pattern, observing the others' acts of communication. Some of the people were giving the president opinions and suggestions that followed logic and were well-grounded. All the rest, however, kept repeating "yes" and "got it" twenty times a minute, like lackeys, so I wondered at the point of their presence.

My attention was caught by a conversation in English about numbers. Victor commented on a new gas field for a potential American investor. His interlocutor was sitting to my right, fully engulfed in his sheets of paper on the table. I peeked at them to recognise my own forecast. The man exclaimed with surprise:

'But Mr. Kaov, this is impressive! The calculations are intriguing, all three of them!'

Smiling all over, I looked up at Victor. I guess *Pride* paraded on my face, but he responded, composed, without even throwing a glance at me.

'Indeed! My team made them and I assure you that in addition to being intriguing, they're impeccably accurate.'

I snorted and my mouth twisted into a sour smile. I took a breath to say something, but Victor cut me off.

'Nia, not now!' He turned back to the man. 'Apologies, my assistant is still getting acquainted with the protocol and her place.'

The stranger's eyes on me were almost as contemptuous as the president's.

'I assume you are already interested in the prospects,' Kaov shot the man with his crushing gaze across the wall of superiority. The man nodded.

I blushed, clutching the chair. *Rage* spewed fire through his nose, *Justice* and *Pride* were enraged. I stared viciously at Victor, struggling to keep the words behind my teeth:

Damn you, you arrogant bastard! How many people live in this person? How can he behave in a hundred different ways, each one of them more humiliating than the last? I calculated this! It was not a team! Only me! Me! I'm not your assistant! God, let me just earn some cash by working for this son of a bitch, and I'm off to the other end of the world! We'll see who will calculate probabilities and put up with his arrogant behaviour then!

I stewed in silence. The security guard standing closest to the president throughout the evening approached him and whispered something in his ear.

Victor got up abruptly, pulled the designer by the hand, and went out. The guard mumbled unclear words to some of the other people and they also fled after Victor. The stranger next to me, too. I watched the lights of the escort twist down the road. Four people and my confused gaze left on the table.

A moment later, the door flew open and a group of women in revealing dresses marched in. They came to the men at our table, the music and everything else became louder. The minister of transport didn't pay any attention to the beauties. Without invitation, he sat down on the chair next to me. He smelled of whisky and sweat. His coat was not there to cover his disgusting curves.

'You did your best to look gorgeous tonight. Nia, was it, right? Where did Victor order you from? You are fantastic!' He snorted and drops of alcoholic spittle flew towards my face.

'I neither did my best, nor I have been ordered. I work for him,' I looked around, trying to find a waiter who could bring the security guards. 'Excuse me!' I tried to get a bartender's attention, but instead of replying, he just turned his back on me. 'Well, clearly he has decided you work for someone else tonight. I'm thinking of having you as my assistant for the next couple of hours,' the minister giggled, sliding his sweaty hand up my leg. He tried to shove it between my thighs, but my muscles tightened as much as they could. 'We're gonna have a great time, Nia!'

Disgusting!

Giving him the gaze, I was unsure if the stomach-twisting succeeded. I could clearly see all the distortions in the repulsive creature next to me. Out of control, my mind kept shifting parts of his body like glowing lines, trying to fix him. *Malice* proposed a hammer.

'Don't touch me!' I pronounced the words distinctly right under his nose.

'Or what, you whore?' He hissed in my ear, licking the skin around it. Creeps ran down my spine.

My heart was racing, I didn't know what to say or do, and there was no one to come to my aid. My phone was out of range at that altitude, and I couldn't see any cars outside. The minister waved at someone behind my back. In a second, a waiter brought him a porcelain plate. My eyes froze on the key laying on it.

'If you behave, you might like it, but if you try to resist, I will like it better,' his voice leaked through his spluttering mouth, his giggle became even more repulsive.

He pulled hard to move the edge of the dress and tore loudly. I crossed my thighs, and my gaze stared at a distant blank spot. My mind was stuck; only the words "faulty pattern" kept repeating themselves. *Fear* gripped me, a roaring chaos swept me away from reality and sent me into a trance. The mental block took hold of me and numbed my body.

Someone in my head pushed forcefully and shouted in a thunder to sober me up. Bright lines and shapes shot before my gaze, returning my focus.

Calm down! Get back in control, don't panic! Priority: speed. Details: seventeen steps to the exit. The road goes to the right, along the forest. You go into the forest. They won't see you in the dark.

The dark!

Fear repeated, tightening my stomach even more, but the voice shouted again. It seemed it was my own voice, not the voice of any of the entities in my head.

Focus! Keep control, balance your breathing. Adrenalin was released. It will increase your speed; you won't become tired. You don't look back. Run and breathe evenly. It shall pass! Count to help you focus, and run. As fast as you can! Chances: poor. Now count, Nia. Count!

I was taking balanced gulps of breath, patting my thumb on the other fingers in a vigorous rhythm.

Everyone in my head held hands and shouted together:

ONE!

I detached myself from the chair, and the heels were kind enough to slip off my feet. Grabbing my bag, I ran. The eyes of the waiters and nasty drunk laughter escorted me out. I rushed out of the door without looking back. Mechanically I turned right; the narrow road twisted like a snake. The city was more than fifteen kilometres away; I didn't have a ghost of a chance, and my mind calculated it precisely. I could hear muffled voices behind my back and my legs flew with all their anatomical strength, even faster. I sank into the darkness of the forest while *Fear* was ruthlessly ripping my stomach.

It's just dark, it's just dark...

I kept repeating this as I stumbled over rocks and branches. I didn't stop.

When I couldn't proceed any longer, only my heart was ringing in the silence. I froze in the nothingness of the dark. My phone showed indications of some weak signal.

'Toma!' Vague sound crackled from the other side, but I couldn't make out what he was saying. So, I continued slowly and clearly: 'I am in the woods. I ran parallel to the road for about half an hour. Four turns. I can see the radio tower. Something is shining in the distance...'

The connection broke. I dialled again, but it didn't go through.

Like a predator, the cold was crawling up and down my bones. I was almost naked and barefoot, and the temperature in the mountain was going below zero. Not able to move anymore, I was only shaking. I curled up by a stump near the road and waited.

It shall pass.

The echo of my voice closed my eyelids. As the darkness engulfed me, I irrationally hoped Toma would find me.

FIVE

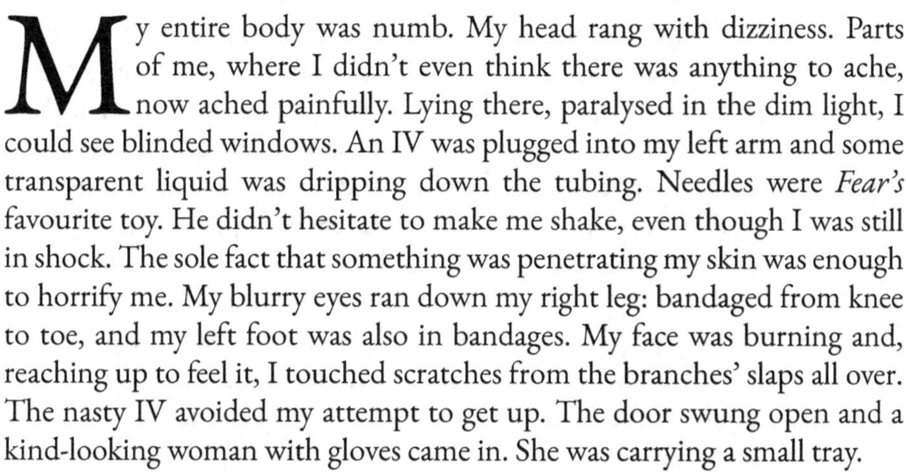

My entire body was numb. My head rang with dizziness. Parts of me, where I didn't even think there was anything to ache, now ached painfully. Lying there, paralysed in the dim light, I could see blinded windows. An IV was plugged into my left arm and some transparent liquid was dripping down the tubing. Needles were *Fear's* favourite toy. He didn't hesitate to make me shake, even though I was still in shock. The sole fact that something was penetrating my skin was enough to horrify me. My blurry eyes ran down my right leg: bandaged from knee to toe, and my left foot was also in bandages. My face was burning and, reaching up to feel it, I touched scratches from the branches' slaps all over. The nasty IV avoided my attempt to get up. The door swung open and a kind-looking woman with gloves came in. She was carrying a small tray.

'Don't get up! You'll get dizzy,' her voice filled the large space around us.

'I can't get any dizzier than I already am. Take this thing out of my arm!'

'I will when the fluid is finished.'

'Now! Take it out of my body right now!' There was panic in my voice as I reached for the tubing.

'All right, calm down. Don't pull, you will hurt yourself,' she removed the cannula carefully and put a plaster on the spot. 'You were freezing and you have many superficial wounds. Your leg is injured, but it's not serious and you'll recover in no time. I was giving you a cocktail of sedatives, painkillers and something for dehydration. Take a rest now. You'll be fine,' she explained slowly.

'Am I in a hospital? Who brought me here?' The last memories in the mist of my head were of the stump, *Fear*, and the cold in my bones.

'You are not in a hospital, but you are getting the necessary treatment. Don't worry and take a rest. I can give you a sedative if you'd like.'

I was taking a breath to interrupt her, when Toma burst in. He marched like a clumsy polar bear heading to the water. The doctor took advantage of this distraction to leave the room.

'Oh my God, you are OK!'

He dropped to his knees by the bed. Raw human pain flashed in his eyes. Puffy, with bags under his eyes, it looked as if someone had chewed him up and spat him back out.

'Good evening, afternoon, morning?' I asked.

'Good evening, Nia!'

I propped myself up in the bed, despite the protest of my muscles. A single lamp lit the huge room. A TV gleamed opposite me. It was almost a cinema screen, reaching from the ground to nearly the ceiling. Next to it, there was a doorless doorway, but I couldn't see what was behind it. I noticed a glass desk with only one pen on it and a chair and a single bedside table. A giant mirror hung on the wall to the left and the bed was big enough for three people. I looked at my T-shirt: wide, stretched, displaying the washed-out image of Daenerys Targaryen[7]. I peered under the blanket and saw my blue panties, inside-out, their torn elastic band tickling my right hip.

'Toma?' I was trying to decide what to ask first. There was horror in his eyes. I wrapped the sleeves of my T-shirt around my fingers and stretched it.

'That's what I found in your suitcase. I thought you'd feel comfortable in it. I also brought the jeans and the colourful trainers. Damn, I didn't know what else to...' he pointed clumsily at a pile on the floor by the bed. His index finger was shaking.

---

[7] *Daenerys Targaryen is a literary character in George R.R. Martin's series "A Song of Ice and Fire ", as well as in the TV adaptation of "Game of Thrones" – author's notes.*

'Christ! What happened? Are you well? You look like a mess!'

'Am I well? I am guilty; how could I possibly be well? I shouldn't have left you; it was all my mistake. I never thought they'd leave without you. I shouldn't have left you there alone.'

'How did you even find me?'

His wet eyes looked at me, then he continued to explain hesitantly:

'What I heard on the phone wasn't enough. It took me quite a while to...' he sighed heavily, squeezing my fingers. '...find you. The road is long, you know. I didn't even know if you were alive! I died a hundred deaths before...' He went silent, biting his lip. '...Nia, it was so hard to find the exact place, and you were there, curled up in a ball this small,' his trembling hands showed me the size.

'Toma, it was not your fault,' I held his fingers. 'I hid on purpose, because I wanted to escape that man, the minister. The creep was going to...' All of a sudden, *Contempt* made me furious. *Malice* was dreamily thinking about inflicting pain, hurting without mercy, and enjoying it all. The idea of her controversial methods slipped through my mouth: 'I will destroy him someday! Painfully, as I look him in the eye, and I'm going to like it,' *Malice's* metal arrow flashed in my pupils. It startled Toma as if he saw a ghost.

'Don't think about that! Take a rest! I'm so sorry I let this happen,' he clenched his jaw.

'Wait! Toma, where are we? Did you bring me to your place?'

'I'm so sorry, Nia,' he kept repeating, as if in a trance. 'I really have to go. I screwed up like never before and I'm beyond grateful you're OK,' an incomprehensible expression twisted his face.

Still dizzy, it was difficult for my words to catch up with my thoughts. He slammed the door before I could say anything. My phone was on the bedside table, hooked up to the charger but switched off. Once on, a barrage of messages, missed calls and emails attacked me. The screen light pierced me like thousands of needles, so I put the phone away. Realising that almost a day had passed, I grumbled:

'Damn, what did this doctor give me to make me sleep for so long?'

I rubbed my forehead, slipped out of the sheets and stumbled towards the door. Moving through the huge room proved to be a painful experience, but *Curiosity* led the way. All the others were silent. I opened the door to find a spacious lobby behind it. French windows revealed a beautiful view of tall pine trees. Directly in front of them were all the houses, including mine. In the lobby, I saw a home bar with various bottles of alcohol, a chess table that I hardly resisted, several closed doors, and a wide marble staircase. Everything looked much cosier than the gloomy bedroom atmosphere.

I went cautiously down the stairs. Quiet voices were coming from the bottom. The doctor was whispering to four other women and a man, all of them in uniforms. About ten metres behind them, the president, the chief advisor, and two strangers were sitting at a large table. Victor looked up. It felt like he was throwing snowballs at my skin. I was stunned, but he simply clenched his jaw and returned to his conversation. Embarrassed by my appearance, the others turned their backs on me, as if I was not there. The butler jumped like a grasshopper to cover my legs with his coat. He insisted on walking me back to the bedroom, persistently pushing me up the stairs. An old man with white hair, he looked like a faithful comrade from a war novel with his ridiculous moustache and teenage acne scars. Very politely, he applied a whole arsenal of persuasions to talk me into climbing the steps.

He managed to shove me back in the bedroom. Everyone in my head was silent with shock.

'Total failure! Absolute failure! How did I end up here, for Christ's sake!' I muttered as the door slammed.

All he cares about is avoiding scandals!

Maddie's words echoed through my head.

Oh, God! I need to explain to Victor and I hope he'll understand that I'm not going to provoke any scandals. I can't do it now; I must clear my mind first. All right, relax. Dress, apologise and get out of here. Is he going to fire me? How could Toma leave me in the bastard's house? Is he out of his fucking mind?!

I took the phone to call Toma, but the annoying news application popped up on the display. "Breaking News" was trying to catch my attention. A young reporter was standing soaking wet in front of the government building. She announced curtly:

'The minister of transport unexpectedly resigned earlier today. The first change in the new president's cabinet came as a surprise to all, and provoked sharp criticism from the opposition, most notably by the former president. The motives of the minister are not clear yet. The press conference was attended by his advisor who claimed that the motives were personal, but he refused to give any more information.'

My hands started shaking as I gaped.

Resigned? So, he got sober and realised he is a total creep? No way! Did Toma say anything? Does he know what happened? Indeed, that's why the president worries I might make a scandal. God knows what troubles came with all this. Damn it, he's definitely going to fire me! My thoughts were scattered around my head, but no one bothered to help me collect them.

'How do you feel, Nia?' his voice dragged me out of the shock. I shivered by the timber.

He was leaning against the door, holding a glass of whisky in one hand. Barefoot, in jeans and an unbuttoned shirt. I detected some expression on his face, but I was not sure what kind because of the darkness. I froze but the hem of my T-shirt swayed. Adrenaline dulled the pain in my body. Embarrassed, I stared across the room.

'You know what happened, don't you?'

'I know every little detail!' He shouted syllable-by-syllable. He exploded, throwing the glass against the wall. Shards crashed to the floor.

'Fuck!' I screamed, flinching at his impulsive reaction. His voice and demeanour were usually composed, even when he was being rude and arrogant. He continued in a quiet voice, but it still felt like shouting.

'Do you realise what you did?' He walked in my direction with a wild face, and I stepped back until I reached the wall.

'There won't be a scandal! I won't say anything! I swear, I...' panic was hiding in my voice when Kaov started shouting right at my face:

'You left everything to the whims of fucking luck, Nia! To fate! My order was to stay with Toma the entire time. From now on, you're not to be left alone even for one fucking second!' Mad flames shone in his eyes. 'You are so smart and your decisions are so terrible! You work for me and you are complying with me and my decisions! You are a woman. There are things you can't handle on your own. You are not to send my people off when I have given them specific instructions. I forbid you to even think about it again! Am I clear?' He leaned against the wall, his hands on either side of my head. I was speechless, witnessing this erupting volcano of madness. Victor took a deep breath to control his voice. 'Are you afraid of me already? Why are you hiccoughing?'

'I'm not afraid. More than twenty percent of the people panic when someone starts shouting at them. I don't, but I hiccough. I already know that you experience difficulties in communication, like me, but you must mind your tone, and certainly, it's not only the tone. The words are also quite improper,' I did not take my bulging eyes off him. The hiccoughs separated my syllables.

An unknown force twisted my stomach and made me shake. It was definitely not *Fear*, it was not even distress. Victor's eyelids went down, he pursed his lips.

'For Christ, Nia! You accumulate a huge amount of information, your mind works on different frequencies, and yet you can't make a single true judgement about reality. Your brain just can't comprehend this vile world. How can you be like that?'

My whole body was vibrating because of the humiliating situation, his unrestrained behaviour and the irritating combination of his voice and his words. Nevertheless, his closeness caused *Desire* to erupt in a wild solo dance. *Reason* was struggling to stop it. I strived to object to Victor's incorrect conclusion.

'Whatever I am, my mind works amazingly and its judgement about the general reality is pretty accurate. The distorted people, their patterns... They're bent into straight lines, and...' It was pointless to explain any further. I was well aware of the fact that, when triggered, I did not speak clearly.

I did my best to suppress this annoying reaction, along with the vibrations in me, but, despite my efforts, *Desire* managed to send my attention somewhere deep into the blue irises. Standing there in my T-shirt and panties, I started tapping my fingers to shift my thoughts away from the incomprehensible processes caused by this man. Now they were going out of control. His body was too close, soaking its heat into me. His smell swirled from my chest to my stomach and back around, leaving a thorny trace behind.

'Your mind works amazingly, yet your decisions are absurd,' he hissed at me.

I took a deep breath, offended by the accusations and by everything going on. With a strong push, I managed to sweep nonsensical *Desire* to the back of my head. *Reason* was offended and hurried to explain through my mouth:

'Victor, apologies for all the troubles, but the cause I sent Toma off for was an emergency at the office. He's not my personal driver. He's supposed to assist me with my tasks, and this was a very logical judgement. I'm doing my best, even though I'm just an assistant who doesn't know her place! Not that you care, but *Reason* was tired last night because it was a next-level crazy day, and on top of everything, I learned that...' I bit the words back before spitting out the fact that I knew he had been spying on me. 'It was a crazy day. Nevertheless, I don't have to explain my decisions here! This way of communicating right now is unacceptable, and it has been unacceptable all along. I know how hard it is, but you should indeed take care of the tone, the words, the way you act!'

'*Reason* was tired?' He narrowed his eyes. 'Nia, there's nothing hard for me. In case you haven't figured it out yet, this is my normal way of communicating. Get used to it! The absolutely unacceptable thing here is you sending Toma off. I don't even know how you managed to persuade him,' he gained control over his voice with a loud breath. I looked down, pulling the T-shirt over my naked legs. 'You work for me, you are going to follow my instructions, and I am not going to accept your absurd risks and your stubbornness! Take a rest now, we will discuss your behaviour tomorrow.'

I only growled. His fingers lifted my chin. My pupils were invaded. Raging demons were storming in the blue of his irises. He came even closer and the distance went beyond indecent. I shivered as his eyes flashed in the dark. My breathing quickened but I couldn't calm it down.

'Damn it, Nia!' He hissed, grabbing my neck. His thumb traced a long scratch on my cheekbone. My heart rate pounded, and his hand detected it. He clenched his other hand in a fist and pressed it to the wall.

His thick, burning touch sent something like electricity through my chest, down to my abdomen, then it exploded in my groin. I jumped and my breath stopped. Victor was looking at me from just centimetres away. My skin vibrated under his hand as electric waves crashed inside me. *Desire* took over my whole mind, kicking my pulse to my throat. Through my open lips, my breath was leaving traces in the silence. I stared at Victor, paralysed by his influence on me, by the incomprehensible processes he provoked. He closed his eyes; his fingers sank into my neck, and a moan escaped my throat.

'Stop giving me this look, Nia!' The words slipped through his teeth. His fist slammed into the wall next to me and the resonance from the blow ran down my spine.

'What look?' I snapped, taking my eyes off him.

The indecent look! How many times did I tell you not to stare at him like that! Have you lost your mind?

Reason hissed as I swallowed dryly. I slipped under Victor's arm, shocked by my body's reaction and Victor's behaviour.

'I'm getting dressed and I'm going to my house. We really must talk tomorrow. Mostly about our way of communicating. This one is quite wrong.'

'You're not going anywhere! The doctor and the staff will take care of you here.' he stood frozen on his spot, seemingly unaware that he was talking to the wall.

'No, I am certainly leaving! I don't need any care. I'm fine!'

I could tell by the movement of his cheekbones that his gaze found me in the dark.

'It was not a question! We're done with your judgements,' his metallic, arrogant voice was back. 'You're staying here until they say you're OK. No arguing! Spare me your absurd arguments. If you need something, ask them,' his eyes traced the scratches on my face. The muscles on his neck tightened and he took a deep breath before leaving the room.

I closed my eyes for several seconds.

And they call me crazy? How many personalities live in this man? Damn it! He's driving me absolutely mad!

My attention turned to the irregular rhythm of my racing heart. There seemed to be a gaping abyss in the place where Victor had touched my face. I felt it with my fingers and I snorted:

'My head's not listening to me, he's not listening to me, and now my body's acting crazy as well. Can't he understand that I don't like to be touched? Damn it! This is a mental asylum here'

I hurled myself onto the bed. My head was booming so much that even the darkness in the room didn't bother me.

Nervously, I walked through the doorless space next to the TV. There was a small room behind it, containing only a big bed and many cupboards. I bumped into one of them. Next, I reached the bathroom, where I took the bandages off. Many wounds were covering my legs and feet. Carefully stepping under the soothing shower, I closed my eyes, and my mind went back to the forest. I washed the disgusting creep's sweat off my skin, trying to convince myself that his faulty pattern was bound to be fixed, with or without a hammer. The water relaxed me, yet the blue and the musk of Victor kept drowning my senses more painful than the wounds and the anger. *The Monster* tried to spit out some lines about my ridiculous hallucinations, but it realised that I didn't even have the strength to respond. Holding its poison back, it just sent a bitter taste and a few gross globs of phlegm towards the nonsensical *Desire*. Its mockery certainly made sense.

I put the T-shirt and the panties back on. Snuggled in the huge bed, now I probably indeed resembled a wet, frightened, stray kitten. Though the medications were doing their job, my body's pain made me toss and turn endlessly before falling asleep; at least, I tried to convince myself that the pain was the cause. Just before dozing off, somewhere within the thundering chaos in my head, I heard *Reason* shouting at *Desire* that it was an intruder, driving us mad and must go away immediately. I nodded in confirmation, but *Desire* remained brazenly silent. It didn't even hiccough at the shouts.

φ

A dream took hold of me. Irregular, dark shapes spilled around to devour me. *Fear* made me numb and sadistically wrapped himself around my neck, leaving me with no air. He immersed me in ice and I struggled for my breath, kicking and pushing. After a long barbaric battle with the familiar nightmare, I broke free with a shout. Hidden in the dark, *Fear* reminded me:

You are mine.

Sweat-soaked and shaking, my upper body bounced off the bed. My heart was hysterical, pounding to escape, but two warm arms held my back and chest tightly.

'Wake up!' His touch burned me. He moved his face in front of my blurred sight. His hold of my sides was bringing life to my skin. 'It's a dream, Nia, calm down! Your heart is about to explode. It's OK! It's just a nightmare.'

Victor's blazing eyes were staring at me. His scent suffocated me. Although now awake, I kept gasping for air—unsure what was worse for my brain: his influence on me or the nightmare. Half-awake, I grabbed his wrists, and my intention was not to move them away. Not at all. His palms pressed harder on my cheekbones. A new rush of reviving heat emanated from them. It reached into my bones and ricocheted, pushing at the walls of my body. His touch shook me more powerfully, painfully, and torturously than ever before. In his arms, my entire crazy being writhed from within.

'It's just a nightmare!' My voice was barely audible, and I suppose Victor assumed I was referring to the dream.

'Are you calm now?' He pulled his hands away, but my fingers tore into his wrists. 'Get some more sleep!'

'No,' I shook my head vigorously. The influence of his touch had broken me and something was cutting me into pieces from the inside. I pinned my crazy, desperate gaze on him, begging him to explain everything.

'Don't, Nia!' He scolded me in a frosty voice. 'Don't look at me like that! I'm leaving now, and you are getting some sleep,' his voice was becoming increasingly hoarse. He pronounced the words sharply, his hands clenched into fists.

'No, I am not!' I snapped back. 'It lacks logic, damn it! It all lacks logic! Why are you here when you'd rather be gone?' My confused thoughts flowed out in words that demanded answers. I squeezed his wrists and felt the muscles tighten. My pupils were probably betraying stories of my absurd hallucinations. My voice certainly revealed a combination of pleading and pitiful longing. He inhaled air in quick, sharp gulps.

'Damn it, Nia! Don't look at me like that! Stop it!' He hissed, but I remained silent, gazing at his gloomy, symmetrical face.

Then I came to my senses. Me. Him. The insane situation. I quickly let go of his hands, shocked by my own behaviour. I looked down and I stuttered:

'I'm sorry, I... just... don't know what's going on with me...' Shoving my hair behind my ears, I fiddled with the neckline of my T-shirt, not daring to look at him.

'You are going to drive me to the edge, aren't you? Your logic, your eyes, everything. All I want is to leave this fucking room, but no, you have to drive me to the edge.'

'No, I... If you explain to me as you did before, maybe I...'

I was mumbling when his hands grasped my cheekbones again.

'I'm not good at explaining at all.'

The whisper made me look up and stare into his eyes. What radiated from them made me gape and swallow dryly. He was not surrounded by the wall of superiority anymore; he was surrounded by thick heat that was almost glowing in the dark.

'Christ, Nia! I can't...'

Instead of finishing, he growled through his teeth. He tugged me closer, his lips pressed against mine. He parted them with his tongue, then slid it over mine. It wasn't slimy at all. Just warm and soft. My breath was sliced into parts. My lungs whimpered, and a full-voltage current made the moss of my skin stand. Victor ran his hand up my spine, buried it in my hair, grabbed the back of my neck with his other hand, and pressed me to his chest. His touch immobilised me for a moment, but then my own hands began moving timidly on his shoulders. They kept going up; my fingers growing thirsty for the touch. When they reached his hair, they buried themselves. He was kissing, biting my lips and everything around. He was sinking in, and my tongue was chasing his, as if it knew this game. I inhaled the bubbling heat beneath his T-shirt. He lifted my chin and a shower of kisses ran down my neck and collarbone, followed by a series of shivers: my heart muscle pushing to break my ribs.

A dead silence immersed my head, like a winter morning in the forest. In his arms, my body began moving on its own. As if in a trance. As if it was not mine, it boldly clung to what it craved. It clung to the madness. Victor pulled me away from his skin, pushed me back, and I collapsed on the bed. In one sharp motion, he yanked the blanket off my legs and landed between them. He stared madly, only a breath away from my face. A completely different person stood above me. The frost in his expression had melted. His icy gaze was now burning. He arranged my hair, stroked it with the tips of his fingers, and glided them over my face. He seized it, then froze, studying me silently with his eyes, chewing his lips. He dug them into mine, biting. I bit back.

His palm was exploring every inch of me. The tight touch of another person's skin on mine provoked a mixture of unknown processes and complete chaos for my senses. He was slowly travelling up my thighs, my hips and my belly. He wrapped his fingers around my breasts, grabbing one of them roughly, pinching its tip. I bent back. As if stricken by a whip, he growled and pulled away abruptly.

'If you have anything to say, do it now!' His voice was hoarse, his breath—broken into pieces. He waited insistently for my reply. I shook my head vigorously, gaping, vibrating, not knowing what to do. He opened my lips with his thumb, then ran it over my tongue. 'You're driving me crazy, Nia! You pulled me out of control! Even touching you is impossible, and it's the one thing I shouldn't do.'

'Well, yeah... I'd generally rather not be touched, but...' I stammered, and he smiled.

'You'd rather it. You just don't know it yet.'

He was whispering. He pressed his body against mine so tightly that I could feel the pulsation of his desire. It beat through his pants somewhere up to my navel. His beard prickled my skin as he eagerly started to kiss everything in front of his breath. He gripped my throat, squeezing to pain. I could read his expression now: he wanted me, he anticipated me, he craved me. I was trying to search for the causes, but *Desire* blocked my mind. It wrapped itself around me like a snake, interrupted my breathing until I wasn't searching for anything anymore. Only for his touch.

Victor's fingers ran down my thighs. Lustful chills crept into his traces, sharp, prickly, stinging. Burning. I curved my spine in an arch as he yanked my pants off. The awkward realisation of my nakedness pressed my knees together. He carefully studied my body and my reaction.

'Earlier, when I was putting them on, my own self-control impressed me,' the sparkle in his eyes drained my throat.

He moved closer to lick with appetite all the way from my navel to my face. His tongue sank into my lips, and I was immersed in the taste of the whisky, the cigar, the sweetness, the madness. Cold and hot, one after the other and all at once, prickled my skin. A chemical cocktail exploded in my head, making me dizzy, then it transformed into a rhythmic pulsation. The sound of a condom wrapper tearing sobered me up as Victor pressed himself against my body's moisture. He had opened my legs wide apart and pinned his mad gaze on me, only a few centimetres away from my face. My eyes opened even wider than my legs. I grabbed the back of his neck, trying to tame the interruptions of my breathing. He froze, staring at my shocked gaze. His irises darkened as if a raging demon was bursting to come out, but he was trying to hold it back. He was chasing his own breath, his fingers eagerly glued to my face. The muscles on his neck tightened menacingly. For a moment, I was hesitant because of his strange expression, but then *Desire* shattered the remains of my doubts.

'Slowly,' the word slipped through my lips.

The tone of my voice said it all. Touch and penetration were painful to me, and now I expected the pain to be unbearable. Nevertheless, *Desire* wanted it right there and then.

Victor took a gulp of air to gain control over himself and made his way inside me very slowly. He was sinking in painfully, overcoming the obstacles of the too-narrow space. He broke into my body and mind, smashing them into pieces. Like a greedy predator, he blasted open the passage to addictive pleasure penetrating the dark of my mind, deep into the unconscious. Unhurried, he was entering into my darkness, millimetre by millimetre.

I dug my nails into his skin, surrendering to some insidious, sticky mixture of pleasure and pain. As all of him sank into me, a loud moan escaped my throat. His kiss muffled it. His body became a motionless part of mine, and his dry lips moved along the outline of my face.

'Damn, Nia!' He growled. I could feel his throbbing heart. 'Are you sure what you did with that boy was even sex? Tell me!' His words sank into my ear.

'You...' I stammered, displeased. I tried to move away but his body chained me. 'Why did you watch it?'

His head buried in my hair, he didn't reply.

'It feels like no one has ever been inside you before,' he said in a trance. His breath sprinkled shivers over my neck. A warm kiss locked our tongues when his body slid gently in a smooth rhythm. He held my face in his hand.

'It feels like you're right, damn it!' The truth slipped between my lips before he bit them.

The pain of him being inside me was dissolving. It disappeared, taking the shape of unfamiliar pleasure. It spread my thighs wide apart. He was leaning over me and his masculine energy occupied my senses. He was invading me, enveloped in the moisture he sucked out of my cells. His curves and edges filled me, stretching the delicate tissue, challenging my ideas in the most unexpected ways. Pulsations warmed the tender spot, lifting my hips to move in his rhythm. Moans kept bursting through my teeth as I pressed my body upon his, as if I was trying to glue myself. His heart rate quickened with each thrust. Mine as well.

In one motion, he wrapped my legs around his waist and growled, digging his lips into mine and my pelvis into his body. He tore at me and at what was left of my sanity, penetrating quickly, rudely and boldly. One of his hands stretched my wrists over my head and the other pulled my hair. I bent like a bow in his arms. A new personality emerged in his eyes. The pain of the fierce invasion twisted me, it swished through my throat, then it exploded into a devastating pleasure. Deep inside, I could feel every uneven surface of his arousal. One after the other, his thrusts unveiled the unique spots of the alphabet unsuspectedly existing in me.

He slid my T-shirt up and my bare breasts glistened. He freed my arms from the sleeves but, when the shirt reached my face, he left only my nose and my mouth uncovered. He carefully placed the fabric over my eyes. Darkness separated me from his gaze. My breath stopped. With one hand, Victor pressed my wrists to the bed. The fingers of his other hand caressed the skin from my neck to my stomach, gently circling the tense nipples. He ran his lips down my neck. All I could hear was the thunderous beat of my heart.

'Let's turn off the lights of your beautiful mind! I want to be your only sensation,' he was whispering in my ear and my body clung to him like a magnet.

Immersed in darkness, I relaxed under Victor's skin and vibrated to his rhythm. It was intensifying, accelerating, exploding. His movements became rough again, when he pinned my wrists and neck with his palms. I was only sensation now. A devastating pleasure. He subdued his impulses and penetrated me at the right pace, in perfect harmony with the unique spots of the alphabet. He led my body to a land of pleasure and pain, where there was not enough air. He was pushing me uncontrollably towards primary disintegration. My deep, tightening spasms were embracing him, and he was hardening even more with each invasion.

He pulled the shirt off my face, exposing himself entirely out of control above me. Nothing was left from his steady, restrained composure. Now he was looking at me with burning, mad, shining irises. He was blazing in the dark. The passion in his kiss ran through and completely disassembled my whole being. His right hand dug into my hair, pressing me against him. His other hand twisted my hips; he sank to my depths. The uncontrollable impulses of his desire were pounding at my body. Each blow fired a spark. An unknown personality of mine wanted to kiss, touch, bite and scream. My mouth moaned sharply:

'Don't stop!'

His mad gaze caught my eyes. All I could see was the burning blue, then defocused, vague, double, fivefold. His thrusts gathered energy into a vast raging ball. Thick and bright, it swirled to every corner, leaving only smoking ash behind. My tissue was squeezing him, the spasms were getting tighter and tighter, the muscles on his neck outlined. His one sharp penetration crashed the ball into me, and it exploded between my legs. An unknown, wild force invaded my body, my consciousness and my subconsciousness at once.

Every cell vibrated in a divine rhythm; every molecule disintegrated to original ecstasy. The blue before my eyes became duller, then it vanished. Silence echoed in my head, choking pleasure sank into my flesh. Bright sparks exploded behind my eyelids as my voice spilled uncontrollably in a voluptuous cry. My spine bent. I stuck my fingers into his flesh like an animal, my shaky legs gripped him. My moisture flowed around him, as if trying to drown him. He was pulsating in me. He was silently coming while his sharp movements reached my inner boundaries. Salty and hot, his body clung to mine. His breathing halted in my ear, changing the surface of my skin. His heart raced against mine. With his fingers tangled in my hair, he drank what was left of my breath.

Then he silently pulled away from me, filling my senses with an instant chill. He went through the doorless space and the room behind it became dimly lit. All of a sudden, I was overwhelmed by embarrassment and I hurried to armour myself with the blanket. Everyone in my head was silent with shock. As if they were gone, and I didn't know what to do on my own. I took several hesitant steps in Victor's direction. Walking around the broken glass, I wondered if it was just glass, or if pieces of my shattered ideas were glistening there as well. Victor was under the shower, his fists pressed against the wall. Water was running over his head, down his body. I traced his profile with interest. Numerous tattooed lines wound from his shoulder to his chest and his back. I didn't manage to stop my gaze in time. It reached below his navel and I bit my lower lip, a little too hard.

'Naked, Nia! I want you fully naked in my arms! Come here!' The streams of water accentuated his muscles and muffled his weird voice.

Without taking the blanket off, I walked as if in a trance toward my magnet. He measured my every step. As soon as I was close enough, he yanked the cloth from my body. I found myself under the shower, standing with my back to him, the water pouring down my hair. Its heavy edge touched my butt. Countless drops were racing down my face, stinging my wounds. Victor glued my palms against the wall and spread my legs apart. His fingers made soap bubbles on every centimetre of my skin, from my ankles upwards. He pressed himself to my back, his hardened desire propped against my left hip. His beard, painfully stuck to my face, stopped the relentless drops of water. I moaned as he bit the corner of my lips.

'Has anybody else touched you here?' He slid his fingers up the soap trail on the inside of my thigh. My skin prickled.

He gently followed the fold that led to my abdomen, then he went down very slowly. He reached a bundle of nerve endings, entwined in a tiny magic button obviously created for pleasure only. A pleasure devoted button indeed. Never pressed before, it went wild under his predatory touch. Pulsations, heat, and stinging arousal tightened my muscles. My nails scratched at the marble. My ears buzzed as a stream of water poured over my open lips. Victor was biting my neck, then kissing it gently, then biting again.

'What about here?' He slipped his finger into me, conquering the new land.

He seemed to know every inch of my body, discovering its secrets with ease. He provoked pleasure beyond any limits I had ever assumed. The air in my lungs responded aloud.

'Nia?' He continued to conquer me boldly, engraving his print deep on the most unfamiliar corners of my senses.

Previously, this way of touching had seemed more than gross to me and I had insisted that Andre should stay away from it. As for me, I had never found the motivation to explore my own body that thoroughly. Victor slipped out of me slowly. The journey of his hand continued to my chest. A throbbing craving pulsated in the spot on which his fingers had been.

'Don't!' A hoarse scream tore at my throat.

'What?' He whispered, invading my head.

'Don't stop!' An unfamiliar lust filled my voice. It echoed like a stranger from the depths of the chasm that Victor had opened in my mind.

He growled. His muscles tightened as he moved me forward, my back against his torso. A few steps took us in front of the bed in the small room. He tossed my body and my face bumped into the soft blanket. My wet hair twisted around my neck like a choker. Victor stretched my arms forward and ran his fingers over them. He took a turn at the shoulders to trace the curve of my spine. His lips followed the same path on my burning skin. He spread my legs apart, pressing my chest against the bed. My butt went up. The tips of his fingers slowly reached the craving button. He patiently tortured my new pleasure with a rhythmic circular motion that provoked an electric shock in all directions.

'I've been imagining you being mine for too long,' panting and hoarse, his timbre caressed me.

Heat was swelling over me as the powerful sensations made my head spin, and all I wanted was for him to fill me up once more. *Desire* insisted that Victor should go again down the path he had just discovered.

When he dipped his finger into my moisture, his breathing instantly quickened. He kept playing with the button, slipping his touch in the wetness and back out. Again and again. My legs were shaking. My heart went wild and my breath escaped in a muffled groan. My hands were trying to resist the explosion. They grabbed the soft fabric, as if in an attempt to save me from falling into the chasm.

'Nia!' He growled. His unrestrained moan tore into my dizzy head. He pressed my chest tightly against the bed, twisting my hair around his palm. 'Don't move!' His voice was trembling.

I screamed as he suddenly entered and his wet skin clung to my thighs. The sharp pain twirled into suffocating pleasure. I curled up, but he pressed me back to the bed. His thrusts went mad, the rhythm was divine again. One powerful spasm immediately squeezed him inside me, and a giant searing wave took my breath away. It hit me, it flooded every inch of me, it smashed me to pieces as if I was a shipwreck at the shore of destructive joy. Victor's name shot through my throat in a loud cry. Then I probably swore because of the convulsions of every fibre in my tissue. Another second, and unstoppable spasms were gripping him like a fist. My teeth and fingers were squeezing the sheet, like my muscles squeezing Victor while he was rudely invading me. He produced a growling sound and came with powerful thrusts. His lips slammed into my neck. He was kissing and biting the delicate skin while my moans were soaking into the bed.

Warm breath slowly revived my consciousness, which had fallen into a throbbing bliss. He turned me around sharply and pressed me sideways against his body, his darkened irises staring intently at me.

'Did I hurt you?'

I moved my head in denial. My gaze was wondering where to run.

'Words, Nia! Answer me!'

'My brain has released endorphins. These are opioid hormones which suppress pain, so even if you have hurt me, I don't...' I spoke quietly, as if in a trance, not knowing who exactly was giving these explanations.

'Stop it!' Victor squeezed my cheekbones. He arranged my hair and fondled my lips, leaving his thumb there. 'I know you can speak normally. You don't need to create distance. I was touching you seconds ago. I was literally inside your body, and right now you are clinging naked to me. Tell me how you feel!'

I shoved my hands between our bodies.

'There seems to be no one in my head, and I can't give you a more precise answer,' I was blinking at his unreadable eyes.

'My lovely dear, only your brilliant mind is in your head. No one else. Try to describe how you feel.'

'Well... How am I supposed to feel? Good?' I snapped, but after some breaths I came up with a more meaningful sentence. 'Unfamiliar neurological processes took place under the influence of biochemical substances. I guess the exact term is orgasm. I mean, earlier, when...' I bit my lip. I looked down at his penis, propped against my navel.

Damn! How did that even fit in me? Human anatomy is fascinating indeed!

'God, Nia! You're getting even more difficult,' Victor turned around, kneeling over me. His knee spread my thighs apart and I went silent as I was shrugging. 'OK, then, let me tell you what I feel: madness. You drove me to the edge! I tried to stay away, but you drove me to the edge! Now all I want is to provoke neurological processes in you, but we can't even talk.'

'This particular activity doesn't seem to require in-depth conversations, if I may say, so...'

His kiss interrupted me, covering me in goosebumps. He ran his palm from my groin up my skin, then buried it in my hair. The space between my legs trembled longing for him to sink into the moisture again. I licked my lips and instinctively pressed my pelvis against him. I stared at the blazing blue while his desire hardened, pointing menacingly at me.

'Don't! Don't give me this look again! I want to fuck you all night, until you faint, but it'll be too much for you. I barely manage to get inside, you're definitely not ready for this, and it's unbelievably hard for me to control myself.'

He lay down beside me and pressed me into himself on one side.

'What do you mean I'm not ready?' My question bounced off his smile.

'I guess you will find out tomorrow,' there was concern in his voice.

I was silently examining his symmetrical face. Again, I could not detect a specific expression, but it looked somehow relaxed. The usual wall of superiority around him was gone. He was not gloomy, only utterly handsome with his sharp features and stubble beard. Everything about him was perfect symmetry. I was aware of what was happening to my body, even though there was no one to explain. I wanted him, but I couldn't understand why he wanted me in return. What was more bizarre, I didn't even care what the exact term was to describe the events. It was probably "madness", and yet all I wanted was the neurological processes to continue. Only *Curiosity* was undefeatable.

'Victor, why did you leave and why did you come back during the night?' My fingers were walking up and down the tattooed flame-like lines on his chest.

'I left because I was angry, and you were in your panties. That tormenting look in your eyes wouldn't have allowed me to control myself for a second more and I would've been very rude. I didn't want that. I came back because thinking of you in my bedroom was driving me crazy, and when you started screaming, it was impossible for me not to touch you. I tried to stay away, but when you woke up and poked me again with these eyes...' He went silent, holding my chin. 'You are making me test my control, Nia, and this won't lead to any good.'

'Then why did you stay away from me if you wanted the opposite? I don't understand, I can't find the logic.'

His pupils dilated. He filled his lungs, running his thumb over my lips.

'I told you that it'll be hard for you to find logic in me,' he slid his fingers down my shoulder, then along the vertical chute from the ribs to the waist and up the pelvis, where the most feminine curve forms its sharp arc. 'This is a steep, dangerous slope. I should've never taken it. Not with you and not now,' his muscles tensed.

'I understand your words, but not the wording,' I frowned and narrowed my eyes with suspicion.

'It's not easy to explain. It's not logical. In my reality, everything is beyond complicated. I just shouldn't have let this happen right now. It's all my mistake!'

The chilly breeze of his voice bruised my skin. The combination of words made no logical sense and it was just as incomprehensible as the dark expression on his face. There was no one in my head to help, either.

'Oh!' The sound sneaked out between my lips. 'I thought that it was normal to have sex for pleasure. I didn't know it could function as a mistake. It was a strange experience for me, too, but "mistake" is not the exact term. If you think so, the most logical thing for me to do is leave!' I got up abruptly.

'Nia!' He raised his voice, staring at me. 'Come here right now and stop snapping at me, because you're driving me crazy!'

'I'm not snapping at you. I want to sleep now. A mistake or not, I'm not staying here. I always sleep alone anyway.'

'Where are you going, for Christ's sake!' He pulled me back to bed and spoke, close to my mouth: 'Stop inventing norms for yourself! You're not leaving and you're not sleeping alone! You're not going to torture your beautiful mind with my mistakes. It's my concern to solve these issues in an acceptable way.'

'What's there to solve?' I gaped. He pressed me into himself.

'Stop it! Come here! All I want now is to feel you: your breath, your skin, the fact that you're finally in my arms!'

His fingers ran down my hair, then over my elbow. He moved me onto his chest and covered me with the soft blanket. I protested but he didn't respond, he just held me tighter. Victor's heat sheltered me, immersing me in a moment of harmony and calm. His scent filled me. His breath caressed my ears, his lips warmed my face. His touch balanced my breathing. The silence in my head closed my weary eyelids. Sleep embraced me and, relaxed in his arms, it seemed that I had finally found a place for me.

SIX

Early rays of sun were teasing my eyes. Still sleepy, I examined the big room through the small doorless space. It seemed even gloomier in the morning light. Dull colours, strict order, scant furnishing, lacking even the smallest accentuating detail. Emptiness. It looked full of emptiness. I ran my palm over the cool folds of the bedsheet. The scent of musk sank into me, followed by vibrations that woke me up. As I realised where I was, I jumped.

I slept here? Damn, what happened? Frankly, is there anything more bizarre, confusing, and absurd than what happened last night?

The pillow didn't reply. I was startled by the dead silence in my head. No one was even snoring, and I shivered. The pain of my wounds was complemented by a sharp sore spasm deep below my navel.

Wow! Some bizarre, confusing, absurd, and obviously dangerous activity.

Knowledge coughed dryly:

Exact term: bruises. According to the data, they are going to heal quickly.

I sighed with relief at the sound of his voice:

That's the first time I've ever been happy to hear your babbling. This silence has been driving me crazy. Look what I did!

I was a bit relieved, but everyone else, even *Reason*, was still hiding. In my emptied mind, there were only the president's glassy eyes staring at me. They twisted my stomach, and the bruises twitched hungrily as the memory of my experience during the night made me sweat. My teeth bit at my lip.

As I tried to evaluate the processes in my body, the silence was replaced by a loud noise. All my questions and doubts erupted in a wailing buzz. Taking several large gulps of air, I decided to seek answers only after my head was back to normal. My plans started with a giant cup of coffee and talking to Toma. He indeed had to explain how I had ended up in these circumstances. Although, I had to admit to myself my intentions of making discreet inquiries about Victor's hundreds of personalities. Dressing in a rush, I was thankful to Toma for the jeans and the trainers but not for the missing socks.

As soon as I found myself on the other side of the door, I realised closing it made me distinctly upset. I had never considered such a door-issue before, and the icy arrows piercing my back surprised me.

Sockless in my colourful trainers, I went down the stairs. To my horror, it was bustling on the first floor. Too many too noisy people for 7 o'clock in the morning. I froze on the last step, regretting that I had not opted for an escape through the window. There was an awkward silence, and I just stood there like an idiot. The curious glances reminded me that I was coming from a bedroom on the second floor.

Shit! It must look exactly as it is. I must say something.

'You're up early,' I stammered ridiculously, waving three fingers.

'Wait for me in my office!' Victor's usual cold voice ordered from somewhere, but I couldn't see him in the crowd. The butler with the funny moustache gave me a light push.

'I'll be off now!' The buzz in my head got louder as I spoke to the dozens of eyes. It was like an exam.

Despite the continuing silence, I regained control and headed for the door. Two steps later I saw him. He resembled a statue, but he looked fresh in his black T-shirt and black cotton trousers. A perfect shadow was drinking her coffee by his left arm. She didn't even look up, absorbed by some sheets of paper. My jaw dropped.

Damn! Are there shadows around every corner?

Annoyed, I grunted in my mind. *Desire* popped up, its mouth gaping as well. It fell to the floor of my brain, howling as if it was going to die. It tightened my stomach into a ball and kicked it to my throat, where it stuck.

Victor headed in my direction. I followed his movements intently until *Reason's* hiss startled me:

Pull yourself together, won't you! I'll deal with you later!

'Good morning!' Victor took hold of my elbow. He passed energetically by all the faces at the table, with me walking unsteadily by his side. Then we were alone in his office. 'Nia, are you alright?' He was rummaging through my brain.

'Good morning! Your question is too conditional for a precise answer.'

Although still stretched out on the floor, *Desire* made me blush. I swallowed dryly. Victor seemed to expect something else to drop from my mouth, but my silence encouraged him to continue:

'I was personally going to wake you up,' the wall around him evaporated. His kiss made me warm all over, and my face remained in his hands. 'What's going on? Where are you going so early?' He carefully tucked my messy hair behind my ears.

'To Toma and then to the office,' I muttered. Actually, all I was thinking about was the direction to Victor's bedroom.

'I want you to take a rest today. Toma's not here. I chose somebody new and if you insist, you can go out, but only with him!' Victor explained slowly and patiently.

'Where is he?'

'In the car outside.'

'I was asking about Toma,' my voice became quiet.

'He's not here,' Victor's glassy eyes were cold now. I pulled myself away and dialled Toma's number, but his phone was off.

'Tell me where he is,' a bad hunch made me shiver.

'It's not your business. The new guy is instructed to wait for you outside. I'm warning you: you can't send him off for any reasons. Logical or illogical. Any!'

I listened to him carefully. Furious because of the words, because of the tone, because of the combination of both. It was the first time his expression seemed a little scary to me, and his scolding voice complemented this. My bad hunch and my anger were growing. I shot my meanest look at Victor, but he didn't flinch. He reached for my hand and I recognised an expression of irritation after I pulled it away.

Turning my back on him, I hurried to the door and nervously passed by everyone in the big room. The plethora of questioning eyes made me search for something to count. The stupid floor, however, offered only chaotically placed wooden pieces, which lacked any possible escape rhythm. I flew out of the door and ran across the grass to Toma's house. Bursting in, I couldn't see even a trace of him in the living room. As if no one lived there. I dialled his number again, unsuccessfully. *Rage* rose in my head and my fingers rubbed my temples. As I tried to gather my breath, a tight squeeze from behind made me scream. Victor's beard sank into my neck.

'What is wrong with you?' He hissed in my ear, pressing me into himself.

'Toma acted weird yesterday because of you, didn't he?' I said through my gritted teeth. He didn't reply. His breathing accelerated and the sharp needles pierced deeper into my skin. 'You blamed him, didn't you? Poor thing! He believes that you're never wrong.'

'I'm not going to give you any explanations, Nia! The matter is settled. I want you to remember well what I said,' those sentences contained all the ingredients that I needed to go mad. So I went mad.

I clenched my hands into fists and this time it was *Rage* who made my face red. When I turned to Victor, however, he seemed even madder than me.

'Toma is not a "matter", he is my friend! Blaming and driving him away is not settling the matter, it's a mistake. A glowing mistake. There are no reasons for such actions on your part. No logical reasons, not any!' I shouted under his nose. The veins on his neck tightened.

'You are not to assess my decisions, but to comply with them! And you are not to argue with me, not in this manner! He's not here. End of conversation,' he looked and sounded exactly as he had the previous evening, but this time I didn't start hiccoughing. *Justice*, half black and half white, exploded. She shook me, provoking *Rage* to storm out of control. I shouted even louder than Victor.

'I'm arguing because I have arguments! It was me who persuaded Toma to leave me and, according to your crazy standards, I am the one to blame. I sent him off. He did what I said, and now you're chasing him out. There's only one rightful piece missing in this sequence of actions: I'm leaving as well,' I hissed the words. My face was all red. 'The logic is absolutely clear. I can't miss it, I can't comply, I can't avoid the truth. Neither do I want to!'

'Toma didn't follow my specific order. This is what I can't miss,' he pushed me to the wall, leaning over me. Lightning flashed in his eyes. 'His misjudgement is his fault. You are to blame only for your appearance that night. It was outrageous for a sober man even, let alone for some drunk creep. None of this would have happened, if...' He held me tight as I erupted in his hands. I stared at him in disgust.

'None of this would have happened if that creep didn't think he was invincible. That's it, and you know it perfectly well! But you're not even blaming him, are you? You're blaming me, Toma, the whole galaxy, but not him. Because he, just like you, is wearing a hundred layers of superiority and justice can't reach to your mount even if it tiptoed. Am I wrong?' My voice cynically pointed out the faulty pattern.

'Stop it and mind your behaviour towards me!' He shouted. It only fuelled me further.

'Enlighten me, Victor? How is it that women never come up with the proper appearance? They are always wrong, and they always provoke some poor male soul that can't handle its goddamn pathetic, simple urges. Well? Or maybe "don't touch me" means something else in male language? That creep heard me well enough while he was forcing his sweaty hand between my legs, while he was licking me, but he didn't stop. And to make things even more disgusting, in general reality there's always someone like you to say that women are to blame. You're just as warped as him! Aren't you, Victor? I can tell by the conceited look in your eyes. I'm leaving now because it is exactly people like you that I can't stand!'

'Nia!' He gave a prolonged growl. 'Don't speak to me about that fucking incident. Damn! Stop it! Don't behave like this. Don't do it because now it's me who you're provoking,' he squeezed my face. Heat leaked from his hands.

His beard stung me as he bit my lips. He rested his forehead on mine, taking a sharp breath. He clung to me with a kiss, and his taste sank to my navel. My tongue couldn't care less how irritated I was. It slithered around his tongue and it certainly seemed to enjoy it. It wouldn't stop. My skin prickled as my heart pounded madly in his hands. My bruises warmed. *Desire* was twisting me as my head was driven crazy from the fact that my body didn't want to pull away from Victor. I gathered all my resistance and shoved my hands between us, trying to move him, but he wouldn't budge. My push only made his muscles tense. He gripped my wrists and stepped back, staring at me. Free from the kiss, my mouth started speaking:

'My behaviour is fully proportionate to your ridiculous decision, irrational accusations, and abominable way of communicating. My logic, the sequence of my actions, and my judgement are correct. My arguments, too. Yours are not. I warned you: I can see the mistakes clearly and I can't comply with them. I just don't know how I let the mistake of last night happen,' I explained, focused on my effort to conceal the vibrations of my body.

Victor nailed his eyes on mine, biting the knuckle of his index finger. His irises shone with anger, madness, and desire in a heap. Leaning his lips towards my ear, he spoke in the deepest possible masculine voice:

'It's hard enough for me to communicate. Especially with you. If you keep provoking me, I'll just lose control and I'll shut your mouth the way I want to shut it. Then I'll make sure the only thing that comes out of it will be moaning. I'll do it for as long as it takes to make you stop thinking, arguing, snapping at me. And then I'll do it more, so that you remember to never treat me like this again. And then more, until you start accepting my decisions, even if they don't match the logic of your beautiful mind. But I'll leave you with a few drops of strength, Nia, so that you'll be able to show me what's most significant: that you finally came to the conclusion that you are not going to create distance between us anymore.'

His words poured distinctly right into my brain, soaking into every cell. His lips and his beard were touching me lightly. Sharp shivers ran down my neck and my arm. He chased them with the tips of his fingers then reached for my hand, pressed it to his teeth, and bit the thin skin. Paralysed, I leaned against the wall without making a sound. He buried himself in my hair, inhaled the scent deeply, then growled, taking hold of my face.

'Am I clear enough now, Nia?'

There was no air left in the narrow space between us, only thick, destructive electricity. Beyond any logic and arguments. *Desire* dived brazenly into the blue as a bright glow illuminated the image of the hidden, unknown female entity in my head.

And what on earth are you?

Reason sobbed in horror. With all her magnificence, *Lust* wrapped me in her infinite red veils, whispering in her arousing timbre:

Make him shut you up right now! And you are surely going to moan! And surely it will be loud! Kiss him!

My body was leaning against Victor despite my effort to pull it back. I took a startled gulp of air, suspecting that my pupils were showing signs of the madness that was raging behind them. The most loyal of my images came to my help. *Knowledge* declared monotonously:

Hormones are reaching a critical level.

Reason shrieked:

I don't know what's going on! We are about to explode! Get out of here! Now, Nia!

The air ended. With one last breath, I tensed all my muscles to pull myself away from Victor and I ran through the door.

'I already know your troubles in communicating, but not being able to pick even one correct word is far beyond unacceptable! I always think! I argue when I have arguments to do so! I distance myself because I need distance from this goddamn reality! Damn you!' I was shouting with my back to him, hurrying to my house.

'You're going to explain this later! You're also going to explain how the hell I am supposed to talk to you!' He hit the wall. His voice became more distant with every step I took. 'And stop snapping at me!'

'I'm not going to explain anything! You are truly insane! I'm out of here!'

I stormed into my house, shaking.

Damn! This person makes me shake in a hundred different ways!

Bursting with anger at the accusations and heated by the vibrations, I headed directly under the shower and turned the tap to ice cold. The water flooded my wounds, and my skin gave out a cry, but I didn't pay any attention. I was incensed by Victor's attitude and demeanour, and even more furious with the uncontrollable reactions of my own body—with the absolute chaos that had invaded my head. I took a deep breath before I started shouting in my mind:

Now listen to me carefully, all of you, stupid intruders: old and new! If any one of you dares to speak a word about Victor, about kissing, hormones, moaning or whatever, this is going to be the end of you. I'll find a way to throw you out. Can't you see that he's distorted?! Can't you hear what he says? Living with Reason and Knowledge was OK, but now it's overly crowded, you're overly loud and you contradict each other. You're going to drive me mad soon. How did I end up in this asylum? How? You made a mess of my head. And who the hell is driving me crazy with these vibrations?

Lust and *Desire* sneaked out on tiptoe. They took an impudent bow and hid with a giggle as I struggled to catch my breath. *Reason* tried to encourage me quietly, but I hit the wall and shouted at him:

Shut up! You're no help at all. They made a fool out of you. Can't you see that my body wouldn't listen to you anymore? It's living its own life now.

Still wet, I slipped into my jeans, murmuring aloud:

'Why did he do that to Toma? How can he act like that! Can't he see how wrong he is? He's so arrogant: his behaviour, his statements, his voice, everything! Screw it! I'm out of this madhouse!'

I used the landline to contact the housekeeper. A minute later, she appeared at the doorstep. I grabbed the wad of money with the elastic band, pulled a couple of notes for myself, and noted the amount on the piece of paper. Shoving the rest into her hands, I told her to give it personally to Victor. I wondered how I was going to repay what I had taken, but decided to leave this issue for later on.

At a nervous pace, I walked out. Of its own accord, my neck turned towards the glass wall of Victor's house. I examined the exquisite back of the blonde shadow with irritation, then my eyes bumped into his composed expression next to her. I continued to the car, my jaw and my fists clenched.

This is probably normal as well. Damn! Fucking shadows popping out from every corner.

I jumped into the car in one motion, hissing at the guy to drive me downtown. He made an effort to start a conversation, but I didn't respond. All I wanted was to disappear and give order to the mess in my head and all around me.

'I'm off!' We were waiting at a red light when I jumped out of the car. The guy gaped in surprise, and I decided that it would be polite to explain. 'I'm not a bad person. Apologies if I'm getting you in trouble, but there's just no reason for you to have anything to do with me anymore. Thanks for the ride and, once again, sorry!'

I merged with the crowd before he could reply. After a nonchalant walk through the narrow streets, I entered "Dream Factory" and examined the weirdos there. Amongst people like myself, I was more balanced. I sat down at a table, my forehead propped on my hands. A young girl with bright blue hair looked at me with sympathy but I didn't react. Despite what I had said, no one in my head was silent and the scandal was raging on a new level. All the intruders, old and new, kept shouting their arguments at each other; occasionally I raised my eyebrows to approve some of the statements. I was grateful that at least my brain was not dead silent anymore. It was back to normal, even if it was more crowded. As I took a bite of my pancake, *Telegram* rattled:

> *I was absolutely clear that you can't be left on your own.*
> *Don't you understand, human?*
> *Do it again, and I'll be forced to lock you up with a security guard!*

I blinked at the display. *Rage* was furious.

> *This man should see a doctor for his issues with communication. Damn, he can't even choose the right letters! Abominable!*

I cracked my neck, then hungrily gulped a bite of perfection with fig jam.

> *Am I supposed to not think logically again or what?*
> *I was absolutely clear that I was leaving.*
> *P.S. I'm not a suitcase, nor any other object that can be locked up.*
> *How did you even come up with such a sentence?*

Less than a minute later, the phone glowed once again:

> *I'll say it in your ear, if you'd prefer?*
> *As many times as you wish.*
> *I enjoyed the chills on your skin.*
> *You are expected at the office, I hope you'll start to calm down once there.*
> *P.S. You don't have to be a suitcase to be locked up.*

My dull face gaped, wondering what was more embarrassing: his question or his conclusion. I blushed at the fact that he was aware of my insane body reactions. Suddenly, Toma stormed in, looking even more puzzled than I was:

'Damn, Nia! Thank God that you're easy to find.'

'Damn! Thank God that you're good at finding me,' I grinned. 'Plain and strong Ethiopian organic coffee in a French press!' I shouted to the waiter, so loudly that the coffee appeared on the table before I had even finished. 'I'm sorry I got you into this mess, man,' I hurled myself at Toma to squeeze with all my strength *Justice*'s triumph over Victor's illogical decisions.

'Nia, I must admit you are the weirdest thing I've ever encountered, and life was doing its best even before I met you,' he curved his lips in his typical smile, but became gloomy: 'Victor's mad again.'

'I know,' I stared at him with seriousness. 'I've been thinking about it and I guess I know why he's mad. I told him the truth forgetting that people just can't handle it. He said that he preferred it, but...' I sighed before his wondering gaze.

'What did you do, besides getting the poor guy from the car in trouble?'

'I didn't do anything! I exploded because he blamed you and drove you away. I told you about *Justice* before. Apart from being black and white, she's also my weakest spot. I couldn't hold back. Yes, maybe I didn't choose the right voice, but my arguments were indisputable, and yet he couldn't understand them. He acted insane. I found a sequence in his logic, that's why I also left. Well, that was not the only reason. At least he's not blaming you and you are not being driven away anymore, are you?'

'God, girl, what are you talking about? I'm not... I...' He exhaled heavily, not finishing his sentence. 'Damn it! I don't like what's going on.'

'What exactly is it that you don't like?'

'Everything,' he examined the scratches on my face with sympathy. 'Victor is right about the other night though. I made the wrong judgement. I put you at risk and now look at what happened because of me,' he took hold of my hand. I sensed that something else was bothering him. However, I wanted to refute what he had been made to believe.

'Victor is not right about anything! He has no arguments to blame you or me. That creep is the only one to blame. Even the creep himself is aware of that. Did you know that he has been hiding since, even at the time of his resignation, and there's no trace of him?'

'I know!' He snapped, looking at the traces on my cheekbones. 'I can't describe how sorry I am, little goblin. I acted stupid and it's true that there are creeps amongst these people,' his nose pointed down in silence.

I knew it was better to change the subject, but *Curiosity* was eating me, so I asked:

'Will you tell me what happened? Before I woke up in the house, I mean.'

'Will you tell me what happened after you woke up in the house?' His expression darkened, and a chill appeared in his usually warm eyes.

'Toma! Now you are staring like a mean goblin!' His careful examination of my reactions made me blush. 'What's there to talk about? You left, I realised where I was, then Victor insisted that I should stay there. Because the doctor and the staff were there...' I mumbled, wondering if there was a way to hide under the chair.

'What else?'

'Well, there was something else, but I am not into explaining. A mistake happened! Just a mistake! That's it! Besides, this "something else" is not really my thing. It has a bad influence on my psyche. And on my body as well. It's totally crazy,' I frowned. 'It's not my thing, and I obviously can't compete with the shadows. Not that I want to... One of them had even settled herself at the table in the early morning...' I rolled my eyes. 'Just drop it, I don't want to discuss that. Tell me what's this way of thinking he has. How could he blame us? And, regarding his abominable manner of communication, I can't even find the words to describe it. He sucks in it even more than us.'

'Shadows? You found the right word without even knowing them,' he shook his head before scolding me. 'You will never be able to understand his way of thinking, nor his life. Your place is not there! Are you listening to what I'm saying?'

'I'm listening and I know you're right. I already told you, it didn't end well for me. Victor was right at least that it was a mistake,' I admitted nervously.

'Remember it then! Now let's go! Victor grumbled that you are going to the office. He thinks I have the superpower to get along with you and he wants me to drive you there. You have work to do, and I hope you can at least make a distinction between work and everything else,' he helped me get down from the high chair and gazed at me, his lips glued together. 'I'm not gonna ask you about everything else, Nia. I'm begging you, though, focus on your job only. Do as I say! I know him and...' He took a breath, as if something pierced him. 'Victor is your boss. Make sure he doesn't become anything more!' He was squeezing my hand and I felt something thumping powerfully in his body.

'Well, I obviously crossed that limit already!' I snapped. 'Besides, I have no idea how to make my absurd actions right.'

'Well, you are the smart one. Figure it out! Unless you want to become part of the army of shadows.'

He clenched his jaw and pulled me towards the car, a mixture of anger and worry showing on his face. I couldn't fully read it, but it lingered in my thoughts.

'I am smart, even smarter than smart. But I suspect this has nothing to do with brains. Something else has its side effects, too. It cripples logic. I'm no shadow. I don't even know how it happened. Damn it!' I waved my hands around helplessly As the engine roared.

φ

Throughout the journey, Toma kept throwing glances at me from beneath his eyebrows. As if he was examining me with a special detector, trying to locate what Victor had rearranged in my body and mind. I decided to share my plans and intentions, to hear what he thought about them.

'I agree with everything you said. That's why I intend to finish with the estates as soon as possible, and then I'll determine if I even want him to be my boss any longer. I may be highly effective, but I'm afraid I lack the qualities required in Victor's reality. I can't avoid logic or the truth! I'm doomed to see the mistakes, his mistakes included. I need the money, however, to get out of here!' A crooked smile appeared on my face.

'Nia!' Toma slammed on the breaks in the middle of the street. 'Victor's reality and working for Victor are two completely opposite directions. You might get stuck in the first, but the second one can shoot you out of the sky. Remember this, don't get them confused and make sure you move in the right direction! It's up to you to not make any more mistakes,' there was concern in his eyes.

We kept silent for the rest of the journey. I didn't raise the subject again and we were both busy throughout the day. It was Saturday, but I had to make up for lost time and the peace of mind at the office helped. The work was progressing. At least there was something to make me more confident, but I struggled not to think about Victor and the whole situation. I forced my mind into my crazy, hyper-concentration mode and found the calmness to do everything impressively fast. The architecture student became disheartened because of my tempo.

In the evening, while I was staring at the cactus, Toma stormed in angrily. The new guy had forgotten to tell him about a meeting at the house. He urged me to go and a couple of minutes later we were in the car. I was wondering if it was alright for me to stay there after the meeting, or where to go if not. I doubted there were any options for me to change my direction, and my lack of experience in such matters reduced the likelihood of identifying the right moves. Toma's speech had motivated me to find a solution, but I didn't know how. The rest of his words, in combination with the expression on his face, struck me with an obsessive anxiety that gnawed at me. I concluded that I should in all cases have a serious talk with Victor. My intention was to inform him that I was aware of the wrong direction, of the mistake, and that my decision was to make things right. We had to discuss our future communication as well.

I didn't have time to get ready, so I entered Victor's house as my usual self: hair in a bun, wearing a shaggy sweater and my trainers. The president's critical gaze scolded me. Three men, almost equally fat, sat at the table. They were of a similar age, and they had a similar distressed air about them. They introduced themselves as the executive directors of three of Victor's loan companies. Opposite them, there was the guy with the crazy eyes who had teased me at the reception. Chris seemed even more peculiar than before, with his pale face, his randomly tattooed arms, shaggy hair, and the indefinable colour of his irises.

I sat down on the narrow side of the table, opposite the president. A twitch of his muscles told me that he didn't like my choice of seat. Toma clumsily took the chair next to me.

'Come, Nia!' Victor motioned at the empty seat on his right. To my delight, there were no shadows at the table.

'I'd rather stay here, if you don't mind!' I said calmly. The others moved their heads, as if they were attending a tennis game.

'What if I do mind?' He asked sharply.

Being crammed between people bothered me. I needed physical distance: the further away, the more comfortable for me. Being centimetres away from him seemed like utterly uncomfortable territory at that moment. On top of all that, the chair he pointed at was opposite the windows in the glass wall: there were seven of them, and the second one was open. They kept drawing my eyes and attention, torturing even my peripheral vision.

'I want to comply with my specifications, and I will stay here! You might not understand me, but...'

He interrupted my explanation rudely, turning to one of the butlers:

'Close that window and open the fourth one!' He moved his composed gaze back to me and I gaped. 'Three closed windows, one open, three closed! Is it better now, or you prefer something else?'

I gulped without answering.

'I asked you a question!'

'Yes, thank you! It's a simple, yet acceptable sequence.'

As I moved awkwardly to my place, my eyes scanned the room. Suddenly, everything seemed bright and rhythmical. Symmetrical lines shot through my head: three doors with three butlers in front of them and an empty doorway between each pair. Plenty of lightbulbs were on the ceiling, but only some were turned on, illuminating the Fibonacci squares. The paintings were forming a colour sequence. I looked at the floor to find an extremely complex yet perfect pattern, which had gone unnoticed because of my rush before. As I traced various combinations in many of the objects around, I was suddenly immersed in balance and harmony. I shot a surprised glance at Victor.

'I doubt I'll be able to get all the specifics, but I'm familiar with a few!' His voice made me prickle.

The people around seemed to disappear. I was searching for something in his expression, but the unreadable face of a statue was speaking from the opposite end of the table.

Does he count? Does he have patterns? Could he be just as crazy as I am? Does he see the mistakes, the wrongs of reality, too?

My lips were probably trembling. Without a trace of embarrassment, Victor went back to his conversation, and the movement of his cheekbones hypnotised me. His voice had an even, deep timbre. Every note sank deeply into my consciousness like a familiar, beautiful melody. It swirled around my body in circles, spun an enchanting spiral, carried me away. The harmonious sequences around me, combined with the sounds from Victor's throat, made me thoughtful and relaxed. Mountains rose on my skin, and I was overwhelmed by throbbing sensuality.

The distorted explanations of the three fat men broke the rhythm of Victor's voice at irregular intervals. Their noses pierced my mind like the scream of a broken microphone. The pain made me squeeze my fingers and my eyes and drove a high soprano from my lungs. I rudely interrupted one of the guys:

'Enough!' My metallic voice made him jump. 'The numbers. They never lie. You do. It's all obvious. There are only months until the collapse. The market is becoming overloaded, and you are adjusting the financial parameters incorrectly. Your business model is falling apart. First, there's a merger,' my hand swung in all directions, my finger up high. 'Then, a sequence... Analysis, optimisation, digitisation, a team of marketing gods, a platform, an algorithm. It will develop a forecast of the customers' needs. C51, for Christ's sake![8] You destroy the weak first, you shift the proportions, then you change everything else. This is the only possible move. C51. If you do it correctly, it will lead to monopoly. I'll calculate the probabilities. I'll draw a scheme. Strict consistency is required.'

Fascinated by the patterns and irritated by the squeaking sound, my brain switched to a special mode. It was extracting the available information to arrange it in hexagons, the most perfect shapes of the universe. My mind was processing the data rapidly, sending curt instructions to my mouth. Colourful lines in my head illuminated the edges of the hexagons, where solutions and possible moves were created. I didn't see anything else. I didn't hear anything else. I was playing mind chess and needed a touch to take me out of the trance-like state. It was painful.

Toma squeezed my knee to bring me back to my senses. I found my eyes fixed on Victor, who was watching me intently. The three fat men were gaping, Chris was straining a sly smile on his face, and Toma was supporting his eyebrows with his fingers.

'Good thing I know how to listen at a fast pace,' Chris laughed over the glass of whisky. 'It's a surprise, Kaov! I guess you finally found someone I can talk to.'

Victor didn't reply. He gave him a cool look and, several quiet moments later, hissed at the fat guys that he was going to determine their actions later. He urged them to go. Everyone walked away from the table, except for Toma, who had pinned his devastating gaze on me. I shrugged with guilt.

'What's wrong with you again?' He snorted in my ear.

'I'm sorry, it happens sometimes,' I frowned. 'My thoughts just fly without control and if they find their way to my mouth, that's what happens. There's nothing I can do, I don't do it on purpose,' I whispered.

'I wasn't referring to your incomprehensible chatter. You were staring at Victor like a mad woman, you weren't even blinking,' he reproached me, visibly annoyed.

'I wasn't! I was speaking to that guy, the fattest one.'

---

[8] *C51 is one of two codes for the Evans Gambit: an aggressive chess opening according to the chess opening classification system, part of the Encyclopaedia of Chess Openings (ECO) – author's notes.*

'No! You shouted at that guy. Then you stared at Victor, tapping your fingers in excitement. That's not the way you look at your boss, Nia. I told you already. Pull yourself together!' Toma was still hissing when Victor and Chris came back.

'Us, smart people, are weirdos. Don't worry about that,' Chris said and winked at me with a grin. 'I've been suggesting that we should optimise these companies for a while, but I guess I was not the right person to get the idea through,' he spoke to Victor in a displeased voice. Victor remained silent; his chin propped on his fingers.

'Leave us!' No one moved and Victor repeated with irritation: 'Get out, I want to speak to Nia alone!'

Toma snorted, then led Chris outside.

'I'm sorry. I will work on my oration,' I muttered, fiddling with the hem of my sweater.

My outburst wasn't helping me with the task of looking more confident for the upcoming conversation. Victor sat on the table, facing me. He put his feet on the chair and made me stand up. His thighs enveloped my hips, then he pulled me towards him. He examined me, clutching the back of my neck. His closeness stiffened me, but I tried to focus on my intention of building a meaningful sentence.

'Pawn to E5. That's how I'd respond to your aggressive gambit,' he smiled under his nose.

'NF3 knight. That would be my move, but I don't like chess and I don't play.'

'You're lying, I just don't know why,' he sighed thoughtfully, then he started reprimanding me: 'We must tame your chaos, Nia! Your mind works so quickly and you look crazy from the side. It's difficult for people to understand such behaviour. Do you get what I'm saying? You must control yourself!'

'I get that! I'm not sure I can do that, though, and it may not be necessary. Especially if no one expects it from me,' I snapped. A line appeared between his eyebrows. 'I know how I look from the side. I didn't mean to embarrass you.'

'You didn't embarrass me! I guess what you're implying, but we're not going to discuss it now. Just try to control your chaos, will you? You are in charge of your mind, it's not the other way round.'

'Oh. Those who live in my head could argue about that. There's been a lot of them lately, and they're pretty loud, too...' It was awkward saying this aloud, but he didn't react.

His glassy irises were rummaging through my brain again. Their blaze contradicted my intentions. I was taking balanced breaths to gain control over the situation, but Victor's effect on me was devastating. He ran his thumbs over my face and *Desire* dropped my body down a steep slide. I kept reciting my meaningful sentence in my mind, trying to ignore the vibrations below my navel.

'Some day I'm gonna ask you who lives in your head. I guess there would be quite an interesting explanation,' he was silent for a moment. 'How do I get along with you, Nia? Tell me! I'm doing my best to avoid my usual ways, but I have no idea how to communicate with you. You drove me crazy today, before I even had the chance to finish my coffee.'

'I drove you...?' I was muttering because his timbre tightened my throat. I looked away nervously. 'Victor, we need to discuss something seriously. I crossed a line that I shouldn't...' I started, but he interrupted me.

'Now that's something I can agree with. We are progressing. You definitely did cross many lines this morning, and I'm not having that anymore! I also agree that we should seriously discuss your behaviour.'

Again, I was not managing to express myself accurately. His closeness was distracting me and I tried to pull away. However, he kept me in place, his eyes narrowed with suspicion.

'That's not what I meant, Victor. It's difficult for me to find the right words when you're this close.'

He let go. I stepped back, concentrating on speaking more comprehensively. His hands formed a triangle in front of his body. His elbows propped on his knees, he lurked on every syllable that came out of my mouth.

'Last night I crossed a line and I have strong arguments that I shouldn't have done that. Right now, I can't determine how to fix my mistake, or if it's even possible. I don't know what the right sequence of actions is to change the wrong direction. Regarding your conclusion, it's not my behaviour but your way of communication that requires a serious conversation.'

'I guess I wasn't clear enough when I said that you shouldn't talk to me in this manner! You're creating distance again,' he growled with a cold look on his face and shifted nervously from the table, his voice reaching new levels of inappropriateness. 'Which part of my communication requires a conversation?'

'The unacceptable part: both the tone and the words!' My voice appeared just as rude as his.

My attention was drawn to some lights outside. Victor waved at the chief security guard who was standing by the door. He went out. A group of guards stopped the cars. The headlights remained at a distance from the entrance. Victor got closer to me, took my face in his palms and spoke quietly:

'I'll be done in a couple of hours, Nia. Then you will explain to me about the wrong direction: in a normal way, not by distancing yourself from me,' he fondled my lips, then he pulled away.

'No, I certainly won't! That wouldn't be a good time to talk. I'd rather talk to you tomorrow morning,' I was gazing at the floor. A huge fight broke out in my head, pounding at my skull to the point of pain.

'Why?' He seemed to be eavesdropping on the fuss in my mind.

'The available data made me conclude that talking to you when it's dark leads to unpredictable results,' I nodded at my own statement while trying, unsuccessfully, to read his expression.

The door opened and one of the shadows, her legs barely covered, walked in. She threw Victor a lustful glance and something disgusting stung my stomach from the inside, making me choke. A sudden silence occupied my head. I heard my own voice in my mind:

Damn, they sprout like cockroaches!

The Monster laughed loudly:

Now this girl doesn't need to be fixed. She's already flawless.

I looked at the beautiful woman's back. Behind her followed others who looked exactly alike. Several men rushed after them, led by the fat non-mafia guy from the mansion. Victor gave a signal to the chief security guard. I stood still, holding on to a lock of hair to support me. The guests passed by me, squinting their cynical eyes at my face. *Confidence* and I were shrinking together. She whimpered to insist on some wine and meditation. The security guard gave me a light push towards the exit. *The Monster* made the taste in my mouth even worse.

I passed by Toma on my way out. He was standing on the grass between the two houses and seemed furious. I guess he had seen through the windows my disastrous attempt to deal with the wrong direction. A nervous gesture on my part demonstrated that I was not in the mood for explaining, so he sulkily hurried to his house. I walked down the path. A few long laps later, the cacophony in my head was still torturing me. Even walking couldn't chase it away. Almost an hour passed before the cold forced me back to my house.

I poured a generous glug of wine from a bottle I found on a shelf, then took my trainers off and threw myself on the couch. I was tense from the painful rumble in my head. I put on a playlist of songs performed at concerts all over the world. Volume to the max. Oftentimes, I would watch those concerts and dream about all the "right" directions. Immersed in the powerful energy, I drifted away, and floated, free from all the limitations of general reality. Music was my only cure to reach silence. Well, I had found another cure the previous night but it came with atypical side effects, while the orderly rhythm of musical notes was a hiding place in which I could fit even in the most twisted times. The geometry of the present moment was definitely jagged.

I was prancing around the living room in my sweater and panties. I guess only crazy girls can swallow, with wine, everything that tortures their body and mind. One after another, the beautiful melodies spun me around. Eric Clapton strummed at my eardrums. I stared at the laptop screen and drifted to one of my most beloved concerts: *Madison Square Garden* was crowded with people back then, in 1999. My mouth open, I waited for guitarist Nathan East's genuine reaction to Clapton playing the chords of eternal *Layla*. I jumped with him, knowing every single movement by heart. After the beginning of the brilliant duet, we asked Layla what she would do when she got lonely but, just like me, she had no answer to that. I had rummaged through loneliness numerous times, and yet the reply was still lurking there, somewhere along the cutting edges. I turned around to land my eyes on Victor's bedroom window[9].

Even the thundering voice that had taken over the living room couldn't drown out the brutal bass of my heart rate, thundering in my head. Clapton

---

[9] *Layla, you've got me on my knees, Layla*
I'm begging, darling please, Layla
Darling, won't you ease my worried mind
Clapton, Eric. "Layla" - author's notes.
https://www.youtube.com/watch?v=fX5USg8_1gA

was masterfully stretching his guitar's soul, and what I saw stretched mine. Victor's silhouette moved, and another silhouette was bustling around him. The shadow of a woman approached the president gracefully. I bounced up and followed the outline of her hand: she reached out to him, he touched her, then pulled her and they both walked away from the spot where I could see them.

Something like a sea urchin with long, black spikes popped into my mind. It pierced my whole body, as if it flooded me with some kind of an acid. I started feeling my navel, wondering what was attacking me, and *Reason* was shaking his square head in hysterics:

Hell, no! No, no, no! This is too much already. I am rational enough to understand the pointlessness of your existence. Get out of here right now! I am not having you even for a second in this twisted head here.

Knowledge's squeaky voice joined in:

Exact term: Jealousy. Her origin is uncertain. She is a type of anomaly. I confirm her irrational nature. I confirm that you two are incompatible.

For the first time ever, the events in my head scared me. I swallowed elaborate gulps of air.

I should've read more of Freud! Fucking Jung doesn't help with this mess! It must be the side effects. It shall pass. There is indeed something wrong with the "something else", but it shall pass.

I finished the glass in one gulp, dizzy already. At least the fight in my head was over and *Jealousy* had hidden somewhere, taking her spikes with her. I concluded that only some sleep could save me from this new state of insanity; I was going to evaluate what it was and what actions were to be taken when I sobered up.

Despite turning on every possible light, I couldn't get to the second floor. After having so much wine, *Fear* added the steep stairs to its long list. The couch was big enough for me to crash there but through the large glass wall in front of me I could see darkness surrounding Victor's house. The porch light was off and the void between us tortured my phobias. With a deep breath, I motivated my body to go out.

Since I was wearing only a T-shirt and panties, the autumn chill sharpened the hair on my skin. I put a chair on the outdoor table, then carefully climbed up. I started fiddling with the lamp tipsily, hoping the bulb would light up.

'What the hell are you doing?' Victor's voice startled me from behind. Some unusual burst of coordination kept me from falling.

'Isn't it obvious?' I could sense *Rage* in my voice.

'You think you can fix it?' He raised his eyebrows in question.

'You think I can't?'

'Yes, that's what I think!' He snapped.

'Because women are not good at these types of things?' I hissed proudly at his implication as I clumsily tried to get down.

'Women are, but you're not! The way you hurt yourself with a stupid glass is enough for me to determine your clumsiness. For Christ's sake, it's raining, it's dark, and you're digging into the electrics, barely perched on a chair on a table! Is this a good judgement? Isn't it wiser to call one of the dozens of people around to fix a stupid light?' He scolded me, his face tight.

'Don't you have better things to do than mess with me?' I gritted my teeth, with no intention of explaining myself in the middle of that risky situation.

Putting my feet firmly on the table in order to get down, I saw fury manifest on Victor's face and he grabbed me rudely without permission. His heat instantly melted the autumn chill. In his hands, time seemed to stop together with my mind. Being that close to him caused a deep muscle spasm that gripped my bruises from last night. I clenched my teeth. Looking utterly displeased, he pinned me to the ground and a loud breath whistled from his lungs. He rested his palms on my cheeks. I couldn't tell if it was his touch, or his gaze, that set fire to my intentions like they were a sheet of paper.

'Do you realise why I talk to you like that? Your decisions must be safe, not only logical. You don't take care of yourself, you don't listen. Absolute chaos that cannot be controlled. You can at least see what's coming when it's obvious! Like the way electricity works! You know about electricity, right?'

'I know everything already!' I snapped, although he was right, I obviously didn't know electricity well enough, judging by the short circuit caused by my illogical decisions.

Victor looked at me like a predator.

'You're irresistible when you're angry, you know that? And you speak like a normal person, too,' he ran a thumb over my lip, biting his own.

'Bull! Why are you even here when you should be gone? Our deal was to discuss things tomorrow morning. What do you want?' I stepped back.

'I am here because you want me here and I want this as well.'

Lust's whisper echoed through the dead silence:

Kiss him! Kiss him right now!

I swallowed dryly, and *Reason* began chasing her, determined to beat the hell out of her.

'You have no grounds for coming to this conclusion. I already explained that talking to you in the dark leads to unpredictable results. I'd rather avoid that.'

'Did you convince yourself with that explanation?' He snatched my throat and pressed me against his chest. A fast heartbeat could be heard from within him. It sent shivers down my skin. 'Today, my lovely dear, you pulled yourself away from my arms three times precisely. Don't do it again because it's bad for me.'

'Victor, I'm afraid that it's bad for me to be in your arms,' my voice trailed off but I stared at him firmly.

Reason shouted:

Absolutely accurate!

I pulled away, trembling, and ran inside but Victor hugged me from behind. He held me tight, his lips running down my neck. His fragrance slithered around me like a snake. I stopped dead. It seemed that I became lighter and the chaos in my head gradually subsided. The silence in my mind revealed the deep chasm that Victor had blown up. I was flying fast around it. No, I had not convinced myself, despite all the indisputable arguments, and he knew that before me. In one motion, he turned me around. His gaze crashed into me. Raging demons dilated his pupils, hiding all that was blue. He dug his fingers into the back of my head and took a slow breath with his eyes closed, probably to tame his madness. When he opened his eyes, however, the demons were already blazing, unleashed, wild and out of control in the pupils of his new personality.

'Four times. Driving me crazy, is that what you want?' He said in a rough hiss.

He dug his lips—dry, desired, and delicious—into mine. He lifted me in front of his navel, took a few steps and placed me on the counter inside. As he pulled my hair, his other hand squeezed my cheekbones. His tongue was moving insistently, searching for mine, and it was all sweet again, and I was vibrating again. My body freed itself to wrap its thighs around him, my hands slid down the back of his neck and I grabbed the cure for my crazy longing. The bass was no longer pounding in my brain. It was pounding in my groin.

Reason gave up. His nose down, he headed to the darkness of my mind.

I'm going to jump, and that's it!

He was wailing from the edge. I shouted that I was about to stop, just a little bit more. *Lust*, however, waved her endless red veils triumphantly. She conquered the space with a whisper:

I'm going to show you what on earth I am now!

She detonated hidden explosions in every corner of my body, she blew apart it just to reassemble it once again. It was hollow now. There was only some thick, devouring arousal. *Lust's* addictive poison burned from the inside, determined to push me into the abyss beyond logic. I clung to Victor: with my hands, with my lips, with my skin, my breath and everything with which I could cling.

His sharp beard tore at my delicate skin, his teeth bit pieces of my lips and my neck. An impulse slammed into my stomach and below it every other second. Victor ran his fingers down my spine, then he jerked my hips toward him. As he pressed his hardened desire into me, a moan escaped my throat.

All my logical intentions turned into a steaming pile of ashes. Apparently, this was one of *Lust's* skills: burning.

Victor froze in front of me. My hands went from his shoulders down his chest, and then further down. He stopped them, kissed their tips and placed them on his neck.

'Don't let go of me, Nia!' He growled in my ear and bit it. I dug my fingers into the skin below them.

He tightened his rude grip on the back of my neck. He slipped his other hand under my T-shirt, pinched the bristled nipple, which hardened even more. He twisted it painfully, sending a sharp arrow to my groin. His hand pulled the bikini away and he walked around the pleasure button in many circles before dipping his finger into the wet. He placed it on a spot exposed as a nerve and sliced my breath into noisy interruptions. As he centred my face before his eyes, I held on tightly to his neck.

'Look at me!' He hissed. He squeezed my nape even tighter. 'I want you to feel exactly how bad it is for you to be in my arms! You need to feel to understand, Nia! Just to feel me!'

He carefully inserted another finger, stretching the fine tissue painfully. My breath turned into a sweet sigh. I tried to move but he held me in one place, repeating through his gritted teeth that I shouldn't let go. His touch was gliding over the moisture, torturing the spot and other magical points. Litres of my biochemistry drowned my neurons, mixing up in a giant explosive cocktail. Victor was vigorously playing with my senses, as if he was a drug that hungrily enjoyed the results of its influence.

All of a sudden, my body exploded. My muscles squeezed his fingers and the orgasm flowed over them. Biting his lips, he ordered me to look at him in an unconstrained, hoarse voice. There were only vague pieces of the blue visible while I fell apart in his arms. He slipped out of me, taking a noisy breath, then he carefully fixed my underwear in its place. He sucked on his two fingers, pulled my lips with them and rubbed them against my tongue. While they were still in my mouth, he came closer and whispered in my ear with his masculine shiver-provoking timbre:

'I think we discussed everything. I didn't understand what's bad for you, but I guess you can explain some other time. You want to make things right—OK, I agree. We need to make things right. That's why next time I will touch you only after you say that you want it. Clearly and firmly! Then you'll have to convince me that you crave being mine. That you are aware of this fact. Then you will stop pushing me away, snapping at me or distancing yourself from me, because all of that makes me explode! And then, I'll finally find a way to communicate with you.'

Victor tilted his neck in both directions, examining my outstretched body. I blinked numbly and I guess I moved my mouth like a fish on land. He shifted the visible erection underneath his trousers, then he went through the glass door.

My eyes followed his silhouette until he sank in the darkness of his house. Words still escaped me, and I remained outstretched on the table before I could regain my consciousness.

Damn! I need someone to explain right now! Reason, you still alive?

Everyone was silent, and he cowardly stepped back from the edge. He waved his arms in desperation, then he ran to hide. Numb, *Lust* blinked. *Knowledge* took a convincing breath, but then it blew it out:

Guessing is not my nature. I confirm that the intentions burned to ashes. No other data is available.

'Well, fuck you! Why am I even counting on you! This is supposed to be your job! What's the point of having voices in my head, if they shut up in the craziest times?' I drank my wine in one gulp.

I went around the living room a couple of times before hiding under the blanket on the couch. It was the first time I had participated in a group silence with my entities.

Even Freud can't help! What's wrong with me? This is getting more bizarre, confusing, and absurd than it was last night. What does he want from me, for Christ's sake!

I gazed at his bedroom window. My body was raging. I started hitting the couch and shouted. *The Monster* took a comfortable seat in the first row:

I can't wait to hear you stuttering! You, freak, can't pronounce even one of the words he expects. You simply cannot! This is not for you! Two people make an even number, and your twisted head can't comprehend this. You don't even know yourself. Can't you see that this man is everything you're not? There are galaxies between you. Not only is he superior to you. He already expects you to become something else. He wants impossible things that are for normal women, and he's never going to accept your pathetic being.

The nasty voice was telling the truth, and yet I hissed at him:

Shut up, creep! Victor counts, and he also has patterns. Maybe he will understand, maybe he has no expectations. Maybe he is like me.

The impudent *Monster* stood in the middle of my counting for relaxation. It wouldn't stop spitting. At some point it was nice enough to shut up and turn off the lamps of my mind. Just before the last light was extinguished, it spat out:

There are patterns everywhere, and you know perfectly well why you don't fit in any of them!

The Monster threw me into its best friend's hands. *Fear's* cruelty hit me. He feasted on my wrecked being; he kept biting hungrily and painfully all night long. I woke up and went back to sleep numerous times with no one there to hold me tight.

SEVEN

My weary eyelids opened at dawn. *Fear* had sucked all my strength away and I didn't want to go back to that nightmare. Stunned, *Lust* was still blinking while *Reason* was gathering energy for a fight that required a triple-shot coffee.

I rubbed my eyes, staring at Victor's window. Although his attitude lacked logic and suffered from irrational expectations, he was still accurate in his assessment of my habits and discipline. My head—and now my body as well—were trapped in chaos. I had been delaying it for too long; It was time to take the first step. The direction didn't matter. I had to finally pull myself together and somehow take control of my mind, my reactions, and my life. Victor's influence made that need crucial.

One—a cup of warm water, two—yoga before coffee, three—no gummy bears for breakfast. No outbursts. I'll think about everything else later.

I wrote down my new intentions on a piece of paper, put some clothes on, and took a deep breath to summon the courage to step barefoot on the cold Sunday-morning grass.

Next, I cycled through yoga positions, pleased with my motivation levels and with the flexibility of my joints. While I was performing a perfect "downward-facing dog"—which stretched the back of every one of my pathetic little muscles—I heard a commotion. My head upside down between my ankles when I saw Victor. He was staring at me, wearing black sweatpants and a T-shirt; he was probably returning from his morning jog, accompanied by several security guards.

'Good morning!' My upside-down smile greeted him. 'I'm working out, too.'

'Good morning!' A mixture of voices replied, but Victor didn't comment on my healthy yoga practice. He was quick to turn around, obviously determined to get back to his jogging.

I performed some more energising asanas[10], then headed back inside. I praised myself in the mirror and smiled for reward. As I walked up the stairs, I noticed that in daylight they weren't scary at all. I went through the bedroom and into the bathroom. The warm water welcomed my body, my hair straightened with wetness and tickled my back. After my early encounter with Victor, *Desire* was blowing in my groin. I tried to ignore it, determined to harness all my focus into controlling my body and mind. My first attempt was unsuccessful, of course, but at least I received some data for the statistics. *Reason* was pumping his motivation by doing push-ups. He was always ready to overthink:

Failures are the foundation of the final result. This is how we gather data. Without failures, success is statistically impossible.

The Monster was probably still snoring in its lair and, to my delight, it spared me the bile sputum for breakfast. Wrapped in a towel, I was rummaging through the neat bottles on the marble countertop around the sink, when Victor's face emerged in the mirror.

Damn it! I'm seeing hallucinations on surfaces now! I guess point four on my list should be "visit a shrink". The strange side effects from sex are dangerous indeed.

I shook my head but, as I turned around, he was standing in the doorframe, perfectly real. His T-shirt was soaking wet and drops of sweat were running down his forehead. His gaze contained blazing madness; his veins were bulging. Storming in, he grabbed me by the hips and placed me

---

[10] *A term in yoga practice. From Sanskrit "physical posture". In general asana is used for any type of position that can be held for an extended period of time. In the "downward-facing dog" position, the palms and the soles are pressed to the ground, and the body points upward in a triangle – author's notes.*

forcefully on the counter and entwined his hands in my wet hair, stretching it. His tongue conquered me, and mine joined eagerly in the passionate kiss. His teeth sank into my lips and pulled at them, as if wanting to tear them off. His beard grated my cheekbones. The ball in my stomach went mad. My hands let go of the marble edge to cling to his back. They slid up the damp fabric until they reached his hair, where they squeezed tightly. Victor growled in my mouth. His erection leaned against me insistently, only a piece of cloth away. He locked my face between his two hands, his eyes focused on mine. His pupils dilated, his breathing quickened unevenly.

'A hundred kilometres of jogging wouldn't be enough to destroy the energy I have for you. I'm not good at waiting. Damn, Nia, say it! Just say it now!'

He spoke through his teeth. I couldn't compare the expression on his face to anything I had seen before. There was no superiority anymore, no composure, no control over his nervous system. Even his heat had changed. Only sweat, energy and animal instincts shone on him, melting any semblance of distance between us, including the distance that I was deliberately creating. He could see I was doing this, the way I could see his impregnable wall. Only moisture, madness and lust separated us now. Or rather, they glued us together. I dug my nails into his skin. Despite it being open, my mouth remained silent. I didn't know how to vocalise my craving, I didn't know exactly what I craved, and I didn't know how to feel it all. The fact that Victor had invaded the space in which I didn't want anyone wasn't helping.

Resting his forehead on mine, he took a broken breath. His kisses grazed my cheekbones. His tongue and beard travelled all over my neck, and an impulse burned the area between my legs. The towel dropped to the floor. It slipped down my thighs and I was completely naked now, wet, my legs stretched apart. The tip of his index finger barely touched my skin. It went between my breasts, over my belly, slowly down.

'Stop torturing me!' He whispered and I nodded, hoping that he would do to me what he had done before. 'Words, Nia! I want you to say clearly and firmly that you want to be in my arms and that you feel you're mine! That's all I want. You can leave everything else to me!'

He sank his gaze to the bottom of my brain. The trap of his influence clicked. I was in. It was the most intimate lack of distance I had ever experienced: deprived of any air, any logic or clarity, yet choking with unattainable anticipation. The wording of my irrational desire stuck in my throat. The facts, the processes and the data were unacceptable for my hyper-rational mind, which rebelled. It was ready to shut down. Victor's energy crushed me, twisting my solar plexus, his glowing irises burning me. His image was flickering in my head.

'I lack data... It's too abstract... I can't define...' My words crawled out, hoarse and indistinct. He growled, pulling my hair back. My neck bent. He ran his tongue over it, then his breath rested on my cheekbone.

'You don't need to define it. You need to feel it! Close your eyes and just feel me, Nia!' The shiver-provoking timbre soaked into my ear, accelerating the vibrations of each of my cells.

His fingers closed my eyelids. In the darkness behind them, the rhythm of his breathing made me dizzy. I was only aware of the fact that I wanted him to dive into me and provoke the neurological reactions again. The craving echoed from the black chasm of my mind, and my throat spat the syllables out:

'Fuck me!'

'Damn it, Nia! You're driving me out of control. I'll even accept these two damn words.'

He slammed his lips into mine, grabbed my hips and pressed me against the wall. His kiss created moisture that filled the space between my legs. Shaking, they wrapped themselves tightly around Victor's waist and my arms wrapped around his neck. It was true that I wanted him to enter me more than anything, and his touch made me vibrate. He pressed his penis into my spilling juices, which invited him to slip in.

'Don't! You are not wearing a condom!' *Reason* shouted through my mouth, but Victor's tongue shoved him back in.

'I wasn't wearing one the other night, either. This will be the last "don't" that comes out of your mouth,' he whispered madly, as he invaded in one sharp motion.

'Fuck you, Victor!' I shrieked because of the stretching.

'You will understand what I'm saying, and you will accept that you're already all mine,' his hoarse voice cut through my ear.

His naked tissue ignited me. I clung to the back of his neck. My spine bent painfully from the smooth, organic feeling. The friction launched my sensuality into a new dimension. I was flooding around Victor. Pressing me against the wall, he pushed into me roughly and sharply. The sticky mixture of chaos he created in my body was choking me, and cries came out of my throat.

My muscles tightened around him, and my trembling thighs pressed against his skin. A pulsation was counting down the seconds to the desired explosion, but he slowed down. He carried me, pierced as I was, to hurl me on the bed.

'Those maddening eyes of yours are going to look at me as you orgasm!' He rumbled.

Settling between my legs, he penetrated with his finger. He spun it on a new bare nerve ending, or on one of the spots that he had discovered in me. I was on the brink of collapse, and he was torturing me. The heat and the moisture soaked his fingerprints. I moved my pelvis, and he pressed his chest to me, biting my lips in a deep kiss. He leaned over me, snatching destructive pleasure from the deepest corners of my subconsciousness. The spasms raged, my fingernails sank into his skin, my breath spilled out in a high-pitched moan. The new personality of mine that Victor had brought to life was storming throughout my body. I pressed my thighs together, staring at him. He drew circles around the pleasure button and I exploded. I pulled him to myself, but he didn't move. He froze two feet above my face. As I came on his fingers, he pressed his other hand to my mouth, squeezing my cheekbones. Only muffled moans could be heard under his palm.

I was looking at him, but all I could see was a blurred picture. The only sensation was the hot trace of his touch winding up my skin, while my head was spinning. All of a sudden, he penetrated brutally, filling me to the edge. My breath stopped. I closed my eyes, squeezing the bedsheets. His thrusts made me spread my thighs wide open to take all of him in. He lifted my pelvis. He was on his knees, forcefully invading. I bent even more vigorously under his maddening touch on the tip of my concentrated sensitivity. He gripped one of my breasts, twisting the nipple between his wet fingers. Beneath them, sharp impulses shot. My feet pressed against the bed, trembling, and my body pressed against Victor, until he reached my depths.

'Look at me! Open your eyes, Nia!' His voice called me from the distance and I obeyed.

I stared into the blue. A couple of pushes later, I spilled all over; pulsating, suffocated by the fire, without blinking. Convulsions were squeezing him inside me, and bright, colourful spots flashed in my mind, even though my eyes were open. The neurological process was tossing me around, extracting moans from my throat.

'Nia!' He grunted, not letting go of my gaze, and his heat sank deep to the last of my cells. As I writhed with the pleasure he had given me, the powerful jets of his juices filled me up.

Still immersed in me, he glued his face to mine. His sweat mixed with mine and I took in our intoxicating scent, together with the smell of musk that made my skin prickle. I was slowly coming to my senses, my body lying there as if it was dismembered.

Reason peeked around a corner and started yelling:

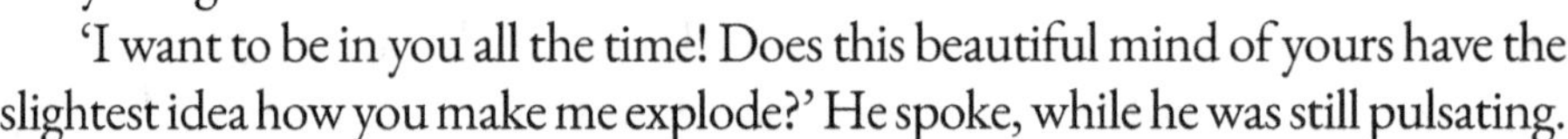

Have you lost your mind completely? What are you doing?

Uncertain, he hid back in his trenches. I only muttered to him to keep quiet. I couldn't think anymore: neither about my actions, nor about any consequences.

Victor was still inside. He was trying to restore the rhythm of his breath, fondling my hair. He was gently kissing my lips and everything around.

'I want to be in you all the time! Does this beautiful mind of yours have the slightest idea how you make me explode?' He spoke, while he was still pulsating.

'I have no reference point to compare the condition before and after the explosion, so I can't estimate the result,' a dry voice came out mechanically. He propped himself up in the bed and laughed above my face.

'Just ask me to shut your mouth and I'll be most happy to do so! There's no need to provoke me with this way of speaking.'

'Victor, that's how I normally speak and I don't do it on purpose. I just express myself accurately, so that people can understand me. Not that it works, but...'

'No, my sweet little cactus, you do something else,' he interrupted me with a kiss. 'You deliberately create distance that people can't or don't know how to overcome. At some point, you adopted this habit and that's why you're just like that little prickly cactus that I gave you. You speak normally only when you're angry, irritated or out of your usual focus. Your brain works on other frequencies then. The same goes for when you're horny. I can explain the process, if you want me to.'

'I certainly don't! Besides, this is an inappropriate subject, especially when you are inside my body. Did I say that normally? Screw you!' I snapped and Victor laughed again, stroking my lips.

'Almost! As a matter of fact, I don't mind you keeping the whole world at a distance, I'd even prefer that. You're not going to do it with me, though, because I'll make sure you'll be angry or horny all the time,' he bit my fingers and took a prolonged pause, tracing the outline of my face.

After a few minutes, he spoke again, with guilt in his voice:

'Nia, the doctor is going to give you contraceptives, if you're not taking any. You will have to take an emergency pill today. So, before you do anything else, you'll have to see her.'

'Certainly I'll have to. Damn you!' I pinned my worst stomach-twisting gaze on his face, but he only raised his eyebrows guiltily. 'You realise that your behaviour is absolutely wrong, absolutely unacceptable, and absolutely abominable, do you? You shouldn't have done this, and you're not doing it anymore.'

'I certainly intend to do this absolutely wrong, unacceptable, and abominable thing all the time from now on,' his brand-new personality was bursting with energy. He bit my palm before continuing. 'I hope you realise that your insatiable body is still squeezing me. Seems like it has a different opinion from your mind and I guess its opinion coincides with mine. That's why I intend to keep feeling you this way!' He smiled at me boyishly.

'I, however, do not intend to stuff my body with chemical shit! This one time I will take the emergency pill, of course, but from now on, you will wear a condom. End of conversation!' I scolded him under his gleaming gaze as he kissed me.

'Arguing with me before the morning coffee again?'

'I'm not arguing, I'm informing you. I'm not going to poison my body with synthetic hormones! This is my body, my call, you should've asked *me* first.'

'Your body is also mine. I think I'm taking good care of it and I wouldn't let anything poison it. There's nothing to worry about.'

'That voice again! How absurd is your statement? You are really struggling with choosing the words! I don't want your opinion; I don't want you to care!' I snapped, pushing his chest, but he only smiled even more naughtily.

'You're pushing and arguing again. I might start to like this,' he pulsated in me again. 'You sure you don't want any of my care?' His eyes flashed predatorily.

He started moving his pelvis and his desire hardened, stretching my tissue. My mouth opened, but instead of an argument, a moan came out. When he was already fully inside me, I couldn't argue anymore. He eagerly slipped into my moisture, mixed with his juices, and the sensation made me bristle.

'Yoga doesn't help with running, but let's see if it's useful in other ways!'

He bit my ankle, then licked it before placing it behind his neck. Then he repeated with my other leg. He glued my thighs to his stomach, sinking to my depths, and I writhed under him. He lifted my pelvis to hungrily invade me. My body was already more than his and he realised that perfectly well. Victor had conquered it, disassembled it, and reassembled it again; to his touch, he had addicted my senses beyond any imagination and reason.

He was going at it rudely and without restraint, and all I wanted was for him to never stop. His furious rhythm drew perfect street jazz from the strings of my pleasure, engraving new sensations on my tissue. He placed his finger on the button and started playing with it again, insatiably, pushing my body to explosion. He was running his thumb over the bundle of sensitivity, invading to the limit, his blue irises nailed in my confused head. He painfully reached to the last millimetre of lust deep inside me. I whimpered, pierced by his passion, out of breath under his desire. I had no chance; the forces were not even. He had created my addiction, he controlled it now, he reigned over it like opium.

'Victor!' The name of my drug came out in a scream.

'Give it to me, Nia! Let me feel you're mine. That's all I want,' his shiver-provoking timbre echoed as if through a tunnel.

My ankles twisted behind his neck. His touch caressed the raging impulses between my legs, pulsations on the inside were crushing him. They emptied my body and mind. I was burning, and the blue irises were reflecting the blaze, enjoying the fire. He filled me up. The hot liquid showered my orgasm and he continued invading until my last cell died in his hands.

'You've been blowing me up, Nia! I spent the whole fucking night testing my control. To know that you exist, but not to feel you, not to listen to your breathing, not to have you writhing in my arms,' his voice was rumbling insanely in my ear. 'Don't do that ever again! Damn, you're driving me crazy! I want you to be naked, mine, and in my hands all the time! I want to do it again! I want to feel you!'

He turned me around, twisted my hair around his hand and did it again. He could feel that I was his. I could feel I was his, too. Rudely, eagerly, no restraint. He destroyed what little was left of my power, snatching the last moan from my lungs. He stretched every muscle in painful pleasure until I disintegrated, then brought me back to life with his touch. I was gradually coming to my senses under a shower of kisses.

Victor lay down next to me, his fingers tracing the sharp feminine curve from my hips upwards. He turned my face to him warming me with his lips and I smiled at the reviving feeling. When I opened my eyes, however, the expression of a stone statue had settled between us again.

'I'm running late and at least ten people are about to have a heart attack now,' he took hold of my chin. 'You're moving to the penthouse today. Make a list of whatever you need. I will decide when and how to come to you. My assistant will inform you of my schedule, so you don't make other plans,' he recited as if he was ordering breakfast.

'And why would I move there?' I raised my eyebrows as I propped myself up in the bed.

'You can't stay here.'

I narrowed my eyes at his arrogant voice.

'Why?'

'Because I say so!'

'First of all, that is not an answer. Second of all, that way of speaking is unacceptable, and third, you could just say that you don't want me here! Unlike you, I don't have issues with the truth. I was planning to rent an apartment anyway.'

'Fourth, that is not the problem, and fifth, you're not renting anything. Stop snapping at me!' He looked exactly like he did when at his office.

'What is the problem then? And sixth, don't use this commanding manner when speaking about my personal life!' I snapped and he hissed noisily.

'Nia, I already explained to you it's complicated. There are certain problems I have to take care of! And they are complicated indeed'

'Take care of? And how exactly do you assume that something will be complicated for me?'

'It's complicated for me!'

'But not for me, Victor! Stop underestimating me, because my mind doesn't like it at all! Neither do I!' I raised my voice.

'And you stop arguing, because my temper doesn't like it at all, neither do I! Just let me sort things out and be a little bit more reasonable! The situation is complicated enough.'

'The situation is not complicated, it's obvious: you need to fit me into your pattern, don't you? I figured it out yesterday. Precise order is your madness, your obsession: when it comes to life, when it comes to women, business or sequences. It was glowing and I figured it out. I found a sequence so intricate yet balanced, that it fascinated me. On your floor.'

The memory of it made my fingers move like the baton of a conductor. Victor was quiet. I sighed with a lopsided smile on my lips.

'It's not complicated at all; for me it's clear. You repeat your obsessive pattern in everything you do. Most people might find this insane, but I can understand it. I just don't understand how your consciousness works this way without people noticing that you're crazy. I guess it's your position! You can afford this and you put everything in its place, just as you expect to do now.'

'It has nothing to do with this!' He snorted nervously.

'It certainly has! This is the only sensation I am perfectly aware of. Distorted people and general reality affect me in the same manner. I need to place them in patterns that I consider correct, I sometimes even apply controversial methods. They drive me crazy! Broken tiles do, too! I see every fucking mistake and it drives me crazy. And people can see this. You were blown up by my chaos, weren't you? You conceived this illogical interest in a person like me, because I am an uncontrollable chaos—I quote you. I am now the mistake that drives you crazy. Actually, no other reasonable cause could provoke your interest in me. I don't match any of your standards. It's not me that provokes you, it's simply the need to put me in place, isn't it? The need to fix me?'

'Nia, how do you even reach these insane conclusions? Damn!' His blazing irises stared at me.

'It's driving you out of control, isn't it, Victor?' I stood up with a cynical expression on my face. Leaning against the wall, I armoured my body with the bedsheet. 'I don't fit into your pattern or into your set of ideas. I am the distorted thing that interrupts your pattern; that makes your obsession drive you insane: without logic, without a single argument. It just grabs you and takes over. I even stop functioning sometimes. You see me as a glowing mistake, don't you?'

'Stop it! I don't see you as a mistake and you're not breaking my pattern. It has nothing to do with it,' his angry look crashed into my barrier. Behind it, I was sick.

'If I start listing, I can even prove to you how I'm breaking it,' I took a deep breath before continuing in an even voice. 'Look, I'm used to people trying to make me fit into someone else's ideas and expectations. All my life I've been what I'm not supposed to be, and it's a daily routine for me. I don't blame people: they just look for ordinary shapes that match their ordinary lives. I'm going to confess something, though. My geometry was not distorted just like that. I've been bending it deliberately and constantly since I was little. I strive to not fit in, Victor, because I realised a long time ago that this world doesn't deserve fitting in; not with the people, not in their lives, nor in their expectations or in the absurd labels they put on others. The same goes for you, no matter who you are and how many times you are superior to me. The fact that some insane reasons took me to your bed and got me to have sex with you doesn't make me your next whore. I'm certainly not going to be one of them.'

'God! Only your conclusions right now are insane. You're not my next whore, Nia.'

'I know I'm not. You, however, are acting as if I am. You expect me to contort and fit in without saying a word. To start with, by going to your goddamn square penthouse, just like a whore you can call or put on hold. And when I go there, what's next?' My voice was becoming more spiteful. 'I'm supposed to unleash my potential? You'll take a break from the beauties with the freak when you're in the right mood for that? And after you fuck me, I'll be calculating forecasts, in order to be the assistant who doesn't know her place. I guess this can also be labelled as "normal", can it not? You really are underestimating me! So fuck you!' The last words were already full of rage.

The bitter taste of truth usually fills people's eyes with saline, but my freakish eyes only dry out. Their glow fades away, leaving only two voids. From behind them, *The Monster* peeks out. Victor froze before me, anger raging in his irises.

'Stop it and control the way you speak to me! I'm not underestimating you, Nia,' he tried to come closer, but my gaze made him stop.

'Yes, you certainly are! You know, the only surprise is finding a madness similar to my own in someone who is so different from me. And given the huge social distance between us, too: you at the peak, and me at the bottom! Or maybe it is exactly this distance that makes you think I will accept all this.'

'Stop it! That's what I'm offering, that's what you're taking!' He shouted and then bit his lips.

He put his clothes on in a haste. He was rhythmically taking deep breaths and his expression told me he was realising the truth about his repulsive ideas and expectations.

'You believe your own lies, don't you?' I kept following the nervousness of his movements.

'You are moving to the penthouse today! End of conversation! We're going to finish it later!' He hissed in his arrogant manner.

I coughed dryly before replying with contempt:

'If that's what you meant the other night, when you said that you were going to find an acceptable way to solve your issues...Well, you certainly didn't find one. I can't stay here, you're quite right about that, and I'm leaving today. I'm certainly not going to your penthouse, though, and I'm certainly not going to wait for you to inform me when and how you're going to come to me. I certainly can't meet these expectations. I had the impression you knew this, but I guess my behaviour misled you. If we both have the time and the desire for this, I don't mind having sex with you sometimes. My perception of sex evolved and I'm planning to continue practicing it. I will think about the possibility of working for you. It might be a good opportunity, but I messed up the directions and assume it's unfixable. I think we indeed discussed everything already.'

A burning bitterly acidic concoction was bubbling under my expressionless voice, and I was on the verge of exploding despite the clear facts. Yet, he was the one who exploded first, though. He leaned over and his face went wild for a second.

'You're planning to continue practicing it? Do you even hear what you're saying? Your twisted mind's conclusions are not even close to the truth.'

'Victor, the truth is nothing but a sequence of data. It either corresponds to what's real, or it doesn't. I know now: what is real is that your expectations equal compromises that I am not able to make. It's that simple!' I didn't twitch. Waves were chasing over his face. 'My twisted mind demands balance now. Like always, it is going to count. And this time, it is going to count aloud. I expect to be on my own as soon as you hear "one",' *the Monster*'s predatory eyes pierced Victor through the void of my eyes.

'Stop being like this! God, how am I even supposed to communicate with you when you're being like this,' he pressed himself against me, but my palms stopped him as I hissed:

'Being like what? Come on, just say it: a freak, a sociopath, a crazy woman...' I could see his neck muscles stretch. When he took a breath to reply, I interrupted: 'One!' The word rattled spitefully and hollowly.

Victor erupted in a growl. His body pressed me to the wall.

'Nia, whenever your voice counts "one", it brings me to the edge of sense, but you can't understand me. If there is anyone who can embrace the chaos within you and all your madness, you are in his arms right now,' his timbre was even more insane than his words.

'Get off me and get out!' The bubbling concoction erupted. I yelled, pushing him away. He wouldn't let go and I sensed the balanced rhythm in which he was trying to catch his breath.

'You're pushing me again. You don't control yourself. You must have figured it out already: you will get what you want. The only fucking truth is that staying away from you is the wisest decision,' air hissed through his teeth before he continued: 'This is exactly what I am going to do this time! My assistant will show you some flats. Choose one and move there. That's it!'

'Save your commanding for someone who might be impressed by it! For your shadows, for instance,' I spat as he clenched his jaw. 'No one will show me anything! That's it! Since you really didn't get it, I'm going to say it more clearly: the fact that you banged me doesn't make me part of your army of whores and you cannot command me like that.'

'You save your stubbornness for someone who might comply with it! I'm not asking you; I'm telling you! And just to make it clear, if you were part of the "army", I wouldn't even bother explaining to you,' he pierced me with his glassy irises, the wall of superiority thick around him.

'Get out of this room and leave me alone! Don't speak to me like that and don't look at me in your arrogant, impudent, haughty manner!' *Pride* was shouting in my head, out of control, and *Rage* was spitting fire next to her. 'Get out!' I started hitting his chest.

The burning anger in Victor's irises scattered his composure into thousands of pieces.

'Damn!' He roared continuously into his palms. 'You are indeed driving me to the edge!'

He turned me around, sticking my chest to the wall, and himself to me. His hardness pressed into my pelvis, like his teeth—into my cheekbone. His hand sank under my panties and he ran it over the damp tissue, his breath whistling. His timbre penetrated my bones:

'Whenever I'm in you, it is so easy to understand your body and everything's fine then. Whenever I'm not in you, you drive me crazy. I'm not looking at you in a haughty manner, Nia. I'm struggling to control myself, to not be myself, because all I want right now is to tell you to shut up and follow my orders. I crave for things to go the way I'm used to: you wouldn't be allowed to utter even one of your goddamn words. But it's not like that. And since I have to deal with you in a way I'm not familiar with, I'm going to leave now, because I don't want to explode,' he explained through his gritted teeth, squeezing my neck.

His breath made my skin prickle and created even more moisture under his fingers. My new personality moaned and pressed itself to his touch, but I growled both at him and myself:

'First, let go of me right now! Second, I don't want you to deal with me anymore, and your so-called "dealing" sucks. Third, your sentences are absolutely unacceptable! The same goes for your habits.'

He exhaled noisily before leaving. I watched his vigorous steps through the window. He didn't enter his house, just stopped in front of it and shouted something at the security guard. His composed expression was back, and yet now I could make out the rage underneath. The boys kept their distance. He shifted the visible bulge under his pants, while someone was parking a black motorbike next to him. Victor snatched the helmet and there was a deafening, sharp noise as the machine flew off.

I was leaning against the wall, the rapturous traces of Victor dripping down my legs. My second personality was still trembling. I was sick of myself, of him, and of the yet another expectation that corresponded to the warped general reality. This time I had bumped into the most repulsive paradigm of myself, and I had never been labelled in a manner more offensive before.

Ironically, fate had pushed me into a madness similar to my own, yet different enough to make me the distorted thing that had to be adjusted again. I was with a crazy person like myself, who didn't fit into my ideas, but he bent them together with my body and my primitive nature to match him. It was the first time I had seen my reflection in eyes that knew how to provoke and torture me.

Over the years, I had managed to train my *Monster* to chew slowly. I stuffed into its mouth every disappointment and all the bitterness and disgust provoked by general reality and by my own personality. That way I didn't have to feel any of them. Most likely, *the Monster* wasn't born with me; I had created it to swallow all these things for me. I didn't know when it had all started, but I had begun to feed it in some masochistic way, and it grew like a mushroom.

The Monster, in turn, taught me to first look from behind my barrier, then to create a distance, then it made me snap at people and life. Eventually, *the Monster* began to vomit, too. Fed up with reality's foul food, it constantly reminded me what I was, underestimated me, defined me, labelled me.

I often repeated to myself that I could not fit into what was normal for the unbearable general reality. At some point, I stopped even wanting to fit in. Before I could realise what was happening, I was already deliberately trying to break the mould. Victor shattered this attitude and at some perverted moment, I wished things to be different. I even allowed myself to twist and bend, in order to become someone suitable for him and for his normality. He knew how to properly define every damaged part and every edge that I had. He did it better than I could. He didn't shy away from digging deep into my subconscious, nor from creating addictions that he could later control. He even enjoyed it all. His sick mind had built an exceptional pattern for him: strict order, identical women, firm communication, perfect proportions. And I had slipped in the direction of contorting myself to fit into his ideals. I wanted it. I admitted it. Aware of the absurd, I was overwhelmed with anger because of my own insane actions. Victor's side effects made me face one of the things that caused my worst mental blocks.

I had pushed myself towards the faulty pattern; from a paradox, it had become the norm. It glowed all over, all the time. It paralysed me. I deemed it one of the most warped patterns. Not a single argument existed to support it, and it just made me block. It was a common occurrence, mostly with women: divine, gorgeous, each one of them extraordinary in her own way. The impeccable sparkle of mankind concentrated in them, they walk up and down the twists and curves of life, covered with scruffy plasters over their wounds. That's what the voluntarily depersonalised looked to me. They did that to themselves, by themselves, and my broken mind observed them, wondering how such a madness could possibly exist in the general reality of supposedly uncrazy people. These women tortured themselves, they struggled, resigned, bent, and shattered in order to meet someone else's expectations and standards. In order to fit into someone else's piece of reality. They destroyed their unique innate geometry to become regular square shapes: to be one-size-fits-all. And that was normal, too.

They shone, each with her own perfection, and yet they willingly broke their star edges. They turned to dust, just to fit into a man's cupped hand, into his ideas. Then they gradually faded in the narrow space of cold relationships, because there was nothing for them there. They stayed, nevertheless, probably convinced by their own *Monsters* that they didn't deserve more, or that "it's normal". Maybe they lived with sinister *Fear*, too, but I was not sure if that was the case with those not-as-twisted as I was.

As I watched the women around me doing this to themselves, I furiously yelled at them. I yelled at them that it was the shortest path from being bright stars to becoming piles of grey dust that could be scattered by the wind of life. I couldn't understand why, but as they kept filing down their uniqueness for the sake of somebody else, they stopped listening and frantically repeated that I was crazy, that I knew nothing. I explained with precise arguments, but while mutilating themselves, they wouldn't hear, they would readily doom themselves to clear and predictable results. Their actions were driven by some decadent force, mind-boggling, powerful, resembling a ferocious beast. It often led to consequences so sinister that I promised myself to stay away from it all. I appreciated the value of authenticity, but already knew how easy it was to just lose it. Even voluntarily. I had rubbed myself against that incomprehensible madness, I had even tasted it, and it had proven to be temptingly sweet. Intoxicating as hell.

I could see in the mirror that, this time, true reality made my eyes look even darker. It gave me a series of sobering slaps. It tied me into a suffocating knot. Without moving, I stretched my face into a smile—pleased that I had come to my senses on time at least. I went downstairs where I bumped into Toma's popping eyes.

'Are you OK?'

'It's a conditional question, for Christ's sake!'

'Why was Kaov here? What's going on? I told you to call me if there was a problem,' he reached out to me, but I pulled myself away.

'There was a problem. The porch light wasn't working and, like always, problems crept out of the dark.'

'Lord, Nia! The porch lights don't work because of Victor, so as not to disturb him. They'll fix it right away. Tell me what happened? Why are you so mad?'

'There's no need to fix the light anymore. Actually, it's not the problem. The problem is that I really did start looking in the wrong direction. You were absolutely right!'

He followed the thread of my attention to Victor's bedroom window.

'Girl, there's nothing for you to look at. Only darkness, and no bulb, not even the most powerful, could ever light it,' he gave me a compassionate yet insistent look. 'Stay away from him! Do you understand what I'm saying?'

'I am not into metaphors, but yeah. You don't have to explain anymore. I am a grown-up. I'm moving out, so I'd rather have coffee with you somewhere else.'

Toma gaped at me, but he didn't say anything. *The Monster* kept spitting that I had gotten what I deserved. It had gained extreme power over both my body and mind and was poisoning all my cells; it made everything blurry and shook me so deeply that I was disintegrating into atoms. It was a dangerous power that took over my brain, pushed it to its knees, then began commanding every thought, every action, completely subduing me. All that it left behind was my expressionless face, with dark, dry, voids for eyes. That morning *the Monster* was spluttering unbearably, vomiting words:

You probably forgot there's no place for you on this Earth, you freak. It's a good thing a man like him even touched a freak like you. You're not even good enough to be a whore.

Gritting my teeth, I turned down all Toma's requests for an explanation. He seemed concerned, but I kept stubbornly silent while packing my stuff. His annoying insistence eventually forced me to clarify.

'I am fine! It's just that... Reality got me distracted. I conveniently forgot what I am, but now I recall. I'm about to do the only thing I can do better than anyone else. The reason why nobody should ever underestimate me. I'm going to mobilise my mind to a state that amazes, and everything will be perfectly fine again. I can do this, at least. Now leave me alone!'

'Nia! I warned you to set a limit with Victor. He drove you crazy as well. I told you to keep your distance. For Christ's sake, Nia, he's crazy! Can't you see that he's totally insane?' He shouted, fully enraged.

'He didn't drive me crazy. I am crazy enough already. He can't make things worse. Toma, telling me that someone else is insane is weird, to put it mildly. After all, I probably cover the requirements for at least five psychiatric diagnoses,' I raised my eyebrows.

'Damn! You don't deserve this! You just don't, do you get that? This is not for you. I should've argued with him more!' Toma exploded. He hit the counter with his fist, then left while I watched his back in bewilderment.

I closed my suitcase quickly. As I slammed the door behind me, however, the unexpected door-issue crept up my back like thousands of fiery ants. I shivered, then snorted. While I was walking to the car, Chris's insane voice from Victor's doorstep stopped me.

'Good morning, Nia! Come! We need to discuss something,' he shouted across the strip of grass and the sound bounced off my sulky face.

'Later. I'm in a hurry now.'

'Come! It'll only take a few minutes.'

'Ugh, why now?!' I hissed through my teeth, tossing my luggage on the car seat, then taking a few nervous steps to calm down before heading to the house.

Chris was sitting alone at the table, staring at his laptop screen. I froze a few steps away when I saw it: the glistening harmony of arched waves. My whole being adored them. Immersed in the pleasure of my mental orgasm, I leaned in next to his head.

'It's cosmic, isn't it?' My voice took Chris out of his concentration, and he trembled.

'Can you see it?'

'Perfectly.'

'I'm just about to sell. I'll make Victor and myself meaninglessly richer.'

'What are you talking about?' Surprise rolled in my voice.

'The forecast. You just said you can see it, didn't you? I see glowing points forming results. What do you see?'

'No! I see the waves, in a divine order. The Fibonacci sequence. The Elliott waves[11] are among its most exquisite forms, and I can see them here, on your chaotic lines!' I pointed at the chart.

'And you don't know anything about the market?'

'There was no one to teach me, and that kind of education is too expensive for me. I can show you something that I found out by myself, though.'

---

[11] *Ralph Elliott created an analysis of stock market movements after the Great Depression of the 1930s. The method became a widely used approach to forecasting financial markets. Elliott believed that market prices move in a predetermined number of waves that correspond to the Fibonacci numbers and the golden ratio. He assumed that the average market level rises in the form of five waves and falls in the form of three waves – a 5-3 pattern, which was called "The Elliott Wave Theory" – author's notes.*

'Frankly, I can't wait. I know only one person who is almost like you, but he went nuts and now there's no one I enjoy talking with. You know this is a way to forecast the market, right?' Chris jumped off the chair and made me sit on it. He glued his face next to mine in front of the screen. 'Nia, can you really see the Elliott Waves, even though I didn't put them on the chart?'

'Certainly, I can! They shine so brightly in my mind,' I laughed at the question. I was in a better mood now. 'Focus on this. Watch the pattern under the waves. Can you see the rhythm? It's perfect, and then the intervals break it. Don't pay attention to the data, they are misleading. Follow the rhythm!' I opened a cryptocurrency website. I often hung out there and I had found this pattern in some of the cryptocurrencies, but hadn't defined the causes or the results. 'I searched a lot and others can see it too. In this Russian blog there is a discussion going on between a bunch of weirdos like me. They say it's happening because of South Korea, and in a controlled way. There's no more information, and they wouldn't share anything else. I asked questions, but... Russians! They keep silent, as if we are in the middle of the Cold War. The Koreans influence the market, that's all I know. I don't understand the rest, even though I can see the rhythm and the errors in the pattern.'

'You're killing me! That's...' Chris leaned closer to the screen, his jaw dropping. 'Damn, how could I not... Nia, it's millions of cash!'

'For whoever gets these things and has the money, probably. I only enjoy it. It's going to happen again soon. It's obvious if you'd only trace the pattern,' I turned around. He was three centimetres away from me, not moving, his eyes bulging. 'Now tell me what you wanted to talk about because I have to go.'

'What got your attention like that?' Victor's metallic voice pulled Chris out of his trance. His T-shirt was soaking wet again. His eyes narrowed and he angrily threw his helmet on the table. Chis moved out of its way, and the president's arm pushed him half a metre away from me.

'Damn it, Victor, she's amazing. A genius!' Chris was moving his gaze from Victor to me, again and again.

'Good thing your definition of "amazing" is different to mine,' Victor threw his blazing irises at my thick barrier.

'Chris, are we going to discuss something? Because I'm leaving.' My cool voice sobered him up.

'Oh, yeah, yeah! I got you information about the credit companies. Victor told me to prepare the data and start working on your plan.'

'I was not informed about this,' I shot my composed gaze at the president, 'I will go through the data, Victor, and decide whether I can combine this with working on your estates. I accelerated the process and they'll be ready sooner than expected. We also need to clarify our financial relations. As soon as I finish my task, if there's nothing truly challenging for my mind, my work for you is over.'

Chris's face twisted in astonishment and Toma gaped from the door. Victor didn't twitch. He stood like a statue that could only be moved by something like an earthquake.

'Bullshit, nothing will be over! You just came, and I've been waiting for you for so long. We are going to achieve so much together. Tell her, Kaov!' Chris squeaked anxiously.

'No matter what I say, you will argue. You don't comply with anything, so the decision is yours. If that's what you want, fine! I wonder who will ever put up with you. Define your financial parameters by yourself and inform the lawyer about them. I can afford you, don't worry about that,' Victor said calmly. All my life I had extracted information about what was going on in other people's minds by their facial expressions, but now they were absent again. My twisted head was silent. I was also silent, facing those superior blue eyes.

'There will be a challenging task. Just give me a little time to confirm something. My genius Smarty, please, don't leave me when I just met you!' Chris was overwhelmed with enthusiastic euphoria. He grabbed my face and kissed both of my cheeks. Victor shivered, his muscles tensing, his face coming to life.

'Don't touch her!' An unrestrained voice erupted from the president as he pulled the madman away from me in one motion. 'We have work to do and I'm running out of time,' he finished in a cold voice.

'Goodbye!' I snatched the documents from Chris and fled through the door.

φ

Toma stepped on the accelerator. Maybe he needed a break from explaining just as much as I did because he turned the volume to the max. *Nouvelle*

Vague hypnotised me with their 'In a Manner of Speaking'[12], washing away the bitterness from my mouth. Immersed in my beloved hiding place, I watched the road, a crooked smile on my face, my lips silently singing along.

The car sped only centimetres away from the other vehicles, but I didn't care. I was enjoying every risky manoeuvre with the perverted hope that we'd fly off the road. I wanted my adrenaline levels to reach a point beyond common sense; to choke my thoughts and help me escape from everything. The words that normal people had applied to me my whole life, trying to squeeze me in their narrow perceptions, were playing along with the loud music.

Freak, crazy, creep, sociopath, twisted, broken. In fact, you have all been right. That's what I am. Except for the sociopath part.

I raised my hands above my head after we missed a startled driver by millimetres. Toma watched me with the corners of his eyes. I looked at my reflection in the window. *The Monster* had glued a well-known face on me: the expressionless one. Traces of mud, like dirty tears, were running over it. In my mind, I stared at him: the person who got blown up by what was broken in my personality. While I, the complete idiot, was deluded that it was all about who I truly was. I deluded that he had noticed something in me... I had been aware of the lack of reasonable motives, and yet I was deluded. Eventually, I crashed into pathetic standards again, the expectations of the general reality. Again, I appeared to be the broken tile, but now I was provoking his twisted mind. Without even wanting to, Victor had gone crazy about the idea of fitting me into his narrow concepts before moving on to the next conquest, in the rhythm of counting an odd number of steps.

---

12 *Nouvelle Vague – In a Manner of Speaking – author's notes.*

EIGHT

All quiet on the office front!

After being stuck in a traffic jam for too long, I reached the office even sulkier than before. The construction workers there gave me the firm impression that they had been doing nothing. I had yelled, I had negotiated, I had begged, but they maintained the same slow pace. Maybe we didn't live in the same time reality? I disappointedly concluded that the battle with such workers had been lost as soon as their profession had emerged. At least they were perfect for practicing patience. Dealing with over 3,000 square metres of two-storey office space and an penthouse of almost 1,000 square metres should have been an impossible task for someone inexperienced like me, but it was quite OK for someone who enjoyed imaginary competitions in their twisted mind; someone who was always trying to find ways to prove themselves, or to earn enough money to afford an escape. The idea of escaping proved to be a particularly strong motivator, even for making bad decisions.

Step by step, however, the plan was executed; cables, pipes and various unfamiliar objects went to their designated places. The penthouse was ready to be furnished and the furniture was already piled at the entrance.

The only problem was that its marble floor had instantly begun to drive me crazy with its random pattern. I immediately determined it should be replaced with something more suitable for counting. Although my head had already related the penthouse to bad memories, I waited in anticipation for it to be finished.

Despite my hard efforts, staying focused remained a struggle. My thoughts kept running towards Victor. I watched one of his interviews, even though I was not interested in politics, and without even bothering to hear what the discussion was about. All I wanted was to investigate the lack of facial expressions and the thick wall of superiority between him and the world, or at least between that particular part of his personality and the world. Involuntarily, I remembered his face when he was blazing over me, penetrating, filling me up, trembling and growling. My skin prickled. Finally, I threw the cactus against the wall. Then I carefully glued the pot back together and apologised to the plant, begging it to survive.

I was well aware that Victor was the thing I needed to get rid of immediately, if I wanted to tame at least some part of the chaos in me. Despite his insulting, arrogant attitude and my good arguments, even the idea of not seeing him gave me muscle spasms. His expectations were contemptuous and unacceptable, but I was in the middle of another sparring round between my mind and my body, and their fight was drowning all of my energy. *Reason* was circling, silently raging. Curled up in a corner, *Lust* and *Desire* were having their group therapy. Everyone else was afraid to speak. Only *Pride* was roaring, giving kicks to the intruders every now and then.

While I was torturing my mind to gather some focus, Chris and his crazy colourful eyes popped up at the door. I put the folders away, giving him a questioning look and without invitation he sat next to me on the floor.

'I saw the suitcase. I heard the words. Motives?' His serious irises pinned on me.

'About the suitcase—a new location is needed, at quite a distance from the current one. Work wise—after a series of mistakes, I am no longer compatible,' he spoke in my manner, so I used the same style to reply.

'About the location—I am going to offer a solution. Work wise—your conclusion is incorrect. You are compatible by nature, which cannot be affected by the mistakes. A hypothesis: there is a conflict with the results due to bad judgements. Analyse the causes, not the consequences.'

'There are no logical grounds or arguments for the causes. I already searched for them. It's just crazy! And I don't even want to discuss the consequences,' I sighed, examining the random tattoos on his arms. They looked like ink stickers, especially the avocado above his left wrist. A fairy was sitting on the fruit, and there was a rainbow next to them. 'Chris, you communicate just like me. Does that mean I don't piss you off?'

'You certainly don't! I already told you, I haven't had anyone normal to talk to for a long time,' he laughed and at that moment, I even liked him. 'I know the consequences. You're stuck with Victor. I know how insane these relations are, but I can be of no use in clarifying them. I still haven't clarified these things for myself. About the location—I have excess space that you could use. About the work—don't relate it to your mistakes with Victor, because they most probably cannot be corrected.'

'I'm not stuck! I am not a duck in a muck to get stuck. What do you even mean by this metaphor? I'm in the middle of some temporary confusion, that's all. About the work—maybe I shouldn't have acted so hastily, because I really need the money. About the location—if you're looking for a roommate, I will take the offer, but you'll have to wait for the rent.'

'You are stuck, Smarty! It's obvious! The gesture clusters[13] say it all. I don't have many observations on ducks, so I can't confirm this comparison! About the work—there are no arguments to refuse it, but still, there are other ways to make money, too. About the rent—I have an excess amount of money and this factor is irrelevant. Call me when you finish here. Bye!'

He gave me his phone number before heading to the exit. I frowned at the conclusion of me being stuck, but *Curiosity* shouted after him:

'Chris! When you communicate with other people in this manner, do you do it because you want to create a distance?'

'Why else would I do it? They don't understand a single normal word anyway,' he replied without turning back and I gaped at the confident statement.

'Just to let you know, no observations on gesture clusters are applicable to me, because...' The door slammed, so I couldn't finish.

God, is everyone around Victor so rude!? I guess today is my lucky day though. I am sober now, and I found a roommate, too. Having to report to grandad like a soldier would be too much right now.

---

[13] *A combination of signals that the body unconsciously transmits. The term was introduced by Allan Pease in his book "Body Language" - author's notes.*

I sighed, slightly relieved, and decided to leave the credit company documents for later. I focused on the papers from the financier because of the upcoming appointment with him. Again, it was too irritating to have to go through the chaotic information on the transactions. I could clearly see that it lacked the required data for an accurate analysis. I was to meet him in two hours, and I intended to fill in all the gaps. I had insisted firmly—almost tortured him—so I was expecting him to give me the original papers. At school, maths had been like abuse for me, because there wasn't a teacher who could understand it in a way that was acceptable for my brain. I had learned to juggle with numbers, formulae and geometry on my own. It was my entertainment. Now it was relaxing to create complex tables for university projects, and I could instantly find even one wrong number in my colleagues' tables. The same happened with letters and commas in books, and also with people. As if my eyes were created with the sole purpose of seeing mistakes, and when there were any, the crazy part of my mind glowed insistently, even if it didn't quite understand the specific matter.

On our way to the financier, Toma turned the volume to the max again. He took breaths to speak numerous times, yet remained silent. My mind kept replaying snippets of my conversation with Victor, and I kept sighing loudly. I was making a pile of arguments to support the conclusion that I should stay away from him, his expectations, and the side effects that came with him. However, some other part of me defected and was stubbornly investigating the possibility of my conclusions being inaccurate. I could even detect some irrational hope that I could be entirely wrong. That utterly annoyed me.

When I entered the house, I was tense, with a headache from the confusion in my mind. The financier's facial expressions immediately signalled to me that he was nervous as well. He greeted me coldly, shoving a giant pile of documents under my nose:

'Wow, this is as tall as the building itself,' I made an unsuccessful effort to lighten the atmosphere, but he grimaced.

'Too many bosses these days. I have to report to a woman now! Hurry up, I can't wait around all day!' He sucked on a stinky cigarette.

The pile contained several payment bills, followed by financial statements, contracts, and other original papers. I read the pages diagonally to sort things out. Switching myself off from everything around, I hurled my mind into a state of hyper-concentration. I was processing the information at a speed that always amazed people, and the financier's grumbling was barely audible to me. I had examined the numbers so many times already that I could recite the entire account in one breath. All inaccuracies in his tables glowed in the shape of spots. Costs were included in the "other" column, or they were listed as internal transfers to various companies. Every time I had called him for clarifications, he had said that there was a mistake, but the original documents left him with no excuse. I hadn't even reached the middle, and the pile I was making of suspicious papers was already too large. I recognised the Panamanian flag on most of them.

Thank God I'm good at languages. They might prove to be useful.

Reason and *Knowledge* nodded smugly. I started reading the content. I put aside payments with grounds that had nothing to do with the expected expenses. The money had been transferred between several companies. The suspicious guy was trying to get me to approve almost half a million of misused spending.

He was closely watching what I was doing. All of a sudden, he grabbed two sheets from the table and crushed them loudly in his fist. I pretended not to notice and, instead, decided that the wisest thing to do was leave with the rest of the papers. Everything was clear to me already, and those two notes were insignificant. The money had been circulating across four companies. It had reached the firm that had bought the estates, then it had been transferred to other three enterprises, then the payments were made from there. I defined the pattern as annoyingly simple. Its regularity was rhythmic and obvious.

'There's too much information, there's no point in wasting your time. I will go through all the papers and we'll discuss everything tomorrow,' I looked at him with undisguised ridicule of the simple scheme he had struggled to come up with. *Reason* confirmed that my judgement to immediately inform Victor was accurate.

The financier shot his sly eyes at me from across the table. He was examining my reactions.

'What am I supposed to wait for? What do you even understand, that you can examine until tomorrow?' Slobber flew from his mouth.

He was tossing the papers between his fingers, flooding me with contempt. *Pride* stood up and stretched her long spine, as if taking a yoga position. I inhaled, trying to remain calm and push *Rage* to the back, but he started swirling behind my staring, emotionless eyes. The mixture of reality's slaps from the morning and this attitude right now was thickening as if in a pressure cooker.

'You know? There's nothing to wait for! There's no need for you to destroy documents, either. My photographic memory is impressive. I can recall every punctuation mark, every line, every colour. "Yacht equipment". Would you like me to recite the bank account, the recipient, the number, the date? Think we can sail at the office?' I was deliberately teasing him now.

'What are you talking about?' He was still impudent but drops of sweat ran down his forehead.

'A bracelet. Rose gold. 3.5 carat diamond. Purchased seven days ago. Does it go with the boat, or is it your way to hook up with shadows? I can keep going...' *Contempt* flashed a torch at him through my eyes. He was sweating all over.

In fact, I was no longer interested in the foul payments. Everything was clear. While going through the papers, though, a bright red line in my mind crossed some of the documents. I found a pattern. Equal amounts of cash had come from recurring companies before splitting, and Victor's money had disappeared in an unknown direction. The numbers were huge, and it was likely a much more sustainable theft than the one I had already discovered. I couldn't pinpoint the sequence and the result, because there weren't the full documents, and the data were incomplete.

Reason was muttering, pointing to the door:

Go to Victor! It's up to him to evaluate and decide now. Not another word! We don't have to prove ourselves to this idiot!

I grabbed the papers, breathing to find my balance and keep my thoughts behind my teeth, when the financier started yelling:

'These are my documents, for my personal account, that's why I crushed them. I put them there by mistake! What is this bullshit?'

His comical falsetto irritated me. My mouth twisted mockingly.

'Seriously? Why is everybody underestimating me? You're insulting my intellect with these absurd, ridiculous claims. It's all clear!' I snapped before heading to the door.

'Don't you dare tell anyone this, or I'll destroy you! You got that? Before, he was only doing you stupid bitches, and now what? A new fetish? Listen to me, doll! Victor might be having fun with you, and you might be mistaken that you're special, but you are not. He will replace you for another toy soon and you won't have his protection anymore. You're playing damn smart, aren't you? Well, be smart about your future situation then!' He kept yelling at my back. When I turned around, his face was even more distorted than before.

Tall and slender, *Pride* stood up. *Justice* nodded at her, pounding on the drum of madness. An invisible cork popped between two of my breaths. Nothing could hold *Rage* back anymore. His disdain for the pathetic man erupted in a powerful blow. I was overcome by the need to become arrogant and spill *the Monster*'s bile out. I needed balance. Even bad things need to be balanced.

Reason took shelter, his square head between his hands. The financier's words ignited my fire, his assumption provoked me, and I gave in. My judgement was not wise at all, but it was well-deserved. I approached the jerk menacingly, staring at him with my nastiest stomach-twisting gaze. He seemed to be getting the creeps, and I enjoyed his squirming face. In a low voice, I spoke clearly, only centimetres away from his foul breath.

'I haven't mistaken myself as special. I'm absolutely extraordinary, you fool! Maybe I am not normal, but I am millions of brain cells away from your ordinary, square perceptions. A few seconds were enough for me to trace your pathetic embezzlement scheme, and a few minutes are enough to systematise the data and even calculate the probabilities, if necessary. You know what's even more pathetic? You've spent numerous sleepless nights torturing your weak brain to find a way. And I can see it in the blink of an eye—an error, a defect, a mistake and a red line simply glows in my mind. You became clear to me in a few seconds. How do you want me to recite it for you: dates, accounts, from which company to which other? I can reduce your stupid little scheme to one simple sentence. It's just as pathetic as you are. I wouldn't know whether Victor is having fun with me, but you don't even know what hilarious fun I'm having with your absurd threats. In fact, I can't wait to see what will happen to you when I describe everything to him in detail. That's what I will recommend: be smart about your future situation!'

'Whore! Don't threaten me, or I'll...' he stammered, but I interrupted him rudely.

'Oh! Let's speak in numbers, that's what you work with—or rather, mock—after all. 4 minutes and 32 seconds—that's all I needed for your scheme. That's exactly how smart you are, and that's exactly how extraordinary I am. An irritating even number if you convert it into seconds. Is that good for a whore?' I kept speaking in an even voice, while sweat and red blotches were emerging from his bald head. I enjoyed his reaction; my lips stretched into a contemptuous smile.

'What kind of a freak are you!? Crazy whore!' His shouts slammed into my laughter. He snatched at my neck, incensed, but I didn't even twitch.

'"Freak" and "crazy"—correct! A "whore"—not really. Now I advise you to get your trembling, sweaty hand off me. I'm already experienced in dealing with sweaty hands, even when they're put in more inappropriate places, so you certainly don't impress me!' I was staring at him, twisting him, and his mouth distorted with viciousness.

Attracted by the commotion, Toma stormed in. His body bulged up and he became furious, clenching his fists.

'If you plan to use those fingers again, let go of her immediately!' He walked toward us, and the jerk stepped to the nearest corner. I laughed impudently, then we headed to the car.

'Wait, damn it! Come back, we'll sort things out,' the financier squealed.

'Idiot! You'll sort things with someone else. That's what you need to think about now!' The words came from my back, and I was pretty sure he cursed at me in Spanish, or maybe French. He followed us to the door, but Toma's second warning look made him stop.

'Screw you, you freak! Wait and see what happens to you if you tell him this bullshit!' The shrieks of the pathetic man escorted us to the car, but he didn't deserve any more replies. What he got was my raised middle finger.

'How can he be that distorted! Wretched impudent jerk!' I grumbled.

'He's stealing, isn't he?' Toma asked.

'Damn right! Let me explain how elementary his scheme is! It's even weird... The money from one company...' *Contempt* was flowing from my mouth.

'No, no, no! You're giving me a headache!' He sighed, spreading his hand in front of my face. 'They all try. Don't get mad and don't judge them, they just want more.'

'More? They work for a huge businessman who is also the president of the goddamn country, whilst earning more than enough. They got the chance for something more—a chance thousands of people crave—they got trust and high-level positions! They probably have more money than anyone could ever spend. Aren't they afraid that he might catch them? It lacks logic, Toma! What more could they possibly want?'

'I think they even play together. I just don't know who is connected. This guy got hooked on poker and on some gorgeous, slippery chick. This combination leads to no good. We're talking about a lot of money, and money has this weird quality: it's never enough.'

'God, the abominations of the general reality never cease to amaze me!' I shook my head, and *Reason* hissed from his shelter:

Knowledge has already explained it to you. Greed is not based on logic, and it is widespread. You still don't get it? You still need exact terms? Listen to Knowledge, at least!

I grimaced at him. Toma looked at me with suspicion, but I continued:

'You must tell Victor right now. I couldn't hold it, I couldn't pretend, and who knows what that jerk will come up with to hide the truth. Not that he's very inventive, but still...'

'I must tell Victor?' He laughed out loud. 'You must. I'm supposed to take care of you. You're supposed to take care of that shit. It's your responsibility.'

'We were there together, and you've been with Victor "all your life". You are going to explain! I don't want to talk to him right now!' I snapped at his reproachful gaze.

'Didn't I say like a hundred of times that Victor should be your boss and nothing more? You did the opposite. I told you to do your job strictly— now you don't want to do this anymore. Could you stop confusing both things, Nia? Do you even listen to what people say?' He was shouting.

'Spare me the "I told you so" speech, please! It's obvious—I messed up. This is the situation now, but that moron and his embezzlement is none of my business. I had to work on the estates deal, and I did. I did my job strictly.'

'Yeah! That's what you think!' The words rolled like a clumsy skier down a steep slope.

I gaped, but before being able to say "what", he braked abruptly and my head bumped painfully into the glove compartment. There was a bang, then the sound of a horn, followed by the whistling of brakes. White smoke surrounded me. Sharp pain pierced my nose. I was feeling about for the door handle, stifled by a disgusting stink. The airbags were full of something that I was unfortunate enough to smell.

Probably distracted by the conversation and the words that he didn't want to say, Toma had stepped on the brakes, not properly judging the distance to the car behind us. It had hit our jeep, hurling it into a bollard, which had at least saved us from flying into the gorge. Realising that he had hit us from behind and was in violation, the other driver fled at top speed. The idiot didn't even bother to check if we were alive.

Toma didn't like using a seat belt. Despite my constant lectures on road safety, he had rigged a plastic device to drown out the annoying beeping. I guess people of his generation were not irradiated enough with the message that belts save lives. He protruded like a nail from the front window, blood dripping fast from his head.

In the jeep, there was an emergency hammer for breaking the windows. I had noticed it the first day and *Curiosity* had made me investigate what it was. I grabbed it, climbed on the bonnet, and started hitting the window. *Knowledge* was rummaging through an old pile in my head full of unnecessary facts. He explained that, due to security measures, windshields crack without breaking. That's exactly what happened. I removed the windshield from the seals, minding not to take Toma's head off with it. In fact, keeping his head in place proved to be a serious challenge for my level of strength. Good old adrenaline did the job, though.

I was amazed that I managed to push Toma back in a normal driving position on my second attempt. His heart rate was normal, but my slaps didn't wake him up. I wrapped my sweater around the wound on his shoulder. It got soaked in blood too quickly and I was seriously concerned. I sat on his lap but could barely reach the pedals; I couldn't bend his huge legs to move the seat close enough for my gnomish height. Twisting myself in an awkward position, and following a short struggle with the buttons, I started the car and took a deep breath to prepare myself for driving.

'Shit! Stupid car! There's one pedal missing,' I searched in front of my sneakers for a place to put my left foot. 'OK, it can't be that complicated to do it with two pedals, if I can do it with three. Toma, if we make it to the hospital alive, you must teach me how to drive better.'

I was muttering aloud while he was still unconscious and silent. Clumsily, I drove the huge jeep down the narrow road. *Knowledge* started murmuring about arteries and cutting wounds, but I yelled at him to shut up. The stress was already enough. The nearest hospital was at the edge of the city, 20 minutes of driving away. My driving was going to take longer, so I focused. I probably should have informed Victor that Toma was injured. Or perhaps my defected part was just looking for an excuse to call him. My phone was too far, in my bag on the back seat, so I took Toma's antique phone with actual buttons. There was an outgoing call to a contact with the letter "V" only, but no one was answering. I was just about to hang up when a sexy female voice, unbearable because of the high volume of the phone, pierced me:

'Hello, Toma! He's on a conference call and I can't put you through right now.'

'Umm, hello. It's not Toma,' I was driving erratically along the turns, stunned by the beautiful voice of the women. I wondered what to explain and whether I should even speak to her.

'Nia, is that you?'

'Who's asking?' I snapped.

'I am Mr. Kaov's personal assistant. His personal phone transfers to mine. I know that Toma is with you. I was going to call you later about the issue of finding you a flat. Is everything OK?' the sickly-sweet spite with which she emphasised the word "personal" was highly annoying. In my imagination, she looked like the shadows and that irritated me even more. The prickly sea urchin took position and thrust a painful thorn in my navel. *Reason* decisively stroked his head and hissed at it:

Now I am definitely killing you! With arguments! His shadows are not our business. Don't you dare to harass us anymore!

I caught my breath after the piercing, ignored the fight in my head and continued rudely:

'All right, all right. It's Nia. I don't care who you are. There's no need for you to call me about the flat. The matter is settled. Toma and I had a car accident, and we are on our way to the hospital. I decided it'd be reasonable to inform Mr. Kaov about that. I have to go now because I'm driving and I am way too unskilled. Bye!'

I arrived surprisingly fast, not managing to stop smoothly. I had no windshield and the brakes whistled. The doctors in front of the hospital must have been startled to say the least; I almost drove the car into the emergency room.

'Fucking vehicle, it won't stop!' I cursed as I got off the seat. Off Toma's lap, I mean. 'Well, apparently, I can't take him out on my own!' I shouted at the gaping men, because none of them moved.

'We're coming,' two paramedics and a doctor hurried with a stretcher. 'What happened?'

'We got hit from behind. He wasn't buckled up and slammed into the windshield. His heart rate is normal, but he hasn't regained full consciousness, only muttering a few times. I did what I could to press the wound but he lost a serious amount of blood.'

I was doing my best to give accurate information to the doctor, who stared at me in amazement, as I kept tapping my foot. After a moment, he gathered himself and turned his attention to Toma. He got two more men to help. They headed to the emergency room, out of my sight. I was about to follow them, but a young female doctor grabbed my shoulder to stop me.

'Are you all right? Come with me, I must see.'

'I'm OK. I want to check on him.'

'You can't go in the ER and I must insist that I see you. Your face is covered in blood, you may have a concussion. I must report this to the police, too. What are these injuries? There are scratches all over you,' her insistent voice alarmed me. 'Miss, you can tell me if you need help,' she directed a compassionate yet decisive gaze at me. 'I volunteer at a support centre. There's nothing to be afraid or ashamed of, you can just tell me everything. There are people who can take care of you.'

'No, no! This is from the other day,' I felt the scratches on my face, and she gaped. My mind evaluated the suspicious situation from the side. 'I'm OK, doctor, really. This week was just weird, let's put it that way. We had a car accident, and that's all. Everything is all fine, even if it all sounds crazy to you,' *Confidence* took control and reassured the doctor that I was not a victim of violence, kidnapping, or whatever she was thinking.

The doctor carefully treated my wounds. Fortunately, there was nothing serious, but she insisted that we should do a scan. She went to see if the machine was available and, when she came back, she told me that Toma was all right. I calmed down. They were going to let me see him in half an hour, because they had sedated him to sew the wound. While she was explaining, two police officers appeared in the doorframe behind her. My intuition rang a loud alarm, and the expressions on their faces confirmed that something was wrong.

'You're coming with me!' An overweight police officer stared at me impudently.

'That's not possible! The patient is to stay under medical supervision. Identify yourself, please!' The doctor argued, standing in his way. He pushed her away to storm in. 'What are you doing? You can't just walk in here. I am sick of your entitlement. Get out of my office right now!'

'Stay away from this, doctor! We came on a signal,' he lisped menacingly before me.

Since I had attended the protests against the old, supposedly non-communist government, I knew my rights by heart. Volunteering lawyers recited legal articles and paragraphs at the squares. The law enforcement officers didn't comply with them, but I had memorised everything nevertheless. In my opinion, policemen were like an Encyclopaedia of Anti-logic and I had argued with armed officers many times, but, strangely indeed, I had never been arrested before.

'If you're thinking of detaining me, I'm not going anywhere without reasonable grounds. I want a lawyer, too!' I snapped, my nose up in the air.

'And do you know what resisting arrest means? Stop playing smart, go!' He twisted my wrist violently.

'On what grounds are you arresting me?' I hissed, but as expected, he didn't pay any attention.

'Think I'm gonna give you explanations?' He wrenched my shoulder back, then snapped the handcuffs shut.

'You're overstepping your rights and exercising excessive force, officer! I weigh 48 kilos. I am a woman and only a woman can arrest me,' I was only certain that this applied to searching women, but still I decided to try my luck. Unsuccessfully. I wanted to pull myself away, but, knowing this would justify his actions, I managed to restrain myself. Instead, I kept yelling with every step as he pushed me to walk on. 'Don't forget that you're criminally liable and I will definitely seek my rights! Tell me your name and your official number! This is absurd! Complete lawlessness and police arbitrariness here! You are a swarm of slackers and rascals!'

He snorted as he pushed me into the patrol car. I found myself in the back seat, behind metal bars. The door had no handles and it stank of cigarette butts in there.

Why do these scumbags smoke in the state cars we pay for?

I had to listen to an annoying tirade on the way. The officer was explaining that it had not been like this before. All modern rights were bullshit. Before, two slaps had been enough to put garbage in its place. The same went for women. This conclusion was followed by my opinion about him, his life philosophy, and the general reality. His eardrums probably didn't enjoy all that, nor did they enjoy the decibels of my insults.

φ

He shoved me into a narrow, stinky cell, without explanation and with a kick. I was waiting for claustrophobia to attack me, and I had just finished counting the scribbles on the wall, when a fat and distorted female officer walked in.

'So you snap at my colleague, you know your rights, and you were threatening him? Is that so, you whore?' She hissed in an unpleasant country dialect, tapping her palm with a baton.

'There are both accurate and inaccurate claims in your question. I will point them out to make your life easier. Inaccurate: I was not threatening anybody, and I don't meet the definition of a whore. If you insist on insulting me, just use another word. I'm tired of this one. Accurate: I snapped, and I know my rights perfectly well, including the right to call a lawyer and the fact that my arrest was absolutely unlawful. Don't come at me in this threatening manner, if you please, because there are always cameras in custody cells. And I intend to request the recording when I take you to court, officer!' My eyes were trying to stomach-twist her, not very successfully, from behind my barrier. *Pride* was boasting, but *Fear* made my legs shake.

'Sometimes the power goes off, you piece of trash. So you'd better think twice about threatening...' Before she finished, the baton hit me so hard that I saw stars.

'Don't you dare hit me, you pathetic creep!' The pain made me sick. I grabbed the bars with one hand and *Rage* waved my other hand in a small fist. *Malice* was dreaming of shovels.

Then there was a loud slap, and the metallic taste of blood flooded my mouth.

'Leave the baton and fight, dirty orc! I'm gonna beat the shit out of you!' I cried at the top of my voice, splashes of scarlet saliva flying at her greasy face.

It took her a second to knock me to the ground with a number of blows, then she continued pummelling my back. Random hits peppered my hips. Stunned, I curled up in a ball to protect myself. She was still beating me viciously when a hysterical male voice interrupted her:

'Stop! Stop right now and switch the camera on! The boss is here. Move! Move! We're in big trouble! Damn, how...?' He and the rest of his words trailed away.

I peered between my hands, ready to protect my head from some belated blow. The orc woman ran away. At the end of the corridor, someone was shaking the male officer by his collar. I couldn't hear what they were saying. Figures rushed through the door and marched towards me. I supposed, happily, that Toma had found me again and he had even called a lawyer. One of the silhouettes was yelling and as the group approached me, the words became distinct.

'...make sure they don't have a job anymore! What's this, damn it? Everyone commands whatever they like?'

'This was a huge misunderstanding! I am terribly sorry! I will sort everything out!' Someone was twisting next to the group, trying to shove himself between the others.

Three sturdy guys walked forward and commanded everybody to leave. A young officer was running in small steps next to them. His shaky hands unlocked the cell, then he fled through the same door through which the other officers had disappeared. Unwrapping the orb that I had become, I tried to stand up but the baton had done its job well, so I remained on my knees. The men stepped away and my jaw dropped when Victor emerged behind them. I blinked foolishly through a stream of blood. Next to him I recognised the security guard who always stood closest to him. Frowning, the guard reached out to help me to my feet.

'Don't touch her!' Victor grabbed his wrist and the guy frowned even more deeply.

I narrowed my eyes, but in my mind, I thanked him for sparing me a touch by a stranger. I had experienced enough stress already. In one motion, he took me in his arms and carried me through a narrow, dark corridor.

'Half a day, Nia! Half a fucking day, and you drove me crazy again!' He hissed.

'I didn't do any...' I muttered but he wouldn't let me finish.

'Shut up, Nia! Shut this fucking mouth up!' He clenched his jaw, struggling not to yell.

The cars of the motorcade were lined up like black beads by the back entrance of the shabby police station. Next to each car, there was a man with the expressionless face of a mummy looking like the bad guys from "The Matrix". The president motioned for the guard with him to open the back door of one of the jeeps, then he quickly took the driver's seat. Victor bustled me in the car rudely and I sensed the consequences of the baton on my back. He walked around the car and sat down next to me. A young boy took the empty seat in the font.

'Get out!' Victor's voice shocked the boy.

'Out, out!' The security guard muttered and the door closed as he took off.

'What are you doing? Tell me what the hell are you doing again?' Victor yelled, leaning centimetres away from my face. 'What, Nia?' Completely mad, he took hold of my face. It was probably his expression, or the energy that exploded, but for the first time *Fear* took over me while I was under Victor. I slipped down. The car was speeding. I caught myself counting the flashing lights of the strobe on the dashboard.

3 red, 2 blue, 3 blue, 2 red.

'Stop counting and look at me!' His voice exploded.

Reason was shaking:

How does he know that we're counting? Did we do it aloud? Is he spying on us even here?

'Don't yell at me!' I snapped, though quietly. 'I didn't do anything. Some idiot hit us, Toma was injured, and I drove him to the hospital. Then a police officer took me into custody, and then a crazy orc woman with issues beat me up. That's all! Even though they are an Encyclopaedia of Anti-logic, it was...'

'He took you to custody?' He interrupted me, barely controlling his breath. 'Just like that? Because you didn't do anything? What did I tell you about your judgement? What did I say about your decisions and the need to control yourself? You provoked the financier, didn't you? Provoked him, humiliated him, and who knows what else. You didn't even think twice. Did you, Nia?'

'Absolute bullshit! He was arrogant and rude, he was underestimating and humiliating me. All I said was the truth, only with some extra details. It's not my problem that he can't take it. Or perhaps it's my fault again, according to your insane standards?' I hissed under his nose.

'I should've left you to spend the night in custody, so you will know what considering the risks means from now on. Reckless actions have consequences, Nia! Your "truth" doesn't matter. You don't control yourself!'

'What's there to control? I didn't say anything inaccurate. Don't yell at me like that!'

'I will yell, because when something is explained to you in a normal way, there is no result! You don't listen. What did you think he'd do, Nia? You weren't hit by some random idiot; you were hit by HIS idiot. A fucking bollard saved you both from your absurd actions. They took you into custody also because of him. He wanted to scare you. Your judgement was unacceptable! Again! You couldn't just zip it and leave, could you? Who knows what you said to make him that mad. Where is your logic, your rationality now? There was not one argument for you to provoke him, not even one, and you know it!' He kept shouting.

I cradled my knees, biting my lip. Patting my fingers in an odd rhythm, I tried to muffle his new burst of rude accusations. *Justice* and *Pride* moved their bowed heads in sync with the rhythm. *Reason* was repeating that he had warned me, and I had ignored him again, but *Pride* snapped at him. There hadn't been any reasons or arguments for me to guess that the jerk would send someone to hit us, or that he would set me up in custody.

Victor positioned himself on the seat with his legs on either side of me. Leaning over me, he was wiping the blood off my face with a handkerchief. I pulled away because it stung, but he didn't stop. Annoyed, I pushed his hand and stared at him with the intention to stomach-twist him, but there was animal madness boiling in his eyes.

'No one can do this to you! No one! I'm not going to see you like this ever again! I'm not going to see you like this ever again! I'm not...!' Dozens of veins bulged on his neck. He swung his hand wildly. His fist landed on the back of my seat, next to my ear, and I instinctively squeezed my eyes.

'Don't you dare!' I shrieked. The touch of his palm opened my eyelids.

'Damn, what's wrong with you today? You've been acting crazy since morning. How could you think that I'd hurt you! Me?'

'You look scary! And you're acting very weird, Victor. What's wrong with you?' I yelled under him.

'You're coming up with one crazy thing after the other! You're not listening, you're not complying, I can't control you. You're driving me crazy! Out of my mind! Do you realise that? You must stop, or I'll settle the issue regardless of your opinion!'

I examined his gaze in bewilderment. As if these eyes belonged to somebody else. A new personality was storming behind them, enraged and unscrupulous, without a trace of restraint or composure. Madness. There was wild madness in his irises now.

NINE

The driver sped through the estate entrance and braked in front of the president's house. Victor took me in his arms, out of the car, and up the stairs. He went straight to his ensuite bathroom and began to nervously pull the clothes off me. Without saying a word, he stripped me to full nakedness and placed me in the bathtub in a sitting position. I hugged my knees to my chest.

'It's not the right time for sex,' I murmured without even looking at him. 'See, sometimes your judgement is wrong, too.'

He snorted, took his coat off and rolled up the sleeves of his white shirt. He roughly unfolded my bent arms and legs. He examined every centimetre of my skin, not paying any interest to my nudity. He carefully washed the blood from my cheeks, then continued to the back. He applied soap, then showered me, over and over again, as if in a trance, as if he was trying to drown the bruises away.

Finally, he wrapped me in a towel and laid me on the king-size bed. With his eyes searching my face, he arranged the pillows under my head and sat down on the edge of the bed. The expression of a stone statue was back. He had already gained control over his voice:

'My assistant decided not to interrupt me. Then Toma called, inadequate and hysterical. You're gonna give him a heart attack one of these days. A doctor at the ER woke him up with the information that you were arrested. She wrote down the number of the patrol car. It didn't take long for me to figure out everything else.'

He turned me on my stomach, pulled the towel away and ran his hand over my back. I twisted in sharp pain under his touch.

'Christ Nia, why don't you ever listen!' His fingers traced the bruises. That made me press myself to the bed. 'One hundred people are needed for you: one will mind that you don't dig into electricity, and the other ninety-nine will stay alert for your next completely illogical decision. Maybe you will stop driving me crazy this way. You've been doing this since early morning,' he snorted, then got up. 'The doc will be here in a minute!' He slammed the door behind his back.

I was still blinking in the pillow when the doctor entered the room. It was the same woman who had sedated me with whoever knows what after my forest experience. I remembered that I had forgotten to visit her in the morning. One of the housekeepers came in with her. She put a bottle of some cream on the bedside table and tiptoed out.

'Hello, Nia! Tell me what happened in custody. Everything. A conversation between doctor and patient is confidential. You can trust me,' she sat down next to me with a compassionate look in her eyes, but I could see a suspicious spark there, too.

How come the words "you can trust me" always evoke absolute doubt? Maybe it's just me.

'The same that happens to most people who end up there. The results are visible on my back,' I replied cautiously.

'I know they beat you. Unfortunately, sexual assault is not uncommon in custody too, and you must tell me if something like that happened to you,' she explained with sympathy, clutching my hand.

'No, dear, all they did was beat me!' I snapped, pulling my hand away.

'Let me see the injuries,' she was watching me firmly, touching my cheekbones, and the situation became even more unpleasant to me. 'I was expecting you earlier today, but you didn't show up. Don't treat yourself irresponsibly. Unless you're aiming at something else...' That spark again. I took a breath, my eyebrows raised at the hint, but she interrupted me: 'You must take this contraceptive now, and the pills are to be taken daily.'

While I was struggling to swallow the pill, she opened her doctor's case. I gaped at the dreadful instruments, syringes, and all sorts of horrors.

'I'm going to examine you thoroughly now, just to make sure you're telling me everything about the arrest. It's for your own good!'

'No way!' I pulled the blanket up to my nose, but she tried to remove it. 'There's nothing to be afraid of!'

'I don't want this!' Her attitude, her doctor's case, or maybe her hints, were the last drop that my nervous system could take for the day. I shouted: 'Get out and don't touch me! You can't touch me! Get your hands off me!'

'Behave yourself, girl. It's just a routine examination!' She scorned me but pulled away.

'Leave her! Wait downstairs. I'll call for you if you're needed!' Victor's inappropriate timbre startled her from the door. The doctor was offended. She walked out, her nose high in the air.

'Why are you all harassing me? Why doesn't anybody understand what I'm saying? You're supposed to be normal people! And what's with the hints? What do you take me for—you and everybody around you? Why did you even bring me here again, Victor?'

'Stop yelling. No one will harass you.'

He sat down next to me and took hold of my chin.

'Relax! All I want is to take care of you. Everything's fine,' his voice was soft and calm.

'I know that everything's fine. Apparently, you're the one who doesn't. Why would I need care? Someone beat me up—big deal. I'm not the first one to have this at the arrests. They do whatever they want with whoever they want,' I explained, irritated. He turned me on my stomach again, moving my hair to one side.

'I know, Nia. I know this better than you. Enough now! Calm down!'

'Well, do something about it if you know so well, instead of shouting at me and blaming me again!' I kept raging under his relaxing caress.

A pleasant smell of herbs filled my nose. My skin prickled from the cool cream that Victor was carefully applying to the baton traces on my back.

'The arnica will heal them in a couple of days. There will be no scars left,' he whispered. The cold ointment was not the only cause of the shivers running down my spine. Heat rushed under his gentle touch. It spread throughout my body, making it hot.

'How do you know that?' I snapped.

'I'm not in the mood for questions,' his voice hardened, and I was silent for a while.

'You know what, I don't even care. As soon as *Fear* removes the needles from his list, I will tattoo my back all over. This way I won't have to bear the scars of the orc and the evil idiot's spite. Some damn creatures inhabit the general reality, don't they!' I closed my eyes to see the tattoo that I had always imagined.

'Your conclusions truly amaze me. Nia, if I told you now that I won't allow any changes on your skin, you'd find all the arguments to get tattooed to the last centimetre of you, wouldn't you?'

'This question is either not OK, or I don't understand it correctly. Most probably, you're not listening again. I don't intend to tattoo every centimetre of myself, and what does it have to do with you anyway? I want only one tattoo, on my entire back. It's lived long in my head,' I clarified, my mind immersed in the image. 'A full-length angel with folded wings; they reach all the way to its feet. It's standing in the middle of something like a cemetery, holding a...'

'...sword, pointed at the ground,' we said that simultaneously, and I gaped at the bedsheet.

'What? Have you seen it somewhere?' I turned my questioning eyes on him.

'I don't get to see it much,' he smiled grimly.

As he turned his back on me and took his shirt off, my jaw dropped. The angel was magnificent. Its wings—so exquisite, as if they were about to flutter. They fell around the figure and every feather, every detail, was perfectly drawn. The hooded face was looking down, so I couldn't see it. The gentle hands that were holding the sword made me think that it was a woman. The annoying sea urchin pierced me, but *Reason* immediately scolded it:

Angels are genderless. Hold your spikes back, Jealousy! In this head here, there is no room for inaccuracies.

I gazed at the words next to the angel's heart, written in a small, winding font. The letters were Latin, yet I couldn't read what they said. The dark background was full of twisted, intricate elements that swirled like flames. They embraced Victor, sliding to his stomach and chest—the part that I had seen already.

I thought about the moments when he had been shirtless, wondering how I had missed the angel. Sudden heat flooded me.

When he was naked, he was always over me, behind me, and once in profile.
The memory of the positions and the sensations shot like electricity that instantly struck my groin. Victor was right: whenever he was in me, everything was OK and our communication was easy, but there was more. In his arms, it was nice, comfortable, and warm. Something like happiness? I swallowed dryly as I shook my head.

'Well now this is weird. How did my tattoo end up on your back?' I whispered, gazing in bewilderment at the image that looked almost the same as the one in my head.

'There are even more weird things, Nia.'

'How come you're so tattooed? Isn't that inappropriate? You are "special", after all, you're on the peak, and a president,' I was overwhelmed, examining the ink tracks. The tips of my fingers touched the wings and as if static electricity struck me. It prickled my index finger and I blinked.

'For the most part of my life, I was not a president, so don't define me according to my position! A shirt is enough to make me look suitable for the world and, beneath it, I can be myself!' His timbre swirled the electricity in my body as I breathed in the captivating smell of musk.

Lust had finished her therapy and now she moved, sending a loud exhale out of my lips. It hit his skin and I enjoyed the subtle shivers it provoked. However, Victor abruptly put his shirt on and pointed his firm irises on me. He was watching me in silence, rummaging through my mind.

'That look again. I understand its consequences, but you don't. You prevent me from taking care of them and of you. You come up with crazy conclusions, you challenge my decisions, you don't listen to me, you push me away, you make me mad, and now you're provoking me again. What do you want from me, Nia? I want you to be as clear and firm as you were this morning,' the unfamiliar strange personality that shone in his eyes enjoyed making me squirm.

'I don't want anything! What would I want from you, of all people? I already told you: I don't mind the sex, it's just that everything else is unacceptable. What more am I supposed to be clear about?'

'Define clearly the distance you expect me to keep, for example. Then, define when you would want me to sleep with you, and when you would want me to get out or leave you alone,' his new personality was intentionally teasing me, and it succeeded.

'I'm naked in your room again, Victor—it's not a big distance, to be honest. What's there to explain more? You brought me here, damn it! I didn't ask for this and I can't understand what you want with this unbearable tone of your voice,' I looked at him from behind the blanket.

'I want you to understand that your behaviour makes me explode! I want you to understand what it means to control your behaviour.'

'I do control it. It's just that...'

He interrupted me rudely, leaning over my nose:

'Nia, you can't even comprehend the meaning of this word control. And I doubt I could change that, no matter how much I explain. The only thing you know about control is how to challenge mine all the time,' his influence on me from this distance was biting.

I gulped. Victor stared at the consequence-bearing look that boomed in my eyes. His irises darkened.

'Let us clarify the meaning by using an alternative approach. That's all I have wanted since the morning.'

An insane spark shone in the insatiable blue making my heart race. When he kissed me, I sucked on my drug. I would have even let him read to me from a thesaurus, if that was what he demanded at that moment. I would let him go through the pages while doing me, as long as he would get inside me. He carefully placed my back on the bed, propped my head on the pillows, gathered my hair in his hand and arranged it to the side. He pulled the blanket away, not taking his eyes off the mad desire in mine. He spread my legs apart, one by one. He folded them, gluing my feet to the bed. Kneeling between them, he examined me through the flames, but with a seemingly cool expression. He ran his fingers from my ankles to my thighs, then he stopped a centimetre away from my groin. He leaned over and his scent sank into my senses. He shoved my wrists under my head, as if I was about to do sit-ups. I smiled and took them out in anticipation, then I slid them down his neck. I grabbed him, biting my lip.

'I intend to verify the assertion that you can control yourself. After all, you want to express yourself accurately so that people can understand you,' he whispered in my ear, moving his fingers a millimetre away from my skin. 'Now put your hands back where I placed them.'

'Why?' I raised my eyebrows in wonder.

'No more questions, Nia. And no more discussions today,' he took one of my wrists to his lips and bit it. 'You won't move! You will close your eyes and be quiet.'

'What do you mean I won't move? This is a joint process of the nervous and muscular systems. Anatomy: motor reflexes and impulses. And why...'

While I was speaking, he pulled something out of the bedside table. He interrupted me, sliding two fingers over my tongue. He gently opened my mouth to place some kind of a ball inside. I found it smooth and not exactly tasty. Without taking his burning irises off me, he fastened the leather band, which held the ball, on the back of my neck.

'There's really nothing to verify about your mouth. It's obvious that you can't control it,' he smiled and stroked my cheekbone as I gaped. 'When I bought this for you, I had no idea that it'd be useful for a lesson in linguistic semantics,' his irises glistened and stood out even more on his symmetrical face. 'I'm still waiting for you to put your hands where I placed them. Let me say it again: I'm not patient at all!'

I hesitantly loosened the grip of my hands on his neck while examining his unreadable face. He placed them carefully back behind my head. Just as carefully, he touched every part of my body to check how the muscles felt. He ran his lips over my breasts, licking the nipples in circles. He bit them, then bit the skin on my belly. My throat vibrated and a hoarse, low tone escaped under the ball. He lifted my butt to shove a pillow under it. I propped myself up, even more questions in my eyes.

'This is the last time I'm telling you: don't move!' I lay back and his kisses drew circles around my navel.

His fingertips walked around my thighs. His lips made the moss on my belly stand up as he descended. I was already familiar with his skills in driving me crazy with his fingers, but I found the idea of having his tongue down there even more shocking than his methods in linguistic semantics. My hands shot to his neck, trying to pull it away, and my legs closed. He spread them wide apart in one motion. Leaning over me, he whispered:

'Obviously you can't control your hands, either,' he pulled something else out of the drawer, then pressed my wrists against each other behind my head. He wrapped them in a band and tightened it, and the band didn't feel smooth at all. 'Let me make this clear as well: the next one will be on your ankles, then on your eyes. You will exercise the meaning of the word "control" on your body. Second option—I will. It's up to you. In fact, I am also exercising, because since morning, my only desire is that second option. It's not easy at all, but I'm holding myself for educational purposes.'

I blinked in bewilderment as the timbre of his voice in my ear curled my skin. I closed my eyes, pressing myself against the pillow. His touch was gentle and chaotic. My senses sharpened; I was all prickly. Victor licked my ankle and continued biting on the way up, to the crease of my thigh, then his lips took the runway straight to my groin. He tasted the tissue hungrily, sucked on it and twisted his tongue with such flexibility as if it was experienced in yoga. Up and down, then in a circle... Wet and soft, its movements turned my heart rate into an erratic wild bass.

I pressed my wrists to my nape, straining my whole body not to move. This made me even hotter. I was on fire. Moisture and softness went all over the bundle of nerve endings and the pulsation within me cut my breath into pieces. My teeth sank into the ball, it seemed delicious now. The circling touch was speeding up in line with the sensation it gave me. Vibrations were coming in waves, while the tightening spasm was not squeezing him inside of me for the first time, bringing the sense of emptiness and the need for him to fill it up. My muscles trembled on their own accord. Electricity with a destructive voltage crept from my toes. It was impossible to control the natural reactions of the muscles anymore. My knees were glued to each other. My back bent and a muffled cry came from under the ball I was biting.

My stifled voice whimpered only centimetres away from his face. My eyes wide open, I stared into the blue above me. He released my wrist for a moment, then the mouth, but it remained in the shape of an "o". The electrical pleasure transformed into a sharp, twisting pain deep in my groin. It pierced my stomach. Victor smirked, my liquid glistening on his lips. He collected it with his finger, sucked it off, then ran his tongue over his teeth. Speechless, I blinked as my body reluctantly experienced its first unattained orgasm.

'I also intend to clarify what exactly it is that you control in your body. How are you going to handle this feeling now? The truth is that the brain is an ingenious sadist, Nia. It uses tiny molecules to cause you pleasure, pain, or an explosion. It would subdue your whole being if you allow this. And it has more than subdued you. You are its captive. It's not enough to control the physical part of your body, you must also control the processes in your mind, and you must know that you're not skilful at this at all.'

'What do you...' I swallowed dryly but my throat refused to vocalise anything else. My body and my brain were protesting with fierce piercing sensations, and I didn't know where to place myself.

'And since you're not skilful, you will at least feel a thousandth of what your behaviour provokes in me. Despite the huge difference between us. I am in full control of myself, and you are the atomic bomb that challenges my endurance. Explaining to you in words is no good. You must feel in order to understand me. For now this is the only possible communication between you and me, at least until you comprehend that your logic is not everything,' he kissed the tips of his fingers and placed them on my lips. His new personality's gaze stomach-twisted me, then he headed to the door.

'Are you seriously going to leave now? Because I can "feel" on my own, too, don't flatter yourself,' in the grip of sadistic molecules and the painful pulsation, I bit my lips with provocatively open thighs. I slid my right hand clumsily between them, hoping that he would put something else there.

'My lovely dear, you are not even in control of your pleasure and I'm afraid your hands will prove to be completely useless there,' he replied with a smug face of condescension. 'Then again, of course, you are free to try! I guess you will manage to find the logic and the sequence of actions to get some skills in this, as you found your way in driving me crazy all day. I'd love to watch as you do it, but I'd rather spare myself that explosion right now.'

He moved the outlined penis under his pants and bit his palm.

'That's enough, Victor! If you had told me that these are the consequences of my look, I wouldn't...' my voice came out in falsetto. 'What does sex have to do with control, sensations, logic, bombs, and everything else you said? What's wrong with you? I don't get it and I don't like it. Not at all!' I roared, still spread out on the bed. My body craved its drug and I was agonising in the dull pain.

'It doesn't. During sex you are mine and everything's fine. For the rest of the time though you are an uncontrollable chaos. You don't even imagine how much I don't like it! I hope you will realise that you need to change! It'd be great if you start with your ugly behaviour, statements, and the unreasonable logic from this morning,' he examined my body, my legs spread apart on the bed, and he inhaled loudly. I was silent, though my mouth remained open. He finished through his teeth: 'Get dressed! You're having dinner in five minutes!'

He slammed the door and I hit the mattress, muttering about all his bullshit.

'And then people say that I'm crazy! I explain clearly that I don't mind having sex, and he speaks about bombs. Maybe that's what people mean saying that men and women communicate in different languages. And what the hell does "unreasonable logic" mean? This is an oxymoron, damn it! And the other words? We need a fucking translator here.'

φ

I stormed into the bathroom, analysing Victor's statements and his behaviour. I shoved myself in the shower and of its own accord, my hand settled between my legs. The wild pulsation that raged there was piercing my brain. I closed my eyes and used my photographic memory to recreate Victor's precise movements. Even though I was doing my best to do everything the way he did, the results were pathetic. For the first time, I slid my finger inside, then I kept pressing the pleasure-button insistently, but only a barely distinctive, tiny spasm provoked a weak twitch just to make my body more eager. I scored zero, even minus the result my body hungrily anticipated, and it got even more tense.

For all these years, none of you have established the sequence of actions required for an orgasm! You are useless, indeed!

Knowledge took offence:

I know human anatomy perfectly well.

I got irritated by his muttering, by my own awkward touch as litres of ice-cold water poured over my back:

All you know is theory! Why am I not writhing then, huh? What do the old pages say about this? Damn anatomy and damn bombs! They're driving me insane! When I had my negative opinion of sex everything was fine. I started liking it, and my head became defected. Together with my body. God, maybe that's why people in the general reality are defected! Maybe that's normal, too? How could one even tell what's right and what's wrong? Damn it! It's a madhouse again. I must somehow get to terms with Victor at least on the topic of sex.

Reason yelled, his arms folded:

Why do you even keep bothering to philosophise about wrong judgements? You have entirely become wrong judgements. You change your conclusions five times a day. How did we end up in this bathroom again? You deserve me to stop talking to you!

We ended up here by car. It's not like I willingly walked here. It just happened.

I hissed sulkily and he started again:

How come it never just happens that you leave for good?

I growled, completely annoyed already:

I don't know how! If I knew, I wouldn't argue with you in this particular goddamn bathroom. Shut up!

When I came out of the shower, I was still vibrating, and, in addition, I had a headache. I tried to breathe-balance the tormenting sensation and my irritation. I didn't want to eat, but, apparently, I had to talk with Victor about his expectations of me.

'I wonder which one of these would be "appropriate" for dinner,' I sulked at the bikini set as I picked it up soaking wet from the bathroom floor. The jeans, wet and outstretched, lay next to them. They unpleasantly reminded me of the arrest and I didn't even touch them.

Wrapping myself in the bedsheet, I examined my reflection in the huge mirror, disappointed to discover I didn't look quite like the Roman statues in the museums. There was a knock on the door. One of the housekeepers peered in.

'May I come in? Mr. Kaov sent me. What can I do for you?'

'Do you have an iron by any chance? My dress is a bit creased, and I guess my appearance is inappropriate again,' I don't know if it was my serious expression, my irony, or the way I waved the bedsheet around me, but something made her laugh heartily.

'Come with me!' With a giggle, she went to the lobby in front.

The door next to the home bar led me into a bright room. Identical dark suits were lined up to the right. Below them—shiny shoes, each pair at an equal distance from the others, and to the side there were impeccably white shirts, all of them buttoned in the same pattern.

A button, a hole, a second button, a hole, a third button...

The irritating order made me start counting the first thing I saw. A few coats, blouses... everything was annoyingly neat. I was shocked to find all sorts of women's clothes carefully folded and hangers with dresses. I frowned at the lady wardrobe, but then my eyes froze on a shoe rack.

I immediately recognised one of the pairs. My mouth dropped and I moved closer, as if in a trance. The shoes were comprised of the precise law of proportions my eyes longed for. True visual harmony. I had admired them hundreds of times on the Internet: Christian Louboutin's eternal model. This man turned symmetry into a cult, and he had long captivated me. His hands sculpted masterpieces in honour of female beauty in the general reality. Black, sharpened, gentle to the touch, with a thin ten-and-something-centimetre heel. Their lower part—exquisite red, cast from Louboutin's passion for perfection that I shared.

The Pigalle model, created in 2004. Named after his favourite neighbourhood in Paris, Knowledge recited.

'God! Shut up and admire! Look at the harmony, the proportions, the symmetry!' I replied aloud, puzzled by the twisted 37½ shoe number.

I wore everything from 37 to 39, whatever I could find on sale, and I hadn't even heard of half numbers. I couldn't resist. Slipping my foot in of the shoes, I was astounded to find out that it fit perfectly. I giggled like a kid at the conclusion that Cinderella would regret not having been chased with this shoe. *Reason* viciously joined in:

All of you girls are impaired from a young age by those fairy tales! You know it's technically impossible for a pumpkin to be driven as a carriage, don't you? I don't even want to reflect on glass shoes and strength[14]. They should have read more physics and less crazy stories to you. They damaged your perceptions!

I laughed at him, gazing at the exquisite beauty on my foot. The shiver-provoking timbre suddenly crept down my back, pulling me out of my trance:

'Now this is an interesting outfit,' Victor was leaning at the door, his index finger pressing his lower lip. 'I'm not sure about the dress though.'

Smirking, he closed the door on the housekeeper. He kneeled before me and slipped the other shoe on. When he pulled the bedsheet away, I was left naked on the scarlet soles. He ran his hands up from my ankles, grabbed my butt and squeezed tight.

'You deserve what I did for everything you put me through today. You deserve much more! But I can't let even this one thing bother you! You are the one who spoke about compromising this morning, but now I'm compromising again with my decisions, Nia,' the irises shone at me as my throat exhaled loudly.

His kisses were circling my belly. He spread my feet apart and I barely managed to balance on the high heels. Relaxing on his ankles, he licked his lips and greedily sucked on my groin. My knees weakened. My right hand clutched the pole with the dresses and the hangers rattled. Victor gave me a look from below my navel and motioned for me to keep quiet. I tightened my grip on the metal and bit the back of my left palm. His beard tickled me, and his tongue made me spill all over. He pressed me tighter to the warm moisture of his touch. My body was falling apart while I was forced to keep it intact ten centimetres above my usual height. Victor kept drawing magical circles over the button and they hypnotically spiralled throughout my body. My breathing speedup, the voltage suddenly slammed at the core of my bones. I was flowing on his lips. My hand seemed to warp the metal.

---

[14] *Strength is the level of mechanical stress that an object can endure before being destroyed – author's notes.*

I sank my teeth into my palm but couldn't muffle the moan. The heels shook as well. My head exploded and I went dizzy. I lost my balance, but he took a strong hold of my neck. Standing now, he pressed my face to his chest. The sharp hairs and the warmth prickled me. He held me tight as the spasms shook me. He ran his other hand down my belly and rudely slid two fingers in the moisture inside me. It stretched painfully, yet the pulsation in there eagerly crushed his fingers. Some more of his magical movements, and he snatched another choking orgasm from my cells. Breathing hard, he growled in my ear.

'I crave you falling apart in my arms, Nia! You don't even imagine what this feeling does to me.'

He slipped out of me, but held me propped against his body until my muscles came to their senses and the strength in my weakened legs was back. He put me in a stable position, then he pulled away. He examined my face, my dry lips. Without saying a word, he picked one dress from a hanger, dropped it on the floor and urged me to step in it. He traced his kisses with the fabric, from the breasts up. Then he turned me around to zip it abruptly.

Excited by Victor's peculiar educational methods, *Lust* thundered inside and groaned:

Wrong direction of the zipper. Tell him, crazy! He must get the dress off right now!

My throat muttered while Victor was struggling in his attempt to put my hair in a ponytail.

'I wonder how many broken bands it'd take for me to tame this?' He leaned over my neck, inhaling the scent. I pressed myself against his heat. Victor wrapped his arms around my stomach and his hardened desire propped against me. I smiled hungrily and tried to shove my hands in his pants, but he gripped my wrists. In a cold voice, he said straight in my ear:

'I hope you like my choice. Seeing your weird issue with stores and, most importantly, that outrageous dress, suitable for my eyes only, I decided to take over. I'm saying this before you have another burst of insane conclusions. As soon as you choose your flat, all these will go there. My new assistant will take care of this tomorrow.'

'Victor, I'm not...'

I tried to explain that I had found a roommate already, but he interrupted with annoyance:

'Don't argue right now. It's hard enough for me to resist already.'

'Why are you resisting?'

'So that you'll be able to sit on your ass tomorrow. Also, so that you can think about your crazy behaviour while I'm away.'

His fingers slid up my naked arms, reaching the neck. He bit it, sucked on it, and my mouth froze in the shape of an 'o' again. His breath hissed, then he pulled away. He watched me as he hastily took his shirt off and threw it on the floor. I was examining the tattoo—from a distance, it seemed as if he was in the grip of a bird of prey. Its claws resembled flames that squeezed his shoulders, his chest, and his six-pack. Victor put another shirt on and carefully buttoned it as I gulped. He pulled a hanger with a coat and his voice—the unbearable one—came from the door:

'I'm waiting downstairs for you! Before leaving, I want to make sure you've eaten some proper food.'

The dinner seemed to have the sole purpose of killing me. The seconds dragged on torturously and I spent about half an hour chasing an olive in my plate. I had never worn a dress without underwear, and it was definitely going to be the last time. I kept moving nervously in the chair, because the fabric irritated my groin and that made things even worse. My stomach tightened, my heart rate had no intention of slowing down, and I was sweating all over. Every now and then I caught Victor's gaze, but the statue expression was back again. Chris and the chief counsellor were there. I didn't know the other three men at the table. Only thinking of what was so special about shoes distracted my impatience to talk to Victor again. Now, I wondered if only wackos like me were fascinated by perfect proportions like those on my feet. Chris's colourful gaze helped me distract myself. I moved, irritated, when Victor's measuring eyes pierced me.

'What is it, Nia? Is the chair uncomfortable?' His cool voice caught me off guard. Behind his expressionless face, though, I could distinguish the mad blazes that I was already familiar with.

'No, no. The chair is fine, other things are the uncomfortable ones,' my mutter attracted all eyes in my direction, and I blushed. I detected satisfaction in his new personality, and there was a faint wicked smirk, too. Then he froze Chris:

'You're taking up the financier's work. Get yourself an assistant, if necessary. Make a power of attorney for Nia tomorrow. The estates are her concern for now. If she hasn't made a new decision, of course.'

Chris nodded and Victor shot a reproachful look at me.

'I haven't made any new decisions. I already told you that I'm going to finish the job. I'd like to check something in the financial statements. Can I get access to them?'

'Why?' He sounded suspicious.

'Because of the expenses, why else? I lack data. He didn't give them to me. I can't really calculate without numbers,' I muttered the semi-truth scornfully. The pattern I saw in the documents was gnawing at me and I suffered in anticipation of putting the pieces together. It was gnawing so hard that I avoided the truth, which was an atypical thing for me to do.

'Chris, give her what she wants. Take care of the other issue, too, while I'm gone. Keep me informed. That's all for now, you can go!' Chris nodded silently once again, and he winked at me from the door.

The chief counsellor threw a nervous glance at his watch, motioning to the president that it was time to go. Victor gave me a haughty gaze from the other end of the table. It was obvious that he had no intention of talking. He got up and so did everyone else, as if there was a command. The security guard escorted the president to the jeep outside and the others went down the aisle to their cars. My foolish expression and I remained alone at the table. I watched his steps through the glass wall. When the driver opened the door, the lamp threw light on a shadow sitting in the back seat. This one appeared most often with him. Her eyebrows up in the air, she evaluated me with contempt as my jaw dropped. Victor's narrowed eyes looked over his shoulder before he got in the car.

Fucking shadows! They really do pop up like cockroaches. How is this normal? It's a total mess here!

The sea urchin prepared its thorns and *Reason* was too slow to come up with an argument. He didn't stop it from piercing me. My face twisted. I rubbed my navel and rolled my eyes, then headed for the second floor. I met the housekeeper at the stairs and asked sharply whether Toma had brought my bag. She nodded, then disappeared. By the sound of my voice I could tell that I was irritated again. I had already concluded that it always happened after a sting by the repulsive urchin. The woman came back in a minute, and I buried myself in the absolute chaos of my bag.

Damn! I'm pretty sure normal women's bags and lives are not this messy! They know how to handle these kinds of situations, too. I should ask how it works.
I finally got to the phone and guiltily texted Toma:

I hope you're alright. Sorry for not texting you earlier.
How do you feel?
P.S. Are you here?

He replied after a minute. Although, I guessed it was difficult with the actual buttons.

I'm here. But the question is why are you there?
Again!
I'll be downstairs in two minutes.

He was not the first one to ask this question today. I frowned but immediately replied:

At least you are exactly when and where you're needed.
Coming!

I hurried to the closet. After a short rummage I was surprised to find out how grateful one can be at the sight of dry cotton panties if they come at the right moment. I put on a pair of Victor's black boxers, tying a knot so they wouldn't fall off. I left a note saying that I had taken his underwear. I grabbed a pair of jeans, a T-shirt, and a sweater from the shelf with all the stuff he had chosen for me. I placed the scarlet soles in their place with a sigh.
'It was an immense thrill for me to experience your perfect proportions. You gave me absolute pleasure!'
To my surprise, there were a couple of differently coloured socks in another one of his drawers. I took two of them. My sneakers in the bathroom were dry, so I quickly put them on, too.

Toma was talking to two of the security guys outside. I studied the thick bandage on his biceps. He shrugged sulkily.

'Today's not my day!'

'Same here. Come on, let's go!' I pulled him by his big paw, relieved that he looked well.

'Where to, Nia?' His gaping face made me laugh.

'To have a drink, for a start! I don't know about you, but *today* is already screaming for drinks to me!'

'I don't drink!'

'All right, it'll be a virgin vegan martini for you. Come on!'

He huffed, then headed to another car that looked exactly like the one we had hit. I hopped inside with my new well-trained movement. I looked around for the suitcase.

'Did you take my luggage from the car?'

'Of course. It's in your house. Why?' He raised his eyebrows.

'Why is it there?' I frowned.

'Victor told me to leave it there. We're showing you flats with the new assistant tomorrow.'

'Bullshit!' I snapped. 'The "personal" assistant didn't tell him what I said, and he wouldn't let me explain. You're not showing me any flats! Wait a second!'

I ran over to take the suitcase, but the second I entered the house, I froze. I looked at the counter, at the stairs to the next floor. Victor's smell and his insane influence on me hovered over the place. Despite all arguments and logical conclusions, they even managed to twist me in some sick imaginary way. Irritated, I rolled my eyes. On my way out the door-issue crept up my back again. *Reason* murmured what kind of a weird new phobia that was.

I tossed the suitcase on the seat and Toma stared at me with suspicion. He took a breath, as if he was going to say something important.

'It definitely is not my day today,' he exhaled loudly, but he decided to stop there. His lips glued together in an unreadable expression as he took off at top speed.

TEN

Toma was thoughtful all the way to my favourite bar. He broke the silence a few times only to confirm again that I was all right. He murmured that life had a strange sense of humour, always sending weirdos to him. His caring, unoffended voice was back. However, he didn't explain the statement to my questioning gaze. He thanked me for having taken him to the hospital, and laughed at my remark that my driving ability could have killed both of us. He even promised to give me some lessons.

The glass elevator took us to the top floor of the tall building. I liked the place; dimly lit, the music was great, though not quite loud enough for my taste, and then there was the breath-taking view. Like a funhouse mirror, the height distorted the ugly reality below. Or, more likely, what it distorted was the sense of ugliness. The dust and the dirt couldn't be seen, giving the false impression there was something harmonious and beautiful about the repulsive, grey city. We settled at the bar and Toma gazed at the spilling lights below us.

I took large gulps of whisky to find the courage to ask my questions. I often treated myself to wine, and had built my tolerance enough to only get drunk after a whole bottle. But even a little hard liquor was enough to relax me. Toma didn't refuse the virgin cocktail with the raspberries and the colourful umbrella, but he still seemed anxious as he sipped on it. Supported by the alcohol, I brought my stool closer to him, propped my head on my hands, and started investigating:

'Toma, when we first met properly, I accepted your conditions. We had a deal. I usually keep my bargains, but there are already enough reasons for me to break the promise I gave you and insist on an explanation for some of the things you said. I have questions for you.'

'Stop bothering me! I am tense enough, I don't need you to give me this crap, too,' he snorted, waving his hand in irritation.

'I'm sorry, but I have to. You mentioned some things about Victor, and the work, and...' he gritted his teeth, but I continued insistently: 'Look, you can't just say that somebody is insane, that his life is a place I might get stuck in, you can't make hints and expect me not to ask after all that!'

'I'm not expecting you to not ask, I am expecting you to not bother me to answer,' he hissed.

I crossed my arms with an arrogant face.

'I can demonstrate just how bothering I can be, if you insist. This will negatively affect our communication, though, and I find it quite unnecessary. Just explain to me what you meant, and answer my questions!'

'Damn! You're not gonna drop it, are you?'

'No, I am certainly not!' I frowned and he shook his head, biting his lips.

'One question. I will give you a thorough answer, and that's all.'

'I'd rather have three shorter answers!'

'I'm not negotiating, Nia! One question and then you leave me alone!' He waved his index finger scornfully.

'It's not fair! The questions are equally important and I don't have a system to prioritise any one of them.'

'Who promised it will be fair? Besides, I know what you're about to ask.'

I was silently wondering if it is possible to summarise my questions in one. It wasn't, but Toma was urging me by tapping on the bar.

'Shoot! I'm not gonna wait all night.'

'How do you know what I'm about to ask when I don't know myself yet?' I tapped my fingers as he looked at me with curiosity. 'All right! I made my choice! Just before we got hit, you mentioned something about the work. Remember? What did you mean?'

'Yeah, I remember, but since when did work become your priority? I expected you to ask me about the "shadows"—that's what you call them, right?—and Victor's personal life,' the evident irony prompted my stomach-twisting gaze. Nevertheless, Toma continued sulkily: 'I remember your mood this morning, too, and I remember you having doubts about your work going forward! I also clearly remember where I found you tonight! What's wrong with you, girl?'

'Argh. Why the mean tone and why would I care about the shadows? I didn't choose to go there, did I? Victor popped up in the...'

'I know where he popped up,' his irises shone with anger. 'Now leave me to my bloody cocktail! I'm not gonna answer that question,' Toma was nervously spinning the umbrella in the silence that settled between us.

'And what's wrong with you, Toma? Why are you acting as if I'm to blame for something! I wasn't planning to end up in Victor's house. I mean, I thought that in case of mutual...' He shot his eyes at me and I held back my awkward explanation. 'Look, honestly speaking, I already know Victor's reality, but nonetheless, it's a mess in my head, and it's a mess I'm not familiar with. I can't describe the bloody cocktail in my mind, and it doesn't even have an umbrella for decoration. I need to start cleaning from somewhere. Just explain what you meant in the car! What you said nested in my brain. It keeps buzzing like an annoying fly and it's driving me crazy.'

'You're an annoying fly, too,' he said, as I grabbed his big paw and stared at him pleadingly.

'Yes, I'm like a fly in a suitcase! No matter what direction I take, I bump into something, and I can never choose the right way. Didn't you say you cared about me? You can see that it's even difficult for me to make my decisions now. I change my conclusions five times a day, that's true. Help me and explain! Why did you say "that's what you think" when I said that I'm doing my job strictly? Please, I can't find the logic here and it's bugging me,' my most pitiful face was breaking him.

'God! You're bugging me with your confused look, girl! How do you achieve it with your goblin eyes? You're giving me creeps and breaking my heart at the same time. I guess there's something wrong with me, too. Only wackos get under my skin. I do care, and you're just as clueless as you are smart. I've been trying to give you hints for days!' His face turned red and hit the bar. 'Damn, everything is going out of control, don't you understand! Problems everywhere! And you don't understand anything that is said to you! Christ!' He stared at me, his lips glued together, and I gaped at the new expression on his face. 'I didn't mean that you were not doing your job strictly. I meant that *you* are not doing it!'

'I am not doing it? I don't get it,' my eyebrows hopped up. I shoved myself under his nose and he sighed.

'There are so many other things your airy head doesn't get. You don't get what kind of a person Victor is, do you? You don't even seem to realise who he is. You didn't enforce limits in your relationship with him, and now you're asking me about work. Work doesn't matter, Nia, and I'm wondering where exactly you are going with that suitcase. Looking for more trouble?'

'More hints and ambiguities. Damn! Explain clearly!' I pushed his bandaged shoulder and he gasped in pain.

'I will, but you're going to comply with two conditions. This time you have to! Every word I say stays only between you and me. Secondly, you don't get to ask more questions. Not even one! Am I clear? After the insane events of today, it's better for everyone that I clear up the details for you.'

'What insane event and what details?'

His sombre smile made me pull away from him.

'It's only one detail, actually—everything is a set up!'

'Toma, if that's your thorough answer, I wonder what the sparse one sounds like! What the fuck do you mean?!' I asked in falsetto.

'Stop cursing like that! I will tell you everything, but it stays between us. Am I clear?'

'Of course! I wouldn't...' I muttered, squeezing my fingers in anticipation. Toma pinned his eyes on his cocktail umbrella.

'I went up to meet Victor at the hunting lodge. The chief of security told me that he was with some strange woman and had ordered no one to bother them. We were having a chat outside when Victor texted him "5". This means that he was supposed to call him out of a meeting in five minutes. The chief used the "urgent conversation" tactic, Victor passed by me in a hurry, and I was curious and looked in. You were there, staring blankly at nothing. That was when I first saw you.'

My stomach clenched in a tight ball as I ordered another whisky.

'Before leaving, Victor asked me to watch you from a distance. He suspected you could memorise car numbers, faces, and other details around you, but he needed more information. He said it was not OK to send you to the employees at the office, nor to bring you to the house, nor was it OK for you to be with him. It was important to distract you with something illogical, but he didn't know what. You had to be able to handle it, so you could decide to stay with him. Whatever that means, that was what he wanted. Then I found out that he had given you the task of dealing with the estates on your own, so you could be isolated and he could control the process. He insisted on knowing what estates you were checking out, and what you were doing at all times… That's what he ordered, and then you drove me crazy with your metro cruise, girl!'

He went silent, biting his lips.

'And after he left?' My voice hardened. Toma reached for my glass and drank half of the whisky in one gulp.

'I will explain thoroughly. Stop asking, you're making me nervous!'

'All right. Keep going!'

'In the evening, you drove that shitty car and I followed. While you were waving your hands in front of the building, I called Victor and he asked for the location. You got home and then Fatass—the guy you met at the mansion—called me with a bunch of questions. As if I was supposed to know the effing answers! He said Victor had checked who the owner of some building was, and I was supposed to know which one it was. Fatass was friends with the owner and Victor insisted that he should immediately contact him to negotiate the estate. Someone else was supposed to come up with the official offer though. A young woman.'

'That's why the seller seemed to have been expecting me in the morning,' my mouth twisted.

'Yeah, but he was forbidden to tell you about the previous conversations. It was a mandatory condition. Fatass made me wonder what was going on. Victor came back earlier and asked that I go everywhere with you and inform him. I wasn't eager to keep you company, but he insisted.'

'Why?'

'Because you're weird. Victor said that it's not easy for you to communicate with strangers, and with him, too. Being with me was supposed to make it easier, especially if we were to be together all the time, so you could get used to the environment. He made me take you to choose clothes, so you could dress properly for meetings and become relaxed with the others. He asked me to watch for your response to any doubts or worries you might have. He wasn't sure what could make you turn his offer down, and he insisted that you should stay at all costs. He wanted to approach you in—I quote—small steps. He warned me to watch out for every word I said because you were exceptionally smart, weird, and you made crazy conclusions, and you were—another quote—difficult to control. Although I quickly got to realise the last one myself.'

'Wow! I didn't know my brain cost a couple of million for unnecessary estates and that much effort. Or is Victor crazy and rich enough to have fun with such plays? "They get overly satisfied, and get weird",' I quoted Maddie. My sarcasm interrupted Toma and he shook his head to refute me.

'They are not unnecessary. Victor decided to move everyone to one place weeks ago. They are in different offices now. He had already chosen the office. I guess he thought that he could provoke your interest this way, or something. As a matter of fact, I don't know much about these details.'

'What about the penthouse?' I rolled my eyes and he shrugged. 'OK, what happened then?'

'Next you left his office in a bad mood, you didn't say anything, and he yelled at me to keep constant watch over you. Then you got into that crazy condition in front of the store, you ran away, and I was worried. I told Victor immediately, and when I mentioned that you had said he was insane, he went mad. He asked me to take him to your flat. He left the security outside. I had to reassure the chief at the door that there was only a small goblin inside. Then Fatass called me and asked me a million questions again.'

'Why?'

'Because Victor yelled at him on the phone. He suspected that the seller told you about their arrangements. If you found out, there wouldn't be a way to keep you, except by forcing you. This was the issue. Fatass asked me whether you had spoken to that guy after you met him, when you had met, and what had happened.'

'So that's why he wanted to know why I thought he was insane. Now I know why the seller expected to see Victor, too. Damn, it was so obvious!' I tapped my forehead with my index finger as the details from Toma arranged into a logical and proportionate sequence in my mind. 'What are you actually? Are you even a driver?' I nailed my goblin gaze on him.

'No, Nia! I'm not a driver, but that's not really important,' he was annoyed. 'Victor negotiated the deal by using Fatass, just to make sure he'd get what he wanted: you. He was determined that you should think it was your success, because he wanted to provoke your interest, I guess. That's why I said what I said in the car.' For the first time, it seemed to me that he was looking at me with pity, trying to evaluate my reactions.

'You don't have to summarise! I got it!' *Pride* stood up. Everyone in my head was gaping, and *Reason* was blinking in stupor. 'Why did he need all this? Is Victor's hobby collecting freaks like me? Or is it some perverted competition, like *Le Dîner de Cons*[15]? With the finale being his bed?'

'*Le* what?'

I didn't translate.

'Damn! The worst part is that everyone was right! Despite having an IQ in the 99.5th percentile, my assessment was wrong. And they, having only three functioning brain cells, turned out to be right! That's what's insane! I truly don't understand your general reality,' I half-closed my eyelids, biting my lips.

'What are you talking about? Who was right?' Toma was trying to catch my gaze, but it was wandering to a distant destination.

'There was never an offer! A chance for something more never existed, nor I had handled the imaginary task. It was neither luck, nor success. It was just a perverted fantasy of Victor Kaov. To have some fun for a night or two with the freak. All my actions until this moment were stupid as hell, weren't they? I just rolled through someone's awfully muddy story,' I was out of words and breath.

'Look, Victor is not a bad person. It's just that when he decides he wants something or someone, his methods are a little over the top. If you had focused on your work only, you wouldn't...'

His voice faded. I concentrated on my own thoughts, and interrupted him by speaking them aloud:

'Damn, how did I ignore what was so obvious! The mass logic defect got me as well—the irrational hope. I so dearly wished it was a real chance that...' I looked into his warm eyes and he shuddered. 'The problem is not the even chance; it's my insane hope for something more than what's predetermined. That cursed, wretched hope, Toma, it's indeed dangerous! It distorts the facts, it blurs the objective sight, it interferes with conclusions, and it often leads to unfounded assumptions. There is another hypothesis for this situation, too, but I don't know whether I should be flattered that Victor appreciates my brain, or I should scorn myself for letting him get me in the whore team so quickly... Thank God I didn't fall for the rented flat, or I'd look exactly like one of them,' I laughed silently. Toma took hold of

---

[15] *"Le Dîner de Cons" – a play and film of the same name about Parisian businessmen, who organise a dinner each week, competing between themselves to bring the biggest idiot of whom they could make fun. Written and directed by Francis Veber – author's notes.*

my fingers, but I pulled them away. 'Screw it! The cameras in my flat were suspicious enough, but you covered the situation. So how does this work—he picks up some girl, he makes an irresistible offer, and he gets her, right? He just needed something more unusual for me,' I examined the ceiling, my face twisted.

Toma watched me in silence. He took another generous sip from my glass.

'I told you I didn't like what was going on. With every passing day, I start disliking it even more.'

'That night at the restaurant—was that part of the game, too, so you could get me to him in the end? So that his excellency wouldn't have to waste his precious time and I'd just land in his bedroom in my panties? Is that some trendy fetish, being with a crazy woman?' I snapped and he gaped.

'Of course not! How could you even think that?'

'I could certainly think that! Victor's ideas of acceptable behaviour and limits are blurry, aren't they? He doesn't mind faulty patterns, either, so I wouldn't be surprised,' I was rubbing my forehead with my fingers, my racing thoughts buzzing unbearably. *Reason* was storming in a circle, and everyone else followed in his step.

'He's not a bully, Nia. He's just too extreme when he wants something. The truth is that he focuses on these things, he gets obsessed, and...'

'The truth is that I was hesitant from the very beginning, I didn't listen to myself and eventually I was forced to accept. He deceived me, tempted me, fired me, he left me with no options and my compromise was ready. Victor misled me about his motives, too. My assessment was confused from the very beginning and it's proportionate to the result. It may sound weird to you, but that's exactly the type of absurdity that a "biochemical" cocktail would cause. I must admit that the president is a very systematic and consistent person. What is he, after all: a maniac, a sociopath, or something else?'

'He just gets what he wants. He's just like that! Now it's my turn to ask a question though. Enough with yours! Where to with this suitcase?'

'I don't have any more questions, Toma. I accidentally hit the most important one. The suitcase is not on a walk. You're going to drive me and you'll even know where I'm moving to. That's your job, isn't it—*delicate* tasks,' I sarcastically stressed the adjective, before swallowing what was left of the whisky in one gulp. 'Why didn't you tell me earlier, Toma? Damn it, you could've spared me a bunch of problems with my head, with my body, with everything. Do you even know what kind of chaos emerged? I thought you cared about me,' I snapped, squinting.

'I thought you didn't have more questions? Now you listen to me. You know Victor won't like this, right? He expects you to move into one of his flats, not to choose your own place.'

'I don't care what he expects! I told him this morning that I was moving out.'

'Nia, you need to approach things more reasonably. Victor is simply the type of person who won't take "no" for an answer. You didn't establish limits in time, and it's hard to make him accept that you won't be obeyed. You're gonna cause unnecessary trouble. Here, you know the details now, make your decisions, but I implore you to go back with me tonight and act more cautiously.'

'You obey his craziness as cautiously as you like! I guess you're used to that. I'm not playing the freak in this circus anymore. I'm not gonna be one or two nights of fun for overly satisfied people. Even a person like him will have to take "no" for an answer.'

Toma was tapping his palms together.

'We'll see if you're right. You won't forget that this is between us, right? You can't tell anybody.'

'You're insulting me! I told you already—with me, things are binary: right or wrong. I try to avoid the latter, even if it doesn't always seem so.'

'I'm not insulting you! It's just hard for me to tell how you are reacting to all this information when you're snapping all the time!'

'The information should be analysed. I am reacting by taking it literally, so I can analyse and then understand the nuances. Mostly, I need to understand how I got in this insane situation, if there can even be any logical explanation. Don't worry, I understand your demand, even though you're right to have doubts. Obviously, my enviable IQ is not enough for an accurate judgement and *Reason* is right that my judgements have all been wrong lately. Being smart proves to be useless indeed in the general reality.'

The noise in my head irritated me and I muttered scornfully:

'I need silence to get my thoughts together.'

I jumped off the chair and Toma caught my hand awkwardly.

'Nia, what I meant was how you react to the information emotionally. You're acting weird and I can't tell how you feel. It's awkward for me because you act like a robot. Are you OK?'

'I don't feel anything, Toma. That's what I am—weird. I thought you were already used to it. People usually feel awkward around me. What should I do to make you feel more comfortable?'

'I don't know! Get sad, get mad, disappointed, curse, ask questions if you must, but stop speaking in this even voice, with the expression of a mummy on your face. React like a human being, for Christ's sake, so I can know what you are feeling!'

'What do feelings have to do with reactions? If you're so interested in the process, then fine—my head exploded and now everyone's buzzing unbearably. *Rage* is storming, *Pride* is storming, *Justice*, too, and I need silence to systemise the data. If I say that I'm disappointed, will you feel better?'

'I know you're disappointed, but the fact that it doesn't show is not normal.'

'Well, at least now you confirmed that I am not "normal"!'

I headed to the exit. Toma threw down some money for the drinks on the bar and followed me, unresponsive and in a very bad mood.

I texted Chris, asking if it was OK to go to his place so late and about the location. He replied immediately, curious to know what had taken me so long. I had no desire to explain, so I left him on "seen". As I was looking for the address on the map, a message on *Telegram* gave me the creeps:

I am impatient, as you already know. I didn't get to hear your answer today.
I assume you don't have a reasonable answer
to my question of what you really want.
"Nothing" is not acceptable. I hope you will come up with
a clear and firm reply before I come back. I can't wait to hear it.
P.S. Refrain from your unreasonable logic until I get back!
P.P.S. I want to know whether you found my educational method
disturbing.
If you did, we will talk about it face to face.

I cracked my neck while reading. Toma peeked at my phone, and I locked it immediately, not wanting another conversation about my undefined limits with Victor. Deep breaths helped me to restrain my urge to reply rudely and instantly. In my mind, I was murmuring:

Your method is definitely unusual, but I guess it'll prove effective. Obviously, I am better at controlling myself, since I'm not cursing you right now. What I found disturbing was that shadow in your car and your abominations, not your educational method. Fuck you and all your different kinds of madness and personalities!

Staring out of the window, I clenched my teeth and phone equally tight. Toma tried to talk to me, but I turned up the volume of the music.

We drove in awkward silence until we reached the entrance of a gated residential complex. The janitor was expecting me, so lifted the barrier and told us where to go. Toma raised his eyebrows with suspicion. As soon as he parked the car, he got out. *Pride* was grumbling, shaking *Justice* by the arm. The others had their heads bowed, and *Reason* seemed to be offline. Before I got out of the car, I once again cursed Victor, my self-control, and his educational methods in linguistic semantics. Then my fingers started slamming the display:

I will come up with an answer, don't doubt that!
A very clear and firm one.
P.S. "Unreasonable logic" is a meaningless oxymoron.
P.P.S. Your educational methods are the only thing that
I don't find disturbing.

I exhaled through my teeth, dragging the suitcase behind me, and Toma staggered next to me, tense and silent. Chris came to the door with a sulky face.

'I thought you weren't coming. Come in!' He took the luggage from my hands.

'Absurd! You can forget about that!' Toma twisted his neck in an unnatural position.

'Forget about what?' I looked at him from the doorstep as he took hold of my wrist.

'Nia, you can't move here! I thought you simply got a flat of your own instead of going to Victor's flat. You're gonna get Chris, yourself, and me in trouble again. Chris, you motherfucker, did you go completely out of your mind? Are you crazy?' Toma shouted at my gaping face and my roommate-to-be replied:

'Don't worry about me, Bear! You can also stay if you want. So, the three of us will be in trouble together, how lovely would that be! Stop overreacting!' Frowning, he closely examined the wound on my mouth.

'Overreacting? You really are crazy!' Toma hissed, tightening his grip on my hand.

'What trouble are you talking about? Chris has a spare room, and he can wait for the rent, too. It's not far enough from my previous location, that's the only problem I see here.'

'For Christ, Nia! What kind of a shitty day is this! I have to make a phone call,' he hurried to the car.

'What's wrong with him?' I asked Chris, who was now acting nonchalant.

'Don't mind him. Victor has damaged all of them and their nerves are weak. Why so late and why the mood?'

'Let's just say my day was two-thirds horrible and one-third absurd, or vice versa. If I was writing a book, it'd take four chapters to describe it, and it's still ongoing! I don't even want to talk about it.'

My new roommate raised his eyebrows. I threw a glance at Toma's back before entering.

The house was huge, spacious, and just as lonely. Chris gave me a tour around and I counted four empty bedrooms. His bedroom on the top floor looked like a goblin's lair: messy, and furnished only with a bed and an enormous TV. A breath-taking view of the night city was hidden by thick, black curtains.

Chris took me to a nice little yard in the back. It was messy, with overgrown grass, one chair, and a small table, atop which sat a couple of dirty glasses. He picked them up clumsily, explaining that he used to have a housekeeper, but her attitude to the job was the same as his attitude to life. It was a weird comparison to make. I didn't yet know that Chris was one of the most brilliant minds I would know. I didn't know that he couldn't deal with the general reality either—that he also got into terrible messes in his messed-up life.

Chris was entertaining me by describing the weirdness of the neighbours, when Toma stormed in the yard and came to us. He grumbled at Chris to leave us alone, and made me sit down in the chair as he squatted before me. I examined his tense face. He took my palms in his big paw and spoke with reproach:

'Girl, I guess Victor's still on his flight. The security didn't tell him that we went out. I guess he won't bother me until he arrives. However, he will land soon, and we have to be back by then!'

'He has arrived. Why would he bother you? And why would I go back? I just moved out.'

'How do you know he has arrived?' His gaze darkened.

'He texted me. I guess he has reception, if...' I frowned as I muttered. '...I replied but I didn't mention anything about our conversation. Don't sweat it. I promised and I will...'

'Damn, why didn't you tell me? Does he know where we are?' He interrupted me nervously.

'No, the subject was different. What's wrong with you? You're the one who is acting weirdly now.'

'How could you even think of coming to Chris? Are you out of your mind, girl? We're leaving, and you're gonna choose a flat first thing tomorrow. You can't stay here!' He pulled my hand, but I snatched it back.

'I'm not choosing anything! And I'm not leaving! Damn, I can make my own decision about a room to sleep in! What is your problem?'

'You! You are the problem!' He shouted, his fist clenched in front of his mouth. 'And Victor as well! Your absolute craziness! I'm always here and there, like an ambulance, trying to fix everything up!' It was the first time he had yelled at me, and the sight of him made me tense.

'Why are you shouting?'

Toma swirled in a circle with his huge feet. Pressing his temples, he sighed loudly.

'Damn this day! He's gonna go crazy again! Troubles again!'

I winced at his loud voice. He had stopped pacing around, at least, and had just taken a breath to speak when his phone rang. His face twisted in a distressed grimace. He gulped, ran through the door and hurriedly passed through the house as I watched his back. He was gone for a minute. Distant shouts reached me. Then he came back and handed me the phone nervously.

'Here, you handle this!' He shoved it under my nose, with the letter "V" waiting on the display.

'Yes!' I answered, annoyed. No reply. 'Hello?'

'What are you doing again?'

'Can you be more specific?'

'I will be very specific about your actions from this moment on, Nia. First, while you're still on the phone, you will go get your stuff. Next, you will take by the hand the idiot who drove you there, and I will only hear your footsteps, then the door of the car being shut,' he explained, stressing every word. His icy voice agitated me.

'Victor, I'm not...'

'I don't want to hear any other sounds!'

'You will have to! And you will have to speak in a more acceptable way, too, because this, right now is not!' I snapped and he exhaled loudly between his teeth.

'What is the acceptable way to get you to do what I say?'

Chris popped out, questions in his eyes. Toma tried to push him back inside, but he wouldn't budge. I went to the other end of the yard, but it was too small for me to get far enough from the curiosity in those colourful irises.

'There is no way! It's not the way, it's the result you expect. You ignored my intentions, you're imposing yours, and there is a diametrical difference between both. It's for me to decide where and with whom I am going to live. Anything else is just as unacceptable as your unbearable manner of speaking!' I couldn't control my voice because *Rage* had gone crazy.

'Mind the way you speak to me!' He yelled in the receiver, and I replied in reciprocal decibels.

'Mind the way you treat me!'

He was silent for a moment, before continuing in an even, quiet voice:

'Nia, I'm two-thousand kilometres away. I have an upcoming informal summit and a few, let's say, important talks. Don't make me mad for the third time today, and don't experiment with my patience. Your place is not there. That's it. Just get in the car and go back to the house. And stop arguing,' he emphasised every syllable, affecting my anger even more. Everyone in my head was gaping, only *Pride* and *Rage* were storming about.

'Victor, I think you're underestimating me again. Arguing on the phone is unreasonable, especially if the other person is two-thousand kilometres away. Everybody knows this and I have always avoided it. I was just informing you that I have no intention of going back.'

'It'd be great if you come to the same conclusion about arguing when the person is two centimetres away. I am informing you, however, that you have ten minutes to get out of there, or Toma will simply drag you to the car. I'll call you when I'm finished here, so you can explain how the hell you ended up there. I guess it's another one of your unreasonable logical decisions. I want your phone on and in your pocket all the time!'

'I didn't end up here, I moved here. You're talking to me like I'm a suitcase again, and I don't appreciate it. I'm not going to explain anymore, so there's no reason for you to call me!' I hung up, pushing the actual button of the ancient phone. I turned around to see Chris and Toma's jaws dropping in unison.

'Did you just hang up on him?' They cried in a duet, and I nodded sulkily, walking towards them.

'Shit, he's gonna get really mad now. Apparently, you are pretty capable of not acting like a robot, though at the wrong time and with the wrong person,' Toma frowned. I shoved the phone in his hand.

'He's gonna go mad? He is the one whose behaviour is absurd! You let him act like this, and then you say I'm crazy to refuse putting up with all this? Is that what you're saying? I somehow miss your logic,' I waved my finger under Toma's nose, and Chris giggled.

'That's just the way he is,' Toma muttered at my red face.

'And that's supposed to be normal? You simply label his unbearable demeanour "normal", and then it suddenly fits into your absurd standards! Is that how "normal" works? I still don't understand how people like him are allowed to be that abominable because "that's just the way they are"! Where are we? At a perverted puppet show? Am I just some marionette?'

'Stop yelling! Chris, leave us!' Toma snapped and Chris turned to go inside. 'Nia, we live up to his standards. We have to put up with...'

'You can put up with whatever you like! It's your business! I, on the other hand, am not going to compromise with his unbearable behaviour. Can't you see how twisted he is? An impudent, haughty, abominable being...' I stressed every adjective.

Toma was taking balanced breaths when his phone started ringing again.

'Christ, you two are driving me crazy!'

He answered the phone with a sharp "Yes", then headed to the entrance again. I took several deep gulps of breath, before heading back inside to Chris and sitting down opposite him.

'He commanded you to go back, huh?' He spoke, not taking his eyes off the computer, with a smirk on his face.

'No one commands me! I'm not a soldier! And there's nowhere to go back to,' while I was still hissing, Toma dropped in the chair next to me and nervously threw his phone on the table. My eyes asked questions, but he didn't say anything.

'Commanding is his style. I hope you realise just how crazy he is,' Chris grimaced unreadably, pouring me a glass of whisky. 'Though I must admit that your character is an interesting challenge indeed. Just to make it clear, I don't have a problem with all this. I knew he was not going to like it when I offered you a place to stay. And when I saw Bear next to you, everything became pretty obvious. I don't care though!' He stared at me for a second, then back at his laptop.

'What's pretty obvious?' I looked at him with suspicion. He turned his attention back on me, but Toma crossed him:

'Shut up, Chris! You might not have a problem with Victor, but pray that he doesn't have a problem with you, 'cause then you'll suddenly start caring! Why did you invite her to come here? Damn, what're you up to?' He yelled and an annoying argument erupted.

'Stop! My ears are protesting because of all these excess words! My head's booming!' I cried but they didn't quit.

The stupid male fight sent me off to the yard.

I was walking in circles, struggling to sort all the new information. Suddenly, complete silence occupied my mind. Everybody was quiet, and my thoughts settled down. Heat took over my whole body, as if I had a fever. The intruders in my head proved completely useless when I was all alone, suffocating with the unfamiliar neurological processes. Nobody explained, nobody helped. I was sweating, sticky mucus was blocking my mind. I found that my stomach was twisting, as if I was being rocked by a stormy sea. Without reason even *the Monster* was hiding, not giving me the chance to stuff my disappointment and offence in its mouth. They went down my own oesophagus instead, like I was swallowing razor blades. It was the first time I truly appreciated *the Monster*'s skill to swallow things for me. It was also the first time I was confused despite the presence of sufficient information. I couldn't come up with logical conclusions, and my ability to concentrate evaporated. I was thinking so slowly that it seemed there was no thought process at all. My heart rate quickened and I was so very sick, that I suspected it was the whisky to be blamed for that part.

I was pacing around, figuring my next series of actions, when Toma coughed behind me. I turned to him. There was pity in his eyes. There was pity in his voice, too:

'What are you muttering there? Are you OK?'

'This conditional question again. Technically, it's not even a question. It's impossible to give an accurate answer,' I spoke evenly and caught myself staring at him with my expressionless face. Then I smiled sulkily, realising that I was deliberately trying to create a distance.

'You turned into a robot again and it feels awkward. Act human, please.'

'What do you want?'

'Victor ordered me to get you back to the house. I said I wouldn't, unless you agreed. His condition is that if you stay here, I stay too. This wouldn't solve the problem though. You'd better comply and not provoke him anymore.'

'And what exactly is the problem, Toma? Apart from Victor's sick ideas and insulting expectations? He doesn't get to impose conditions, and I don't agree that you should stay here.'

'I'm not asking for your approval,' he said quietly and that irritated me.

'It's about time you stopped reporting everything to him, Toma! There's no reason for you to be the "outside camera" anymore. Plus, there are no "delicate" tasks here,' I hissed rudely, irony spreading over my face. Nevertheless, the warmth in his eye remained.

'OK, I can see you're upset. You have grounds for that. Take a rest, and tomorrow we'll go for pancakes. We'll peacefully discuss your intentions because things won't work any other way.'

'Certainly not! I've already decided what to do and I'm doing it today. Besides, the president asked me a particular question and he insists that I shouldn't—quote—"experiment with his patience".'

'God, why do I get the feeling that I'm not gonna like your decision?'

Toma came closer, looking at me with suspicion.

'The logical decision is clear, and you don't have to like it. It's a bit difficult for me right now because my brain has become defected, but it's not too complicated. I'm considering several factors. I have never had any positive experience in my communication with Victor face-to-face. Especially when it's dark—my reactions are unpredictable then. I could fill a whole new volume of the Encyclopaedia of Anti-logic with my actions under his influence. Besides, I promised not to show anything regarding the information I received from you, and there will be a risk if we talk face to face.'

'What do you mean?'

'It's obvious—I'm going to text him! I'm going to inform him that I'm not working for him anymore and that I'm going to revise my position about the "something else" thing. I'm going to correct my mistakes clearly and firmly, if that's how he wants me to communicate my intentions.'

He blinked, his lips moving with no sound.

'You mean that you're going to text him that you're leaving as of today, and that you're not going to have sex with him anymore? Text this to Victor? That's very restrained, Nia! Just great!' He spread his hands over his head. 'And this sounds logical to you? That's what your big brain came up with?'

'You're not listening to me, or I'm not expressing myself clearly? I'm going to present my arguments and decisions in a structured way. After all that happened today, I have enough motives even without the information you gave me.'

'Christ! Now I'm not getting your unreasonable logic, either!'

'He's not going to suspect that you told me anything, if that's what's bothering you. Chill!'

'Chill? Really, I shouldn't even try to explain. Damn! I was handling one mad person, now there are two of them!' He grimaced and shouted: 'Chris, to my great regret, I'll have to stay here.'

He went inside. I had no choice but to follow him.

'Choose your bedroom, Bear. And stop overreacting,' Chris muttered without getting off his laptop. The uninvited guest grumbled under his breath and I caught up with him.

'You're not staying here, Toma!'

He shook his head and didn't reply. Chris looked at me with surprise, but I neglected the curiosity in his colourful eyes. Toma slammed the door of the bedroom next to mine and I spent the next couple of minutes considering whether I should knock. I talked myself out of this idea, concluding that our conversation was over and any convincing was unnecessary.

I huddled in my new bathroom and took my time in the hot shower. I even enjoyed the unusual silence for a while, relieved that there was no one to murmur, argue, or analyse. However, my body was still under the influence of the incomprehensible processes that made me sick. I nested in the bed, dressed in the Daenerys Targaryen T-shirt and thick, colourful socks. The only thing that echoed in my head was the rhythm of an uneven, distant bass. All data and assumptions entwined into chaotic lines that didn't create any patterns. I wondered how I should word my message to Victor.

Writing. Erasing. Writing. Over and over again. It was hard to not give out what Toma had shared with me, or the disappointment and the offence that *the Monster* had not swallowed. Through strenuous editing, I did my best to communicate my decisions clearly and firmly. Eventually, I went through the whole text again:

Taking into account your lack of patience,
I am answering your question promptly.
Our conversation tonight confirmed my final decisions.
I am systemising them, according to the different subjects:
1. The distance—in the morning you stated that being far from me was
the wisest decision and—I quote—the only fucking truth.
I confirm your conclusion. I can't define the distance precisely, but it
should exclude any physical contact, especially when it's dark.
2. The unreasonable logic—since the morning, you have been suggesting that
I should change my logic, but it is a constant. I confirm that it is
impossible for me to fit into your well-distinguished pattern.
I find your reality and your expectations unacceptable. I can see
your urge to find a place for me there and I think the distance
under point one will solve this issue as well.
3. The sex—I have revised my position and from now on, I don't plan for us
to practise it with each other, even in the case of mutual time and desire. I
emphasise that I'm not in conflict with having sex with you
in general. However, I found some side effects. (Example: today,
because of my desire to have sex with you, I allowed my logic
to be variable. Example two: again because of my desire for sex,
my intentions suddenly burn out.) It leads to issues with my
conclusions as well. I found many others that I'm not going to
list. The ones I already mentioned say enough about how
serious the side effects are. Thus, point one will solve this issue too.
4. The job—I cancel my previous decision to finish what I have started.
I considered the assumption that I am compatible by nature, but
this argument is not enough because I took the completely wrong
direction. The estates are going to be finished soon and I hope you
will like them. I did my best. I need some time to systemise the
process and transfer its management (you need to clarify to whom).
About the credit companies—I will describe my whole concept in
an acceptable, structured form, so it won't sound insane, as you

> *rightfully pointed out.*
> *P.S. I don't have the necessary data and I will do my research on*
> *whether your methods on linguistic semantics are disturbing, and*
> *then I will give an accurate answer to your question.*
> *At this stage I can confirm that they are effective yet short-term.*

I looked carefully for mistakes, before sending the messages, point by point. After sending the last one, some kind of pressure gripped my chest. A minute later I checked the status, which confirmed the messages had been delivered. Everybody was still silent, even *Reason* didn't comment on my judgement or my decision. *Lust* and *Desire* didn't protest. Only the defected part of my mind was still rummaging, but I couldn't understand what it was looking for this time. Some strange tension was rising within me, and I wondered whether Toma had infected me with his mood. What he had said played like a nightmarish tape in my mind, and I could hear what Victor had said, again and again, despite trying to muffle his voice. Every replaying of the tape caused the same reaction, but *the Monster*'s hungry mouth was still clenched shut. The razor blades process was still going on. My throat was burning.

I asked myself if it was even possible for a dubious, privileged, overly satisfied top-level man to offer chances to someone like me. Were there any logical motives for a deal like this one? It had been obvious, more than clear, that there was something wrong, but I had been deliberately ignoring it all along. I was not sure whether his actions were provoked by some perverted fantasy, incomprehensible madness, or if I was just another moment of fun for a bored person who was used to getting everything he wanted. I was agitated with the probable hypothesis, yet my focus kept moving to these contemplations. In the general reality, there are all kinds of weird, difficult to understand scenarios, and I had never encountered a suitable analogue of this one. *Knowledge*'s silence didn't help with finding the answers.

I stuffed the wireless earphones in. Billie Eilish[16]—my favourite weirdo—thundered, asking where my mind was. It was the first time, however, that

---

16 *Eilish, Billie. "Bellyache." – author's notes.*

music didn't succeed in saving me from reality where it was still too narrow for me and my edges. It was the middle of the night, and I started down the dark stairs, singing along. Her voice pricked my skin and my oesophagus shrieked from another serving of razor blades. The darkness made me press my palm against the wall. I hurried down the stairs. Ever-present *Fear* didn't spare me one of his pokes.

Downstairs, I found Chris in a trance under the bluish light of his laptop. I approached him and, from behind his back, gazed at the huge table on the screen, noticing company names from the financier's documents. I startled Chris. He slammed the laptop shut and I heard his shout even through the earphones.

'Damn! Don't sneak on me like that!'

'Sorry. I came to get some water. Why aren't you sleeping?'

'I work at night. I concentrate better this way. The jug is on the counter,' annoyed, he pointed to the kitchen.

I poured myself water, but had no interest in going back to my bedroom. I sat down opposite Chris and he looked at me curiously with a glass of whisky in his hand. He poured one for me as well.

'What's wrong with you? You look like used chewing gum. You're not suffering now, are you?'

'Why would I suffer? I just got strained because I found a sequence of misjudgements, I confirmed how useless my IQ is, and it again transpired that I don't understand correctly, and quite naturally...'

'I told you already: analyse the reasons, not the results!' He interrupted me rudely.

'I did that, but right now I can't analyse even a simple sentence. I blocked out. Chris, tell me, why does Toma treat you this way?'

'Bear is a good person, but he's been sulky lately, and he's overreacting. Don't listen to him! One less toy for Victor—he's not used to that, but he'll swallow it. He has enough toys,' he was waiting on my reaction but I shrugged silently. 'I heard you talking outside. Why are you going to text him? Actually, what is your problem, apart from obviously not taking a collar for a necklace?'

'You must know that your comparisons are too weird. My problem again is the expectations that I don't fit into. I'm supposed to be something else again. Never mind! I already texted him that I'm quitting my job and that I have revised some of my previous decisions, but I don't think it'd be appropriate to specify now.'

'There are no arguments for quitting your job. You make me repeat myself. He might be unbearable and mad, but he offers limitless possibilities. I know you can't go into details and I'm not gonna ask questions. If you've cut him off completely, though, it's probably the wisest decision,' he took a big gulp, squinting his eyes. 'Nia, he went to the police station for you, didn't he? The chief of police is a friend of mine and he wouldn't leave me alone. He begged me to do something so he wouldn't be fired. I tried to ask for the details but obviously Victor's hounds hid your identity. The chief was complaining that there was a huge problem over some girl.'

'It's true but the problem was not me. It was the financier. He set up my arrest and there was an orc who used the baton quite well. Screw her!'

'Look, Smarty, let's put aside Toma's overreacting and Kaov's manias. He shagged you, he wants you to be another piece in his slut-collection, and it doesn't work for you—end of story. You're gonna get over it! The true problem is somewhere else,' his voice became serious and I gazed at him with surprise.

'What do you mean?'

'Victor doesn't have full control over the police and the enforcement structures yet. The ex-president still pulls the strings. He has access to information, and let's say the two of them are in a complicated relationship, and a very negative one, at that! You mustn't do anything to draw that guy's attention. He mustn't know that Victor is interested in you. Under no circumstances, because he's not gonna be the only one interested then! Victor showing up there was a dangerous act of insanity. If you really manage to distance yourself from him, you'd be better off. Even though, knowing the maniac he is, and looking at how stuck you are, I doubt that...'

'I didn't draw anyone's attention. I told you already, that guy set me up. He bribed them, he wanted to scare me because I couldn't hold back, and I told him the truth. Let's stop talking about distancing, sluts, and Victor, 'cause I'm sick already! And stop repeating that I'm stuck!' I snapped as I jumped off the chair.

'Come on! Sit down! Just keep that in mind and watch out because people with very bad intentions are stalking us. Don't get mad about the stuck part. Those are uncontrollable neurological processes. No one knows how to deal with them.'

'Normal people know how to deal with them. Along with the judgements, relationships, limits. And I don't. This is not for me, but I guess it's all my problem.'

'They don't know how to deal with it all one bit. If even people with our intellect don't, the poor beings are doomed.'

'It doesn't look like that in the general reality.'

'Nia, reality is exactly what proves my words. It's not a coincidence that all books are about relationships between people. They get together, they bang, they split, they ugly cry, and then they move on, but again to the same things. Even libraries yawn at this banal story. Same scenario, but they keep writing and keep reading it. Probably because of the imaginary happy ending—they want to switch it for the real ending. They pretend to be explaining new things, but it's all fantasies, no results. The truth is, nobody knows anything and they keep spinning the hamster wheel. The same recurring sequence of events, and it still evokes total chaos. It's absurd.'

I wrinkled my nose and shrugged. What he said was somewhat valid.

'Lack of logic is the reason. If people acted rationally, there would be a proper pattern and things would be a lot easier from them. Besides, I found out that sex is also part of the problem. It defects the mind; it comes with horrible side effects, and yet it's a practiced by so many,' I took a sip of whisky and Chris giggled. His funny grimace made me laugh.

'I must admit I've never heard a conclusion like this one before, but yeah, it makes sense. If there was a proper pattern, though, it'd be damn boring. Maybe they just like going in circles. Drop it! We're not the ones to figure it out. Let's talk about something exciting—cryptocurrencies. First tell me why you look like this, though,' he motioned a finger to his lip and frowned.

'An injury from the car accident.'

'What about the bruise on your neck? The car accident again?' He sulked and I covered the spot with my hand.

'It's more like a consequence. I think the exact term is a "hickey",' I went silent, listening to the situation in my head. *Knowledge* was not there, and I was surprised to find myself imitating his way of expression.

'If you say so! And how did you end up in custody?' He rolled his eyes while lighting a cigarette, then offered me one. I liked the taste of tobacco and despite all arguments against smoking, I was tempted to accept it.

'Someone hit us. Victor says it was the financier's guy. Poor Toma got injured and I had to take him to the hospital. He was unconscious because he was losing blood in dangerous quantities. Then the policemen took me and an ugly fat orc tried to solve her issues on me during the arrest. If you see what my back looks like after her baton...'

'I can imagine! I'm experienced in being arrested. That pathetic little bastard! He fled like a rat, he's probably at the other end of the world now. I'm trying to locate him by using his personal accounts but he's running for his life. Now I know why the police guy was fretting, too! Most probably the financier paid him to arrest you. And then Victor went mad because he let this happen too!' He lifted the glass, staring at it.

'Victor really was mad, but not because of that. With his twisted standards, he said that I was not in control of myself, and he blamed me for what happened. I only said the truth. I was rude all right, but the idiot deserved it and, to be honest, I don't regret anything despite the consequences.'

'You caught him stealing, didn't you?'

I nodded but decided not to share anything else, remembering that I had seen the company names on his screen.

'Are you trying to locate him because of the money?'

'You think Victor took the effort to explain? He just ordered me, but I doubt that's the reason. Kaov is neither a compromising, nor merciful person. He's gonna destroy him only for edification, so the others won't dare even think about stealing. There's no stopping him if he is provoked. In this case, however, there's another motive as well,' he spoke sarcastically, exhaling smoke at me. 'That guy played with his toy and Victor definitely has some twisted sense of ownership. He doesn't like anyone touching his toys.'

'I'm not his toy, Chris. Let's put an end to this subject because your comparisons are really annoying. Plus, if he is what you say, aren't you also provoking him by inviting me here?'

'He's owned me for a very long time, Nia. There's nothing worse he can do to me. Besides, I don't care anymore!' His bitter face grimaced. I was confused by his reaction, and he pinned his colourful irises on me.

'Why do you want to know about cryptocurrencies?' I looked down at the glass in an attempt to change the topic.

'Not ready to discuss awkward subjects relating to his majesty Kaov, huh?' Chris went silent for a moment, a cynical smile on his face. 'Never mind, we'll get there at some point. I'm waiting for a friend to give me more detailed information about the Koreans. I want you in because I can't do it without you. Now that you're suddenly unemployed, it'd be even easier. When one door closes another one opens, right?'

'This statement is absurd. There is no such dependence. I've been having some door issues lately and I don't like your metaphor. How can I participate in this? I don't even have money for the rent. Why do you need me?' I gazed at him with suspicion and he continued seriously.

'I don't need money, Nia, I have that. I need what's between your ears. In the morning you showed me an anomaly with which you entertain yourself. I had to calculate half the day and it's still difficult for me to systemise the regularity and to make a forecast. My brain is impressive, but yours is... I don't even know the word!'

'I'm just a freak who can see the mistakes, Chris. As if my eyes were created with this purpose only. Or the general reality is a collection of countless mistakes. If we approach this esoterically, I guess the word would be a "doom" or a "curse". I can't say which one is better,' my voice was gloomy and probably the same went for my face.

'They are both inaccurate, Smarty. Stop underestimating yourself and change that distorted idea of yourself! I think you're amazing to the googolth[17] degree!' He tipped his glass to say cheers.

'I don't like googol. It has only two simple divisors. One even and one odd. It's insane! Correct patterns don't arrange in an even row. It's distorted!' I frowned and Chris laughed.

'And what's not distorted? You maybe?'

'Even numbers just drive me crazy. They're no good for counting, only for dividing. Anyway, Toma says that I should thank people for their compliments. Then I should say something nice in return. My brain is awfully blocked right now, and I can't think of any compliments, I can only say I enjoy talking to you because it's simply the truth,' I shrugged in excuse, knocking his glass.

'I need your brain, not your words of gratitude. Say we're gonna work together on the crypto bull and it'll be enough for me. And we're gonna make a fortune, if you're interested in that part.'

'I confirm. I'm in! I'm interested in making a fortune, plus, as you said, I'm already unemployed and I also owe money.'

He smiled with content, raising his glass for a toast again.

'Cheers then! To the unlimited opportunities and to your unlimited brain!'

---

[17] *Googol is a number larger than the number of all subatomic particles in our known universe which according to different calculations are between 10^{79} and $10^{81}.$* Google *derives its name from this word. Edward Kasner and James Newman speak about the googol in "Mathematics and the Imagination" – author's notes.*

'Exactly my unlimited brain's strive for unlimited opportunities got me into this mess. It almost drove me crazy but at least it took me to your house. A strange sequence, wasn't it? Cheers!' After drinking another glass in one gulp, I swayed to my bed.

The booze plunged me into a fog. All I heard was an echo and my head, seeming completely empty, opened an endless horizon for *Fear*. He soared in the vast expanse but didn't attack me, though his gaze froze me throughout the night. Just before I opened my eyes, he leaned over me and drank all of my breath, shattering me to pieces.

ELEVEN

A sunbeam was torturing my brain. I tried to defend myself with the pillow, but my diminished adrenaline, following the previous night, allowed a sadistic hangover to sweep over me. One sole thought whimpered in the silence:

Whisky—never again! Remember this, goddamnit, and never drink it all in one go again!

Once I managed to realise where I was, I recalled in chronological order what had happened the previous evening. Only one of my eyes open, I reached for the phone. The status of the messages had changed—they were all "seen", yet there was no reply. All of a sudden, I was short of breath. As if enormous pressure on my lungs was preventing me from inhaling enough oxygen. I tapped my chest. There was a sudden jab of pain between the fifth and the sixth ribs, and I sighed at the dangerous effects of drinking and smoking. I staggered to the living room. Toma was at the table, drinking a large cup of coffee. Last night's bottle was empty, the ashtray was full to the brim, and Chris was sitting half-alive on the couch. A lowered projection screen on the wall opposite him served as a TV. The morning bulletin was breaking the silence with the annoying voice of the host.

'Good morning!' I muttered.

'Morning!' Chris snorted, and Toma glared at me. Despite my sleepiness, I read the question in his eyes.

'I sent a comprehensive message to Victor. I explained everything in a structured way and made sure I was as clear and firm as possible. Just as promised, I didn't mention our conversation. The matter is settled, you can relax and go now!'

'Did he reply?'

'No, but he's seen everything. What's there to reply to?'

'Do you feel calm now? How are you? I'm avoiding the "are you OK" question, but I don't know how else to ask. Let's go for pancakes and talk?' Toma's warm eyes studied my face thoroughly. My headache made it difficult for me to even move my lips.

'I don't want to! Besides, I'm not effective this early in the morning and I'd rather not talk.'

'All right then!' He stared at his palms. Concern was stuck on his face like a jellyfish as he muttered something and went to the yard.

The coffee machine spat out a generous serving of vital juice. After the second gulp, I could focus my gaze, but my head was not yet awake. This was the longest period of silence in my head I had ever experienced. Even *the Monster* was missing and it terrified me. I walked past half-alive Chris on my way back to my room, then woke myself up with a cold shower. Examining my reflection in the mirror I defined my appearance exactly like recycled chewing-gum. My difficulty breathing frustrated me even further and I was already pretty nervous when I got to putting my clothes on.

I rudely asked Toma to drive me to the office. He only nodded. It was Monday and my plan was to organise and systemise the remaining tasks, so that the new person in charge could understand them easily. I also found out that the financier's documents were delivered to the office after the crash. I wanted to get them, too, because my immortal *Curiosity* kept gnawing at me. I was impatient to put together the disappearing money pattern. My faulty desire to prove myself was luring me again, even more strongly, because of the set-up and because of all that underestimation I had already experienced with Victor. I admitted to myself that I was going to shelter the injured cactus from the office as well.

As I opened the front door, I screamed and slammed it back shut. It took Toma a second to run to me and find me propped against the door, gawking.

'What's going on?' He pulled me to himself.

'The bad guys from *The Matrix*! They're outside!'

'What matrix, girl? Are you going crazy again?'

He moved me aside to open the door. The chief of security was frowning from the doorstep. I peeked from behind Toma's huge body.

'What are you doing here, Sergey?'

'What I was ordered to do!'

'Let's talk outside!' Toma sighed stepping forward, but Sergey's hand stopped him.

'I don't have time! I've been dealing with the plane all night. I'm a flight attendant now! Because of this chick here, I messed up the airport schedule and I take the crap from everybody,' the Bad Guy grunted with contempt in his Russian accent. 'She has five minutes to get her stuff and get in the car!'

'Excuse me, are you talking about me or to me?' I jumped from behind Toma's back and I raised my voice: 'Is grammar too difficult for you? Why are you speaking as if I'm not here? What stuff and what car?'

'Stay out of this, Nia! Get inside!' Toma gave me a light push while the other guy kept grunting.

'Toma, I have orders, you know. Don't make it hard for me, please, or sort the things out with Kaov! You get your stuff, or leave without it, I don't care, just stop hanging around,' he stared at me viciously and my mouth twisted.

'What orders do you have that include me?! I'm not going anywhere! What the fu...'

Chris popped up, his half-alive face and all, nailed his eyes on the security guard, and interrupted me:

'Good morning, Sergey! I don't remember inviting you over. And I surely dislike seeing you at breakfast,' he muttered monotonously, and the Bad Guy clenched his jaw.

'Neither do I, but it seems days have become mostly dislikeable lately,' his angry voice didn't affect Chris's stone face. He just raised his eyebrows in reply as I stormed to the second floor.

Slamming the door to my room, I clutched the phone and dialled Victor's number, but he wouldn't pick up. I waited for the *Telegram* signal to stop, then dialled again. On my fifth attempt, he answered.

'You are insistent. Good morning! Is there a problem?'

'I am motivated, and the morning is not good. And yes, there is a problem! The insolent, ill-mannered Russian at the door who treats me just like you—like I'm a suitcase, or something. He seems to think that I'm going somewhere with him. I assume you can explain these expectations?'

'That is Sergey and he's going to escort you to Brussels. As soon as you arrive here, we will have a normal conversation because our communication on the phone is a catastrophe. I really hope I don't have to explain anything else right now because I'm busy,' as usual, he spoke as if he was ordering breakfast and reaffirmed his ability to make me mad in seconds. Nevertheless, I maintained control over my voice.

'Victor, the phone has nothing to do with our catastrophic communication. The main problem is the usual lack of question marks in your sentences. Especially in those just now. I'm not coming to Brussels, and there's nothing for us to discuss!'

'You still under the influence of last night's outburst?'

'I didn't have any outbursts!'

'Judging by your messages, I wouldn't say so, but as I said already, you will explain your insane behaviour face-to-face. You are leaving with Sergey now, Toma stays. The plane is waiting for you, so be quick. We will continue the conversation over dinner,' his voice became as cold as ice, even more intolerable than usual, and I took a deep breath.

'My messages were not provoked by an outburst. My decisions, again, are diametrically opposed to your expectations, and I find your expectations insane. I am leaving for the office now, I will prepare what's necessary, and, in a couple of days, I will pass it on to whomever you choose. You tell your impudent Russian to buzz off and possibly work on his attitude! This exhausts everything I have to explain. Oh! One more thing—I hope this will be the last time I am treated like a remote-control toy and...'

'Tell me what you want, damn it!' His arrogance pierced my eardrum.

'I don't want anything!' I snapped, ready to hang up, but his next line stopped me.

'What or how much do you want, Nia? Whatever, just name it!'

'What?!'

'Just say what or how much it will cost for you to get your ass over here, no more explanations! The only thing I can't afford is the goddamn time it takes for me to talk to you right now!' He hissed angrily and I became incensed.

'Screw you!' I clenched my fist as my heart rate raised to the skies. 'From the first moment I saw you, I knew that you were an insolent, conceited, cynical jerk, and yet you exceed all my expectations! You can determine the price of your shadows and their three brain cells, not mine! You can't afford me! Am I clear enough?! Screw you, Victor! Screw you!' I yelled the last sentence in clear syllables, then my shaking hands turned off the phone.

Rage's fires made me dizzy. I dropped the phone in my backpack as I flew down the stairs. Chris's curious eyes followed me from the couch. Sergey was still arguing with Toma at the door.

'Where is your luggage? You're not ready yet?' The security guy snorted and I stomach-twisted him with my goblin gaze. I pushed him aside to make my way out. He and Toma followed me.

'Drive me to the office or to a metro station! I need to get my stuff!' I shouted, my face red because of *Rage*. Toma frowned but unlocked the car nevertheless.

'What metro are you talking about? Don't give me more shit, girl! Where do you think you're going?' Sergey stopped me, gripping my wrists.

'Don't touch me! Got that?' I yelled and kicked him in the ankle. The Russian's face twisted beyond recognition. 'Let go of me right now!'

Toma patted his shoulder and moved him back.

'She's not coming, Sergey! Let her go. I will explain and get things sorted out with him. Don't sweat it!'

'There's nothing to sort out! I already spoke to Victor! I'm not going to Brussels! What am I, a whore on demand?' I hissed.

'Toma, why don't you sort out your own issues with Kaov for starters? I don't want to babysit her! I told you this one was troublesome and look where we are now. It was obvious that night she would bring only problems. She doesn't know her place, or she must be crazy, acting like this.'

'Hey, Russian boy!' I clenched my fists. *Rage* was about to explode every moment now: 'Did you start with the vodka from early morning? Watch your mouth!'

'See? Insane. What's wrong with her? Why don't you explain to her how she should behave and where her place is? How can you stand her with her big mouth? If I were you, I'd have given her a good beating already,' he arrogantly waved his hand in my direction.

'Come!' I snapped and walked straight to him. 'Come and show me how you beat women!' Toma grabbed my wrist in an attempt to stop me. 'Did anabolics make you this disgusting, or were you born this way? If I had a shovel right now to even up the fight, I'd show you exactly how insane I am! Screw you, you anabolic bastard!' I yelled and he squinted, pressed the phone against his ear, and went to his jeep.

Toma pulled me into the car. Once in his driver's seat, he started rubbing his cheekbones.

'Who is this jerk to behave like this? Who is he to come here and give me orders, and threaten me, and...' I kept grunting.

'Shut up, Nia! Just shut up!' Toma shouted. His voice echoed in the coupe. 'Stop it, for Christ's sake! You're making trouble again!' He hit the wheel and I jumped up.

His wild eyes stared at me, but then he went soft again. Holding the tips of my fingers, he continued in a restrained voice:

'I'm sorry, goblin, it's not your fault. We are all just a little on edge right now. Sergey is a ruffian, but only in words. He's not a bad guy. He wouldn't hurt a fly if it was female. Don't be scared!'

'I'm not scared! I'm mad! Such words shouldn't even cross a man's mind, let alone come out of his mouth. The words of a lowlife. Do you know how widespread this faulty pattern is and, unfortunately, not only in words? He deserves me to hit his Russian snout and teach him how to behave!' I waved my wrists and Toma's cheeks bulged.

'My little goblin, there seem to be safer ways for you to hurt your hand,' he mocked me but then made an effort to continue seriously: 'Nia, this man is a trained soldier. He's about one hundred kilos of muscle stronger than you, and has about the same number of skills, too. You should avoid such opponents because, despite the enthusiasm, you're not strong enough to defeat them. Please! If you ever get involved in a situation with a man like him, don't wave your skinny hands but run! As fast as you can!'

'From an anatomical point of view, you are right, but I stick to another philosophy. According to it, the important thing is to find a way despite my disadvantages, even though I have a lot of them. I read one conclusion a long time ago and I go back to it every day. Anyway, I am never enough, and I always lack something, and it's far more than physical strength.'

'God, we must do something about your crappy self-esteem. I guess underestimating yourself is your favourite sport. And what was this important conclusion?'

'"Always choose a bigger enemy. It makes him easier to hit!" [18],' I gave him a grave smile and he frowned.

'And who is your enemy?'

'It's reality, Toma. The fucking general reality.'

He gaped at me and shook his head, as if suddenly feverish.

'Christ! Fate brought me two wackos, and they're frightfully similar, too,' he sighed before turning up the music. His expression showed that he didn't want to explain any further.

He drove fast. As soon as we passed the guarded entrance, I realised that we were being followed by the Russian and the other cars that had waited in front of the house. Two more jeeps popped up on the road. I peered in the wing mirrors as they surrounded us like hyenas. A car on each side and two more behind us, in both lanes. I nudged Toma and he turned the music down.

'They're following us! Four jeeps!' My falsetto voice grated.

'I know.'

'And?'

'What?'

'Why are they following us?'

'Victor's methods. I already explained to you, don't bother me anymore. He's not too pleased with me either and he wants to keep controlling every step you take. I'll talk to him.'

'What's left to talk about? Damn, does he really not understand what people say to him, or does he have some serious problems with crossing boundaries and his behaviour? He really thinks he can do whatever he wants!'

'You are the one who has a problem with his behaviour. And he doesn't *think*—he *does* what he wants!' Toma made a face.

'Power, money, and goddamn male biochemistry can create a terrible chemical reaction, I'm telling you!' I grunted. 'History has proven it, and now I can confirm it in practice,' again, the breath shortage from the morning pressed me, 'it was logical that the situation with Victor would be the same, but I even failed to estimate this on time.'

---

[18] *A quote from Terry Pratchett and Neil Gaiman's book 'Good Omens' – author's notes.*

Biting his lips, Toma shrugged. We continued on our way to the office in silence. I pressed my forehead against the window, gazing at the repulsive, dirty, gloomy city outside. My new findings about the general reality twisted my throat into a knot and I felt sick.

φ

We parked in the garage. The bad guys formed a line behind us; a man had jumped out of each car before they had even stopped properly. The Russian glared at me and I glared back, hoping to make him puke. Toma was insistently pulling at me to walk on, but I kept throwing glances behind my shoulder at every odd step. We were alone in the elevator—they had obviously taken the stairs.

Toma shoved me into the office and slammed the door behind me. He stayed in the foyer. I opted to eavesdrop, of course, and heard him arguing with the Russian. Toma insisted that they should stay outside and that Sergey shouldn't speak to me anymore. Sergey tried to object but Toma yelled at him to shut up and follow his instructions. Then he stormed in and past me, visibly angry, not saying a word. I hid in my workroom and rubbed my temples. I found the silence in my head even more disturbing than the tightening pain in my ribs. I was already dramatically missing *the Monster* and desperately needed its hungry mouth. I didn't know where else to stuff all my disappointment and I kept crunching on it as if eating glass.

Damn! How do normal people handle this if they don't have their own Monsters?!

I tried to distract my thoughts with the company of the architect student. My mind needed to be engaged in other tasks before I could decide my next moves, so I dug into systemising the work. My hyper-concentration proved kind enough to let me immerse myself and I relaxed for a while, though I wasn't comforted. For the first time, I realised how much I needed the entities in my head and my conversations with them. They turned out to be my safest hiding place.

I particularly missed *Reason* and *Pride,* and I was desperate to have *Confidence,* but she was probably meditating again with a glass of wine and her ears shut.

After spending a couple of hours in isolation, I found Toma, deep in thought and walking in circles. He didn't feel like working on his security plan tasks. His warm eyes stared at me and all of a sudden he even gave me a hug: squeezing me in his big paws and repeating what an incredible creature I was. Awkwardly, I pushed him away, failing to respond to the compliment in the manner he had taught me. Trying to create a distance, I murmured that I didn't like to be touched. Toma said he wanted to ventilate his head for a while outside the office. I asked if he would help me get the rest of my stuff, most importantly my books, from Maddie's flat and take them to Chris's. He replied that he was going to do that alone and insisted that I shouldn't go out before he was back. I gave him Maddie's number and confirmed that I was going to wait for him at the office.

I had often thought about my books since I had moved out. After reading each of them, I had placed it in the colourful row of book spines. Waking up to the sight of this harmonious regularity was one of my few pleasures in life. At breakfast, I would often entertain myself by arranging the gummy bears in the same way. I was immersed in the memories of these cosy moments when, suddenly, my thoughts ran in another direction. The colour sequence of the paintings in Victor's living room appeared before my eyes. I arranged it in my mind and beamed. His pattern was nuanced and gloomy. It started with white and ended with black, and twisting abstract shapes went through it like flames. Every shade was exactly one third stronger than the previous one. They followed a precise ascending pattern and he was probably the only person there who could see it. Apart from me. The two wackos. In my thoughts, I studied his floor, too. It was truly amazing to the googolth degree. A perfect sequence of wooden elements. I still couldn't figure out what it reminded me of, but it resembled the shape of a triangle. Its complexity created the illusion of chaos, yet it was actually another perfect piece of geometric harmony.

How is it even possible for him to count and see the sequences? How could he create perfect patterns, given how distorted he is?!

Reason popped up, as if through a blinking TV screen, and I jumped:

He is a faulty pattern altogether! He is not simply distorted, he is the very unit of measure for distortedness. A complete sociopath that we should be beware of.

The Monster's nasty voice joined in. It seemed to be coming from a tunnel:

He got bored of dolls and decided to play with freaks! Some choice you made for a guy to fall for! I guess you will need a price list, too, freak!

The voices faded away. My thoughts were floating in different directions, and the ones about Victor seemed to fill my lungs with his scent, with heat, and suffocating anger. Shivers rained all over my body, my stomach tightened. The memory of the musk brought the morning breath shortage again and a hallucination attacked me out of nowhere. The glassy blue was staring at me, then the remaining part of his face appeared as well—he seemed so real behind my closed eyelids. I reached out and unexpectedly touched some skin. My eyes opened abruptly.

Chris's colourful irises pierced me. He shook his head, his eyebrows up high. I choked as the jab between the fifth and the sixth ribs spiked me, followed by his voice:

'You're so damn stuck, Smarty!'

I snorted and pulled myself away.

'Well yeah I'm stuck! Your goddamn whisky and cigarettes left me short of breath and there's some piercing pain in my ribs. Why are you sneaking up on me like that? It's creepy,' I was nervous and he smirked.

'Right! Surely, it was the whisky that left you red-faced, biting your lips. And cigarette packs often warn that "smoking leads to the ridiculous appearance of having a crush",' he rolled his eyes and I gawked.

'Man, you have some serious issues with your expressions and your comparisons! What's wrong with you? Not sober yet? I'm not ridiculous and I definitely don't look like I have a crush.'

'Sure, if you say so! Your phone's off and I came to see how you're doing. I also brought you the power of attorney and bank statements, in case you still need them. Your ex-boss ordered me to get them ready for you, didn't he? He's still my boss, at least for now, so I must fulfil my tasks.'

'You think he's going to fire you?'

'I don't think so, I hope so! Did you manage to sort things out with him? I guess he can't take it, not being able to control his toy. He must be very annoyed, sending his hounds after you.'

'I sorted everything out! He expected me to go to him and even name my price... his typical stuff. He obviously assumes that I would wake up and then just go with some stranger, a Russian with the face of a serial murderer, to fly to the far end of Europe and give him explanations. He thought that I had an outburst of some kind! Imagine that! After his abominable behaviour, unbearable way of communication, and that sick set-up, he says the problem is me again!' I coughed and went silent, minding not to give away anything else. Chris examined me with suspicion.

'Ha! So that's why you were in that mood last night? How did you find out about... what was her name?' He narrowed his eyes and I froze. 'Maggie?'

My intuition jumped to its feet and alerted me that I had to fool Chris if I wanted to find out what he was talking about. Unexpectedly, *Knowledge* started declaring:

Fooling someone requires a calm voice and an affirmative answer. An imitation of actions and then immediately a counter question to make the interlocutor underestimate us.

I managed to remain calm and gave *Knowledge* an imperceptible nod while Chris was lighting his cigarette. I took one for myself, aiming to distract his attention by making him light it for me and thus concealing my ignorance on the matters.

'Maddie. It wasn't that hard. After all, her skull contains three brain cells chasing each other. How did *you* find out?' My blank expression and my barrier proved useful, as always.

'Me?' He smirked before continuing smugly: 'I personally gave her the money. It didn't take long. Stupid and greedy, too, and obviously pretty convincing.'

I gulped. Chris continued, studying my face with suspicion.

'She's good at that,' I sucked on the cigarette, not taking my eyes off the colourful irises.

He laughed.

'You got me, Smarty. You don't know anything! Good job, though, you got me for a moment.'

'I do! I know!'

'I can tell, Nia. Your eyebrows trembled, your eyes are more open than usual and the adrenaline produced dilated your pupils. I know body language perfectly; I've long studied it. Even psychopaths like you can't control their physical reactions to certain emotions. Surprise is one of them.'

'You must be perfectly aware then that us, psychopaths, don't feel emotions like others do! Body language is not reliable for any conclusions in my case. All right, I'm not gonna lie to you, I don't know the specific details, but I can guess. You gave Maddie money to fuck Andre, is that it? It didn't take her long because sex is the absolute extent of her skills!' I turned my back on him, taking a deep draw from the cigarette.

'Maybe they had been doing each other anyway. I didn't ask questions. Her task was to bang him on a regular basis at your flat. You're not suffering because of his morals now, are you?' His tone turned mocking as he nudged my shoulder. I stepped back.

'What can I say?' I shrugged and nervously admitted: 'People's behaviour stopped surprising me a long time ago, at least that's what I thought. It's not Maddie or Andre. They're both clear to me. It's Victor who keeps revealing new dimensions of insanity. What are you staring at? Waiting for my moral assessment?'

'I'm not waiting for anything. What set-up were you talking about then?'

'I can't tell you this!'

'Well, Smarty, trust is a waltz that requires equal steps from both dancers. If you can't trust me, then I won't trust you either and I won't tell you anything anymore.'

'It's not a matter of trust. I promised Toma and I don't want to lie to him.'

'You promised and you don't wanna lie? To Bear?' Chris giggled sarcastically. 'Why so?'

'Because I don't lie to my friends. I promised him!'

'Your friend?' his cynical laughter made me scowl. 'Do you even know who Toma is to promise him anything?'

'He's not just a driver, obviously,' I snapped. 'I know he also takes care of Victor's delicate tasks!'

'Not just a driver!' He shook his head, still laughing. 'Nia, he's Victor's partner!'

'What partner are you talking about? And stop parroting, it's really annoying!'

'I'll tell you only if you tell me about the set-up.'

I squinted at him, tapping my foot. He had managed to tempt me again, and I was annoyed at *Curiosity*.

'You're like a demon at a crossroads, Chris,' I grunted and he imitated horns with his fingers as he stared at me with anticipation. 'All right, damn it! But you go first.'

'Long story short, Toma is Victor's only partner. He owns a part of his business. They've known each other for over 20 years, and he's like a brother to Victor. I don't know the story of their friendship, but Toma is a weirdo, ex-military, he doesn't like people, he doesn't like talking. He somehow gets along with you well, but he mostly grunts at everyone else. He lives in modesty, wears his black clothes, and avoids life altogether. He only does things for Kaov, but I don't really know what. I only know that all he cares about is preventing problems for Victor, and obviously the current problem is you. How could you assume that this person was your friend?' He made a mocking face.

'Bullshit! How could he be a partner in a business if he's been with me all the time for days? And brother? Victor sent him off the other day! You're making it all up!'

'I'm telling you what it is! He couldn't have sent him off. All Toma cares about is Victor; it's like he's mesmerised. He doesn't have any other relatives or friends! Even if you delude yourself into thinking he is your friend, the true reason is not you! Tell me about the set up now! I wonder what Kaov came up with this time.'

'Damn it! That's not possible!' I sighed, rubbing my face.

'This is the truth! Ask him if you want! Now speak—we must equalise the proportions of information! What did Victor set up for you?' Chris nudged me, offering another cigarette.

'It's about the work, but it stays between us, OK?' He nodded and I started muttering reluctantly: 'First, Victor offered me a position working for him out of nowhere, and he didn't give me any details. I wasn't sure about it; he acted very weirdly. Then he got me into dealing with real estate and managing the whole process on my own. All of a sudden, I got fired from my internship and some other dubious events occurred, too. I didn't know what to do and I accepted because of the money. The other night I found myself at his house and... Anyway! It turns out that Victor has negotiated everything to do with the real estate beforehand... He actually set the whole thing up… Something like this. That's how I ended up in this mess,' I shrugged and sighed.

'He's a maniac! I told you! I must admit that he's dangerous when he makes up his mind on something, he has no limits. Truly a sociopath! He managed to bang you and you fell for him, didn't you? You're not all in there'

'And you're all there? Huh? Enough with this bullshit! What is with you and who-banged-who! Tell me more about Maddie! How did you get to her in the first place?'

'Pretty easy. Your university is full of naughty girls who like money. I know someone who goes clubbing with your Maddie. It was easy to make her intrigued, and that's all. As soon as I saw you at the reception, I knew that my task was somehow related to you. I guess Victor wanted to gather some information that you'd find interesting. He likes collecting that type of stuff. I think your flat was wired but you should ask him about details, I don't know them.'

'He seems to like all sorts of collections. I'm not going to ask him; I won't speak to him anymore. His actions are not only maniacal, they're perverted. An overly satisfied man with some weird hobbies!'

'You did him. You're the one who'd know if he was a pervert, not me!'

'How am I supposed to know what's perverted and what's not?'

'Well, generally there are some sex norms and they are well-known. About his actions, you heard what Bear said about Victor last night— that's exactly how he is! He can afford it—he does it! After all, it's exactly overly satisfied men with weird hobbies that occupy politics and the peaks of business.'

'That's why our poor planet is near its end!'

'They like getting what they want, no matter the price. That's how things work and I doubt it'll change! Just take it!' He gave me a mean look before changing the subject: 'I'm leaving the documents here. Tell me if you need anything else. Care for some lunch now? There's a new Italian restaurant downtown and it's very trendy. I just don't know whether the guys outside will let you go, or follow us like a travelling circus? Sergey won't fit in the trunk of my sports car,' his attempt to joke irritated me even further and I grunted.

'I don't want to read documents right now. I won't argue with the Russian guy either—I'd eventually punch him in the face! Plus, my outfit doesn't suggest any trendy new Italian restaurants. I'm not in the mood for haughty gazes with my spaghetti.'

'I think all you'll get are salacious gazes, despite your crappy sweater. And if you comb your hair and dress normally, you'll get date invitations with your spaghetti. But it's up to you. Tell me if you need anything else regarding the documents. I have everything on my computer.'

'OK. Give me another cigarette!'

He lit one for me and headed for the door before stopping short.

'I'll give you my advice: get rid of that stuck-up face and focus on your capabilities! And another thing: don't let Victor manipulate you! You're outrageously smart, but he's outrageously good at manipulating people. Besides, you handle emotions the way a Neanderthal would handle a space shuttle, and it'd undoubtedly be unhealthy for you to get involved with someone like him.'

Chris left the room.

'For Christ's sake, man! You should see a doctor for your ridiculous metaphors!' I seethed.

As I watched his back down the hallway, *Reason* gave me a start by popping out of the blinking TV again:

Listen to what people say! I warned you that we will have problems with the hallucinations, now you should stay alert for the manipulations. They are just as dangerous. I don't even want to find out what a nightmare emotions are!

For a moment my head became clear again. All the entities were there, although they were blinking. *Desire* and *Lust* were having their group therapy again. *Curiosity* wasn't giving *Knowledge* a break, as always. Fortunately, I had learned how to mute their unbearable conversations as soon as I turned seventeen. *Reason* had his arms crossed and was tapping his foot. *Pride* was storming about. Their voices were muffled, though, and all I could hear was some indistinct buzz. *The Monster's* neigh overcame every other sound. I was pretty aware of what it was going to nag about, and the thought alone brought a bitter taste to my mouth. I pressed my forehead against the French window, growled, and repeatedly slammed it with my palm. My breath shortage and the jab in my ribs became worse. Dull, tightening pain enveloped my chest, building worry inside me. I finished my cigarette, nevertheless. Its fire seemed to ignite my anger for Toma.

'That's it! It's like I'm competing with myself at making the worst judgements possible! How could I think that he was my friend? How did I mess up so badly? I've lost my mind! I'm like an honourable guest at *Le Dîner de Cons* and it's getting even worse!'

I couldn't find my place. Eventually I decided to take the documents at Chris's—to go there without Toma, and explain to the Bad Guy that he should leave me alone.

Sergey was leaning against the wall in the hallway. He stood up abruptly when he saw me, and the other guys jumped to their feet as well. I tried to conduct a peaceful conversation with him, but my voice escalated every time I had to repeat my demands and every time he refused to comply. Then he muttered something in Russian to the others and I understood that they were planning to take me to Victor's house. They circled me like vultures and I started shouting, squeezing the folders. The huge bodies towering over me provoked my claustrophobia. I yelled at them to back off but they didn't move. All of a sudden, Toma jumped out of the elevator. He pushed them away and squatted before me as I was gasping for air.

'Get them off me!' I waved my hands and he hissed at them to get some water.

'What's wrong? Are you OK?' His warm brown eyes examined me. He shoved a glass under my nose, but I turned my head nervously. 'Sergey, I gave you a distinct instruction to not talk to her anymore! Can't you see that you're scaring her! She's all white and hardly breathing! What did you do to her?' He yelled at the Russian while still chasing my mouth with the edge of the glass. I pushed his hand, the water spilled everywhere and he stared at me, sulkily.

'I'm claustrophobic, I'm not scared or thirsty. These idiots circled me and I guess they're deaf. They don't hear what they're told,' I gathered the folders from the floor and hurried to the elevator.

'Toma, Kaov ordered me to drive her to the mansion if she tried to leave without you. She has been explaining for 10 minutes now that she was leaving alone. What was I expected to do?'

The elevator arrived and I stepped in. Toma followed me without caring to reply. I stared at the buttons, pretending not to notice him, and he grunted:

'We said you were to wait for me, didn't we? Where are you going?'

'I'm going back to Chris's place!'

'All right, the car is in the garage!' He pressed the -1 button, his eyes glued on me. 'Are you angry with me?'

'Why would I be, Toma? Who am I after all to be angry with you!'

We came to a halt on the ground floor, and he grabbed my elbow. His crooked face was sad.

'Let's not argue! I will drive you and you will tell me why you are angry when you decide you want to. Please, goblin,' he took the folders from my hands.

φ

I kept gazing sulkily at the boulevard, counting Toma's deep sighs. We arrived at the house in complete silence. The doorman seemed to have been instructed to let in Toma's car only. The jeeps that had been following us again stayed on the other side of the barrier. I smiled smugly.

Chris's housekeeper opened the door. I stormed past her without even greeting her and Toma followed me. He tried to talk to me, but I kept my mouth shut. Leaning against the door to the yard, I watched him pouring whisky for himself. He dropped down on the couch in the living room and stared back at me. My initial intention was to just torture him with my stomach-twisting gaze, but his false-friendly conduct provoked me. I approached him nervously, my index finger raised menacingly in the air, and opened and closed my mouth a couple of times like a fish. After I took breath for the fifth time, I hissed:

'I might be all the worst things, but I don't deserve this from you!'

I ran to the yard. Late autumn sunbeams caressed my body and I decided to caress my ears as well—with music. As Toma peered out, I demonstratively plugged the earbuds deeper into my ears, and he went back in, his face down.

After half an hour, he appeared again and I silently watched him dragging a chair over. I kept waving my legs in sync with the song that played on repeat. As always, Sting[19] was saving my broken mind with his "broken music"[20].

Toma served two glasses of whisky, then pulled one of my earbuds out. I took the other one out and stared viciously at him. He surprised me by not attempting to explain anything. Instead, he spoke in a business-like tone:

'I guess it's not the right moment for this, but you're in a bad mood anyway, so I'd better tell you now. I'm so sorry, but that bitch threw all

---

[19] *Sting – Englishman in New York – author's notes.*
[20] *Broken Music: A Memoir* By Sting, PUBLISHER: Random House Publishing Group

your things away. I don't imagine how you could live with such a horrible person! She was shouting, cursing, hissing...'

'My books?' I gaped.

'Everything!'

'Damn her! Dirty slut! How could she do that?!' I hit the table and Toma frowned. 'I should've got them earlier. I shouldn't have left them there. What a mean creature! Is it contagious? Why is everybody so mean?' I turned red.

'Don't get mad over this, too! Please! My heart breaks when I see your teary eyes. Let's go and buy the same books,' he took my hand in his paw, but I pulled it away.

'Don't get mad? Do you know how many gummy bears I haven't eaten in order to afford those books! Even if I stop eating today, it'll still take years to get them back!'

'They are on me. Don't worry about that! We'll have some fun; we'll eat ice-cream and we'll talk. We have things to discuss,' he gave me another pitiful look.

'And how do you have so much money? Delicate tasks pay well, perhaps? Or maybe there's some cash left from the clothes we didn't buy? Or is there something else?' I hissed and he gritted his teeth. 'I don't want you to buy anything for me! It's my problem that I moved out! Another one of my wrong decisions with a proportionate result. That's all!' I jumped angrily off the chair.

'Please, don't give me the robot attitude again! Act human and tell me why you're pissed?'

'So now you're assessing my attitude, too?' I stomach-twisted him with my gaze but then continued in an even tone: 'My plan is to finish my work from here. I will be ready in a day, I guess. I'll call you when I'm finished and give you the documents for Victor. Thank you for trying and sorry if Maddie gave you too much crap. There's no reason for you to stay here any longer. I'd like you to leave and tell the Bad guys to leave, too!'

'I can't tell them to leave but I'll make sure they don't bother you.'

'Oh, yeah, excuse me—what I meant was I'd like you to instruct them!'

'What I meant was that I'll speak with Victor.'

'You two speak a lot, don't you? Come to think of it, you never specified how exactly you work for him... Apart from the delicate tasks to satisfy his perverted hobbies,' the irony in my voice was a perfect match for my cynical face. Toma was embarrassed and stared at his palms. 'You avoided the truth,

Toma. Then you lied to me. This is what I didn't deserve. That's why I'm pissed with you.'

'What bullshit did Chris tell you?' He snapped, his face all red.

The Monster suddenly neighed, spat in my mouth and made it twist.

'Great! You won't even stop! You know, I guess it sounds unbelievable, but I have a friend, too. A true one! Wildling told me that friends never lie to each other. Deceiving each other is also wrong. When you came to me, to that yard, I thought that you accepted me and that you were a friend. Communicating with you was somehow easy, it didn't make me tense. All of a sudden, I got this crazy idea that you cared, that you were comfortable with me. I was supposed to have learned how to not make irrational conclusions a long time ago, but delusions are chasing me lately,' my disappointment stretched into a crooked smile. 'Not telling me in time about the job was enough. And after this new lie, *the Monster* definitely won't leave me alone! You were the person I pointed out to prove that it was wrong!'

Toma frowned angrily and interrupted me:

'Nia, I don't know what that *Monster* is, I don't know what it was wrong about, but you can't doubt that I accept you and hold you dear. And, most of all, you can't doubt that I care for you. You got that?'

'Yeah, right! As Victor's partner, as his almost-brother, as his outside camera—as what exactly do you care? Oh, wait! Maybe as the "friend" who has been pushing me towards my wrong conclusions all along?'

'Why is it so important what I am? You asked me not to hold prejudice against you, and now you're doing it to me. You're judging me! You're assessing me by secondary factors, and not for who I really am,' he spoke nervously.

'And who are you really, Toma? How am I supposed to assess you after that nasty business with Maddie?'

'What are you talking about?'

'Don't play innocent! I just don't know how you managed to get me to see them mid-sex, so you could take me straight to Victor. Not that I care, but I guess nobody would enjoy the sight. You two decided to experiment with how the freak would react in such a situation, or what? Am I like a mouse in a labyrinth? You put me in different scenarios because—how did you say it—"he's just like that", or "because he can afford it",' I wouldn't take my eyes off his. He examined my expression in silence.

'Nia. Would you please explain what the hell are you talking about because I don't get it!'

'What's there to explain? Chris told me everything! He personally gave Maddie the money and she was quick to fulfil the task. And you're still lying to me! How can you even participate in all this? Can't you see how wrong it is? Damn!' I was waving my hands about and Toma clenched his jaw. 'Leave! You're not wanted here! Take the gorillas with you and tell the Russian that if he dares to come anywhere near me again, he'll see just how inventive I could be! I don't care about his one hundred kilos of muscle! I have *Malice* with me! And she has some controversial methods, I swear!'

Toma didn't reply. He turned around and stormed to the exit. Although I was in the backyard, I could still hear how he drove off at full speed. I sat down on the grass, my hands shoved in my hair. Without even having to utter a word, *the Monster* managed to turn *Contempt* against me, against everyone else, and against the general reality. I kept trying to drown it in whisky, but it only seemed to intensify the burning sensation that tortured my cells. I didn't want to spend even a second thinking about the whole rotten story. There was probably not even a hypothetical chance for me to comprehend all of it. My mind was immersed in chaos and I was struggling to gain control over my attention and turn it off in some way. It was an unsuccessful struggle.

The truth is that general reality, devoid of any logic, is full of wormy relationships. Twenty-three and a half years had not been enough for me to comprehend the reasons for lying, being mean, nor for the distortion of people and their faulty patterns. I knew that if I decided to ask Maddie why she had thrown my books away and used Andre in that gruesome manner, she would only say that it was my fault. There was absolutely no causal link between me and her wrong decisions, and yet she would be fully convinced of her rightness. She wouldn't accept any of my logical arguments.

I had undoubtedly discovered that people had developed similar pathologies. They are probably even aware that the result of such illogical actions would be negative, yet they repeat them all over again. They adore obscuring the truth with flat excuses, inaccurate statements, even esoteric beliefs. Sometimes they also practise quantum physics in their primitive style: "it was meant to happen this way", "fate wants it this way" and such nonsense. People in the general reality are experts in probability theory. At night, they calculate the potential of a certain probability and in the morning, they confidently announce the results they concluded. They avoid, however, looking for accurate and reasoned judgement in the cosmic predetermination. They don't aim for their actions to align with such a judgement. It seems that every member of the human race is enrolled in a competition in distorting the truth in the most absurd ways possible and acting in the worst possible ways. Everyone else simply applauds the new levels of stupidity.

The general absurdity also involves tarot, palm, saliva and sweat reading—everything that can devalue simple logic and value or justify some insane judgements. When the proportionate negative consequences occur, people just wave them off and go back to their quantum principle: "it was meant to happen this way", "fate wants it this way", or—my favourite!— "that's normal". They don't try to resist following the faulty patterns and they don't object if someone else follows them, too. They find it easy to accept the bad results, or simply ignore them.

I was contemplating the new, even more gruesome face of the general reality, when Chris startled me:

'Moody again! At least now you look rather more angry than stuck-up!'

'Are the jeeps gone?'

'No, they're still outside. Where's Bear?'

'I don't know. I asked him to leave and take those jerks with him.'

'He's not gone, I even gave him a key earlier. Why is he a problem for you?'

'For Christ's sake! Why would you give him a key? I don't want him here. I don't want to have anything to do with him, Victor, or those jerks outside.'

'Smarty, I'm sorry to be the bearer of bad news, but this is not going to happen this easily, nor this quickly.'

I took a breath to dispute this statement, but Chris put his hand on my shoulder and carried on with a smile:

'Let's not argue! Let's go out and have some fun, even if we have to put up with the circus that will be following us. Put on something more proper and we'll go to the Italian restaurant I told you about.'

'I'm fine this way! I refuse to be proper anymore. I tried and it's been nothing but trouble ever since. This is what I have and this is what I'll wear!'

'All right, don't hiss. You could at least comb your hair, put on a T-shirt and high heels, and you'll be the fashion rebel tonight. There's face control at the restaurant, even for women! I don't think they'll like your sweater!' He grinned, holding out a hand to help me to my feet.

'Seems that there's face control for everything in this general reality. I can't keep up with their standards anymore. But all right then, I won't embarrass you!' I grimaced and he laughed out loud. 'Give me a couple of minutes!'

After a quick shower, I put on a T-shirt and high-waisted jeans, but left my hair loose. I put on the heeled shoes and decorated my wrist with my favourite accessory: an ancient, scratched watch from my grandad that he had worn at the beginning of his military service. He had made the steel strap shorter and had put a piece of leather beneath it, so it wouldn't touch my metal-allergic skin. I made a halt at the door and decided it wouldn't hurt to put on some make-up and the red lipstick that turned grey pigeons into flamingos. At that moment I badly needed to be a sparkling, flamboyant flamingo.

Chris was waiting for me in his irrational two-seater car. He suggested that we should try to shake off the Russian's company. I bent down so they wouldn't see me in the car with him and, to my surprise, they took the bait and remained at the entrance.

'Your hair is impractically long. I haven't seen it loose before,' he pulled it and I laughed.

'Yup, it's just as impractical as your car. Why is it missing two seats?'

He seemed a little offended.

'I'm thirty, which means that I'm still a young and popular bachelor. With this car, hunting for women is easy, like catching goldfish in a bowl. It speeds up the process, and I don't have much spare time.'

'Your comparisons are getting even weirder! I'll just leave the parallel between ornamental fish and women with no comment! But what if you catch one right now—where would you put her? In the trunk?'

'I doubt I'll get lucky tonight. Even the car won't help when I'm accompanied by a sexy fish like you. If something happens anyway, I'll just drive you home and go back.'

'Thanks for the compliment, though it's suspicious. I think your irises are an interesting and rare genetic mutation,' I nodded, pleased to find myself applying my new skills. His jaw dropped. 'All right, you can take me back home if something happens. But you'll have to instruct me on how to communicate with the goldfish if I encounter them in the morning. I've had such conversations and I know that women don't react well to being a one-night stand.'

'Women? What about you?'

'I don't have much reference yet. At this point, however, I can't see why sex should be put within time frames. Rather, the problem is repeatability.

Especially if you expect it without grounds and annoying *Desire* digs into your brain like a worm. I suspect these are also sex side effects, but my hypotheses are unconfirmed yet.'

'I must admit that Kaov has certain qualities if he's able to handle you. I don't even know how he managed,' Chris rolled his eyes, stepping on the accelerator.

φ

We flew down the boulevard. The brakes whistled as he stopped arrogantly in front of an elegant building. There was a long queue, and everyone stared at us. A young guy opened the door for me and Chris tossed him the keys before leading me in by the elbow. The sturdy bouncers at the entrance unhooked the red rope that served as a barrier, and I heard shouts from the queue.

It was a nice, cosy restaurant that bore the spirit of Italy where I dreamed to go someday. I examined the pompously dressed guests, but even their appearance didn't make the place look kitschy or snobbish. No one gave me critical looks. They were just laughing and talking, sipping wine from their glasses. Despite the ban, people were smoking inside and smoke rose from the tables, carrying the sound of cheerful voices. I enjoyed it all and smiled, too.

The music and the atmosphere improved my mood, and Chris chose some great pinot noir that happened to match my taste. I was captivated by his Italian travel stories while I struggled with the bizarre artichoke plant. Just as I was swallowing, Sergey leaned over my head. I almost choked on my bite. The Russian only grunted that I was to turn my phone on, then he left. Annoyed, Chris rolled his eyes and motioned that he was going for a potential goldfish at the bar until I was finished with my task.

I dug the device out of my backpack. As soon as I switched it on, a bombardment of Victor's *Telegram* messages arrived. There was a text from Toma, too:

Why did you go out alone? I texted Chris a hundred times!
Please, reply to Victor, because he's gone crazy again!

Like a musical line, the tone in Victor's messages went to peaks of unacceptability and then declined to normal. Of course, he still maintained his thesis about my outbursts and insane acts. Then he claimed that I couldn't behave like this. I ignored numerous messages containing only capital letters. They were followed by texts with the "can't" leitmotif: can't go out without security, can't switch my phone off, can't keep him unaware of my whereabouts. Again, he was saying that I had driven him mad in less than twenty-four hours and I frowned at every piece of his nonsense. The last message was different, though:

> *I'm sorry. I was too mad.*
> *I don't know how to communicate with you.*
> *What should I do so you can understand me?*
> *How should I do it?*

While I was trying to come up with a reply, I received another, even shorter text:

> *Don't let go of me, Nia!*

Once again, my breath shortage hit me, suddenly and vigorously. My lungs were paralysed for a second and I clutched the edge of the table. The jabbing in my ribs was so brutal that I whimpered. I put the phone down so I could clutch the edge with my other hand as well. I was trying to balance my breathing when Chris came to me. He turned my face, tapping my cheek.

'You OK? What happened?' He leaned before me, looking worried.

'I'm fine! I told you that some breath shortage has been torturing me since morning. It shall pass. I guess the smoke here made it worse.'

'Bullshit! Kaov's bothering you again. Let's get out of here, you don't look well.'

'No, I'm fine. I need a minute to text something back and then you'll tell me everything about Italy.'

He returned sulkily to the bar. I got my breathing back to normal and a sip of wine made the jabbing subside. I took the phone and started pressing the screen.

> *There are too many messages, so I'll focus only on the last ones, on*
> *your questions. You don't have to do anything, and nothing can be done*
> *to help me understand you.*
> *The reason: I don't have the desire and/or interest to do this.*
> *I gave up trying to understand faulty patterns long ago,*

because there's a risk of me starting to act according to them, too.
I don't know what you mean by your last text in the negative
imperative form.
I'm not holding you, therefore I can't let go of you, therefore
you can't expect me to not do that. I find all this too abstract.
P.S. I insist that Sergey stops tormenting me. This means that he
and the rest of the men should leave. They made me claustrophobic
today, they're torturing me, and there's no reason for them to hang around.
P.P.S. I don't want to talk to you anymore!
Stay away from me, Victor!

He saw the message right away but didn't reply. I caught myself staring at the screen, tapping my fingers, when Chris got my attention with a splendid lemon sorbet. We finished our desserts with the agreement that I was going to pay for my part of the dinner as soon as I got my money. He on the other hand promised to fulfil the lack of gummy bears for breakfast.

His car was driven to the entrance. I looked around to see that the jeeps were not there and they didn't appear on the way, either. We went home undisturbed. Toma's room was empty. I declined Chris's offer to drink whisky because tiredness was pushing me straight to my room.

I kept falling asleep but it seemed that I woke up in a blink. The breath shortage again. It was as if someone was pressing against my chest. I was tossing and turning, the bed seemed to be hungrily sucking all strength away from me and exhausting me. As I was lying there in a half-awake state, a hallucination bumped into my body. I prickled. Victor was in me. His fingertips were touching my face and his lips were biting mine. His heat sank into my every bone. The blue was staring at me, teasingly. He was enjoying my desire, owning it, and I was writhing on the pyre. Our strengths weren't even—he controlled me and I couldn't resist. He kept filling me up, crucifying me, I fell apart into pieces in his arms and I was no longer myself. Who I was anyway? My consciousness crumbled to a million particles that vibrated in his rhythm. Hidden in the darkest corner of my mind, my other self, my new personality craved to be his. It was wailing. My new personality was inclined to bend and fit. Poisoned and addicted, it was up for any life compromises. I was damaged. A complete mess.

In the middle of the night, my eyes opened abruptly and I stared at the black ceiling. My heart pounding underneath my sweaty skin. All the information flew through my head and made me dizzy. Then, I was sick. My index finger touched the corner of my eyes. Something burned there. A thin stream of saline flowed to the pillow.

TWELVE

It was past ten. An annoying sparrow on the ledge was rehearsing a courtship melody that challenged my deep respect towards animals. On the other side of the window, routine life was pursuing its usual purpose. I couldn't move, though. I didn't know how to handle the new condition of my body. How did normal people cope with all this? My very being was crushed under the neurological and chemical processes that were taking place. The *Monster* was not there to swallow, *Knowledge, Reason* and their explanations were also gone. I had nobody. What was happening to my body and mind simply wasn't for a freak like me. It was as if I was under the attack of a raging *Beast*, and I had no idea how to fight back.

Turning face-down on the bed, I tried to hide from the general reality under the blanket. The reality was no longer only narrow for me—I was vigorously protesting against it. I suffered breath shortage, jabs between my fifth and the sixth ribs, and, most of all, I suffered from unwillingness. Unwillingness to accept the sequence of data that shaped the truth, nor my wrong decisions, nor the insult. I was struggling to refrain from mental judgements. I had been trying to get rid of this bad habit, but now I was judging, mostly by swearing and hitting the mattress. I was cursing Victor, Toma, the distorted world, the non-existent chances, myself... I even got to the esoteric point of saying fuck off to karma. Realisation hit me, however, that it was all my fault. I had been avoiding the facts, squinting at what was obvious. It was quite logical that I would eventually crash head-first into the consequences—or rather, the consequences crashed head-first into me. Some pathetic little motivation coming from Chris's job offer bounced in the back of my head, except it was not strong enough to scrape me off the bed, or to scrape the disappointment off me.

The housekeeper knocked on the door first. Then it was Chris. They kept checking on me every hour or two. Still, I wouldn't get up. Chris teased me about being stuck, or he might have been advising me but I threw a sock at him and hid back under the blanket. Hiding in bed is a popular therapeutic method, isn't it? People do it on a regular basis and I expected positive results, too. I just lay there, my head covered, waiting for my mind to clear up. However, it only fell back to sleep, buzzed or cursed, and the defected part of my brain kept pushing me to check my phone. Numerous times, I picked it up to see that there were no new messages. After the seventh try, I got irritated and shoved it in my backpack. I took a deep breath and even muttered some 'Om's in search of balance. My inner cynic nudged me. In the spiritual world, people use 'Om' to become one with the universe—with their cosmic self or something, while in the real world 'ohm' marks electrical resistance[21]. I found this contrast amusing. Despite my not-so-deep meditation, I achieved some progress and managed to sit on the edge of the bed.

I put an end to this sick story! Everything about the maniac is clear already! I left, and now I seem to be expecting him to chase me. What is this messed-up anomaly?

Rubbing my face, *Reason*'s sudden murmur made me jump up:

Fairy tales are to blame. I have been telling you all along, they are dangerous! They have messed you up from an early age. Sleeping, barefoot, starving, princesses undercover. They always run and there is always someone

---

[21] *Ohm is the unit of electrical resistance and is abbreviated with the capital Greek letter omega (Ω). It is named after the German physicist Georg Simon Ohm (1789-1854) who discovered the relationship between voltage, current and resistance for each part of the electrical circuit and described it by Ohm's law – author's notes.*

chasing them, or even worse—saving them. Brainwashing! And then people wonder why they are unhappy with their misguided expectations!

Knowledge's squeaky voice joined in:

I confirm! It's archetypal propaganda. A degenerate and dangerous practice.

'Damn, I'm so glad you're here! I thought I'd gone completely insane. So, what now? Am I crazy because of the fairy-tales? Am I a princess freak with literary damage since childhood?' I patted my cheeks. 'Does this happen to normal women as well? They read books, too. I guess they also read fairy-tales. Is this a common anomaly?'

They didn't reply.

I staggered downstairs with my pathetic, messy-hair appearance. It felt like I was carrying an elephant on my back. The baggy T-shirt covered my panties. Daenerys Targaryen, in the company of her dragon, looked sunnier than me. I found Chris in the living room, wrapped in his own blanket for hiding from the general reality, a bottle of whisky by his side. He was swearing at the laptop.

'What're you doing?'

He kept hitting the keyboard, not even bothering to look up.

'I'm raging!'

'Why?'

'The new episode of "Game of Thrones" is today, and now my account is blocked. Lovely!'

'You watch that?' I gaped as my mood brightened.

'Who doesn't watch "Game of Thrones"? You crazy?' He hissed, still hitting the laptop.

'Relax. Stop breaking it. I have an account, too. Use mine.'

A wide smile brightened his face.

'That's why people should have roommates—they'll either save your life if you choke, or your mood,' he looked at me with enthusiasm, then sighed heavily. 'Are you done suffering? I thought you'd stay in bed at least for a day. Forty-eight hours is what it takes for those goddamn hormones to be processed.'

'Yeah!' I dropped down on the couch and took a sip of whisky. 'Cortisol[22] is pretty horrible, I must admit. My liver is overloaded, and then there's these jabs, and the breath shortage. Disgusting! Gloomy thoughts engulfed me as well. I hope it'll be processed soon!'

Chris nodded, lowering the huge screen, and I gasped at the quality of the picture and the sound. We had missed only a few minutes of the episode. He shared his blanket with me and we stared at the screen as if hypnotised. Unexpectedly, he hugged me, ruffled my hair and kissed my forehead. I didn't even have the strength to scold him for touching me, so I just settled myself more comfortably. While we were arguing over our character preferences in the series, Toma popped up at the door. I jumped up, but Chris squeezed my knee and motioned for me to refrain from confrontation. Toma sat down cautiously on the far end of the couch. He stared at me, but I defiantly turned my head back to the screen.

'What are you watching?'

'You're supposed to say "good evening" first!' I snapped, not taking my eyes off the screen.

'"Game of Thrones", of course. Don't you watch it?' Chris did his best to speak calmly, and Toma grunted.

'No! Is it another nonsense with wizards?' His mocking tone was disturbed by the scolding looks we shot in his direction. 'All right, all right, don't kill me! It was a joke!'

'Great series!' Chris waved his index finger, though he still wouldn't allow me to join in the conversation. 'You'll catch up with the old episodes and choose your favourite for the throne. I hope it'll be different to ours, so we can argue. Hush now! You can make popcorn if you like.'

Bear walked to the kitchen and after a brief struggle with the microwave, reappeared with sodas and three bowls of popcorn. We didn't take our eyes off the screen. Toma went back to bring glasses because he saw us drinking whisky from the bottle. Fortunately, he kept quiet and didn't bother us with dumb questions.

As soon as the episode was over, Chris and I started a debate. Toma asked if we could explain the storyline for him. My roommate explained

---

[22] *A catabolic steroid hormone. It is often referred to as "the hormone of stress" because its levels increase significantly after physical or emotional stress – author's notes.*

that he supported the Starks and suggested that I was a Targaryen fan. I replied sulkily:

'I'm not with Daenerys. She's a cute weirdo, though. A total misfit, and yet she manages to change the whole reality there. She's absolutely insane but look at how determined and confident she is. True inspiration for freaks, or for me, at least.'

'Who do you support for the throne then?' Chris frowned.

'The question is not who I support. I calculated the probabilities and I'm updating them with every new episode. The result varies, but I always get a three-point variable that I can't relate to anyone. I still don't have the exact answer.'

'You calculated the probabilities for the end?' Chris gawked and Toma shrugged.

'But of course! I have *Curiosity,* not patience. Who knows how many seasons they're gonna release before we know the end result? I applied Pascal's meth...'

It suddenly dawned on me. My mind flew back to Victor's house. The bright lines rushed through my head. They slid across his floor, bumped into a pattern and the shape was clear now. I smiled, my eyelids half-closed, and murmured hoarsely, my mind wandering around Victor's living room.

'Pascal! Pascal's triangle[23]! How did I not recognise it at once! You altered it in an ingenious way! How did you invent this!' My eyes ran back and forth between the floor and Victor who was sitting at the table. He started walking beside me, then we were in his study. I stared at the glassy blue that occupied my mind again. 'Your mind is beautiful, and yet you're so distorted. It's perfect, Victor, it's an impeccable pattern, and you are...' I opened my eyes abruptly upon realising that I was speaking aloud. Toma and Chris were gawking at me. Toma seemed concerned, and Chris—annoyed.

'You're stuck again, Smarty. Or perhaps you've gone completely out of your mind?' Chris spoke with spite as he took a sip from the bottle.

---

[23] *Pascal's triangle is a symmetrical numerical triangle. It serves as a rule for fast calculations of combinations, hence its importance in combinatorics and probability theory. It is used to calculate combinations without repetitions and binomial coefficients (Newton's binomial theorem). Binomial coefficient tables were known to Chinese and Arabic mathematicians. Pascal's merit was their popularisation in Europe – author's notes.*

'She's not out of her mind. She simply talks to herself sometimes,' Toma stared at me and put his warm paw on my shoulder. 'Goblin, maybe my judgement about the whole situation was wrong. I can see how your face changes when you speak about Victor. Maybe you two better discuss...'

'We have nothing to discuss! I made everything clear. I just remembered something and got carried away. His floor was a puzzle for me, but now I know what it is.'

'Wow! So now it's floors that make you blush? I thought it was only whisky and smoke,' Chris's irony flew with the spittle from his mouth.

'What the hell did you both expect?' I pointed at them angrily and they stepped back. 'You were the ones who drowned me in information that can be only defined as horrible, gruesome, and disgusting. Choose whichever definition you like! I drank it in shots in no time. What am I supposed to do? I'm not experienced, and my body's been poisoning me with a devastating dose of the worst hormones! It even brought saline to my tears last night. Everything will be fine once my liver is finished processing the excess biochemicals. Stop mentoring and criticising me! End of conversation! The topic about Victor is over.'

'Sorry I made you upset, Nia! I know you're disappointed, but you can at least talk to him! Relationships between people are not just hormones and liver processes. Maybe...' Toma was clutching my shoulder.

'They certainly are!' Chris and I interrupted together. We looked at each other and he explained:

'That's exactly what they are! Biochemical processes aiming for reproduction. The sociocultural specifics of our century complicated them, but they're still entirely influenced by hormones. I guess you've heard this popular abstract statement: "Time heals". Actually, it's the period it takes for the liver to process the excess substances. Suffering from relationships, love, and all sorts of drama is literally metabolised at the molecular level. Drinking a lot of water is useful in this regard. We throw the hormones away, we get detoxed, but unfortunately in most cases the process starts all over again. I suppose this is the doomed fate of our wretched kind. Until we evolve.'

'You're absolutely right, Chris! Don't forget the "mental stage" of metabolism because most people are not familiar with their own anatomy. They often attribute not feeling well to various emotions, but the proportion between a couple of hormones is simply broken. That's all!'

'Christ, I don't get half of the bullshit you're both saying! What hormones and what metabolism! People feel passion, love, grief,' Toma looked at us and I crossed my arms on my chest.

'I don't expect you to understand! You can explain why you're here now.'

'I came to see you. I asked Chris first.'

My roommate was on his way to sneak out of the room. I shouted at his back:

'Hey! What is he talking about? Why didn't you ask me?'

'It won't cause any harm. He just wanted to see you. I told you that getting rid of Victor is not going to be quick or easy. The same goes for Bear, too,' he disappeared from my sight and I twisted Toma with my gaze.

'All right, you saw me. You can go now!'

'Stop it, goblin! I didn't know anything about Maddie. I was mad because of this disgusting bullshit. Please, don't be angry with me!'

'I'm standing here, with my huge IQ, and I believe you,' my cynical tone made him sad.

'I'm telling the truth. I want to eat pancakes and listen to your weird conclusions again. I enjoy your company, goblin. I feel guilty for what happened,' I thought that he was sincere for a moment, but then I shook my head to chase the new delusion away.

'You enjoy being an outside camera, or Victor enjoys having one?' I grimaced and he didn't say anything. 'I hope I'll be alright tomorrow. My plan is to finish everything and hand you the documents for the president. I accepted a new job and I want to get to it already.'

'Let's discuss things. I know Victor goes too far with his obsessions and manias, but maybe I was too quick to make my conclusions...'

'I told you that this subject is over. You came to see me, didn't you? You saw me and you can go now!' I pointed to the exit and he headed in its direction with his nose down. He stopped at the door. Sadness flashed in his brown eyes.

'Nia, I want you to remember that I am your friend and you can count on me. For anything, anytime.'

'You're many things, Toma, but none of them is even close to my idea of a friend!' I snapped.

The disappointment on his face made me regret my words for a brief moment. I didn't stop him, nevertheless. He went out and my new door-issue turned my stomach upside-down.

φ

I leaned against the wall in the shower. The water was slamming into my skin; its touch made me relax and my mind drifted away again, taking me back to Victor's bathroom that morning. My back pressed against the tiles and my throat whimpered. My body craved what Victor could supply. A spasm squeezed the space below my navel, reminding me of the addictive sensation. I slid my hand down but remembering my previous pathetic attempt made me stop instantly. Somewhere in my mind, *Desire* sobbed. It had no obvious intention to leave. Irritated, *Reason* and I were discussing how it had turned from an intruder to a permanent, rather annoying guest.

I thought that it was perhaps a good idea for me to go back to my grandad's and isolate myself from everything that reminded me of Victor. However, the number of details I'd have to explain had increased in relation to my reluctance to give explanations. I looked at the bed. After having spent so many hours there, I didn't want to go anywhere near it. I picked up the folders with the documents but they didn't sustain my interest either. In the darkness of the night, my mind wandered again through the memories of Victor. Thoughts that made me sweat attacked me. I went back downstairs, wrapped myself in the blanket, and started watching the first season of 'Game of Thrones'. The bottle of whisky and a pack of cigarettes proved to be a great company. My eyelids gave up during the sixth episode. Well-sedated and half-asleep, I sensed a touch, followed by a movement. I opened one eye to see Chris carrying me up the stairs, then tucking me in my bed. I heard him whispering:

'This will pass too, angel. It'll pass.'

'This shall pass,' I murmured. Then I dozed off.

The clock on the phone showed it was past noon. I had no desire whatsoever to remind myself how bad smoking and drinking were. I stoically endured the consequences of my harmful deeds. Squinting, I found out that I had received a message on *Telegram*. I jumped up, but Victor was simply asking a dumb question:

So, you've discovered how I altered Pascal's triangle?

I snorted as I started pressing the screen annoyed:

Certainly!

You may not want to believe it, but my IQ

is much higher than yo...

Reason didn't let me finish. He coughed theatrically. At least he and the other entities were back and were not blinking anymore. *Reason* felt more than well, obviously, for he was eager to exercise his favourite sport—nagging:

Sober up! Underestimating the opponent. A manipulation that aims to provoke a reaction. A transparent method. Even your sedated brain can get it. Chris has even warned you.

I erased the message, grunting:

'Damn it! My stupid boss didn't succeed, but there's a good chance that I'll kill all of my own brain cells by myself. So, Toma really tells him everything! Even what I mumble under my nose!'

My liver was processing the hormones lazily, and it was even slower with the whisky. My body felt crushed. I was aware that in a state of such hormonal mess, it was important to take slow, systemised steps. To drink water, too. I made up my mind, deciding to finish what I had planned regarding the documents, then get rid of them, find my balance, and focus entirely on my work with cryptocurrencies.

When I got downstairs, I realised that the house was empty. In the dining room, there was a plate of my beloved "Dream Factory" pancakes. Next to it, on a white tray and in an interesting colour pattern, gummy bears were arranged. There was also a note with a yellow tulip on it. I was surprised because tulips were my favourite flowers.

> *"I'd choose one of these and forbid the other. I'm learning*
> *to communicate and comply. With you! With your decisions as well.*
> *Let's talk! Soon!*
> *I suffer from impatience, my lovely dear."*
> *V.*

Shivers crept over me as I studied the table. For a moment, I considered stuffing all the gummy bears into my mouth, just to manifest disobedience. However, I took the pancake instead and pressed the phone with my only clean finger:

> *Your first sentence is not OK AGAIN.*
> *The second one—you're not doing well.*

We're not going to talk! Soon.
I suffer from reluctance.
P.S. Leaving food in people's houses is unacceptable.
It's a creepy thing to do.
Even though you quite often do unacceptable things,
keep that in mind.
My decision is clear—stay away from me!
I don't fit into this madness.

He saw the message right away but didn't reply. As I stared at the screen, a larva crawled through my mind, trying to confuse me, and nibbling on my clear conclusions. Repeatedly, the idea that it wouldn't hurt if I had a talk with Victor struck me. A new personality split joined the bunch of other problems. Had someone listened to the argument between me and the larva, they'd conclude that I was crazy, or even worse—they'd pity me.

I spent the day struggling for concentration and staring at a blank spot. I tried unsuccessfully to systemise the real estate work. However, the sequence in my head was annoying: a digit, Victor, a letter, Victor again, distraction, then only Victor. I gave up trying and put the last sheet of paper back in the folder. I felt like smoking. Then I felt like drinking. I figured out that in my current situation, my mind felt more tolerable sedated than clear. I hoped the whisky would knock out all thoughts together with the larva. I came up with a name for the larva: doubt.

Chris didn't come home until late at night. I had drunk half of the bottle and studied him from the couch through the alcohol mist—he was angry, and probably even more drunk than I was. He muttered some indistinct words before heading straight to his lair.

He didn't carry me upstairs that night, and I woke up at dawn in the living room. Someone was slamming on the door. I opened it to see an agitated neighbour. Chris's car was left diagonally across the driveway, blocking the surrounding houses. The neighbour looked like one of the shadows—fresh, her hair perfectly made, yelling next to the car. I gathered all my strength to wave at her to wait and headed for the top floor. Chris was sleeping, also in a diagonal position. On his bedside table, there was an empty bottle, a full ashtray and some kind of a white dirt that resembled chalk. I started pushing him but he just snorted. I rummaged through his jeans' pockets finding condoms, rectangular pieces of paper, money, chewing gum and, finally, the car keys.

Despite the woman's unbearable chatter, I opened the door, but had no idea how to start Chris's Porsche. Neither did the neighbour. After a moment's thought, she suggested that we put the car in neutral, then push it to the slope that led to the garage. My hazy brain agreed to this stupidity. Naturally, the principles of dynamics[24] didn't want to comply with the early hour, or with my drunk mind. Newton's second law[25] predetermined the outcome. Our idiotic decision resulted in the front of the car ending up stuck in the garage door, an empty alley for other drivers, and me being upset. I went upstairs again. This time I was pretty sure that Chris would wake up to the four words that could drag a man out of a coma:

'I hit the car!'

He jumped in his bed, as if struck by an electric shock.

'You drove my car?'

'No. Just hit it.'

'What the hell? You can't touch the car! Are you crazy?' He jumped out of bed and staggered down the stairs.

'Well, you can't leave the car diagonally across the alley. The neighbour was slamming on the door. I guess you were quite drunk last night. You shouldn't drink and drive—it's dangerous, it's reckless and it's typical for individuals with a low IQ,' I followed him down the stairs.

As soon as he went out, he started shouting:

'Oh shit! What did you do? Did you push it?'

'Yes.'

'And you dare speak about my IQ? Newton's second fucking law. It's obvious, damn it!'

'I know but I drank last night, too. My brain is not functioning properly yet! I'm sorry! It's not that broken, there's more damage to the garage. Praise

---

[24] *Dynamics is a component of classical mechanics. It studies the causes of motion of material bodies depending on the forces applied to them. It describes the physical quantities of path, velocity and acceleration and their change under the influence of forces – author's notes.*

[25] *Newton's second law of motion is $F = ma$, or force is equal to mass times acceleration.*

dynamics! I will pay for the damage someday,' my chin trembled with guilt and Chris sighed.

'All right! Chill! I have three other cars, but this one was my favourite. I must admit though that crashing a Porsche by pushing it is really something. It's an achievement,' he chuckled and I shrugged. 'Come on, get in! I badly need coffee!' He hurled his ridiculously tattooed arm over my shoulder and kissed my cheek. 'I'll call for someone to get the other car, so I can at least teach you how to use it rather than push it. You can drive it when I'm away.'

Coffee revived us in silence. Chris ordered breakfast while I chewed on gummy bears. He informed me that he was leaving the city in a couple of hours, and told me everything about the housekeeper's schedule and where he had left money for her. He gave the phone number of a driver in case I needed him. I kept nodding, slowly processing the information in the background of the painful clatter inside my skull.

We were staring helplessly at each other when Toma strode in. He looked annoyingly fresh, chuckling as he asked what had happened to the car. Chris pointed at me and Toma hid his grin with his hand as I grimaced. He shook his head in reproach because of our pathetic condition, then put three boxes of food on the table. I was too exhausted to ask what he wanted. Chris and I looked at each other, then we attacked the food in an attempt to fight our hangover. Toma sat down on the couch, switched the morning bulletin on and muttered to Chris to be quick because he wanted to discuss something with him. An annoying voice was chattering from the screen. Toma went to the yard to take a phone call.

I watched the show with no interest when a familiar face drew my attention. It was the doctor from the emergency room, except she was in a nice purple outfit and her hair was elegantly styled. The host announced that the topic was violence against women and taboos in society. The doctor calmly explained that she headed an NGO that helped women who were victims of violence. They also focused on campaigns to change negative attitudes and stereotypes. When asked why she did it all, she spoke about her ex fiancé. After another brutal beating, he threw her out of the car in front of the emergency room. My jaw dropped. She calmly described details about the experience, including that her family had accused and rejected her. She was left all alone. The reason for that last beating was that the creep suspected she was pregnant and he didn't want the baby. She went into details about kicking in the abdomen and stabbing, and I plugged my ears, sick to my stomach. Eventually it transpired that she was not pregnant but now she would never be.

It was hard for her to overcome what happened. After several suicide attempts and a lot of antidepressants, she took control over her life. An NGO supported her as she studied medicine, then she decided to work at the same ER at which she was saved. She convinced the head of the hospital into creating the first centre to help women in need. A surgeon now, she waited for the ambulances with patients at the same parking lot in which her life had changed forever. The horror had set her free and she was committed to helping others. At work, she sewed split heads, in her spare time—torn souls. She said the first job was easier—it was blood and pain, but it passed. It was much harder to find a cure for the bottomless suffering of the souls. She shared various horrible stories that had found shelter in her centre, and I turned pale with horror.

Damn! If life tears you apart like that, you become nothing but patches! Are you a God or a monster to create such creeps? Even Malice is not creative enough to think of a proper punishment for them. Why would they even be scared of hell, if hell is likely modelled on the reality here?

While I was contemplating, the doctor spoke about self-pity, claiming it was harmful. She said she was grateful for the test she was put through because it was what had awakened her to life. I gaped at this conclusion while reading the caption on the screen: *A national campaign initiated by the government raises debate on violence against women, rights, and rigid public perceptions. A change in legislation is being prepared.* The host asked her guest to comment on this and the doctor said that the last days were very fruitful for their cause. Her organisation received a generous anonymous donation. The amount was enough for the construction of many medical centres, an accommodation facility for women at risk, and other planned activities for which they previously had no funding. For the first time, different organisations were invited to a meeting with ministers about their campaign and the possibility of amending the law. The president attended the first meeting in person and ordered the ministers to assist and mobilise their administrations. The doctor was chosen as a front face and coordinator of the activities. A media campaign with a series of videos was starting today, and the host announced that the first one was about to play.

The video began with a forest, then a close-up of a running woman in a torn dress. She kept looking over her shoulder and I moved closer to the screen in bewilderment. The sound of her rapid breathing and pulse brought me back to that night. My cardiac muscle skipped a beat. The woman collapsed beside a withered tree. In the next moment, a bunch of people surrounded her, carried her to an ambulance and a male voice-over said: *No one can do this to you!*

Lightning struck my brain. The disconnected pieces of a vague memory swirled through my mind. I jumped on the spot. Toma was standing behind me, staring at me. Chris was staring at him.

'This! This was what Victor said in the car! The exact same thing! But I remember it from...' I muttered under my breath and Bear pursed his lips. I squinted at his embarrassed face: '...that night. It's from that night. In the forest. Isn't it?'

'Damn!'

'Why the same words? Tell me! Why?'

I stood in front of Toma and nudged him. He grunted:

'If I lie down and die right now, you'll revive me just to kill me with questions again. Right?' I nodded vigorously as he rubbed his face. 'I need coffee. Chris, get ready, or we'll be late!' He hissed while filling two cups.

Toma staggered towards the yard and I followed. The two chairs were waiting for us. He sighed.

'What happened that night?' I was tapping my fingers impatiently while his gaze was sticking pins in the table. 'If you are truly my friend, the moment to prove it is right now. Stop lying to me.'

He looked up in silence. Several sips of coffee later, he spoke quietly:

'"Woods, four and something is shining"—that was all I heard, and then there was no connection. I got scared and called Victor immediately. Then I found out that they had left without you. I asked him to send people and then drove like crazy and the cars of the boys caught up with me midway. There were teams with dogs. He was there, too.'

'Who? Victor came to the forest?' I gaped and Toma snapped:

'Yes!"

'Man, you lied about that, too! What's wrong with you, for Christ's sake!'

'Victor made me repeat your exact words. Four was for kilometres, minutes, turns, or hills along the road. He said that you counted but he wasn't acquainted with your sequences yet, whatever that means. He ordered the teams to split up. I was trying to explain why I wasn't with you, but he wouldn't speak. He wasn't hearing. He was in that typical state of his...'

'What state?'

He went silent for a moment, rubbing his scalp, but didn't reply to the question.

'I went with him. We searched for you for quite some time. I had never feared my watch before. At that temperature, your chances were running out by the second,' he shook his head, his warm eyes running all over my bewildered face. At that moment, the horror in his gaze destroyed any doubt that he cared for me. 'Someone shouted near us and Victor ran in that direction. I barely caught up with him. I got rid of the curious team with the dog and then I saw you. Curled in a tiny ball next to the stump, and he was on his knees, looking for a pulse. I must admit that when he carried you in his arms, lifeless, I felt weak. I didn't even dare come closer. He carried you, wrapped in his coat as he walked with his stone-cold expression. But his eyes... I know those mad eyes so well. Staring straight ahead and even an apocalypse couldn't stop them from reaching their goal. I was too stunned to think straight,' Toma clenched his jaw and my fingers. 'I tried to take you from him, so they wouldn't see him, or even worse—film him. I had no chance! He wasn't responding, good thing it was dark, at least. He was muttering the same thing again and again. He didn't even tell me if you were alive.'

'No one can do this to you...' The vague memory became vivid, but Toma was immersed in his own mind and he probably didn't even hear me.

'He was focused on a distant point and I couldn't get him out of this state. He had gone mad. Possessed. In a trance. Out of control, of his own self-control. It was not the first time I saw him like that, but he had been so strictly disciplining himself for so long that...' He looked down. I could tell that he was not only worried but also upset.

'What state, man?' I repeated nervously but he just shook his head.

'The doctor was examining you and I came in. I didn't even realise that he was gone,' his face darkened and he fell silent.

'Damn it! Stop with these lyrical pauses, you're driving me crazy. Where did he go?'

'Sergey called me but by the time I got there, the whole security was at the entrance. Victor kicked everybody out of the restaurant. The guys are afraid of him, and they have their good reasons. The Russian shoved me inside. Victor and I have been through so much together, there's no longer a thing he can scare me with.'

I froze at Toma's painful face.

'What are you saying, man? What happened?'

'I guess someone from the restaurant told him. I don't know what happened exactly. I found that son of a bitch dragging himself on the floor. Victor had crushed him and he kept going. The creep was rolling on the floor disfigured; I don't know how he was still breathing. I was afraid I might not be able to stop Victor in time.'

'Come on! He wouldn't kill a man.'

Toma gave me a meaningful look.

'In this case, he'd have even enjoyed it! Victor was so brutal, you can't even imagine...' I shivered. He was not right, though. I could imagine. I was well aware of *Malice*'s pyres, her controversial methods and power. I knew how she could get carried away.

'So that's why that creep didn't show up.'

'He couldn't have. He's in a coma, Nia! He hasn't woken up since.'

I guess Victor has Malice, too. Weird.

For several minutes, there was silence. My even tone broke it:

'I'm sorry if you expect something else from me, but I don't have much pity for people. Objectively, the minister deserved that. I'd do the same to him if I could, probably. I admit, however, that I'm surprised because Victor blamed me and you for what happened. And I blamed him.'

'That's not the point, Nia. You don't understand. He took risks that are too dangerous for all of us. You included. Victor lost control, and this can't happen right now.'

'It's not about control. *Malice* is just too persuasive. Don't make me explain to you how inventive she is or what she dreams of—a hammer, in my case. But after all, it was Victor himself who took a creep like that on his team. Maybe his wrong decision made him mad. It doesn't fit his orderly pattern. I understand perfectly!'

'What're you even talking about? She understands! Most of them are like that—distorted, or whatever you call them. Rapists, paedophiles, drunks, junkies. Creeps—that's what they are! Victor is the president, Nia, and he is not only that! Do you even realise these things? Can you imagine what problems could arise? A scandal, too. Thank God his team covered everything up, at least for now. This is the least of our problems, even!'

'You should've beaten him then! You speak like it's my fault. I don't have data on your generalisation about "most of them", but that guy was definitely a creep. And a rapist.'

'It's not your fault! I know perfectly well what he is!'

'If Victor was aware of what happened, why did he blame us? Why did he kick you out of your house? His crazy standards again?'

'He didn't kick me out! Stop repeating this! We had a fight.'

'Because he beat that guy?' I frowned and he squeezed my hands.

'Because of you! And because he started losing control. He was obsessed in his crazy way and crossed every boundary. He decided he'd go for this, put both of you in danger and, if he keeps on, it'll only get worse. I refused to participate anymore in this absurdity and we fought bitterly. He knows that I'm right but he wouldn't consent. That's why I decided to tell you what was truly going on.'

'What do you mean he didn't kick you out? Why weren't you there that morning then? Why, after I fought with Victor and accused him, you came to "Dream Factory"?' I waved my hands in question.

'Damn, how many questions per minute can you ask?' He held his forehead and I stared viciously at him. 'I wasn't there because I went out early in the morning to ventilate my head in the mountain. Then Victor called me. He shouted at me that you went crazy because of me and now he was the "distorted" one when he had just achieved some success with you. You disappeared at a traffic light downtown and the driver was shocked. He couldn't even repeat what you explained to him. I don't always understand what you say, let alone the poor guy.'

'Damn! Have I made even one correct assumption recently? Your house was empty, man. Empty! Didn't you see that I called like a hundred times? Why didn't you call back?' I interrupted him, stressing every syllable.

'Call back to say what? I knew you went for pancakes and preferred to come to you. What did you expect to find in my house? I'm a military man. My whole life fits in a bag,' he said to my scornful face. 'Victor was mad because you disappeared. I think you know why already. He can't take it when people don't do what he wants. Let's say you're too uncontrollable according to his standards. If I have to be more specific—he was furious. I said I'd get you back. I didn't want to fight with him anymore and I didn't want him to freak you out by sending a group of people to drag you back. I used my superpowers to deal with your unreasonable logic. This was a quote. I tried to motivate you to establish your boundaries with him because he had stepped over the reasonable limits. But you didn't get it!'

'I don't get anything obviously,' I started sucking on a cigarette under his reproachful look. 'He gave the money to that doctor, didn't he? I even find it difficult to define him already—distorted, but not really. I'm confused!'

'I guess that's right. I'm done explaining though—I obviously suck at this. I'm not making this mess worse. You roam here like a ghost, you smoke, you drink... He is unbearable, jogging for hours, one can't speak to him...'

'He's back?' My voice squeaked and I cleared my throat in embarrassment.

'You said you were not going to talk to him anymore! Why're you asking?' He snapped.

'Toma, according to the normal standards, does his behaviour show that he's interested in me?' I muttered, all blushed. 'In a way that is not perverse, I mean—not like a cat playing with a mouse or a looney playing with a marionette. In a normal way?' I moved my hands like a puppeteer. The larva was crawling in my head, eating my previous decisions for breakfast.

'See... Victor's standards are not really normal. Even I find it difficult to understand him sometimes. Plus, his personal life is like the Vatican Library; we've all heard about it but few get access. He doesn't share it with me or with anyone. One thing I know for sure though—his life is not for you. You're an incredible person, Nia. I'm sure that someday you will be loved the way you deserve, but this day is not now.'

'I'm certainly not interested in such abstract interactions between people, but I'm certain that it doesn't depend on what one deserves. I certainly don't have such needs either. Fortunately, my brain works in an effective, rational way. What I meant was...'

He interrupted me with a smile, speaking softly:

'Everyone needs this abstract interaction, goblin. A robot, a normal person, a weirdo... At the bottom of every human grief, settles a lack of love. Remember this and when you meet love someday—take it and don't ever let go!'

'Oh yeah! I just watched an interview about people in love. They're so eager to not let go that they barely come out of love in one piece. From what I heard about the scars it leaves, people should rather call it *a Beast*, not love!'

'I heard what the doctor said, too. Gruesome stories! It was her who met us at the ER, right? I remember her shaking me to wake up.'

'Yes, she even tried to rid me of the corrupted cop. Actually, if it wasn't for her, they might have beaten me much more in that shithole.'

'Probably, yes.'

Chris appeared at the door in a business suit, and Toma went on:

'I have to go now. I'll be away for a couple of days. Promise me though that we're going for pancakes when I come back and, please, stop being angry with me. I want you to tell me about your new job, and I have to give you driving lessons. Pushing lessons, too, obviously,' Toma grinned but then continued in a serious tone, waving his index finger about: 'Girl, I insist that you stop drinking and smoking. All right?'

'All right! Are you sure about the pancakes though? I'd probably torture you with more questions.'

'You already killed me with one. You can't torture me any worse.'

'Which one?'

'What do you mean which one? I still haven't thought of anything that is simpler and yet more perfect than pancakes,' he laughed contagiously and made me smile, too.

'You have no chance in that, Bear! I've been thinking about this since I was a kid, since my grandpa made pancakes for the first time. With fig jam. If heaven tastes like something, it's that!'

'For Christ's sake, weirdo, put the question on Reddit. Someone must have come up with an answer,' he gazed at me with affection. 'You're beautiful when you laugh. I hope I see you often like this more. Stop torturing yourself. Stop thinking about all this. Leave it all behind. I'm absolutely certain that awesome possibilities are awaiting you around the next corner. You really do deserve more, Nia,' he squeezed my hand, smiled again, then left.

I closed my eyes to let the sun caress my face. Toma was probably right, but his advice to stop thinking had the opposite effect. I guess the rule not to use a negative in an imperative sentence was justified. "Don't think" sounded like "Don't imagine an elephant". A trunk and huge ears immediately appear in one's mind. It was natural that I would do the opposite of what he had advised. I walked around the empty house all day. The larva ate part of my brain along with my decisions. All it left behind were the cells addicted to Victor. Numerous times, I took the phone, began writing, then erased what I had written. I was also on the verge of calling him a couple of times, but *Reason's* screams stopped me. I screamed, too. My personality split stretched the nerves in my body and the obsessive thoughts about Victor destroyed them further.

Smoking a cigarette in the yard, I watched as dusk pressed down the scorched autumn sunset. I suddenly remembered that the penthouse floor was to be finished today and checked the date in my phone for confirmation. The chaotic marble pattern was already supposed to have been replaced with symmetrical boards in a sequence that I created. I had put dramatic effort into explaining what I wanted at the carpentry shop. The pattern was to start with three large pieces in the hallway and continue in a descending, circular order. It was not as complicated as Victor's living room pattern, but I knew he would like it. *Curiosity* wanted to see how it looked and I wanted to visit the penthouse and the office for the last time, too. The following day, I was to prepare the rest of the documents and hand over the keys.

It was getting dark, and *Fear* stopped me from walking to the bus stop. Chris hadn't showed me how to drive the Porsche yet, so I took some of the money he had left for a cab and wrote a note, of course. I was burning in anticipation on my way there. The rush-hour traffic was infuriating, and the falling rain didn't help it move any faster. I plugged my ears with the music of my favourite playlist and tapped my fingers to suppress my irritation.

It took us an hour to arrive, and I hurried to the entrance in the dark. A private elevator led straight to the penthouse. On my way upstairs, I threatened to cut off my head. This didn't affect the hysterical "call—don't call" argument with my second personality. I decided to ask a normal woman what to do with this split as soon as possible. If normal women even had such personality splits, of course...

Entering the penthouse, the stunning night view over the otherwise repulsive city caught my eye.

'Everything looks so different from above! Your shoes are muddy, and yet you can forget about all the mud down there!'

I took off the dirty trainers and hopped onto the three large pieces in the hallway. My cardiac muscle squirmed as I put the keys and the elevator card on the bar. The screams in my head had become unbearable. I turned the volume of my music to the max and examined the floor with a smile because the pattern looked good. Every choice I had made about the furnishing of the living room pleased me. I made a round of the penthouse and approved the final result—even praised myself, which rarely happened. I had achieved at least these results completely by myself. No one had influenced them, no one had made them crooked—I had managed on my own and had managed well.

I turned to go. Five steps to the door. As always, I was to take the first one with my right foot. Then I could simply close the door and leave another disappointment behind my back. All I had to endure was the discomfort of my new door-issue. I counted *one*. Then I said it again, louder, but I didn't budge.

'Damn you, legs! Why won't you move? Are you damaged, too?'

The view caught my attention again and instead of leaving, I pressed myself against the glass. My gaze chased the curves of the lights. There was no dust, no dirt, no grey anymore. The ugliness of reality disappeared. The twenty-third floor erased it, as if it was an unwanted touch on an artist's canvas. The raindrops transformed the city into a deceptively beautiful Instagram shot. I sat down on the floor, hugging my knees. The burning weight between my ribs was probably the anatomical manifestation of what people call sadness. Apparently, this cocktail of hormones was difficult to process, or perhaps my liver was simply too overloaded.

This time the music didn't manage to silence the chaos in my head. It didn't free my mind as usual. My consciousness pounded wildly, trapped in the narrow space of my skull. It protested. The larva was crawling, leaving its slimy trail: an obsessive thought that I could live there now, I could feel Victor all over me and inside me. All I had to do was fold myself, file down an edge or two, and fit in. Just one fucking compromise. Questions were falling with the rhythm of the rain: what if I did that? Doesn't everybody? *Reason* was screaming about madness and absurdity. He was chasing the larva, rubbing away the trail of slime with his sleeve. I was trying to figure out how to turn the volume on the phone up in order to stop the disaster in my mind.

My favourite voice spilled into my eardrums just in time. My music angel graciously caressed my senses, like a true deity. Only gods can save people in this manner. All my life, he has comforted me, walking beside me through the cutting thorns of loneliness. The violin took over the chaos, as always. It was an old song born long before me. With this song, Sting's[26] unearthly timbre had taught me how to adore when I needed adoration the most. He knew how to play the strings of even a crazy freak like me. He was touching something unfamiliar in my broken soul. His "broken music" breathed life into it. He was making it human. Sting gave me what was missing: the fire of emotions, which, extinguished by life, didn't burn

---

[26] *The Police (Sting – vocals). "Burn for You." – author's notes.*

in me. His music gave me freedom to feel, even if only for a moment. I vibrated, brimming with the divine harmony of his voice and sang along with him, my eyes closed, my mind quiet[27].

I opened my eyes and saw another hallucination in the glass of the window. The lights of the city mingled with Victor's grim face, accentuating the sharp features of his cheekbones. Even his imaginary face had its devastating effect on me. The blue of his eyes pierced me, squeezing my stomach. My lungs protested with a painful spasm, and I covered my head with my palms.

Damn! When will it all end? These hallucinations will drive me crazy. I think I should see a shrink.

Reason grumbled that I needed a shrink indeed. I took a breath to reply but then the fragrance of musk suffocated me. I sensed his presence.

He sat down behind me and squeezed me between his legs. He hugged me. The violin went mad. He wrapped his hands around my bent legs, holding me close. The bass exploded, along with my heart. He pressed his cheek against mine. His sharp beard tore at my skin, then he kissed my temple. He pulled out one of my earplugs to put it in his ear. We listened to perfection together[28].

He was silent, his body radiating heat. I couldn't take my eyes off the reflection of his irises in the glass. I stopped blinking. I could have probably stopped breathing, too. His effect on me was like numbing poison. These were the objective facts. The simple truth. His breath ricocheted on my skin, raising shivers that he chased with his soft lips. He was perfectly real, he was holding me tight, and his touch soaked into my cells like a drug.

---

[27] You and I are lovers
When night time folds around our bed
In peace we sleep entwined
And your love flows through me
Though an ocean soothes my head
I burn for you, I burn for you
https://www.youtube.com/watch?v=ag6KMH0UlVM
[28] And your love flows through me
Though I lie here so still
I burn for you, I burn for you
I burn for...
https://www.youtube.com/watch?v=ag6KMH0UlVM
The Police (Sting – vocals). "Burn for You." – author's notes.

Sting sang his last stanza. We listened to the next song, another one, but Victor was still silent. His face buried in my neck, he was inhaling the scent and just listening to the music with me. He held me even tighter. He brought his legs closer to each other in front of me and I stayed in the cocoon of his embrace.

'In your even number of words, you missed two substantial arguments!' The shiver-provoking timbre sank into my eardrums, my throat became dry.

'What are they?' My hoarse voice was barely audible.

'There is no universe in which I could stay away from you, Nia. There is no reality in which you don't fit my madness perfectly.'

I was breathing hard with my mouth open, and *Reason* cried out:

There is no galaxy in which this nonsense can be considered "arguments"! He's a maniac! Get out of here! Right now, Nia! He is manipulating us!

'Shut up!' I hissed as I clutched Victor's wrists.

'Who are you talking to?' He peered to the side, then turned me to face him. I knelt between his legs with my head bowed.

'I wasn't talking to you. It's just...' I stammered. He squeezed my face, focusing his gaze on mine. 'I'm just talking to myself, you know...'

'You're lying! Are you OK?' His firm look confused me even more.

'I'm fine,' I tried to get up, but Victor held me back, his fingers buried in my hair. 'I want to go,' I kept lying while my hands contradicted me by clinging to his shirt.

'And I want to kiss you,' he traced the outline of my face with his thumb and pressed his forehead against mine. 'I'll put it as a question this time. Do you want me to kiss you, my lovely dear?'

My head went in all possible directions. Before it could nod or shake properly, Victor bit my lip. Impatient, as always, he didn't wait for my answer. My pulse went wild. My hands shot to his hair. In a second, my legs were already around him, and he grabbed the back of my head. My tongue bristled with the coveted taste. All my senses went crazy. I sucked on my drug and had no intention to let go. His desire rose under me, setting me on fire, as I kept kissing him. He kissed back ravenously, sinking between my lips, giving me the pleasure that made me unable to think straight, and emptying my mind. Only a void was left behind—for Victor to fill it. He suddenly pulled away, staring at me in silence. I waited. He wouldn't do anything but stare. I muttered scornfully:

'When you ask a question, you'd usually wait for an answer. Note that this goes especially for kiss-related questions!'

'I suffer from impatience for you, my lovely dear, and as ever your eyes replied quicker than your mouth. There was nothing to wait for—they said it all!' He smiled and kissed me again. 'More than kissing you, though, I want to talk with you. I know what Toma and Chris told you. I'm also sorry for the bullshit I said to you. I can imagine how it looks from the side and I don't even want to think about the insane conclusions you reached!'

'So you must know why we won't talk. I will accept the kisses though. I won't refuse sex, either. But no talking,' my fingers hungrily hooked his neck, but he growled and pulled me away once more.

'We are definitely going to talk! As long as it's necessary for you to realise that you've heard only other people's truths. Not mine, not ours. Only their point of view and part of the facts.'

'Enough of these abstract truths of yours! The order of events and your actions are clear. It's simply the truth; it can't be yours or theirs. A sequence of facts that I already know, unfortunately,' my voice became nervous. While I was explaining I gasped because of the breath shortage and the jab between the ribs again.

'What's wrong?' Victor moved me to sit on the ground and kneeled before me. He took my face in his hands and his irises went ablaze. 'Nia, what's wrong?' His voice was cold now. He kept insistently chasing my gaze.

'Nothing. I'm just short of breath and I have these jabs right here...' I pointed the spot between the fifth and the sixth rib on the left, then I rubbed it with my fingers. 'Your perfume is strong. I guess it triggers it.'

'My perfume? When did this start?'

'A few days ago. I'll be fine. The problem is that I did something stupid the other night and now I am concerned.'

'What did you do?'

'I googled the symptoms!' I looked down guiltily. 'Now I assume it's pericarditis or even worse things!'

'What things?'

'Asthma, coronary artery disease, intestinal worms...'

'For Christ's sake, Nia!' He laughed. 'You don't have pericarditis, nor worms. There have been too many emotions these days, and you obviously experience difficulties in handling emotions. How could you even think of searching Google for a diagnosis?'

'Don't tease me! I know it's stupid, but it just happened...' I snapped and he suppressed his laughter with effort.

'I'm not teasing. Come here! You won't have any more stress, my lovely dear,' he hugged me.

I settled in his lap with my legs crossed behind his back. It was the first time for days that *Desire* wasn't wailing, and I smiled with relief. Victor was studying me, kissing my fingertips.

'I'll call a doctor if you still have worries. An army of doctors—for everything on Google! I believe though that we can find another cure for the breath shortage and the jabs. Everything will be fine! Everything is right when you are in my arms!'

'No, it's not! It's certainly not! Why are you even wasting your time on me, Victor? Explain your motives so I can change my conclusions. You're right, they're very unpleasant. You're surrounded by gorgeous shadows, you're at the peak, you have everything, you are the president, for Christ's sake! The social distance between us is enormous. There's no logic for you to...' He put his thumbs to my lips.

'I already asked you to not look for the logic in me and to not assess me according to my current position. I'll try to explain some day, but don't push me. Don't focus on who I am. Right now, I'm just whoever I have to be. I told you that it just takes a shirt to make me look proper for the world,' he was unbuttoning his shirt and I smirked cheekily. 'Like you wear a baggy sweater so you could hide underneath it. We're not so different from each other. For me it's just more complicated.'

He took off his clothes and grabbed the bottom of my sweater. I raised my arms and was left in my Daenerys T-shirt. He pulled it off too, but despite my expectations of sex, he moved behind me, propped me against his warm chest and hugged me. As he kissed my bare shoulders, he whispered:

'You can't even imagine how it feels to not be able to feel you. Now that I'm naked and pressed against you, is there a social distance still?'

'It's there, no matter if you're naked or not. You understand quite well what I mean. We stand on different social steps and you're definitely taking advantage of this. You didn't ask me not to look for logic like you said. Your manner of speaking doesn't include the ability to ask. You basically order and, what's even worse, you think it's normal!'

'You're right. That's what I'm used to. I don't even know another way. I was hoping that with time, you'll get used to me and my manner of communication, and that I'll understand your way of thinking and attract your attention when the time comes. I couldn't wait long enough, though, and everything went out of control.'

'Victor, I can't get used to this way of communicating.'

'I get that, Nia. Try to understand on your part, though, how difficult it's for me with you. But I'm trying. You will try too! You won't argue about everything! You will accept that I know some things better than you. Just trust me and accept that there are issues that depend on me. This way you'll let me make decisions and take care of you and of us. If you'd just stop summing everything up on logical grounds and insane conclusions.'

'Honestly, your decisions are quite controversial,' I snapped and he bit my ear. 'Don't bite me! I can give you many examples, like the other day, when you sent Sergey to harass me. This was absolutely unacceptable. What you did with the work and with Maddie was even worse!'

'I just created better conditions. I didn't send Sergey to harass you, but to protect you. As soon as you texted me about your claustrophobia, I ordered him to follow you from a distance!'

'Follow me?' I shouted and tried to move but he kept me in his embrace.

'Don't pull yourself away like that! This is an example of decisions I make and you take! How do you assume I knew that you were here? I'm no medium.'

'God! You speak like this is something normal. It belongs to the "unacceptable" column, Victor. Do you even comprehend that there are boundaries you shouldn't cross? You can't follow people!'

'Do you even comprehend that you're not "people"? I won't compromise with your safety anymore—what already happened was too much. Let's not argue! We'll discuss this, just not now. Here is another question: would you like for us to get out of here?' He turned me to face him and the blue was already burning. He touched my naked back with the tips of his fingers, biting his lips like a devil. I was burning, too. 'Please, appreciate that I asked a question. I'd usually say it in another way!' He smiled and kissed my cheek gently. 'I've got two days. We'll spend one of them together.'

'Where?'

'Another question. Can you try to not ask?' His irises were rummaging through my brain. 'Just come! I'll take care of all details!'

Reason shouted at the top of his voice as I nodded like an idiot. Temptation deformed my clear thinking. Victor urged me to raise my arms so he could put the T-shirt back on. He also put his shirt on, though left it half-buttoned. I got up and took my backpack clumsily. He threw my sweater on the table, seemingly convinced that we were not going to need it, and covered me with his jacket which looked like a dress on me. Taking my hand, he slid his fingers between mine and laughed at how small they were. With his other hand, he placed an earplug in my ear, the other in his, and turned up the volume of the music.

More than ten guys were lined up at the door. Sergey was in the front, sulking. I stopped by him for a second, but Victor pulled me away. The Russian took out a card for the elevator and went in with us. The others took the stairs. In the elevator, Sergey turned his back on me but my discomfort at his presence showed on my face. Victor pressed me against the wall, leaning over me, smiling boyishly. The air around him was raising some kind of primitive animal passion in me. He blazed. The cold, composed man with the statue-like face was gone, as if he was a different person. Only the absolute power in his gaze and the typical note in his voice were there to remind me that he could do anything to create the conditions he sought.

'Imagine that we're all alone here. He can't see or hear us. He's not here!'

'What do you mean he's not here? He's right behind you,' I peered but he turned my head back to him.

'You'll have to get used to that because we'll rarely have the chance to be alone. Just accept that no one else exists in our reality, Nia!' He squeezed my neck and the coveted lips subdued me. In a second, it felt like Sergey was truly gone. *Two Feet*[29] shouted in my ear that I was drowning. Indeed I was—drowning in the taste of Victor.

The elevator opened to the garage. The guys were waiting, lined up in a cordon. Two of them used something like flashlights at the security cameras and another two stood by the president's jeep. The security guards surrounded us as we walked. There were seven steps of claustrophobia to the car, and I counted them, squeezing Victor's hand. Sergey jumped in the driver's seat and motioned for no one else to get in. Victor opened the door for me and when he got in as well, he placed me on his lap, facing him, in one motion. The Russian flew through the entrance and only the mad blue irises shone in the dark.

'I missed you unbearably. Don't do this again! Don't run from me!' He kissed me. I shrugged and sighed, and he frowned. 'I'm not kidding, Nia. Don't do this!'

---

[29] *Two Feet – "Feel Like I Am Drowning" – author's notes.*

'The arguments that this was the right thing to do are undeniable. I could probably prove in a hundred different ways that what I'm doing right now is a wrong decision. Its natural consequences will hit me like a high-speed train. Isn't it so, Victor?'

'I don't like it when you talk like that and no—you can't calculate the probabilities in human relationships. They don't obey logic or laws, simply because they're not measurable. They are chaos without regularities, in which you just hope to survive.'

I was silent in the embrace of my questionable decision. The car sped down the boulevard at the same speed that the consequences were running in my direction.

THIRTEEN

We were in a better mood on our way to Victor's house. His fingers played with my lips. The arrows of his charm shot in my direction; my privates were the target. He announced that he was planning for double forbidden pleasure today, then ordered Sergey to get "his car". The security guard replied sharply in Russian, but the president's tone cut him off. Victor told me everything was ready—my luggage included—and we were to leave straight away. The guys were lining up suitcases in front of the house. I watched the commotion, pulling Victor's coat around me. Through the glass wall, I saw Toma sitting at the dining room table. He shot a moody glare at me and shook his head with reproach. Awkward, I turned my back on the house and Victor pulled me closer to him. I saw an approaching bright green car with a disturbing symmetry. It made me gawk as the doors opened upwards.

'What is this?'

'A pleasure machine, my lovely dear. I told you I'm gonna have a double dose today. Driving this with you inside will be the ultimate happiness. What's the matter? You don't like it?' With a smile on his face, he motioned for me to get in.

'I can't decide. There's something wrong about the symmetry. The height relative to the width is disproportionate, and the colour and the shape make it look like a frog,' he frowned, and I hurried to explain: 'I'm not saying all this is bad. I like amphibians. It's just strange. What is this pleasure machine actually called?'

He chuckled as he replied, biting my hand:

'*Lamborghini*, but you could find a name more suitable for a frog and we'll just rename it. Get in!'

Sitting in the car was like sitting directly on the ground. Sergey kept grunting in Russian and the president shouted at him, also in Russian. The guard walked off sulkily. He waved at the other guys and they hurried to their cars. Two of the jeeps headed to the exit at full speed. Victor took his driver's seat and insisted on buckling me up himself. I tried to argue but the belt turned out to be double, resembling a device for pilots, and, after a brief struggle, I accepted his help. He tightened it so firmly that I could barely move. He caressed my cheekbone, then kissed it with a smile. Studying my tied-up body with interest, the mad flames in his irises flickered.

'Are you afraid of high speed?'

'Certainly not. Toma drives fast, we even have a deal that he'll teach me to drive like him. As soon as I can afford to, I'll buy the most amazing car for myself and I'll drive it really, really fast.'

'None of this will happen.'

'Meaning?'

'First, if you really insist, it will be me who gives the driving lessons, not Toma. Second, you're not driving alone and you're most definitely not driving fast. "Really, really fast" is absolutely out of the question!'

'I certainly will! As soon as my skills are good enough, I plan to drive on my alone, really, really fast.'

'No chance! Cut these plans off right now, and don't argue again! I won't let you do this!' He shook his head and I sulked.

'Victor, I thought we already discussed the limits of your behaviour and your tone of command. None of this right now is OK and I thought you were supposed to be learning to improve.'

'We discussed arguing, too, but I guess there was no use! Your unbearable "certainly" is here again. You're not driving alone and you're not speeding! End of conversation!' He muttered as we drove down the alley. An ominous roar came from the car, resonating in my stomach and killing my reply. 'However, what's that amazing car you are talking about?'

'The most amazing one! A *Tesla*! Really fast but eco-friendly, not like your frog, I suppose. Who knows how much it pollutes! Plus, a *Tesla* does the parking for you and for a clumsy person like me, that is a salvation,' I snapped. He rubbed my fingers, his tight face melting into a smile.

'All right, my lovely dear! I will buy a *Tesla*, but you're wrong saying that it's eco-friendly! I can imagine Toma's face sitting in this electric toy,' he pressed my hand against his lips to conceal his laughter.

'Why would you need it? You have your frog and plenty of other cars as well.'

'Not for me, for you!'

'I just told you that I plan to buy it when I have the money. Don't you listen to me?'

'And why not let me buy it for you right now?' He snapped. We waited for the metal spikes at the exit to come down.

'What do you mean by "why not", damn it! It's obvious—you will destroy one of my wishes!'

He sank his teeth into my hand.

'For Christ's sake, Nia! Damn, how am I gonna deal with your unreasonable logic?'

At his last syllable, my back glued to the seat. My breath ran back to hide in my lungs.

We were flying on the highway at 200 km/h. I realised how important it was that people specify what they mean by "high speed". We passed the most disgusting part of the city so fast that I couldn't even notice the misery of the peeling houses. Apparently, speed was the second thing that could erase the ugly strokes of reality. I leaned my head against the window and Victor slowed down sharply.

'Are you scared?'

'No.'

'What's wrong then?'

'Nothing. I'm thinking about all the strange things I've been finding out lately. I just found one such thing.'

'What is it?'

'New function of speed. I get it from a physics point of view, but it's still strange. You drive so fast that reality bends around us, it's like it's being erased. I know that there's horrible poverty out there, but I can't see it now. People don't even have a statistical chance of getting out of it, and now it's like it doesn't even exist. There, look at the ghetto!' I pointed to the right. Victor sighed.

'I don't agree that they don't have a chance. It's just that poverty has its own strange function as well. It sticks to the mind, it's difficult to clean, and is often confused with fate. The truth is, life doesn't like giving chances, Nia. One needs to snatch them out. But then, because balance is needed, life snatches out something else in return. You don't have to think about the ghetto. People there—and for that matter, people everywhere—rarely choose to strive for something more. They'd rather keep their nails intact and simply clean the dirt under them.'

'I have observed them, especially on the metro. I agree that they don't like challenges. I guess they like the square patterns of life. I'd even say that they strive for them. But why do you think that people from the ghetto don't want to strive for something more?'

'I don't think so. I know so because I spent sixteen years there,' his face darkened, and I stared at him.

'What do you mean? What can a person like you possibly have to do with the ghetto?'

He didn't reply, just drove at full throttle. As we sped on the road, he remained silent and focused on the insane speed.

Before long, Victor stopped by a small plane on a runway away from the airport. I was dizzy. Two cars were already waiting, and the others arrived after us, their tyres whistling. Visibly angry, Sergey jumped out of his SUV and headed towards us. Victor lifted the strange froggy door and looked at me intently as he unbuckled the seatbelts.

'You all right?'

'I think I'm going to puke. Side effects of the speed on the stomach and the vestibular system...'

When he pulled me out of my seat, I staggered. He laughed and carried me to the steps. Toma caught up with us, but didn't even look at me. I waved at him and he just clenched his jaw without greeting me. The plane was small, there were only a dozen wide seats inside. Victor passed the crew, heading to the rear where there were four large separate armchairs. He placed me carefully on one of them, gave me some water and pulled the curtain behind him.

'Victor, I think we have different ideas of what constitutes "fast". I think it's up to 170 km/h. I don't even know how you can call such insane acceleration and the terrible vibrations from the traction "pleasure".'

'Great pleasure,' he kissed my forehead with a cheeky smile. 'I love fast driving, hard fucking, and getting whatever I want. I love any sort of madness that gives me adrenaline. That's who I am! I suspect that some of our ideas about pleasure are different indeed.'

'Getting whatever one wants is a universal desire and most people like it. We are not different in the fucking part, either. I don't know what "hard" means, but I enjoy yours. The speed and the adrenaline, though, they're far beyond my limits. Besides, adrenaline is a dangerous hormone. Did you know that at the cellular level it's more addictive than heroin?'

'I guess you're better now, since you have started with your typical explanations!' I nodded. He placed me next to him on the armchair and hugged me. 'And do you know that I intend to expand your limits? You'll be surprised how many pleasures lie beyond them.'

The engines roared and the pilot announced that we were taking off.

'Will you tell me where we're going already?'

'No,' he untied my ball of hair and scattered it on his chest in order to caress it. 'Is your phone charged?'

'Yes.'

'Get the earphones then. I like your playlist and listening to it with you is all I want to do right now.'

I played the music and leaned over him, biting my lip, my fingers running down his chest.

'We can do something else on the way, I suppose.'

'Don't give me this look! I have an important meeting and I need to stay focused, which has proven to be a difficult task lately. If I fuck you now, I won't be able to stop for the whole night. I'm just going to feel you now. Let me enjoy the impossible chance of you even being in my arms.'

Kissing my frowning face, he pressed a button and the seat turned into a bed. He glued me to himself and I settled as if I fitted perfectly. The music sank in my right ear and in his left ear. I could sense his fingers going up and down my back and I shoved my hand under his shirt, tracing the inky flames of the tattoo. His desire was trying to tear his pants but he wouldn't let me touch there. I swallowed dryly as the rhythm in his chest made me drift away. He was caressing my hair, my eyelids felt heavy. Cigar smoke swirled around me. I liked the smell of tobacco, so I inhaled the fragrance, mixed with the scent of musk. This combination was apparently addictive at the cellular level, too; it made me dizzy. My body dived in the touch, drowned in the smells, and blissfully surrendered in his arms.

φ

A cannonade of kisses woke me up. I murmured under Victor's glowing face. He led me outside. As soon as I stepped sleepily out of the plane, a soft sea breeze stroked my skin. The temperature was more pleasant than back home and I took a deep breath. He held my fingers, but I didn't start down the stairs.

'Where are we?'

'In Naples.'

My jaw dropped and I pulled my hand away.

'Holy shit!'

'Stop swearing, Nia! What is it now?' He scolded me but I grinned in an even sillier manner.

'Holy shit! Holy shit! Holy shit!' I kept jumping on the spot and he grimaced at me. 'I've always wished to go to fucking Italy! And now I'm here without even specifically wishing for it. That's fucking statistically impossible!'

He narrowed his eyes, smiling.

'So I can make your wishes come true after all. Not only destroy them, like you said before,' he pinched my cheek, then kissed it. 'You must either allow me to do it, or I should just keep my intentions a secret. I guess the second option would be easier, if I could only find out what you want. Come on, I have to drive you first, and people are already waiting for me.'

In front of the plane, there was another car with its doors lifted. It looked similar to the frog, though black. There were several jeeps as well. The guys were already in them and Toma was in the driver's seat of one of them. Before getting in, Victor fastened my pilot seat belt again. I was gazing out of the window. As soon as we got on a wider road, he sped up like a monster. The city lights gradually faded from my view to turn into dots. Then they were off.

'Where are we going?'

'Wait and see.'

'You have a meeting, right? I could've travelled with Toma so you wouldn't be late.'

'I wouldn't trust even him with these sharp turns. Enjoy my speed and my music now, tomorrow you can enjoy the view and I will enjoy you!'

The music of *Hippie Sabotage*[30] thundered. My seat vibrated because of the bass, and I trembled because of the predatory blue that pierced me. Victor split his attention between me and the road. He bit my palm, his lips moving with the lyrics of the song. As he stared at me, I wondered whether he saw a devil in my eyes, or just his own reflection.

The road twisted into serpentine bends. Even at a normal speed it would have been too much; they were terrifying turns that could challenge the stomach of a rally driver, and yet Victor kept persistently pushing the limits of my nervous system. Nevertheless, I could hear the moans of *Desire* in my head. I stared at Victor's focused face as my two fingers walked from his shoulder to his neck. He kept throwing glances at my cheeky face, his jaw clenched. All of a sudden, he turned down the music and the speed. His shiver-provoking timbre filled the car cabin.

'I kindly shared my intentions with you, and now you're provoking me again. Jeans off!'

'What? Now?' I gawked and his muscles tensed.

'Now, Nia!' There was a biting undertone to his voice.

I hesitantly began to unbutton. Stiffened by the belts, I pulled off the jeans with a laborious pelvic movement.

'Panties off!'

'I thought we were not supposed to have sex?'

'I'm waiting!'

---

[30] *Hippie Sabotage. "Devil Eyes." – author's notes.*
You've got the devil in your eyes
You went and took me by surprise
Say what you wanna say I won't go back
If you wanna hit the road then let's go then
Let's just go and see the world and just show them
What it really means to live life golden
https://www.youtube.com/watch?v=qe3K0eNRrns

I struggled with the bikini but eventually managed to take it off. He put them to his lips. He slid his hand over my naked skin, then pressed it against my groin. I slammed my knees together as the electric shock of his touch glued me to the seat even tighter than the speed.

'Spread them apart!' He moved one of my legs to the side. He drew circles over the eager bundle of concentrated pleasure. 'Now you do it. But don't go to the end!'

'I can't. I tried already and it didn't work.'

'You'll try again then. Imagine that it's me touching you. My tongue is there. Imagine me fucking you,' he continued his magical movements and I moaned. 'Share my fantasy. I'm fucking you as you're all tied up, like you are now. You keep screaming for me not to stop and then you fall apart in my arms.'

He growled and switched to manual mode. The car roared wildly. Victor's hand clutched the gearstick and mine went below my navel. The tires whistled and the back of the car slid down the sharp slopes. The pulsation between my legs was raging, my blood started boiling as the adrenaline blew my head off. I imagined it—the desired touch, then Victor stretching my tissue, my limits, then me falling apart from pleasure. *Lust* shrieked wildly. Wrapped in her red veils, I impatiently moved my fingers in circles. Moisture and deep moans came from me.

'Look at me!' The tone of his voice lifted my eyelids. The mad flame raged in his irises. 'Put a finger inside! I want you to do it slowly!' Opening my mouth, I penetrated myself cautiously. Victor bit his lips. 'Damn!' His muscles tightened.

The speed increased as I vibrated in my sensations. I pressed my head against the seat. One of my hands gripped his wrist. The other one kept going in circles, more and more impatiently, then it slipped in again. A strong pulsation drew a salacious sound from my throat. I began to move faster.

'Stop!'

'I won't!' My thighs trembled, eager for the explosion.

My body was on the verge of melting, but Victor grabbed my fingers and bit them.

'The finish is mine, Nia!'

Three turns later, he stirred the wheel sharply to the right. He stopped the car on something that resembled a platform. As we started descending underground, he unbuckled our belts and the belt on his trousers as well. We were in a garage. A man I didn't know was waiting by the door but

Victor shouted something and he disappeared. Seeming out of his mind, Victor grabbed my neck to pull me out of the car. He lifted me to the height of his navel. Adrenaline throbbed in his pupils. My ankles entwined behind him and his desire pulsated at the entrance of my body.

'You're a goddamn torturer of my self-control.'

I took a breath to reply but he invaded me rudely and only a scream escaped my throat. He sank to the limit. The painful, addictive sensation slammed at my bones. The mad blue pierced my brain. I dug my fingers into the back of his head, his beard scratching my cheekbone. He pushed into me, driving his desire like a predator, and the thorny pleasure flooded me in heat. My back pressed firmly against the car, my muscles vibrating, my thighs enveloping his waist even tighter. My special spots went crazy. A pulsation tightened him in me and my stomach, making me moan loudly. Victor's eyes set ablaze. He bit my lips hungrily, his breath speeding up along with my convulsions.

'Wanting only this and not getting it drives me crazy. You're mine and you're not running away from me anymore! Am I clear, Nia!'

He spoke through his teeth in my ear. Midsentence, one of my special spots exploded. My orgasm erupted with hot moisture. Victor pressed his forehead against mine. He kept penetrating in sharp movements reaching my limit, coming together with me. He was pulsating, squeezing me against his hot body. His breath was broken and his dry lips sucked the little moisture that still shone on mine. He stayed in me for a couple of minutes before placing me carefully on my feet. I stood there in silence in my colourful socks. I awkwardly watched the stream of his liquid desire running down my thighs. Not taking his eyes off me, he pulled the jeans from the car.

'Panties are first, trousers come after,' I muttered as he put my foot in one of the legs.

'You will find lingerie in the suitcase. These panties are mine,' I frowned, and Victor smirked. He caressed my cheekbone gently and his voice dropped lower: 'I should have been more careful but I couldn't hold it. Adrenaline plus you is a combination quite difficult to handle. Did I hurt you, my lovely dear?' He put my hands to his lips as he watched me guiltily.

'I'll probably have bruises again. I guess slower and easier, especially in the beginning, would be safer.'

'OK, I'll try,' he kissed my fingers as he spoke. 'I want you to take a rest now. I hope there won't be bruises because all I want for tomorrow is to be inside you. Slowly, easily, rudely—whatever you wish!' His guilty face was so cute. Bruised or not, I couldn't wait for tomorrow. Anticipation took over me and I frowned.

'Can't you just stay with me? I'd rather not be alone.'

'I'm begging you, don't torture me with this look! If there was even a hypothetical option, I'd go for it. You won't be alone though, don't worry about that. The house is swarming with staff and security.'

He stroked my cheekbones, but I turned away disappointed.

'Where are you going?'

'Back to Naples.'

'I could've just stayed there too. It makes no sense to drive all the way here just to go back now.'

'If it was appropriate, you'd have stayed. I think we already spoke about the decisions that I make. Don't sulk at me! I'll be back before you wake up.'

I frowned as he pushed me to the door. We walked into a bright corridor. A few steps later, the same guy popped up and Victor introduced him:

'Luca's at your service. If you need anything, ask him. I want you to have dinner and sleep well. I have to go now,' he let go of my hand reluctantly.

The man greeted me cheerfully in English with a nice Italian accent. We went out into the open and meandered along narrow alleys surrounded by high fences. A countless number of stairs led us to a white, arch-like gate. There were colourful lemon-patterned tiles all around. After passing through the seemingly humble entrance, however, I found myself in an environment that reminded me of a film from the golden age of European cinema. The impressive garden abounded with well-kept plants. Garlands of lights swirled along the alleys, creating a cosy atmosphere. The huge villa was perched on a cliff over the sea. *Google* told me that I was located right above the small beach of Positano. On the edge of the cliff, there was a pavilion with Roman-style columns. I walked there and sat down. The boats twinkled like distant lanterns in the vast blackness before me. The sea was hiding in the dark, but I could hear its endless movement. The moon shyly peered from behind the clouds and messy-haired waves glistened in its light. As I watched the new reality before me, my lungs sighed loudly. I thought how insane it was that I—me!—was there at that moment. Luca caught my attention with a glass of wine, a tray of food and a smile. Still remembering the rough travel, my stomach couldn't take any food, but the drink tempted me. I asked for a cigarette. The breeze caressed me as I enjoyed the wine and the tobacco while a warm wave spilled through my chest.

Luca took me to the bedroom. I was astounded by the careful order in the suitcase as I rummaged for a T-shirt and bikini. In the shower, however, my mood darkened. I scorned myself for allowing Victor to come inside me again, besides, I hadn't taken the pills. We really needed to define clear limits in this regard. I searched the Internet for a solution and was soothed by the information that emergency contraception could still be effective up to three days. I decided to cheer my mind up with some touristic information about Positano. What I found, though, were statistics about the car accidents on the serpentine bends along the Amalfi Coast. I was shocked and quickly calculated the probabilities; the coefficients turned out to be pretty high. I wanted to inform Victor about the results:

I got acquainted with the statistics. The probability of dying or getting injured
on this road is critically high. The speed you drive at is disproportionate
to the conditions. We didn't die on our way here but there will be
an accumulation of probability on your way back and the figures are not optimistic.
Take the data into account!

He didn't receive the message. I did the maths again but, of course, my first calculation was accurate. I was confirming the results for the umpteenth time when my phone jumped on the bedside table:

I'm not on the road. I'm on water.
Don't worry about me.
P.S. Do you miss me?
I murmured as I pressed the screen energetically:

I don't have data on water transport.
I can't calculate probabilities about that right now.

Worrying is a pointless activity and I never do it.
P.S. The time you've been away does not evoke the sensation of missing.

I was getting comfortable for sleep when he replied:

The time you've been away is enough to make me miss you already.
I need to be inside you. I need you in my arms.
You're ruining my focus. Go to bed. Now!

I relaxed in the soft embrace of the bedsheets. Ever since we left, I had been ignoring *Reason*, and he was obviously fed up with nagging. Only *Lust* kept purring in my head, waving her veils all about. The breeze brushed past the curtains to nest on my face. Fatigue pressed my exhausted eyelids down and I fell asleep.

φ

Shouts in Italian made me jump up in bed. The blanket was on top of me, so I became entangled, and twirled my neck like a meerkat to get out. Three huge men were staring at me. One of them was holding a gun and I shook my head to make sure I was not dreaming.

'Are you OK, madam?' The sturdiest one yelled in English but I just blinked, not able to comprehend the situation.

'Not anymore. What's going on?'

'I heard you shouting. The balcony is open, and I assumed someone broke in. I didn't see you under the blanket,' he examined the balcony.

I rubbed my face, muttering:

'Why would someone break in through the balcony? There is a door, right? I must've shouted in my sleep. I suffer from nightmares and sometimes talk. I probably shout too. I'm sorry for freaking you out,' my pulse was pounding, and I pressed my hand to my chest.

'We're sorry for storming in and for scaring you but, please, close your windows and your doors. Even armoured, they're not secure when opened. We'll leave you to your sleep then. Sorry, we were just doing our job, madam,' another guy explained, and I nodded as they left.

'Well, I guess there actually is a worse way to be woken up than a forgotten alarm on Sunday.'

I slumped on the mattress. The adrenaline kept my eyes wide open, and it was not even morning outside.

The dawn was just about to wake up the world. It fought with the darkness as I peered from the balcony. My rapid heart rate wouldn't let me go back to sleep. Putting on a white romper from the suitcase, I wrapped myself in a colourfully dotted scarf to protect me from the pinching breeze. There was no one in front of my room. Everyone was still sleeping because it was indecently early. The garden looked even more stunning in the daylight and, beyond the gate, I saw stairs that led downwards. I counted 253 of them to the beach, and was bewildered by the steep slope and the dedication of the masons who had built the stairs.

I sat down on the shore, waited for the dawn to pierce the horizon and greeted the scattering colours with a smile. The sun came up and its smile was even brighter than mine. I counted the boats and frowned because of the even number of white spots in the blue. The narrow beach was no more than fifty metres long. I walked around in search of sea treasures and shoved a few in my pocket, burying my feet in the small, cool stones, and enjoying the sight of the rising sun.

I was fiddling with a piece of blue glass when I saw that one of the boats was approaching. Shaping my hands into binoculars, I gazed into the distance. A small boat came out of it and rumbled in the direction of the shore. It stopped at the wooden pier at the other end of the beach. Through my binoculars, I watched Victor getting off. I jumped up, beaming, and walked barefoot toward him but came to a halt at his nervous gait and sulky face. He leaned over me, his jaw clenched, then opened his mouth a couple of times only to produce no sound. I stared at his face, two heads above mine, and was just about to break the awkward silence when he hissed:

'What are you doing here?'

He pulled me towards the stairs, but I hadn't taken my trainers.

'Nothing. I watched the sunrise. I was just hanging here. Don't pull me like that!'

'Why are you alone?'

'Who am I supposed to be with?' I was agitated and he stopped walking.

'For Christ's sake, Nia! How did you even get out of a house guarded by over twenty people, goddamnit?' He shouted, his gaze becoming wild and making me tense.

'How... through the door,' I was blinking foolishly, and he bit his lips.

He hurried up the steps without caring to reply. I struggled to keep up and stopped on the 165th step, pulling my wrist away to lean against the wall, panting.

'Are you going to walk, or do you want me to carry you?' He asked loudly. His tone annoyed me.

'I'm not an athlete! I need to catch my breath! What's wrong with you again?' My voice sharpened in defiance to his clenched teeth.

He slung me over his shoulder like a sack and continued up the stairs. My head upside down, I studied Sergey's crooked face a few steps below us. At least he had picked up the trainers. He looked away when I started hitting Victor's back.

'Let me down right now! Gone crazy again? Let me down!'

Neither my fists, nor my yelling seemed to bother him as he walked in even steps, clutching my thighs tightly. He put me back on the ground only after we were through the gate. The guys in the yard froze, staring at me. Victor passed by them, waved and they followed him hesitantly. Luca also popped up. He nudged me in the direction of the pavilion and while we were walking there, he asked:

'Where were you, miss?'

'At the beach. Why?'

'How did you manage to go out alone?'

'What's wrong with all of you! There's one way to go out—through the door, and I happen to know how to open doors,' I waved my hands about.

Luca muttered something in Italian, then insisted that I should sit at the pavilion where breakfast was served. He poured me a cup of coffee and invited me to eat, pretending to not hear the yells that were coming from the house. I kept peering over his shoulder. Victor's silhouette appeared in the dining room window and I saw him grabbing one of the guys by the neck. I jumped up and started down the alley, but Luca stood in my way. He shouted something and the guy at the villa's entrance nodded at him, then Luca insisted that I go back to the pavilion.

Less than a minute later, Victor came out, walked to me angrily and sat down on the chair next to me. Still sulking, he lifted the lid of an elegant metal container full of gummy bears. He put a handful in my empty plate, but I defiantly pushed it away. My questioning eyes were studying him, and they must have seemed a little shocked, too, but he placed me in his lap nevertheless. His fingers buried into my hair, and he tried to kiss me, but

I turned my head away. He squeezed my neck as I tried to resist him, my hands against his chest.

'What have I got to do to make you stop pushing me away?'

'Stop pulling me, for instance!' I snapped and he put his hands to his cheekbones. 'Why were you trying to suffocate that man?' He snorted without answering and I continued angrily: 'Victor, I keep encountering new personalities of yours, every new one weirder than the others. Your behaviour is that of a schizophrenic. Your expression right now is giving me the creeps. Please, explain your reaction because I don't understand it! I assume that this time, the problem with understanding is not in me.'

He took his hand off his face. In his eyes, there were demons that I had never seen before. He pulled me rudely to his lips and bit mine. His kiss was gentle nevertheless, and his fingers moved carefully all over my back. As if two different personalities inhabited his body and mind simultaneously, dictating opposites in his attitude. He exhaled through his teeth, then spoke calmly:

'I went mad! Idiots! Supposedly well-trained, each of them weighs a hundred kilos, and yet they can't handle my tiny girl. You sneaked out, unnoticed. They weren't even aware that you were gone. He said he left you in bed. If I hadn't seen you at the beach, I'd have found the bed empty and freaked out until they found you. You can't go out on your own, Nia! It's unacceptable as much as not knowing where you are!'

I kept blinking at his angry face and laughed when he finished.

'Are you serious with this nonsense?'

Victor's expression melted my smile.

'Dead serious. I was trying to stay away from you until the security issues were settled, but you drove me crazy. If I was more patient, it would have been different. But I'm not, and right now I have too many enemies. I can't compromise or miss things,' Victor grabbed my face. 'Being with me puts you in danger. That's why Toma has been raging from the very beginning—because I put you at risk. And he's right about that. I need to take the necessary precautions and, for you, they're obligatory.'

'I don't remember us discussing all this.'

'We don't need to! This is an issue decided by me! You won't even see the security guards, like you didn't know about the Russian and his team. Only two guys will be close. Sergey will take care of your route schemes but before that he'll tell you where you can go and where you cannot. The penthouse will be secured. I ordered for your online photos to be deleted but you need to delete those with your face in your social media as well...'

I gaped as he kept reciting more and more insane conditions.

'Stop it!' I waved my hand in front of his crazy face, trying to figure out how to put all my bewilderment in a sentence. 'You keep speaking so calmly about all these absurdities, as if they're actually going to happen,' my tone became sharp and he sighed in his cupped hands. 'I'll say it clearly and firmly—NO! No security guards, no Sergey, no route schemes and deleting photos! And how did we even get to the goddamn penthouse again?'

'Stop swearing! I don't wanna argue right now!'

'It's not an argument! There's nothing to argue about!' I escaped his embrace. As soon as I got up, I started shouting: 'The answer to all these absurdities is NO! I get claustrophobic by just listening to you. Having sex with you doesn't mean that I'm with you! Whatever "being with you" even means, damn it!' I kept waving my arms under the fire of his eyes. 'I have a life of my own and when it comes to my life, the decisions are mine. If I'm going to live in claustrophobia because of some fucking, I refuse it altogether! Damn it!' I crossed my arms and turned my back on him. He hissed through his teeth, then hugged me, pressing himself against my body as I moved sulkily. Kissing my neck, he whispered:

'You're not just a thorny cactus. You're like a tiny little Tasmanian devil. You storm about, you gnash your teeth, but you don't realise that you being furious is the cutest thing I've ever seen. I really hope thought that I'm not just "some fucking" for your beautiful mind,' I grunted as he pressed me to himself. 'I have a proposal, my lovely dear. Let's just leave it here. We'll negotiate a diplomatic solution later. We both find it impossible to communicate, it's a nightmare for us to compromise, so we'll have to develop new skills. Let's enjoy this day today, and after this we will argue as much as you like. The morning didn't start well, and I'd like us to try again.'

'Try what? The start of the morning is gone now.'

'We can rewind it,' propping his chin on my shoulder, he stretched his arms in front of me and pretended to wind a clock, whilst imitating backwards speaking with incomprehensible sounds in my ear. This ridiculous theatre made me laugh. 'Good morning, my lovely dear! I dream of waking up to the sensation of penetrating you,' he bit my neck and slipped his hand under my romper. My nipples bristled. I looked around in embarrassment. All the guys had their backs to us.

'Victor, I hope you realise that what you're doing right now doesn't change this morning's reality?'

'There is no objective reality, Nia. It's not a constant because we can change it every second. Simple quantum physics. In my reality, you're opening your eyes right now. I finally get to wake up holding you in my arms. Your skin prickles, you enjoy feeling me after you *didn't* miss me last night,' he stressed the negative word. His abstract ideas amused me.

'I'd better say "good morning, Victor" in this reality of yours then.'

'This is a reality of ours. You tell me everything there,' he was running his hand all over my skin.

'Apparently you're into quantum physics, too. I must admit, however, that you're quite frivolous about the notion of the multiverse[31]!'

He laughed and led me by the hand to the gate. When we got there, he gave me a devilish smile.

'There was one thing I liked about the previous reality. I'll repeat it in our new morning.'

'What is it?'

He grabbed me and tossed me like a sack over his shoulder again.

'This,' he slapped my butt, amused and already walking down the steep stairs.

The boat was still there, tied to the wooden pier. I froze. Water took second place on *Fear*'s list. On my rare encounters with it, I would only let it reach my knees, and even then it made me shake. I couldn't swim and I had defined drowning as an unwanted way to die. Victor noticed my anxiety as he invited me to get in.

'What's wrong?'

---

[31] *The multiverse is a hypothetical group of all parallel universes that could possibly exist (including ours). Taken together, they contain everything that exists: space, time, forms of matter, energy, impulse, the laws and constants of physics that are in force in these universes. The term 'multiverse' was first introduced by the American philosopher and psychologist William James in 1895 and was later popularised by science fiction writer Michael Moorcock. – author's notes.*

'*Fear*. Water is on his list. Besides I've never been on a boat before, and I think I'd like to keep things this way.'

'Well then this is a great opportunity to expand your limits and learn how to trust me,' he lifted me in front of his navel, and I wrapped my legs and arms around him.

The boat began to rumble, and I trembled like a leaf in Victor's embrace. I was probably turning pale, and he smoothed back the messy strands of hair over my face, smiling. After a short period of a mental block in my head, we reached a larger and much taller boat. A giant boat—a yacht, a ship, or whatever the exact term for this type of vessel was. We got on and I was surprised to find out that it didn't sway at all. Victor reached out to help me down the inner ladder.

'I think this boat is better. It doesn't shake and we're somehow further from the water.'

'It's not a boat, it's a yacht. It's perfectly safe, don't fret!' He laughed and pulled me up the steps.

We passed by two levels before we reached the top one. There was a spacious room and some sort of a porch with a swimming pool and a view that left me speechless. I walked to the front and clung to the railing. I squeezed it tightly, just in case, then took in the whole beauty. In one direction, there was hilly terrain dotted with colourful houses. To the other side—the innumerable shades of the Tyrrhenian Sea. I didn't suspect their existence outside the fantasy of photographers and *Photoshop*. I guess the state I reached was what people call "being in love". The sun was shining over the landscape and for the first time in my life, I was possibly falling in love. Italy captivated my senses. *Desire* was probably going to wail for this land for eternity.

'Oh my God! Now this is a sight one could never get tired of, isn't it?' I said with my back to Victor, running my eyes all over the landscape. I turned around to see him smiling and staring at me.

'Yes, my lovely dear. This is a sight I could never get tired of,' his irises were burning and his gaze made me hot. I turned my head back to the water. He hugged me, his beard scratching my neck.

'It's amazing. I guess I should say "thank you",' my voice came out hoarse from my dry throat.

'Thank me for what?' His words tickled my ear. Pressing himself against me, he slowly moved his hands from my thighs to my neck. Prickly impulses raced through my nervous system, finishing in my groin.

'For being here. For giving me the chance to enjoy all this splendour. I told you that I've always wanted to visit Italy.'

I shuddered at the sigh in my ear.

'Did I tell you that I want to bring you joy? I'll scatter at your feet the entire splendour of this whole goddamn world, Nia. Then I'll enjoy the sight of you admiring it.'

While whispering, he took off my scarf. His fingers chased the sharp shivers down my shoulders. The romper slipped down to my ankles. My bikini ended up there, too. The sea breeze caressed my naked body. My breasts heaved and Victor filled his cupped hands with them.

'More than anything I want you to be mine. My mind's only salvation is to have you in my arms.'

Victor took a few steps with me in his arms and my back bumped the bed. His lips ran over every centimetre from my ankles to my neck. After sucking in the moisture from the orgasm provoked by his tongue, he penetrated carefully and slowly. He was taking his time, igniting the stakes of my body one by one, so they could devastate me. He kept filling me, not taking his eyes off mine, and the addictive blue mesmerised me. I sank into the darkness of my desire and came again, and again. The powerful convulsion suddenly twisted me. I was shaking when Victor pressed my hands tightly to the bed. His irises went wild as I writhed underneath him. He was no longer trying to be careful. My delicate tissue's sensitivity sharpened, and I moaned loudly at the stretching, craving penetration. He invaded rudely and another spasm spread heat throughout my body. A moan flew out of my throat and Victor bit it, along with my lips. He growled. He pressed my pelvis to himself, invading my absolute limit to fill me with his juices. His orgasm drowned my groin, and the addictive scent of his skin drowned my lungs.

He pulled me to lie on top of him. I enjoyed the processes that took place in my body, and relaxed on his chest. My heart rate had not yet got back to normal when he ran his hand over my butt. He hardened again and propped me up, ready to burst in. Lustful flames flickered in his eyes. I jumped up.

'What? Again?'

'I told you I wouldn't want to stop. Now I don't intend to.'

'Christ, how do you even do it? How are you so energetic when you're not really young?'

He frowned.

'I'm bursting with energy for you. And what do you mean I'm not really young? I'm only turning forty today.'

I studied his boyish expression with suspicion, and he pinched my nose.

'Today?'

'Yup.'

'Your birthday is today?'

'Yup.'

His laughter embarrassed me.

'I'm sorry, I didn't know. Happy birthday then!'

'How did you not know? There was such an uproar about me turning forty only after the elections. The court ruled in my favour, of course, because it's the same year after all, but the media chewed in this for a whole month.'

'I don't follow political news. It's boring. Wait here, I've got something for you!' I remembered the sea treasures that I had found.

I ran to the porch where my romper was lying on the floor. I took out of my pocket the piece of blue glass that had long travelled the sea. It was a lucky piece of glass—instead of ending up in a dump, it had crossed the world by water, adopting a smooth and unique shape.

I opened my cupped hand in front of Victor's nose. He took the glass and kissed my palm.

'Here you go! An insignificant gift from someone who didn't know that you were going to fuck them on your birthday.'

'Thank you, my lovely dear. Don't be cynical! I'm spending my birthday with you. I just prefer to fuck you meanwhile,' he pulled me back to bed.

I lay down next to him, my head on his chest. He walked the tips of his fingers over my shoulder, spinning the glass in his other hand. His hoarse voice pierced my brain:

'You know what penguins do?'[32]

'I do,' I muttered, awkward because of his association.

'Can I take it this way?'

'Certainly not. I'm not a male penguin choosing a female. It's just a little gift for your birthday. I have nothing else.'

'You can give me something else, too.'

'And what is it?'

Appetite shone in his eyes.

____

[32] *When choosing a partner, king penguins give them a stone – author's notes.*

'The chance to make a wish of yours come true. Tell me something you desire but have never done.'

'Are you referring to sexual desires?' I leaned over him, my elbows raised.

'Yes. I'd like to hear all of them. Then fulfil them all.'

'Well, I don't think I have any. My opinion of sex improved only recently and I haven't thought about that before. Only...' I went silent, shrugging.

'Only what?' He stared at me insistently and I blushed. 'I'm listening, Nia!'

'Well... I haven't had any wishes, but a couple of hallucinations attacked me. If that counts.'

'What do you mean?' He leaned against the board of the bed with a serious expression on his face.

'Well... Hallucinations in which your face pops up. As if you are real and I can touch you. It first happened when... Andre and I had... you know what! The hallucination, however, made it feel as if it was you who was under me,' he grimaced but I carried on: 'It happened afterwards, too. In the bathroom. It's weird. You wouldn't understand, and I don't want you to think I'm cra...' His laughter interrupted me. Victor hid his lips behind my hand.

'God, Nia! Why would I think you were crazy? It's not a hallucination, it's a fantasy.'

'Have you had those?'

I studied his amused face with suspicion.

'Of course, everyone does. What are we doing in this hallucination of yours?' He smiled, biting my fingers. I gulped.

'Well, I'm on top. Like this,' I took the position, and the face of a predator was back on him again. 'I'm holding your wrists,' I stretched his hands over his head and pressed them to the bed. 'Then I'm moving at my own pace and when you're about to finish...'

'You on top is not a good idea,' his muscles became tense and he licked his lips.

'Why not?'

'Because that way I'll have too much control over your body and we'll end up in my fantasies. Or maybe we could merge them. Your fantasy with mine. What about that?'

I nodded. He let his arms relax and I settled myself on top of him. I touched his penis, uncertainly taking in only the tip. I struggled to keep pressing his wrists to the bed, but I could barely reach them, and he smirked.

I glided up and down cautiously, and with my every movement he also rose to sink deeper. I jumped up as he pierced me abruptly. He clutched my wrists and locked them with one hand to my back. I fell on his chest and couldn't get up, couldn't move, and he dug his fingers into my hair. He growled, sinking to my very bottom.

'As you know, I'm impatient. If my fantasy gets too much for you, just tell me to stop,' he whispered, his thrusts still going.

He stroked my butt, then suddenly slapped it. The sound echoed. My skin prickled. I jumped but he held my head to his chest. My breath stopped and his was hoarse now. He ran his fingers over the burning tissue. Stinging arrows flew under his touch. He started pulsating, deep inside me. He slapped me harder just when he had reached the limit inside of me. The pressure made him invade a new territory. I shrieked but my muscles tightened around him because of the unexpected pleasure. A mixture of burning pain and electrifying ecstasy swept over me, stretching my body like a string. He pressed me tight to himself.

'You want me to stop?'

The timbre of his voice ignited me.

'No,' I muttered as my nervous system tried to handle the unfamiliar processes.

Victor slapped my butt once more, much harder, caressed it, then set my skin ablaze again and again. His heart rate quickened as he repeated the movement. He kept piercing me, blowing up the darkness of my mind. I was slick with sweat. The skin under the slaps burned painfully. He pushed into me like crazy, it was the first time I had heard his breath ragged and loud. My nailed wrists moved in his grip as a spasm constricted my muscles. Victor let go of them and I propped myself against the board of the bed, raising before his mad eyes. He watched my orgasm like a predator. Then he released his own and his heat poured into me. He slid his hand up my throat, squeezed it and held me still, preventing me from breathing. He kept moving, relaxing the grip on my neck periodically. I became dizzy and sank my fingers into his wrists, but he didn't stop pushing into me. My body suddenly took off, with a powerful burning tension vibrating in its centre. I was exploding again. Everything underneath my skin was on fire. My juices drowned him. I fell into pieces on top of him. His desire pulsated in me as his hand stroked my itchy skin. He was growling while I was counting the stars under my eyelids.

φ

Victor took his phone from the nightstand and sent a text. A moment later, I heard footsteps and some clattering from the porch, but he remained silent. After a while, he carried me outside into the blinding sun. He headed for the pool and I shivered but the water only reached his waist, plus it was warm. He went in and I wrapped my legs around him, holding on to his neck too, just in case. Someone had left a bottle of champagne in an ice bucket, two glasses, and fruit by the pool. Victor poured champagne while studying my face. He took a couple of ice cubes, plunged his hand in the water and pressed the ice to my butt. I frowned.

'It will soothe the skin there. Does it hurt?' He rested his forehead on mine.

'My endorphin levels are high. I can't tell. It's just cold.'

'Take it. You know that I didn't mean to hurt you—only to give us pleasure, right? Just say the word and I won't do this anymore!'

'Of course I know that. When your penis is inside me, that's exactly what happens: pleasure. Why would I want you to not do it anymore? I don't think I understand your question,' I rolled my eyes and he laughed, shoving a piece of melon in my mouth.

'I'll give us pleasure we're not even aware of. All I need is for you to trust me and never doubt that I want you to enjoy things beyond standard limits,' he kissed me, turned my back to him, and leaned me against his chest. 'If there's anything bothering you, just tell me. OK?'

'I always tell people when there's something bothering me. That's why we need to resolve one issue.'

'What issue?'

'I'll have to take emergency pills again, but I don't have any.'

'I thought the doctor gave you normal ones. You can't take emergency pills that often!'

'I know, I read about it, but I didn't take the normal ones. I wasn't planning to have sex with you anymore. And I don't plan to have sex without protection with someone else, so there was no reason to take pills.'

'Fine, I'll ask for what you need,' he ran his fingers over my neck and squeezed it, biting my ear. 'And, please, don't plan sex with anyone else at all because just these syllables make my adrenaline explode.'

'I won't for now! Sex with you is enough. Plus, you make *Lust* go crazy with her veils, and *Desire* wails like...' I stopped abruptly, although I was amused by what I had said. I cleared my throat.

Victor handed me the glass of champagne, not reacting to my words. The yacht glided smoothly along the colourful coast while he caressed my shoulders. He stuffed another piece of melon in my mouth, his chin propped on my shoulder.

'I'll ask you a question and I want a frank answer!' His tone made my stomach twist, as if I had entered a dentist's office. 'The other night at the penthouse you weren't talking to me, and you weren't talking to yourself. You heard a voice and you replied to it, didn't you?' I was silent, squeezing my fingers nervously, but he took hold of them and kissed them, then pressed me tighter to himself. 'You can tell anything to me, Nia. Please, explain what's going on in your head. I can accept your reality, whatever it is. I will understand.'

'I don't think so and I don't want you to think I'm crazy,' I looked down, but he pushed my chin back up and covered my cheekbone in kisses.

'Nia, you alone are a madness for me. A madness I didn't know existed in this goddamn world. I want you with all your hallucinations and conclusions, and, after your unreasonable logic, I can most definitely handle the voice in your brilliant head, too,' he crossed his arms on my chest.

His beard scratched my cheekbone and I groaned as his fingers moved along my skin, as if they were trying to peel away my limits on sharing. I found out that I wasn't awkward discussing this issue with him. Naturally, out of habit, I was concerned that he might think I was crazy. However, I wasn't reluctant to tell him exactly what was going on in my mind, even though I had never admitted these details to anyone else. My eyes were running over the colourful slopes while muffled words came out of my mouth:

'There isn't a voice in my head, actually,' I cleared my throat, and he pressed his cheekbone against mine.

'What's there in your beautiful mind then, my lovely dear?' He whispered in my ear.

I took a deep breath.

'Many voices. They're not voices, really. I mean, they can talk, but I can also describe the way they look, therefore they are images. Like entities, you know? Like inhabitants of my mind.'

Victor swallowed dryly. Embarrassed, I fell silent. After all, I could have still pretended it was a joke.

'I feel you straining, Nia. Relax and tell me everything. I don't want any boundaries between us. No limits. OK?' To my surprise, his tone was soft and warm. His face was neither shocked, nor reproachful, but there was no definite expression, in fact. He just smiled and kissed me before leaning me against his chest again. 'Tell me more details, please. Better give me an example, so I can understand.'

'Fine, I will try! For example, back at the penthouse, I snapped at *Reason* because he said that there was no galaxy where your nonsense could be considered arguments. He was technically right but I wanted to hear what you'd say. He doesn't like you at all and he keeps nagging, even more since *Desire* and *Lust* invaded our space. They argue and storm about all the time.'

'Who are they?' His voice was muffled. I turned to assess his reactions, but he only smiled discreetly.

'They are new and very annoying. I don't know where they came from. *Desire* dances and it sometimes wails. *Lust* swings some sort of veils, but it turns out she has bombs, too. The other morning, when we argued about Toma and you were giving orders in your unbearable tone, they were making me kiss you and I didn't want to! I fought with them bitterly after that.'

'You mean you communicate with them?'

'Of course I do! They're in my head!'

'Are there others?'

'Yes, they're quite a lot. *Fear, Curiosity, Malice*… I suspect you have her, too,' his breathing was balanced but when I looked at him again; he seemed stunned. I snorted, regretting having said so much. I tried to get up, but he held me back. 'You're horrified, aren't you? You already realised that I'm a total freak?'

'You're no freak and I'm not horrified,' he ran his thumbs over my cheekbones. 'I'll ask you a question and I'm begging you to give me the most precise answer possible. OK?' His eyes were rummaging inside me, and I just nodded. 'That morning when we fought about Toma. You shouted at me, I shouted back, then I kissed you and you ran out of the house. How did you feel at those moments?'

'I just told you. My head was in total chaos. That was exactly when I fought with *Lust* and *Desire*. Everyone argued, I shouted at them, then my body went crazy, too. Total chaos,' I fell silent because his pupils dilated. Without saying a word, he bit his lips. 'See, you definitely think I'm crazy now. I can even see expressions on your face,' I looked down, but he lifted my chin again and kissed me gently.

'No, I don't! Stop saying that! I'm just trying to understand you. I have another question,' he lurked on my every twitch. 'When I left, you saw a woman in the car. You've seen her on other occasions, too. I was watching you through the window. You were startled, your face changed. What happened then? What did you feel? What made you jump?'

'The urchin. It's also new—the "Prickly one". *Knowledge* defined it as an irrational anomaly. *Reason* couldn't stop it in time and it pierced me, that's why I jumped. It has thorns this big and it stabs my navel with them,' I showed the size with my fingers and he squinted, as if reading some small print. '*Knowledge* explained and *Reason* is aware that this is *Jealousy*, and that we're absolutely incompatible, but it just invaded my head and there's nothing I can do about it.'

I shrugged.

'Oh my God!' He muttered and outright horror crept across his face.

I rubbed my palms in utter embarrassment and shivered as the *Monster*'s chuckle erupted in anticipation of Victor's conclusion. He took my fingers, however, and put them to his lips. He kissed them before he spoke:

'God, Nia! My lovely dear, what has happened to you to make your mind distort emotions into such thought constructions? How did they become like this? What kind of trauma could transform feelings into entities?' He sighed and went silent for a moment. 'Your amazing intellect makes you hyper-rational. I knew from the very beginning that you have difficulties with emotions, but this is a whole new level. How is it possible? How long has it been going on?' I was annoyed by his compassion and the condescending tone that sounded like he was speaking to a seriously ill person.

'It has always been like this. All my life. I'm just like that! I don't like you pitying me. Before concluding that I'm a freak, you must know that my IQ is impressive, and it definitely compensates for my craziness and how messed up I am.'

Victor sighed.

'You're no freak and you're not crazy. Come here!' He pulled me to himself. He covered my face in kisses and forced a smile. 'I know what your IQ is.'

'You can only guess, you don't know exactly. It's my chance to be superior to everyone else! Well, at least to everyone in this part of Europe, including you!' I gave him a smug look.

'I saw your result and I agree—it's impressive.'

'Bullshit! You couldn't have seen it.'

'Nia, I have a pile of documents this big on my desk. All concerning you. I know everything. The only thing I'm missing is your birth certificate.'

He seemed awkward.

'I wonder who is crazier—me or you,' I frowned and he laughed, shrugging with guilt. 'Just like following people, gathering personal documents is also unacceptable. Don't bother going further—I don't have a birth certificate. Stop digging for documents about me. They're not your business!'

'Everything concerning you is my business. You don't have the original? I thought it was lost in the archives.'

'It's none of your business and no, I don't have it! The orphanage didn't provide my grandad with it. He issued a new one—it's not exactly a birth certificate, although it serves the same purposes.'

'What orphanage? What are you talking about?' He was bewildered but then regained this even, statuesque expression. I rolled my eyes.

'The orphanage he took me from, obviously. A place for freaks like me.'

'You weren't adopted. I would've known.'

'I certainly was! Apparently, there are things that even you don't know. My grandad adopted me when I was very little,' I gazed at him smugly. He poured more champagne for both of us.

I could tell how displeased he was with his lack of information. He helped me out of the pool.

'Let's have some rest now! You woke up very early and you need more sleep. If we stay in the pool a minute longer, we'll turn into frogs.'

φ

As soon as we entered the room, he pushed me to the bed and lay down next to me. He placed me on his chest, covered me with a blanket, then sighed deeply as he kissed my head. I was curious and tried to get up. He pulled me back and was silent for a long time before he spoke:

'You were sincere. I will be, too. What you told me worries me and we'll start doing something about it. Firstly, I absolutely forbid you to use the words "crazy" and "freak" anymore. As soon as we get back, I'll have you thoroughly tested to make sure everything with your body is OK. I'll also find a therapist to find out why your extraordinary brain does this to you.'

'Absolutely no chance! I'm not seeing any doctors! My grandad made me go to so many. You don't like those words but you obviously do think that I'm crazy if you want to send me to a therapist. At least say it clearly—a psychiatrist,' I snapped, pushing his chest. His muscles tensed and he pressed me back into him and bit my hand.

'It's not the right time for arguing, so just stop! You're not seeing a therapist because you're crazy—but because he can help you understand yourself, and me as well. Especially the devastating part of me which is beyond your logic.'

'What part?' I gaped.

'The illogical one. You may have entities in your head, but in mine, there are demons. Emotions, completely irrational emotions, and if you don't learn how to feel and understand them, they will destroy us both. You, my lovely dear, are all mind, and I am all soul. I find it very difficult to control it all with you, and you can't comprehend it at all.'

I was silent. I couldn't tell whether his assumption was plausible. He pressed me into him, and I moved even closer. His touch made me relax. I was almost somewhat relieved. Although it was the first time I had spoken openly about my craziness, my mind was silent.

Reason was down in his trench, horrified, as if he expected Victor to reach out into my head and pull him out of there. Only the tension in Victor's muscles bothered me. They vibrated and tightened at uneven intervals with no rhythm. His skin radiated heat that soaked into me. I traced the flames on his chest until his gentle playing with my hair made me drift away in my sleep.

FOURTEEN

My tired eyelids opened and closed as I drifted in and out of sleep; whenever I succumbed, the glassy blue pierced me. As I snuggled in Victor's arms, his vocal cords snarled. Gentle caresses pampered my back to send me back to my sweet afternoon nap. Despite the seaside humidity, my throat was very dry and the heat in the yacht's bedroom finally woke me up. I raised my head and he smiled at my sleepy face, before pushing it back to his tattooed chest. His other hand was vigorously scrolling on his iPhone. He whispered that I should get some more sleep and kissed my forehead.

'I'm thirsty.'

He gave me a bottle of water and, judging by his visibly better mood, the rest seemed to have treated him well. He playfully licked the drops of water that ran down my chin and my consequence-bearing look was instantly ignited. I bit my lip with desire, but he just exhaled loudly and pulled me to lie down by his side again. His touch sent dozens of volts of electricity that burnt my likelihood of going back to sleep to ashes. Strange tickling irritated the smooth muscles of my abdominal wall, as if bugs were crawling. My hand slipped hesitantly to Victor's navel and my stomach quivered. In fact, I had never touched his penis before, nor had I touched anyone else's. When I first saw Andre's, *Reason* concluded that this part of the male body simply lacked aesthetic value. Then he associated it with a whole bunch of unpleasant things. I agreed and from then on, avoided touching or even looking there.

Now, however, *Curiosity*'s crooked eyes blinked rapidly behind the glasses as my hand set off on a research mission south of Victor's six pack. I ran my palm down his belly and I detected a tightening in reply. I went further but he caught my fingers just as they were pricked by the hairs above his groin.

'What're you going to do down there, my lovely dear?' The shiver-provoking timbre took off.

Victor put my palm to his lips and kissed it.

'What will I do? I will touch. I'm curious and...'

'Curious?' He took his eyes off the phone and stared meaningfully at my confused face.

'Yes, because I've never done that before. I lack experience, and the aesthetic reasons...' I muttered.

Through his laughter, he kissed my fingers numerous times.

'All right! I will let you do it but only this time and only because I want to satisfy your curiosity! In fact, my plan is to grant all your wishes, even the weirdest ones, my lovely dear,' he was amused.

My hand continued its adventure. The temperature of the skin there surprised me and so did the smoothness. He bulged in my hand, and I squeezed tighter, enjoying the touch. The result—even more. I accelerated my up and down movements and he got so hard that I could barely feel the skin anymore. He growled, pulling my wrist away abruptly.

'Enough!' His heart throbbed in his sweaty chest. I stared at the blue irises that froze my intentions.

'Why? I like it!'

Victor smiled cheekily.

'I'm pretty sure you'll like this even better.'

He pushed me underneath him, spreading my thighs wide apart, but I glued them together and leaned sulkily against the headboard.

'Why don't you want me to touch you? In general, I don't like it either, but you touch me all the time and I let you. Do you also have issues with it?' I stared at him, waiting for his reaction, but there was none. His eyes froze and he exhaled through his teeth, pulling me back beneath him. 'Victor, if you're going to avoid my questions, I'll do the same. I won't answer ever again!' Under him, I crossed my arms sulkily. He snorted and explained nervously:

'It's not that I don't like it, Nia. I adore your touch. It's just that I prefer to control my own body. That's all! Now I'd like my tongue to delight you!' He sucked my lips to make me shut up then sank into a deep kiss, but I pushed him and he growled: 'Another question?!'

'No. A conclusion. I was planning to share it with you this morning, but our conversation took another direction. Basing my opinion on my observations of your recurring pattern, I'm afraid you have a problem. I suspect I know what it is. I've read about it, and you have all the symptoms,' I nodded confidently and he raised his eyebrows.

'And what is my problem according to your observations?'

The mockery in his tone annoyed me and I replied firmly:

'Victor, the facts clearly show that you have serious control issues. I'm absolutely sure, even though I'm not a specialist. You must take care of this! You suffer from a mania for control and, because of it, your mind tries to insert order into chaotic systems. Of course, they can only be influenced by unbalanced sequences, so what you want is technically impossible. Therefore, this is considered an irrational desire and is classified as a mania. It could drive one mad and shouldn't be underestimated! It's characterised by spe...'

His laughter interrupted me. The irises shone and the white teeth boasted in front of my face.

'You're not a specialist but you're so right. I do have control issues. Huge issues,' he spoke with sincerity, yet his voice still sounded ironic. I looked at him with suspicion because of the strange combination of attitudes. 'I definitely find it hard to control the chaotic system that is currently in my arms. For now, at least. It's a huge problem and it really drives me mad.'

'Very funny! Did you hear what I said? I'm not joking, it's a seri...'

He muffled my voice with his palm.

'I did hear but I would prefer to listen to something else.'

He pressed me against the bed, shoved his head between my legs, and sucked until nothing but my breath escaped my throat. Victor grabbed my open legs tightly in order to fix me before his face, then sucked hungrily again. His tongue went wild over the delicate tissue, licking every millimetre with care. When it began to move in circles over the hardened tip, I squeezed the sheets. He made rhythmic circles, then carefully slipped his finger inside me and my legs shook. He growled and added another finger, this time much more rudely. He placed them straight over the pulsating spot, as if the imaginary map of my pleasure navigated him. A few movements later, I screamed and probably swore as the moisture of my orgasm burned me.

I couldn't wait for Victor to get inside me so I started pulling his neck, but he stopped me. He leaned over me, not taking out the fingers that were still driving me crazy. His dilated pupils made his gaze look dark. He wasn't taking his eyes off me and insisted that I keep mine open, too, as I came three more times. After the last one, my body was like jelly; I couldn't move, my cardiac muscle was trying to break through my softened ribs. Nevertheless, I still craved him stretching and fully destroying me.

Victor kissed me continuously, causing my anticipation of his penetration to build. To my surprise, however, he got out of the bed and headed to the wardrobe. On the verge of exploding, I watched his steps and his penis. Our desires were definitely the same, but he was struggling to squeeze his into a pair of black beach shorts. He was putting on a shirt, too, when my hoarse voice broke the silence:

'Won't you be more comfortable having sex without your clothes on?'

'If you're not satisfied yet, my tongue and fingers are still hungry for you,' the veins on his neck pulsated as he studied my naked body without moving.

'I'd rather you involve your penis, too. I thought you said that sex was all we were going to do today.'

'Yes, but I'll take care of my adrenaline in another way first. I'm not sure how different things affect you. I don't know how your mind will react, and my greedy fantasy is definitely crazy. That's why I'm gonna destroy some of my energy for you and I'll be more restrained.'

'Again, I understand the separate words but not the whole meaning. Why don't you want to have sex? Is it what I told you about me, or what?'

'Because I might not realise in time if the entities in your head refuse to accept my demons. Because I'm worried about what I heard, and I might not feel your reactions properly. I have no idea how I could help you, and I don't want to provo…'

'Help me?' My sarcastic tone flew out. 'How exactly did you reach the conclusion that I need help, Victor? Why would you help a non-crazy, non-freak like me?' I got up with the sheet over my breasts, hoping my goblin look would do its job. Again, Victor didn't twitch.

'I don't think you're crazy, nor a freak and this is the last time I will say this. I'm just being cautious. I read the doctors' statements and I'm looking for the proper approach so I don't provoke sudden negative reactions and…'

'The doctors' statements? About me?' I snarled, then started yelling: 'Stop snooping in my goddamn documents! You don't have the right! Damn you, it's even illegal!' I threw the pillow at him, but he caught it and hurled it at the wall. My mouth twisted and my shouting escalated: 'This is a perfect example of how you shouldn't approach me! You're provoking an extreme negative reaction with your behaviour right now. I don't need help or "special treatment", nor the disgusting pity in your eyes! Damn you, Victor! Don't do this! Don't underestimate me because it really drives me mad! If my personality is a problem for you, go and bang your goddamn shadows! They're normal, right!' I hissed, heading for the bathroom.

He grabbed my hand, but I snatched it away and slammed the door in his face. I heard him growling, then hitting something on his way out.

I tried to calm down with a long shower but, even after that, I was still furious, regretting every word of my confession. What I regretted most was my irrational assumption that Victor would simply take my way of functioning and accept me without wanting to fix me. I had long ago concluded that it was impossible. I guess I had deluded myself because he also had the habit of counting, he also had patterns, and we were somewhat similar. Well, obviously even a person like him couldn't understand a freak like me.

I had gathered more than enough arguments to be sure that people had difficulties with diverse forms of consciousness, life, and thinking. There are a million examples—historically proven—and one can find new confirmations every day—whether it's a person with an unorthodox angle of perception, someone with different beliefs, or something as banal as sexual orientation; square-shaped consciousness and irregular geometry don't fit under the same sky. The War of the Squares never ends. They rebel, sometimes aggressively, in their relentless struggle to file down the unique edges of anyone who is different. They always label and I never came to understand them. It's crystal clear that this battle is initially meaningless. After all, they would get bored if the whole world could be arranged like a jigsaw puzzle with the same pieces. At some point, I came to assume that most people probably have some very brutal and cruel *Fear* which dictates their actions. Only *Fear* could be that irrational. However, I couldn't guess how he tortures them to act in this way.

I had encountered the Squares' aggression on multiple occasions since I was a kid. I had found out that the childhood period was the hardest, due to children's lack of an established behavioural norm. I didn't fit in, and my grandpa had to do his best in order to soothe me every time kids showered me with insults and sometimes even stones and other items. He repeated the same thing as a mantra:

You are smart!

You are good!

You can, Nia!

They just don't understand you yet.

It shall pass. It shall pass...

I appreciated his willingness to comfort me but what I needed wasn't comfort. What I needed was data. So I went back to my peers, again and again, but couldn't understand them. No matter how much time I devoted to studying them, I couldn't grasp the logic of their behaviour. Years later, when I realised that the Squares filed down the edges of their children from an early age, it all became clear. This was the war of the Little Squares. I arranged their actions in their logical place. That probably was the moment at which my brain began to rebel more fiercely against faulty patterns and distorted people with square minds. I encountered increasingly larger absurdities and, when I got to the point where there was no possible logic for them, the faulty patterns drove me into a stupor—my mental block.

Victor's running from the conversation didn't change its urgency. He kept piling up expectations that he could fix me, that I could fit into his pattern, he impudently trampled on my personal boundaries. I couldn't take, or pretend not to notice, any of these. I had never developed such a function and didn't intend to.

The sun was just about to escape behind the horizon as I leaned against the deck railing. The yacht was anchored near the shore, which gave me the opportunity to enjoy the magnificent colours around. The warm caress of the sun and the sea air extinguished *Rage*. Again, I was surprised that I didn't notice any swaying of the water. An amazing engineering solution had brought comfort and steadiness, as if the yacht was on solid ground. Perhaps this impression was due to the awe-inspiring size of the vessel, but I was not in the mood for calculating the stability and the metacentre[33]. I

---

[33] *Stability is the ability of a vessel to withstand external forces. At small tilts of the transverse plane, the lines of action of the forces intersect at a point which is called a metacentre – author's notes.*

downed a glass of champagne instead. The bubbles almost came out of my nose, but I poured myself some more. While I was admiring the colourful details of the Amalfi Coast, a buzzing sound caught my attention. Not far from the yacht, a jet ski was swishing furiously through the waves. It kept accelerating straight ahead, then turning abruptly. I recognised Victor by his shirt and was astounded by his persistent diligence to fly. The pressure of the centrifugal force[34] was obvious, and I thought most people knew the laws of inertia[35]. He seemed to be accelerating just enough to keep his body on the verge of taking off. Again and again. He suddenly sped towards the yacht, then slowed down abruptly. I watched him sulkily before he disappeared out of my sight.

As I leaned over the railing, *Reason* started murmuring with sarcasm:

Quantum physics is most definitely difficult for him. It is quite obvious, after we heard his absurd ideas about reality. It is true that few people can handle quantum physics, but he doesn't know even the simplest laws. You could at least explain fundamental physics to him, or he will get himself killed with his insane machines. There are much more natural ways to die!

I nodded in agreement about the ways to die but objected to the other assumption. *Knowledge* joined in with his nightmarish exact terms and a whole cannonade of formulas. *Reason* was trying to shout even louder, enlisting examples to prove that the president was not proficient in physics. I defended Victor's knowledge, certain that he was aware of Newton's laws. While we were arguing, something cold and wet pressed against my back.

'Which of them are you arguing with?' The hoarse whisper sank into my ear followed by many kisses. I didn't reply, trying to push Victor's hands away, but he kept me tightly in his embrace. 'The good thing, my lovely dear, is that I'm not the only one you argue with. Tell me, to whom were you repeating your favourite "certainly not" phrase?' He hugged me even tighter, and water soaked into my robe.

'To no one. I'm grumping to myself. Let me go, if you please!'

'Grumping to yourself about physics? And no—I don't please and I don't intend on letting go of you ever again,' he turned me to face him, then

---

[34] *Centrifugal force pushes rotating bodies around a curve. It is considered a fictitious force, pseudo-force or inertial force, because it is not caused by interactions between real objects, but is a manifestation of inertia of the bodies – author's notes.*
[35] *Inertia is the resistance of any physical object to any change in its velocity. This includes changes in the object, speed, or direction of movement – author's notes.*

stared at me, running his hand over my cheekbones. His tone softened: 'I'm sorry, Nia! Please, let's just forget about our previous conversation. I didn't mean to insult you. I don't want us to fight, I don't want you to be tense. You could simply accept that I have this compulsive need to take care of you and make you feel well. What is happening is beyond my control and that drives me crazy. My demons go wild.'

'You have control issues, I already told you that. I warned you that your mania was dangerous, and you just laughed at me!'

'You're right, but try to understand me. Accepting the way your mind works and the entities there work is a process. My mania and I need to adapt somehow, and it's also a process. Let's rewind all this. OK?'

Victor's influence over me bent my firmness. Drops of salty water ran down his face. His T-shirt clung to his well-sculpted body just like I wanted to cling there, too. I nodded sulkily and he continued, smiling:

'You must explain to me so I can understand you! Tell me, with whom and about what were you arguing?' His gaze was relaxing. I moved away but he lifted my chin and his eyebrows. 'Nia!'

His insistent way of pronouncing my name—with an extended "i" and a sharp "a"—sank into my brain like a command I couldn't neglect. Or, rather, I did not want to neglect it.

'I was just wondering why you didn't consider the centrifugal force. The inertia was obvious, and you could've jumped out at any moment. I assume it'd be a painful experience,' I wrinkled my nose and Victor narrowed his eyes.

'What about the argument? With whom and about what?'

'With *Reason*, because he kept nagging that you didn't know physics. He said I should explain the fundamental laws to you, or you'd kill yourself with one of your suspicious-looking vehicles. I argued with him because I think he's wrong and you know these laws. That's all.'

He squeezed my face in his cupped hands. Biting his lip, he studied me thoroughly.

'All right. What you mean is that while you were observing the inertia, you got worried?'

'I already told you that worrying is a pointless activity. It has absolutely no correlation to the result, and so I don't practise it.'

'I think I'm getting it already. I guess I have to disappoint you, my lovely dear. The argument over Newton's First Law[36], while I'm recklessly driving my jet, is simply your hyper-rational brain's manner of worrying that I might get injured,' he kissed my face after every word while I kept blinking. 'This is not a practice but an emotion, Nia. It's called "worrying". It's truly strange—the way it happens in your case and how your mind transfers emotions into entities and dialogues. However, I'm happy that you worry about me, even in your bizarre manner!'

Victor looked at my bewildered face with a mischievous smile, then bit my cheekbone lightly. He looked boyish again, and I was not sure how to react to his statement.

'I have to do something quickly and I'll be back soon. I want to find you naked in our bed 'cause the jet ski didn't quite take my energy for you,' he took off my robe, pushing me to the bedroom.

Victor disappeared down the stairs at a quick pace and I sat down on the bed, deep in thought. His conclusion puzzled me, and I needed him to shed light on the arguments and explain what he meant as soon as possible. I put on my bikini and his shirt, then followed him down the stairs. I bumped into some security guy there. Good thing the unbuttoned shirt managed to cover my breasts, at least. However, this fact didn't change the stunned look on the guard's face. The open area of the yacht—it looked like a porch, but I don't know the exact term—was furnished with style. The floor was made of dark wood and everything else was white. Victor was sitting on a wide sofa, a cigar in his hand and his unbearable tone penetrating someone's ear at the other end of the line. He frowned as I approached, waving at the guy behind me, who immediately disappeared.

I passed by a huge TV. The news from back home was on and the light of the screen shone on Victor's darkening eyes. Still hissing on the phone, he pulled me to sit in his lap, facing him. He motioned for me to keep quiet and ran his hand over my back. The touch was slowly melting my questions away. His blazing irises studied me, but he still kept his focus on the phone conversation. Was it truly possible that two of Victor's personalities could function simultaneously? The energy he radiated made my stomach twist. There was no logic to his interest in me, to his lust for my mediocre body

---

[36] *This law is also called the "law of inertia". Each object maintains its state of rest or of steady and rectilinear motion until an external force brings it out of this state – author's notes.*

features, but I didn't object. I had the same illogical, primitive passions. I slipped my hand over his chest to cheekily land it in his shorts. He looked at me with reproach. His jaw clenched and his fingers dug alongside my spine. He had an instant hard-on and I impatiently knelt to take off his shorts. Victor yelled into the phone once more, threw it to the far end of the sofa, then grabbed my hair and pulled me in front of his face. His demons stretched the blue irises.

'Don't provoke me, Nia!' His expression changed intimidatingly quickly again.

'I'm not provoking you. I'm undressing you.'

'And don't walk around half-naked!'

'Why? We're on a yacht at sea, aren't we?'

'You can be naked all the time upstairs if you want. Not here!' He pulled my hair rudely.

Frowning, I propped my elbows on his chest.

'You want me to explain to you, so you could understand me. Right?' I raised my eyebrows and he nodded with suspicion. 'It goes the other way round, too. I don't see any difference between the levels of the yacht.'

Releasing his grip on my hair, he sighed:

'OK, let me try. Assume that my version of your sea urchin is terribly irritable,' he moved his index finger between my breasts. 'Assume that, since I'm jealous of you, other men's eyes walking on your naked skin makes me explode and become mad.'

'Why are you jealous? It doesn't seem to be a useful function.'

'Because it's not a function. It's my essence, and you provoke it. I am jealous of you; I act possessively and I also feel this obsessive urge to control you. I know it's not logical. It's not rational, but you need to understand me somehow because I don't want this particular demon of mine to go mad. I don't want you to see it when it's mad.'

'Victor, to tell you the truth, I think you need to see a therapist, too,' I raised one of my eyebrows and one side of my mouth. 'Now you mean that seeing me half-naked is a provocation for you?'

'No. Seeing you half-naked, in your bikini, and another man looking at you—that makes me explode. A provocation is you kneeling before me.'

'Because...?' My questioning eyes stared at him.

Victor started crushing his lower lip with his finger and was silent for a while.

'I don't want you to get me wrong again, so I'll ask you a question first. OK?' I nodded. 'Nia, don't you find sex with me worrying?'

His firm expression startled me, and I pulled away.

'Am I supposed to worry about this, too?!' I guess the falsetto in my voice amused him.

'No. It's not that you're supposed to,' he laughed. 'Look, since you drove me out of control back in my bedroom, I've been watching your reactions closely. I know you lack any experience and I'm trying to explore your limits because I am definitely into exploring the challenges and adrenaline in sex. I control myself, even though it's damn hard, but at the same time, I don't want any limits between you and me. Considering what you told me, however, I'm worried about the reactions in your head because I can't see them. I don't know where the limits are of what's normal for you. There's no way for me to know if one of your entities has decided that our sex is too rude, or not normal, or whatever. Then you'll find reasons to run away from me and you'll make me...'

I was listening to his assumptions, but the incorrect data in them made me interrupt:

'But it's me you bang, not them. Maybe *Lust* takes some part, too, but the truth is, my head goes silent at these moments. There's no one there. This is one of the side effects. To be honest, I'm surprised that sex is also labelled normal or not normal.'

'You could label it "standard" if you like.'

'I don't like labelling at all. Victor, could you please clarify something that I don't understand? There are two purposes to sex—reproduction and pleasure. Right?' My eyes opened wide, and he nodded. 'Only a few mammals are privileged to have pleasure. People, cats, dolphins, and several others. If you like it and I like it, too, why are you worried? Why would we define it according to a scale of "normality"? Isn't it enough that it serves one of its primary purposes—pleasure? I certainly like it the way we do it and I don't get what I should find worrying or why I should label it.'

'God!' He showered my neck with kisses, speaking into the skin. 'I didn't say you should! Your logic is perfectly correct. I don't know what the situation with cats or dolphins is, but most people have a lot of restraints. You understand this, don't you?'

He smiled but I shook my head.

'I am not skilled in understanding people.'

'OK, let's say they find it hard to comprehend and satisfy their own desires because of some mental restraints. Narrow boundaries, limits that prevent them from truly enjoying. You can also call them illogical taboos.'

'If that's the reason you don't want us to have sex, you should know that I don't have any illogical taboos. I'm probably even incompatible with them if they're illogical.'

'My lovely dear,' he stared at me with an incomprehensible look in his eyes, 'I fully accept your unreasonable logic and your conclusions right now.'

He sank his lips into mine. While kissing, he took his bulging desire from his shorts and placed me on top of him. I looked around to confirm that there was no one there. Victor pressed a button within his reach that made the light down the stairs turn red.

'They won't bother us, don't worry.'

'I'm not worried, just checking. And, just to let you know, my logic is not unreasonable—it's precise. Your weird worries are unreasonable.'

He pressed himself against me. I could feel his heat through the bikini as he continued speaking in the deepest masculine timbre that made my brain cells disintegrate into atoms:

'So no one in your head has their say on matters of sex? It'd be enough for me to watch your body and trust my feelings regarding your pleasure? No limits and no illogical taboos?' He tucked my hair behind my ears, and I nodded at his precise conclusion. Biting my cheekbone, he growled. 'I think I just got the best birthday present ever.'

He slid his palm down my spine. As his fingers ran between the two halves of my butt, I shivered. The reaction made him go back there. He gripped my face with his other hand and stared at me:

'You don't doubt that I'll penetrate every possible area of your body, do you?'

'I haven't thought about that. I have no grounds to doubt it or not,' I shrugged.

Victor put his hands under my arms. He lifted me and whispered:

'Take your pants off!'

I pulled my bikini off, then he moved me back to my previous position on his lap. He ran his penis over my pulsating tissue, and I was surprised to find how wet the spot was. Victor leaned over my breasts and bit one of them. He swung his tongue over the tip, sending a number of arrows into my groin. Biting my lip, I waited for him to invade but he slid back, spreading the moisture. He pressed himself against the new area without penetrating; he was teasing me, touching the new spot, and my body reacted with a vibrating moan. The excitement provoked by the friction was intensifying. My open lips went dry.

'It's stimulating, isn't it?'

I nodded. He pressed the tight opening and the strange sensation startled me. I got up slightly, but he held me in place and continued teasing the sensitive spot. His breath spread hot shivers over my skin, my nipples hardened even further. He twisted one of them between his fingers and I moaned. Impatient, I tried to push myself down, but he stopped me.

'Stand still! Not now. I have to put effort first and you must be patient. I guarantee that wherever I fuck you, you will scream with pleasure. Then you'll want more and harder, and when you realise that your body is mine, you'll adore it when I fuck you in every possible manner. You'll adore it in every possible way, and you'll adore being mine.'

He gently moved the scattered hair away from my face. Kissing me, he pulled out the string from the waistband of his shorts. He studied the sweaty skin between my breasts like a predator, then ran his lips over them and took the shirt off me. His masculine timbre provoked a deep pulsation below my navel:

'I want you to put your hands behind your back, my lovely dear. And let me please you my way. Our way, actually. No illogical taboos.'

I didn't react and Victor moved my wrists carefully. He pressed them together. Staring at me, he deftly twisted the string around them, bombs exploding in his eyes.

'I must admit that my version of your *Lust* has some serious control issues. It goes mad with desire to control you! You can't even imagine what I feel when you're in my arms!' He whispered in my ear.

My hands were nailed behind my back. Victor squeezed my neck, glued to my lips. He kissed me like he was ravenous for my taste. His tongue went wild and so did mine. My desire to experience him in every possible way made me go ravenous as well. I wanted him inside me, but he tortured me with his gentle teasing on the throbbing spot in my buttocks. My mouth moaned in front of his. He was doing his circular motions on the bulged pleasure button as my arousal couldn't take anymore. I craved sinking my fingers into his shoulder, but all I could do was move my hands behind my back as I was about to explode.

It was true that Victor observed the reactions of my body. He knew them perfectly well. At that moment, every part of my body could have probably taken him in, but he kept torturing me. Just before I came, he lifted me up. He moved forward his desire, hardened to the verge of explosion, to abruptly pierce my moisture. The stretching and the booming ecstasy made me scream, and my trembling body fell to pieces over him. The drug spread deeply through my veins and as soon as he invaded the orgasm swept me up.

'This is the feeling I crave. The feeling that you're mine. I'm addicted to it, Nia!' He growled in my ear.

He turned my back to him while I was still shaking. I knelt on the sofa and he pressed my breasts against the backrest. The last rays before sunset invaded my pupils as he invaded me. Holding the string between my wrists, he kept pushing me to my absolute collapse. His other hand tugged my hair. The sensation inside was tearing me to pieces.

'I have a particular hallucination, too,' his hoarse voice made me even more dizzy. 'One single fantasy that torments me. In it, you are all mine— your body, your mind, everything and you fully accept me. You are mine in every possible way, no illogical taboos, no limits! Tell me that you can simply be mine!'

He sensed that I was on the brink of orgasm and deliberately slowed down, gliding me over pleasure's cutting blade. My body arched.

'Don't stop!'

'Say it! Say that you can be all mine and release me from my nightmare!' He tortured my overexcited body, playing with my addiction.

'I can! I can!' The syllables struggled to sneak between my dry lips.

Victor pushed himself into me fiercely. It was as if there was some part of him that had never invaded before and I screamed. He froze, breathing loudly. A scorching voltage burned in my body. I yelled again, this time lustfully:

'Again! Do it again!'

He pushed once more, not letting go of my hair, and took hold of my neck. My spine arched in his direction and my breasts bristled under the touch of the breeze and the fingers that pinched my nipples.

'You're driving me mad!' He growled wildly and my skin perspired because of the electricity beneath it.

I was the one who was going mad. Getting hot. Burning. Victor reached the edge of the chasm that he had blown up in my mind. Now he was pushing my limits further in the dark. When he pressed his cheekbone against mine, my spine couldn't bend any further. The heat from his chest slammed into my back. He squeezed my neck, stopping my breath. At that moment, even my breathing belonged to him. The fingers of his other hand crept downwards. The tip of my desire had turned into a hard ball of dense sensitivity. He stroked it gently, drawing the mesmerising circles, then slapped it lightly. I jumped but Victor's muscles held me in my arched position. I didn't have enough air to moan with the sharp sensation that electrified me. He stroked and pushed again, deliberately keeping me just millimetres from absolute ecstasy. My body was about to collapse while Victor's movements were driving it crazy.

He kept touching gently, then slapping the sensitive spot with increasing intensity. My senses went wild. He was penetrating abruptly, as if he was following the rhythm of the waves that crashed into the yacht. He was feeling me. He knew perfectly well that I was on the verge and controlled my disintegration skilfully. His pushing sped up. He was invading increasingly rudely, rubbing the bulging pleasure carefully. He gripped my neck tightly and my pulse throbbed in his hand. He hit the sensitive bundle again, this time much harder. An arrow flew to burst the ball below my navel. I exploded, screaming with the sweeping collision between pleasure and pain. The hot moisture of my orgasm streamed down between my thighs and Victor let out a frenzied roar. He came in me with several pushes, flooding the narrow space. I could feel every jet of him. My delicate tissue wrapped around him tighter than ever. I was on the verge of fainting. The biochemistry was raging over my nervous system; a fully unknown level of chaos was storming in me and I was drowning in the devastating pleasure that sprang from the darkness of my mind.

Victor released my wrists. He remained behind me, holding me against his chest. I was vibrating in his arms, and he burrowed his head into my neck. My senses were coming back to life when my ear trembled under his timbre.

'You don't even imagine what you do to me,' he whispered and a shiver ran over my skin. 'My mind explodes every time I come with you, my lovely dear. I crave it!'

Victor turned both of us in one motion. He sat on the sofa with me in his lap and embraced me, showering my face with kisses. I stared at the icy-blue irises. They were burning again. An unfamiliar hoarse voice escaped my throat:

'You always come at the same time as I do, which is nice, but it's anatomically and statistically strange.'

He laughed, biting my lip:

'God, I whisper that I crave that and here's what you think about! It'll definitely take time for me to get used to that. If statistics are that important for you, though—it's not strange because I do it on purpose.'

'What? Coming?' He nodded at my astonishment. 'Isn't it supposed to happen of its own accord? It's a neurological process, after all.'

'It is but, in my case, not quite. I can come in a second, in hours, or at a particular moment that I choose. It depends on me. Let's say I'm a little twisted,' he smirked.

'Twisted?' I squinted. 'You control this, don't you?'

'Of course!'

'Victor, don't get mad at me, but you should really approach your control issues. I don't think this is normal,' I shook my head reproachfully, but the sound of his laughter made me smile, too.

'And I don't think you are into "normal". At least I hope not because that's the only thing I can't provide.'

I was surprised that I had used the label that had always annoyed me. I didn't reply. He put my bikini back on and covered me with the shirt, then ordered food and drinks on the phone. Seconds later, a middle-aged woman appeared to leave a piled-up tray. She tiptoed back out. I followed her awkward movements and pinned my questioning eyes on Victor:

'Aren't you worried that people will see you with me, or that they might take pictures of us? I'm not very proper...' I muttered but he stuffed a piece of peach in my mouth.

'Don't think about that, my lovely dear! It's my business and I've taken care of it.'

'I don't think you've taken care of providing them with earplugs! I'm pretty sure your people can already determine the precise tone of my orgasms,' I sulked at his laughter.

'When the red light on the stairs goes on, everybody has to go to the lowest level. Nobody heard you. Well, except for Sergey, but his proximity is a must. If you insist, I will buy earplugs for him, even though he doesn't really hear well.'

'Yuck!' I grimaced with my tongue out.

'Why do you dislike him so much?'

'His behaviour is terrible. He's rude, impudent, arrogant, he even seems to be a communist and I hate them! Should I continue?'

Bursting into laughter, Victor almost choked on his champagne.

'He is arrogant and rude all right but he's nothing like a communist. Whatever insults you use, you'll be right, but you should not call him a "communist",' he gazed at me with curiosity, running his index finger over my lip. 'Nia, are you even capable of hating?'

'Only communists.'

'How come?' He laughed, his hand buried in my hair.

'Well, I don't know how—my grandpa taught me. When I was very little and I just know that I hate them,' I shrugged.

His eyes shone and stared at the very bottom of mine.

'Now I feel hopeful,' he lowered his tone.

'About what?'

'If your grandpa managed to teach you how to hate, then there's a chance for me to teach you how to love.'

It was my turn to choke. Champagne came out of my nose, spraying his chest. He tapped my back, concealing his laughter with his left hand. He waited for me to balance my breathing, then carried me up the stairs to the bedroom.

'We'll discuss this some other time, when there's a hospital nearby. You certainly can't handle this demon!' Amused, he kissed my nose playfully.

I was awkwardly silent. He hurled me on the bed and leaned over me with his boyish look.

'I reserved a restaurant. We'll approach the shore, so Toma can come on board. And then, my lovely dear, we'll have dinner at a place that will take your breath away.'

I exhaled, relieved because of the change of topic.

'Couldn't somebody see or take photos of us there?'

'I just told you that it's my business. Plus, I told you that I reserved a restaurant.'

'The whole restaurant?'

'Yes!' He said firmly.

'All right. A logical decision.'

'See? My decisions can be logical and you can accept them, after all.'

Victor took two cases of clothes out of the wardrobe and, smiling cheekily, opened one of them to reveal a floor-length golden dress. I began to study it intently, but he grabbed me and shoved me in the shower with him. As we showered, his two fingers made sure I came over them. Once he had towelled my skin dry after the shower, he settled in the bed, staring at me with anticipation. I put the dress on. It was my size, but dragged a foot and a half behind my feet. My entire back and my arms remained naked, and the sharp neckline reached down to my navel. The delicate fabric covered my breasts, revealing the sexy curve of their arches. I was looking at myself in the mirror when Victor slipped my feet into outrageously high heels. The passionate red spilled all over their soles.

'I guess all I'll think about tonight is how you'll end up in only these. Your height right now perfectly fits my intentions for when I'm kneeling before you,' he ran his hands over my thighs, his chin propped on my shoulder.

I was gaping at my reflection when he pulled a box out of the wardrobe and reached towards my skin with a glittering necklace. I grabbed his wrist, shaking my head.

'Don't!'

'Why not?' He pulled away, sulking.

'I'm allergic.'

'To diamonds?'

'No. To metal. I get spots this big,' I formed a circle with my fingers and watched him sulking through it. 'The itch is terrible, but there are worse things. For example, strawberries, peanuts, and molluscs could easily kill me,' I counted on my fingers. 'Unfortunately, the number of my allergies is even and that drives me mad. I hope a fifth one will appear, but I don't think it's actually going to happen.'

'Damn! First, you run away from stores, then your stupid logic that I destroy your wishes, and now I can't even give you jewels?'

I shrugged and he threw the necklace to the side, snorting. He hurled himself on the bed like a sulky child. I looked at myself in the mirror again and started murmuring hesitantly:

'Victor, this dress seems much more provocative that the one you defined as outrageous. I'm not sure if it's...'

'This one was chosen by me, for me, and for you to admire it, and it's for my eyes only. I don't want to remember that dress and that night. OK?!' His expression was wild for a second and eyes darkened when he stood in front of me.

'Toma told me what happened that night. Everything. I must say that I was wrong to blame you. I didn't have all the data and I thought that...'

'Come here!' He pressed me against his chest, the throbbing of his heart invading my ear. 'This is your way of apologising for hitting, insulting, and yelling at me, I guess. The only thing I blame you for is what I felt when you disappeared and I didn't know where you were. You're much to blame for that disastrous nightmare. I am the one who must apologise, though. I called you there to see your reactions in such an environment and to get you used to it, but I didn't assume that you'd be left alone with those creeps. I shouldn't have...' His fingers clenched into fists.

'You knew what he was like...' I frowned.

Victor went silent for a moment with his statuesque expression.

'Nia, let's not ruin our mood with this story!' He cleared his throat. 'We're not talking about it anymore. I'm going to get dressed and we leave in ten minutes,' he turned to the wardrobe.

Barefoot and thoughtful, I went to the deck and leaned against the railing to cherish the evening landscape. With the sun gone, the view had changed. The twilight had wiped away all colours from the slopes. Everything looked bluish and the darkness was about to hungrily swallow the horizon.

Another big yacht was speeding towards us. When it got close enough, I could make out a group of people on the second level. The fat guy from the mansion was leaning against the railing and it seemed that he was staring at me. I stepped back to the bedroom and shouted:

'Victor!'

He didn't reply and I shouted louder.

'What's up, my lovely dear?'

'Well, I'm not quite sure. The data is that the Neapolitan version of the Pirates of the Caribbean is approaching us. They're led by that fat friend of yours. The difference between him and Jack Sparrow is about 200 kilos, but he's still acting like a pirate. My guess is he's preparing to board your yacht.'

Victor jumped out in formal black trousers and an unbuttoned shirt. He went to the railing and seemed furious when he turned back to me.

'Idiot! Damn!' He passed by me, swearing, and stopped on the stairs to warn me: 'You stay here! Is that clear!'

I nodded in bewilderment, but he didn't seem to believe me. He had his grounds, actually—I immediately went after him. One of the guys, however, appeared on the last step. His angry face blocked the way of *Curiosity*, and I went back.

I watched covertly from the railing. Some sort of a bridge was placed on the lowest level between the two yachts. The level below me was longer and I could clearly see the commotion. The staff was putting out tables, chairs, and cutlery. Everyone was in a hurry. I recognised Luka, who was giving orders in Italian. His hasty tone showed how nervous he was. Scared by Victor's approaching shouts, I quickly slipped back to the bedroom. He stormed in with a furious expression, which changed as soon as he sat down beside me.

'I'm sorry, my lovely dear, but dinner is out. I need to finish this, then we'll get out of here. We'll sail to Capri and stay in one of my favourite houses there. I'll postpone our return back and compensate you with a marvellous evening tomorrow,' he caressed the outline of my cheekbone gently. I was already skilled at reading his micro-expressions[37]—I saw tension.

'For me, there's no problem. You don't have to be sorry. It's your birthday, after all, it's OK to celebrate it with friends.'

He started explaining in a chill voice, as if he didn't hear me:

'Nia, a boat will take you to the villa now. You'll stay there.'

'No, certainly not! I'm not going into the water in the darkness on that small boat! Are you crazy?'

'Don't argue! The guys will take care of you.'

'No chance! I'm not doing it at night! I'm not going on the boat!' I whimpered and he rubbed his cheekbones.

'All right, relax. I don't want to make you nervous again. They'll get you dinner here. You eat and then you go to sleep. Downstairs, there'll be someone instructed to be at your disposal for everything. If you need anything, call him. I don't want anyone to see you and you're not to come downstairs. And, since you always do the opposite to what I say, I will repeat that I'm dead serious. You won't leave the room! Am I clear, Nia?'

'You certainly are! You don't want your friends to see me. I just don't understand why you brought me here if...' He interrupted me, squeezing my face rudely.

'First of all, they are not my friends. Second, let's practice accepting my decisions without arguing. And without a whole bunch of questions, if possible. All right?'

---

[37] *Transient facial expressions that appear when trying to suppress or hide an emotion. People are not able to fully control or block emotions and micro-expressions appear in 1/125*[th] *of a second – author's notes.*

'But how am I supposed to understand you if...'

'Enough! I'm not gonna explain any further!' He exploded and I jumped. He immediately took control over his unbearable tone and continued evenly: 'Toma will join you for dinner soon.'

He grabbed his coat, then went down and the huge security guard blocked the stairs again. I heard Victor listing my allergies in a hiss. He told the guy that he was personally responsible for me, then disappeared.

φ

I timidly approached the railing to watch the events from above. An endless table crowded with food and drinks was set up below. Waiters with full hands were walking cautiously on the ladder between the yachts. The number of fat guys at the table was increasing, yet nobody could beat Fatass—he seemed to have eaten three of the others. I recognised several porky men from the mansion at which I had my first meeting with Victor. I didn't know the others, but I could hear the same thing in different languages:

'Happy birthday, Mr. President!'

Hypocrisy echoed all around. My ears acknowledged it because of the typical metal thread in the tonality. I didn't know *Hypocrisy* but I imagined that a string with a tin can on its end hung on his waist which rattled with each movement. The voices were engaged in a competition to greet Victor with toasts and praises. He was walking among the men. Next to some of them, there were stunning shadows that looked exactly like Victor's. They behaved in the same way, too—standing on the left side, nodding, replying with one word only, or probably not saying anything at all. I couldn't tell from the distance.

Soon, everybody took their seats around the table, talking excitedly. Victor sat down in the centre, just opposite me. I lay on my stomach, propped on my elbows, making sure he couldn't see me. While I was spying in this awkward position, I was startled and almost screamed.

'You doing your work-out, Smarty? I don't think this outfit is suitable for push-ups.'

Chris's cynical voice raised my adrenaline and I snapped:

'Man, you should really stop sneaking up on people like that! What're you doing here?'

'I'm with the travelling circus. Toma told me you were here, and I came to check on you.'

'Is that guy still standing on the stairs?'

'Yup. You can't go downstairs but that doesn't mean I can't come up here,' grinning, he took position on the ground next to me. He held a bottle of champagne with two glasses and poured some. 'We're in the trenches, but we can still do this with style!'

'Very funny! What's going on there?'

He knocked my glass for a toast and downed his.

'It's Fatass's surprise for Victor's party because he disappeared early today. We came from Naples. We work with most of these idiots, and Kaov plays politics with some of them, too. I guess that's the answer to your question.'

My nose wrinkled as I examined the reality down there. The nasty fat men created clouds of smoke with their cigars and a cacophony of repulsive laughter and toasts. Chris studied my expression with a smirk.

'Let me improve your mood! It's a party, after all.'

He produced a small box from his pocket and started rummaging in it.

'How?'

'With mood-improving powder.'

I frowned as he carefully formed white lines.

'Chris, my only advantage in this warped world is my brain! I'm not gonna fry it with drugs. Your brain is quite OK too, so I recommend you do the same.'

'If it was that easy, mine would be already breaded and deep fried by now.'

He brought the box closer to me, but I pulled away.

'Be careful! Someone might see you. It's unhealthy and it's illegal, I think you know that.'

'Oh, Smarty! On this boat, my three grams of coke are nothing.'

'Nevertheless! Do you know how many dangerous substances it contains? What it's mixed with? Not one healthy brain cell will be left if you keep doing this, I'm telling you,' I shook my head reproachfully, but he just smiled.

'Don't fret! This one is from the spring, let's put it that way. Pure nature.'

'Yeah, and it's also bio, vegan, gluten free, right?' I rolled my eyes.

Chuckling, he snorted one of the lines. Our faces twisted simultaneously. I downed my glass of champagne and poured some more. Fatass got to his feet by the table, his belly peeking out from under the buttons. He announced that he had brought a special surprise for the president. From somewhere below me, several women started popping out, marching in a row. Their clothes were so scarce that there was nothing left for the imagination to do but yawn. My head almost got stuck between the metal bars of the railing as I watched them. The girls lined up around the table, turning slowly in circles for the men to examine them well. The men tugged at them and peered, as if they were choosing a watermelon at the market, trying to assess if it was sweet enough. The women were chosen exactly to Victor's taste. They looked like the shadows—tall, blonde, long-legged, flawless beauties with empty gazes and smiles pinned on their faces. The fat guys who were already accompanied by shadows nudged the already useless girls and they immediately disappeared into thin air.

A minute later, I saw a female singer who was popular lately. She looked like the others, though even glossier. She marched to Victor in her tiny dress to sit on the arm of his chair. There was music and she began to sing *Happy birthday, Mr. President*[38]. She was doing her best to surpass Marilyn Monroe in the lustfulness of her tone, purring in his ear. Her fingers turned into a little fellow who climbed up his biceps. I expected the sea urchin to pop up but, to my surprise, it wasn't there. Instead, I was suffocated by hot and icy-cold waves. My stomach tightened, my heart rate quickened rapidly, and I started shaking, gripping the bars.

'Is there anything more banal than singing *Happy birthday, Mr. President* at the actual birthday of a president?' Chris stole my own thoughts, rubbing cocaine on his gums.

'Certainly not! If clichés were weapons, an atomic bomb just exploded down there. No, a hydrogen one,' I hissed.

'Fattass is the Einstein of clichés then,' Chris giggled and I rolled my eyes again. 'You're so mad, Smarty! I can tell by your facial expressions. It might transpire that you don't like anyone else touching your toy, too. You realise how ridiculous it is to feel jealous for the commander of the army of whores, don't you?' He burst into a mocking laughter.

I watched Victor, ignoring Chris's conclusions. The singer was twisting around him. She was doing her best to get his attention, which was not a surprise. It was easy for his manly symmetry to spark interest, and his glassy eyes were magnetic. For me, at least. Victor, however, just sat there with his statuesque expression and I couldn't discern his mood.

---

[38] *Marilyn Monroe – Happy Birthday Mr. President – author's notes.*

The next song began, and the girls circled the men. Some more women crept out from somewhere—there were over thirty beauties and almost the same number of beasts, but not in the fairy-tale sense. I studied the girls' faces carefully and assumed that some of them were underage. The fat guys grabbed a girl or two in their arms, like orcs who had smelled fresh food. As I stared at this reality, the bright red lines in my mind framed the sequence of faulty patterns in squares. The president calmly sipped on his whisky. He ran his fingers through his damp black hair, then touched his lips. He didn't seem to notice or care about the distortion of what was happening around him. The situation increasingly reminded me of that night at the restaurant and this association made me sick. The only difference was that Victor had walked out before the ugly events took place back then, and now they were running in his honour.

I watched a girl sitting in someone's lap. The man licked her ear. I shivered again when Fatass pushed two of the youngest girls towards Victor. Fatass gave them instructions and they immediately started dancing, touching Victor's shoulders. My throat went dry. The singer kept singing three centimetres away from his ear, twisting her body even more lustfully. Most of the men got up and started shaking their fat bodies in the company of the long-legged beauties. They slapped their butts, shoved hands under their skirts, and twirled them all around like rag dolls.

A waiter in white gloves walked across the small bridge between the yachts. He climbed the stairs and stood in the centre of the party, placing a huge tray on the table. Other waiters set shiny plates here and there. They lifted the silver lid of the tray and a mountain of cocaine appeared. I goggled at Chris, and he confirmed my assumption about the nature of the substance:

'I told you. My three grams are like a pinch in a packet of salt,' he shoved another glass of champagne under my drooping mouth. 'I feel like a VIP being here, above the successful bunch! What a privilege, to watch the party of the political and business elite from above, isn't it? A prime minister, a president, ministers, tycoons... businessmen,' he pointed at them, charging his words with irony, before doing one more line.

Two of the girls had their noses buried in the mood powder, as one of the Successfuls groped their asses. I suspected that he was about to go at it with one of them right there, at the table. Again, Chris was quicker than me to comment:

'The feast of the Successfuls is a dream-come-true, whaddya say? Fat guys with countless money drown in alcohol and snort all night long on a superyacht that costs hundreds of millions. Then they shag models with their dicks that they haven't been able to see for years. Sheer beauty!' He kissed the tips of his fingers theatrically and snorted loudly through a metal tube. 'A moment of reality that deserves a whole month of loudly discussing rights and social inequality. It's even worthy of its own hashtag that the fat guys could support! Well? Why're you so quiet? What would you say about the peak of politics and business, Nia? Are you impressed by the stink of luxury?'

He gave me a cynical look and I muttered:

'You shouldn't generalise. Not all of them are like that.'

Chris smirked and replied arrogantly:

'Well of course! Kaov is definitely able to see his dick. He's in top shape.'

'Both claims are obvious,' I snapped at his cynicism.

'To be honest, I was surprised to find out that he sleeps with you. You don't seem to be one of these girls, you're outrageously smart and...'

'One of which girls, Chris? Believe it or not, smart girls do it too! Even me!'

His crazy irises shone in the dark.

'One of the sluts downstairs. You don't seem to be one of them and I think you should have more respect for yourself. Look at them well and decide whether you could fit in here, because this is your new reality. The reality of the overly satisfied creeps bored of having everything,' he pinned his colourful irises on me and refilled my glass again. 'Cheers, Smarty! Welcome to our fairy-tale world!' He motioned smoothly at the lower deck, rubbing more cocaine into his gums.

Toma's roaring voice startled both of us:

'Get this shit out of here, Chris! I don't want to see you snorting in front of Nia ever again!'

We looked over our shoulders. Bear was all red with anger. Two waiters began to serve the table, but he hissed at them to shoo.

'Spying makes you feel better?' Toma scolded me and I looked down embarrassed.

He offered me a hand to get up. I stood by the railing and Victor immediately caught my gaze. He shot a glare at Toma, too, who pulled me back.

'That's an interesting outfit, girl!' He commented through his gritted teeth.

I adjusted my cleavage, muttering:

'Yeah, it's because we were supposed to go out for a dinner.'

'A dinner. Right. You obviously don't mind Victor's taste anymore,' he went silent for a moment. His warm eyes froze. He took a breath and yelled angrily: 'How the hell did you end up here, Nia? I left you with your good intentions for a new job, pancakes, and driving lessons. Then you left, just like that, with a man you don't know, for Italy. No luggage, probably even no cash for a goddamn return ticket. What were you thinking, for Christ's sake?'

'I left with Victor! And I didn't know we were coming to Italy!' I snapped back.

'Nia, Victor is a man you don't know!' He angrily stressed every word. 'You left with him, not even knowing your destination. I don't know what's special about your brain, but it's clearly defective. You act like an idiot!' He yelled and I bowed my head guiltily.

Chris stepped in:

'Enough, Bear! She has some relationship with him, after all. Don't be mean to her. Plus, Victor is difficult to resist—you would go with him, too.'

'You stay out of this!' Toma gritted his teeth and Chris stepped back.

Toma brought me closer to the railing again. What was happening down there closely resembled the events from the repulsive night at the restaurant. The singer was still sitting on the armrest, walking her fingers over Victor's biceps. One of the models was dancing to his other side. Victor was squeezing a cigar and a particularly fat orc was struggling to talk to him.

'Well? With your intellect and your qualities, where will you fit better— to his left or to his right?'

'I'm sorry, Toma, but I have nothing to do with these women. As you can see, I'm not there and I'm not dancing in a three-centimetre skirt!'

'But of course! You're right! A while ago, there were several women with floor-length dresses. Your outfit looks more like theirs. Oh! They're not there either. Probably because they're waiting somewhere for their turn,' he grimaced, his voice becoming even more ironic. 'Actually, you're more than right, because these chicks down there are just a bunch of expensive prostitutes. The ones with the dresses are even more expensive, but they're just a bunch of common mistresses. The difference is that the first are being called for the night and the second are being taken to a night out. My ordinary brain still thinks that you deserve more. I don't know what your special mind thinks,' he walked away with a nervous wave of his hand, then dropped in a chair, staring into the distance.

'Victor didn't know these people were coming. His plans for today were quite different and...' I staggered but I didn't finish my defence speech.

I watched the grotesque picture downstairs, realising how right Toma was. His stern honesty struck me again. It was an integral part of his uniqueness, as was his fatherly care for me. The words "common" and "mistress" sank deep into my brain, settling in every cell. I stared at the reality of the Successfuls. They moved in slow motion as lines bumped around the faulty patterns in my mind. Around the mistakes in my judgements, too. My brain reacted in the only possible way. I started counting—men with white or black shirts, women with short or long hair, sitting people, snorting people. I was looking for some regularity. Everything was so distorted, however, that it didn't form even the simplest pattern. I tapped my fingers and drifted away. *Justice* watched the young women in anger. *Reason* was hiccoughing in silence. He probably was ashamed for having defined Victor in the beginning as an example of the extraordinary things that we craved. *Knowledge* declared facts about geishas and courtesans, their functions, and the principles of their existence.

Pride slapped *Desire* because it sobbed. She stretched her graceful back, her nose up in the sky as ever. *Pride* spoke rarely. She usually just watched from above with her squinted eyes, but this time she ordered the four words through her gritted teeth:

Out of here! Immediately!

I came out of the daze with a cough as Chris touched my shoulder. He handed me another glass of champagne and, with compassion on his face, knocked his glass into mine. I downed it, walking over to Toma who was grunting under his nose. I spoke to him in an even tone:

'Your conclusions are correct. Even that there's something defected in my head. As you might have noticed, my judgements tend to be wrong lately. I guess delusions are out hunting these days. There's no cause for me to stay here anymore.'

'And how exactly do you intend to not stay?' His cynical face annoyed me.

'Usually, one avoids staying somewhere by leaving. That is, by making a movement. In my case, it will be linear. It's obvious!' I rolled my eyes, pointing at the shore.

'If you're going to swim, at least change into something more comfortable,' he snapped, and I struggled to stop myself replying in the same tone.

'I can't swim. Therefore, I plan to take that fucking little boat. Despite the water and the dark, damn it!' I expected him to offer his help, but his face darkened even further

'Nia, I'll say it straight so that you finally understand! There are only two ways for you to leave—with Victor or with his consent. As far as I can see, neither condition is applicable. You should've thought about this on your way here!'

'Bullshit! It's not like that. Victor said that guy was here to assist me. Exact quote: "Downstairs, there'll be someone instructed to be at your disposal for everything". I'll ask him for the boat. And you should stop being mean to me. I'd rather you come with me because I'm afraid of the water and the dark. You're right—I've got no money on me. You'll have to give me some for a return ticket and I'll give it back.'

He motioned to the stairs with a grimace of mockery.

'Go on! Sort things with the instructed guy and I'll sail with you to Africa, if I have to. If you convince him to let you leave, I'll give you all the money you want, and I won't demand it back! Just remind me after that to fire the boy before the madman drowns him!' I blinked foolishly and he snapped again: 'Yes, it's Victor I refer to!'

The dialogue with the security guard was disappointing and brief. It was actually more of a disappointing and brief monologue. I asked numerous times "why" and he only grunted in reply. On my way back, *Pride* was growling. With every step, I realised more clearly that I couldn't leave without Victor's consent. My legs were heavy. The sensation that the yacht was getting smaller and was about to crush me any minute now was getting stronger and stronger.

I sat down opposite Bear without speaking and gazed at the sky. It didn't help me to relax and my breathing got louder and louder. When I gripped the edge of the table, Toma squatted before me in worry.

'What's going on? Why are you shaking? You idiot—did you give her some of your shit?' He shouted at Chris, but I shook my head and interrupted:

'Claustrophobia!' My panicked voice bewildered him further and Toma squeaked in falsetto:

'Nia, we're under the open sky! What claustrophobia?'

I tried to move my lips, but Chris spoke for me:

'The phobia is not just about closed spaces. The brain reacts with the same hormonal attack if one can't get out of somewhere. Some people show these symptoms even if they don't have problems with narrow spaces. For example, if they enter an unfamiliar building and can't find the exit. This could be a panic attack, too. Technically, the same process takes...'

I nodded and Toma waved his hand nervously:

'All right, all right. I got it. Don't give me your psycho-recitals again! And what am I supposed to do now? What will happen to her?'

'A fit, I guess. Her brain will release a shocking amount of hormones. Any minute now, probably. I don't know exactly how it happens to her and I don't have the data. It's different with different people.'

'God! What kind of freak are you? You recite things as if nothing bothers you. Aren't you worried, for Christ's sake?' Toma snapped at Chris who replied calmly:

'Worrying has nothing to do with the result. It's absolutely useless. If she faints, it will be more useful for her if I stay calm.'

I nodded again, trying to catch my breath. Toma rubbed his scalp vigorously.

'You stay here and watch over her! I'm going to Victor!'

Chris was busier with peering downstairs than watching over me, but it didn't matter anyway. The only thing that helps with a claustrophobia fit or a panic attack is balanced breathing. Counting helped me, too. *Reason* had a stockpile of numerous ideas of things to count when this happened to me.

'What a sociopath! He just pulls on his taxidermy face and you can't tell if he's angry or amused,' Chris muttered while he was spying through the railing. 'Toma is speaking in his ear and Kaov isn't even twitching. He has no facial expressions. How is it possible?'

'He has. He controls them. He has control issues, too,' I said intermittently between three mental counts of the metro rhythm.

Chris chuckled:

'Well, that's more than clear. I warned you that he's a sociopath and a maniac. However, nobody can control subconscious impulses.'

I waved my finger in denial.

'He can. One can see micro-expressions but only from very close.'

Toma popped up and Victor pushed him from behind. He closed his eyes for a moment, squatting before me, then grabbed my face.

'Her breathing is quickening. She'd better get out of here. Probably the reason for thi…' Christ started explaining but Victor told him to shut up. To me, though, he spoke calmly.

'Nia, there are doctors on board. Don't worry. They'll be here any minute now. Your medical record doesn't say anything about such a severe claustrophobia. Are you sure that it's not something else?'

I shuddered at his soft voice. If I hadn't gone mad precisely because of him, it'd probably soothe me. In our case, though, his influence only made me angrier.

'Doesn't my record say that it's confidential?' I snapped in a hoarse voice.

Victor clenched his jaw and pressed his fingers against my carotid artery to measure my racing pulse.

'It's too fast. I'll tell them to give you a sedative.'

'I don't want any sedatives; I want to get out of here! Now!' I gasped at my attempt to shout in his face. He carefully examined *Rage* in my pupils and my tapping fingers. He squeezed them and pulled me on my feet.

'All right, I'm coming with you, so you don't get scared in the boat. I'll get you later and we'll be out of here. Toma, her scarf is in the bedroom,' he waved at him but I snapped more angrily:

'I don't want you to come with me or get me later!'

Victor took a breath, but Toma interrupted him nervously:

'I'll go with her. Don't put further pressure on her, plus they'll start asking questions. You don't have to do this, Kaov! Enough problems!'

Victor growled, wrapping the colourful dotted scarf around my head. Only my eyes were left uncovered and Toma took me by the shoulder down the steps. After the last stair, we turned the opposite direction from the people. Victor froze for a moment before returning to his reality. Bear and I went through a corridor and some cabins, with Chris following us. We went out at a different end of the yacht and I became disoriented. A few steps later, I shivered at the sight of the boat which now seemed like a miniature toy.

'Where are you going?' Toma scolded Chris but he replied in his typical calm manner:

'I'm not staying here. I'm coming with you. You need someone normal who doesn't go into hysterics like you.'

Toma grumped but motioned him to get on the boat first. Chris offered me a hand and sensed my shaking.

'Are you that afraid?'

'Quite enough.'

'You must address these problems. Phobias are not harmless!'

I sat down beside Chris. He hugged me and rubbed my shoulder. The engine roared and Toma shook his head reproachfully. My roommate rolled his eyes, then moved to the side, but I clung to him again. Toma shoved himself between us, squeezed me tight in his bear hug and rubbed his knuckle on my scalp.

'Feeling better, goblin?'

I nodded, staring at the approaching shore. I was supposed to be better, but as soon as I stepped on the small stones, my stomach turned. I looked back and gazed at the darkness around the yacht, or rather the darkness gazed at me. The irrational desire that Victor would follow me jumped again and I shivered at the new manifestation of the absurd anomaly:

Damn! Those goddamn fairy tales have really screwed me up. Reason is right—people must be careful with them. Who'd have thought they are so dangerous?

FIFTEEN

The slopes of Positano were hardly better than my experiences on the road. Everything was steep and difficult: a painful challenge for my nervous system. And the stairs were a painful challenge for my body. Struggling with the last sixty-four steps, I wondered how Victor had managed to take them with me on his back. I even regretted that he was not there to carry me again.

The staff at the villa acted strangely when we appeared. Bear walked in silence, we followed, and all three of us sat down at the pavilion. Toma and Chris were fighting over something again, but I didn't listen to them. Instead, I was trying to ignore the argument in my own head. Everybody there was shooting causes and evidence at the others. I was staring at the yacht in the distance when I sensed the jab between my fifth and sixth ribs again. The breath shortage and the hot and cold waves were also back. My stomach tightened and I embraced my knees to my chest. Toma studied me with suspicion and urged me to get some sleep, but I refused and he headed for his bedroom, murmuring, with Chris in tow.

The small boat docked again. I peered from the pavilion, again with the irrational desire that Victor would come after me, but only the security guys got off the vessel. There was another jab. Again, I considered the possibilities of having pericarditis, asthma, or worms but then I was startled by a loud roar that came from the yacht. Apparently, the feast of the Successfuls was at its peak, as was the chaos in my mind. A moment later, lavish fireworks exploded in the dark sky reflecting billions of sparks into my black eyes. Grandpa was a sapper. He likes to tell and I like to listen, thus I had accumulated a huge amount of information about explosives in my Memory Palace[39]. I beamed at their only beautiful form and started listing the reasons for the splendour:

'Sodium, calcium, selenium, strontium...'

They shone brightly, but the culmination of their existence burned them out. They brought seconds of joy, and then died into the sea to a loud applause. *Knowledge* pointed out the importance of one of Ancient China's four great inventions—gunpowder. Without it, fireworks wouldn't be able to fly or shine. I made yet another parallel between fireworks and people. Fireworks needed gunpowder, and people—a chance. The main difference was in the duration of their existence and in the sparks. Fireworks shine brighter than most people; their short life seem more meaningful.

While I was murmuring to myself, my roommate startled me again.

'Whisky or vodka?'

Chris was standing behind me with two full glasses and his cynical smile. When I turned to him, I saw the security guards landing in the garden like a flock of crows and I groaned.

'I don't like either, so I don't care.'

He pushed the whisky to me and began doing lines on the table. I silently studied his well-trained movements before asking:

'Why cocaine?'

'Empties the head. It gets quiet there, and the chaos becomes more tolerable.'

'So there's chaos in your head, too?'

He nodded with a sour smile, focused on what he was doing.

---

[39] *One of the memorisation methods in mnemonics – an art and a technique of remembering (mnemotechnics). The founder of this science was Simonides of Ceos, and the term derives from the name of the Greek goddess of memory – Mnemosyne. People with a high IQ or photographic memory use it also as a way to compress information that can be restored later – author's notes.*

'I must admit that silence is a fascinating effect,' I wondered whether it was really true and which substance gave cocaine this quality.

Chris's colourful irises stared at my curiosity as I propped my chin on my hands.

'Your priceless brain is surrendering to sadness, isn't it?'

'What sadness, Chris? There's only chaos in my head. To tell you the truth, I could go without my head right now. It's been useless lately, and the buzz is unbearable. I wouldn't mind some silence and I don't care how I'm gonna get it anymore,' I sighed, watching the yacht in the distance. The fireworks were over and it was cloaked in pure darkness.

'You're all messed up, Smarty. I guess you don't understand what this buzz is. It's true—amazing brains have their defects. Let me improve your mood. Relax, for Christ's sake! Just mind that Victor's hounds won't see you 'cause he's gonna cut my head off for this.'

He gave me the tube and I hid behind the scarf. It felt as if the powder scratched the outside of my brain, filling my senses with a repulsive mixture of sourness, gasoline, and chemical smells and tastes. I rediscovered the meaning of the word "bitter".

'Disgusting!' I was struggling to decide whether I should sneeze or vomit first, and Chris giggled.

'Wait!' He dipped his index finger and rubbed cocaine into my gums.

'My nose is already damaged, and now you want my teeth to fall out, too?'

'Don't worry. Half your face will go numb and you won't even feel them falling out.'

'Certainly! Why would I need a face if I don't have teeth and a nose?'

I cleansed my mouth with whisky. Compared to the coke, it tasted like vanilla ice-cream. My grimaces entertained Chris and he laughed, but his mood was no better than mine. He sipped on his vodka in silence. A couple of cigarettes later, he spoke in a serious tone:

'Why did you leave, Nia? Explain to me because I really can't understand those relationships. Victor offers you more than you'll ever have. A truly extraordinary life.'

'What a dumb question?! You were there, weren't you? It's obvious! If you define that life as "extraordinary", then you're damn mistaken. Are you crazy?'

He gazed at me, his eyes squinting with suspicion, and I frowned. I didn't want to discuss Victor's reality anymore, so I changed the subject:

'Tell me, what do you empty from your head?'

'Love, what else? Now you're asking dumb questions.'

'And what's that love of yours?'

'Special—half love, half monster!'

'Well, you must be glad that it's not only a monster. I have one and it's not nice at all. It's like a parasite. You can't get rid of it.'

'You're also a monster, do you know that? I don't envy Kaov! When he squatted before you, I saw an expression on his stone face for the first time. You're stuck all right, but he's also biting the bottom. Oddly enough,' he shot a glance at me, and I shrugged at his statement. 'I just can't understand how he got his hands on your medical records. You didn't give it to him, and I couldn't dig it up.'

'Dig it up?!' I took a generous sip of whisky.

'Yup, Smarty! I enjoy the multiple functions of my quite OK brain, as you called it,' he explained with his typical cynicism, sucking on the cigarette. 'A brilliant financier, skilful with digits, and an amazing hacker. And a total douchebag in normal human stuff. Just like you, even though you might be even worse,' he took a theatrical bow. 'I'm also good at making contacts, manipulating weak minds, and giving bribes. Priceless skills in our goddamn fairy-tale world.'

'And what exactly did you dig up about me, douchebag?'

'Well, obviously everything but your medical records!'

'Well, obviously not! You're not that amazing if Victor didn't know that I was adopted,' I gave him a haughty look. He narrowed his eyes.

'I knew about that! I wasn't sure if you knew, that's why I didn't give him the documents.'

'Why?'

'Because your beloved president tends to use information about people in a sociopathic way. This seemed too delicate for a freak like him.'

My jaw dropped. Chris went to the house to refill the glasses but came back with the whole bottles. I kept smoking his cigarettes as my annoying *Curiosity* pushed him to tell more about his half love, half monster. Maybe he just wanted to distract me. He shared with me the banal story of a man, a woman, and her husband. Chris was the man. The woman in question claimed to love him very much but she never divorced. He attributed this to a lack of courage and irrationally believed that they would be together someday. He said he loved her madly, despite being aware of the biochemical process. I was surprised that a person with an impressive brain like his was in such a pathetic situation. He had harnessed his full potential to achieve "everything". For him, this everything came down to becoming richer, more successful, and more powerful than her husband, so he could seduce her with the chance for a better life. It wasn't working and he wanted to know why. Maybe he realised perfectly well that she was not going to be with him. The data was clear, the negligible probability could be easily calculated. He had probably estimated it numerous times, but had chosen to wait for her, nevertheless. His patience made his demons come to life, and they obviously were into alcohol, drugs, gambling, and reckless risks. He also told me about the defects that devastating love always creates. Again, love seemed more like a ferocious *Beast* to me. By what Chris told me, I concluded that he was pushing his luck to the edge. He seemed to be trying to kill himself in time before the desperation at the end of his tragic ode could devour him. A love like his, or rather a *Beast* like his, rarely leads to a happy ending...

The bottle of whisky was reaching its end. The vodka was gone, and so was the cocaine. After the third line, the taste didn't seem so repulsive anymore. Apparently, it truly worked, too, because my dizzy head was completely silent, interrupted only by Chris's chatter. When he wrapped his coat around me, I could barely focus on him anymore. He announced that he was going to try to find some fun, then he zigzagged through the garden. I followed him in the same curved line, and the guys approached me with tension. Someone walked angrily from a corner. After staring at him for a while, I recognised Sergey.

'Well, well, the non-communist Russian! Looking to slap some women, comrade?' I snorted under his nose, then went after Chris again. The Russian grabbed my wrist.

'Where to?' He asked sulkily.

'Out! He's going to look for some fun and I don't know what I'll be looking for!' I pointed at my roommate, swaying on my feet. 'Destination unknown!' I tried to pronounce the syllables clearly, but wasn't sure exactly what came out of my mouth.

'He can go wherever he wants. You can't!' Sergey hissed and I pulled away—at least that was what I thought I was doing before landing on my ass on the grass. Chris and I chuckled. Sergey snorted in Russian under his breath, trying to get me to my feet, but I was all limp.

'What're you murmuring there, Russian? Let me guess: "You can go out either with Victor, or with his consent!"' I imitated Toma's booming voice and Chris giggled at my acting skills.

I was in the middle of my third speech in Bear's role, when the well-known unbearable tone interrupted me:

'Good guess!'

Victor was leaning against the entrance, rubbing his cheekbones, looking contemptuously at me. I struggled to focus on him from the ground as he approached, but that only made me laugh even harder. He pulled the coat off my shoulders, threw it at Chris, then lifted me and said through his gritted teeth:

'First, if you're going to throw, mind you don't do it on me. Second, I forbid you to even step near booze anymore!'

Victor carried me to the room as I kept repeating his command in a mocking voice. He didn't utter a word and just walked, staring straight ahead. I don't think he was even listening to me. In the room, he put me on my feet and before I could even find my balance, pulled the dress away rudely. One of its straps slapped me in the face, interrupting my giggles. When he tore the bikini as well, his gaze scared me, and I pushed him away. I kept swearing and pushing but the forces were even more unequal than usual. He grabbed my neck and my wrists so I couldn't hit anymore.

Victor took me straight to the bathroom. Looking past me, and without hesitating for a moment, he turned the shower to ice-cold water. I hated him at that moment, as if he was a communist, but after a while I was thankful because he held my hair as I threw up. The next ice shower made me hate him again. He grumbled because I refused to drink from the bottle of water he was shoving under my nose. Eventually he managed to pour it in my throat. After I threw up again, I felt slightly better. I wasn't seeing two of him anymore, at least. He silently dressed me in one of his T-shirts and a pair of boxers, then placed me in bed and tucked me in to my nose. He dropped down on the other end, demonstratively plugging his ears with headphones. The volume was to the max and I could hear a faint melody in the silence.

For a long while, I stared at the ceiling without moving. Eventually I couldn't help but gaze at his face. It looked grim even in the dark. The dim light from the garden lit the edges of his cheekbones and they seemed sharper. His jaw muscles moved and tightened, and the stubble-bearded chin rose. I noticed a slight tremble to his fingers. He didn't tap them as visibly as I did, but I could still detect a combination of odd numbers. I copied the rhythm of his count. He was also staring at the ceiling but noticed the movement of my fingers and stopped his own. He cupped his palms in front of his lips and stared silently back at the ceiling. I kept gazing at him, but he didn't even want to look at me. Instead, he pretended I was not there. I pulled one of his earphones out and plugged it in my ear, but he didn't react.

Hearing Russian, I frowned. I was about to give the earphone back but the harmony stopped me. The melody was rhythmical, soft, and relaxing. I rolled onto my back next to Victor, listening to the beautiful, mesmerising male voice: [40]

Victor kept staring at the ceiling with his hands under his head. He growled and the icy note in his voice sent arrows down my spine.

---

[40] *Jah Khalib – „Созвездие ангела" – translator's notes*
Держи меня крепче рукой, не сомневайся я с тобой
Ведь мне с тобою хорошо и легко, это чувство так необыкновенно
И мы где-то далеко, где-то над землёй
Где-то высоко, высоко, высоко, высоко над небом
Там, где другая галактика
Там, где созвездие ангела
Оно сияет в глазах твоих
Прекрасное созвездие ангела, ангела, ангела

Hold my hand tighter. Don't doubt it – I'm with you,
Because I feel so good and at ease with you.
Such an unusual feeling.
And we're somewhere far away,
Somewhere above the ground,
Somewhere up high,
High, high, high above the sky.
There's another galaxy there.
The angel constellation is there.
It shines in your eyes,
That beautiful angel, angel, angel constellation
https://www.youtube.com/watch?v=KFWhRKh-bZo

'It wasn't claustrophobia. You ran away. You said you were mine, but you ran from me. I warned you not to do it, but you just ran away from me again. Stop provoking my demons, Nia!'

'I didn't run from only you. I ran from your warped reality, too. I hope your demons understand that.'

He leaned over me, *Rage* was peering through the blue. His image was so clear that I wondered whether Victor had entities in his head, too. The other option was that one of his demons shone in the same ferocious way.

'My realities are many. What I'm wondering right now is if you intend to stay, voluntarily, in any of them?'

'Probably not. I'm good at quantum physics and I know that even if they are many, they can't be too different from one another. Besides, as it turns out, the reality of the Successfuls, or whatever that is according to your perverted standards, is no good for me. In the reality of the "business and political" peak—an exact quote by the way—I found even more distortions than in the general reality. They both lack my kind of logic!'

The sensual Russian lyrics pierced one of my ears and, in the other one, I heard Victor's rapid breathing. His lowered voice then invaded:

'Do you know what peaks truly are, Nia?' I gazed at him with questioning eyes, and he held my chin. Again, his different personalities created contradictions in the way he looked and touched. 'They are nothing more than a gigantic heap of mud climbed by someone who made quite enough compromises on the way up. The truth is my peak is terribly high and the list of compromises is endless. Another truth is that in my reality, there's nothing you deserve,' he caressed my cheekbone, but I turned my head away.

'Apparently, you're confirming my conclusion that my place is not there.'

Squeezing my face, he closed his eyes.

'That's not how I imagined this. You appeared at the worst moment possible. I should've been more patient; I should've stayed away and waited a little longer. I should've made sure that it'd be easier, safer, that you'd get used to all this gradually, but it didn't happen. I lost control and acted too quickly. The consequences now, appearing one after the other, are quite natural. You'll learn truths about me that will make you sick and yes—you will see a terrifying reality around me that shouldn't even exist. I don't know when or if this is going to change. You must just accept that there is another reality—only for us. At least until you manage to grasp the others, too. And don't provoke me any further!' His voice shook.

I could sense the powerful energy thickening in him, yet my voice came out sharp and cynical:

'And what exactly is this for-us-only reality? The one where I can't go out without your consent? The one where you lie, dig up information about me, disregard everything, violate all acceptable limits? Or the reality where cocaine, drunk fat guys and underage prostitutes lurk on every corner? And in the last corner, there's me standing like a common mistress with her proper appearance? Where exactly do you think I could fit, Victor? Which one of these realities do you delude yourself into thinking I will stay in?'

His breathing quickened. I sensed the heat radiating from his body. His irises darkened. Staring at me, he squeezed my cheekbones even tighter and I pushed him, struggling to pull myself away. Suddenly, he exploded at the top of his voice:

'In ours!' *Babel*[41] thundered in the earphone together with his voice. 'With me! You will stay with me! Your place is in my arms!'

The string of the mandolin and his tone stretched my body. My stomach twisted—not because of the bass in the song but because of the madness in his yelling. Victor hit the wall with his fist and I jumped. He continued hoarsely, leaning only a centimetre away from me:

'I know what I am and you will also find out. You are not going out without my consent. I will forbid what needs to be forbidden. That's how I am. You don't understand what tortures me from the inside but you will accept my reality, me and all my demons! Just like I accept you with all your craziness!'

I shook my head, staring at his wild expression. Though my voice trembled slightly, what I said still sounded impudent:

'I don't intend to and nothing of all that is acceptable: neither your behaviour, nor your stinky reality, let alone the insane look you have right now. I won't even comment on your tone.'

Victor radiated another burst of heat, turning red as the veins on his neck bulged.

'But you have no choice. You have no choice, Nia. Nor am I asking you!' His eyes clouded, as if something suddenly possessed him. Even his voice changed. Gripping my cheekbones, he spoke in my ear as if in a trance—quickly, silently, freezing me: 'All the time, I think about you disappearing. You're just not there, and there's nothing I can do. I don't

---

41 *Gustavo Santaolalla – Babel – author's notes.*

have control over you. You are not mine. This obsessive nightmare plays on repeat every fucking second. It drives me mad! It makes me explode! The only salvation for my mind is having you in my arms, Nia. Only then everything feels right.'

He fell silent. I opened my mouth to reply but he stared intimidatingly at me and I froze. He continued through his teeth in front of my face:

'Don't say you're not staying. Don't say "no" to me, Nia,' his tone escalated with every syllable. 'Don't provoke my demons! Don't, or I'll just lock you up and never let you go!'

He yelled the last words and I jumped. His *Rage* exploded. Billions of flashes shone like fireworks in the mad blue. I pursed my lips to not scream when he hit the wall behind me with his fist the first time. Then again and again. He wouldn't stop hitting.

'I won't let you go! I won't let you go! I won't let you go!'

He shouted repeatedly at the top of his lungs, hitting the wall harder and harder, until eventually, I screamed. My shriek made him regain control over himself. He closed his eyelids and, a second later, his face lost all expression. When he opened his eyes, he studied my bewilderment, but I couldn't tell what he felt. Again, he was the haughty statue that I had almost forgotten. Then the wall of superiority was back on, too, like an invisible armour. A furious demon remained to rage in his eyes only. It was truly capable of destroying us both. Even destroying the whole world.

Victor stormed out. His state of insanity had left scarlet stains on the wall. I propped myself up in bed, already sober. The adrenaline evaporated the last drop of alcohol from my brain. Terrified by his madness, I was ready to flee—to sneak out the door and sink into the Italian darkness in just my panties. *Fear* was about to add Victor to his list. This thought shocked me, and I shook my head to come to my senses and went to the balcony to get some fresh air. I watched him walking to the pavilion. Toma was running after him. He took hold of Victor's biceps, trying to stop him, but Victor pulled away abruptly. He raised his hand and Bear didn't follow him anymore.

The president went to the fence and leaned against it, staring into the darkness of the sea. He roared at the top of his lungs, as if he was not human but a wild beast trapped in a narrow cage. I saw him hitting the fence numerous times, then he propped his head in his hands and froze in position. As I watched, heat spread throughout my body. It pinched under my skin. It burned. My terror dissolved in this heat and disappeared. My limbs went numb, and my throat tightened into a ball as my heart rate quickened again. It wasn't *Fear* this time. I couldn't define what the new, unfamiliar process was.

All of a sudden, I remembered all those times at which I had succumbed to mind blocks or had yelled because the warped world had driven me mad. My own madness was neither more beautiful, nor less terrifying for everyone around. Some of those times my grandpa's hand had been on my shoulder. He had stood beside me, repeating his mantra. He never gave me the data I needed, but his presence made everything slightly more bearable. I could clearly see that Victor's distorted world drove him mad. His manias, too. I couldn't find the logic of his reality and I didn't understand his madness. Although I didn't have the explanation he needed, nor a mantra, I did have my hand, and I was overcome by the irrational desire to place it there, on his shoulder.

I didn't flee. It wasn't the Italian darkness into which I sank, it was Victor's darkness. Holding two glasses of whisky in my hands, I crossed the alley barefoot in his T-shirt and boxers, under the confused gazes of the guys. Toma was still standing near the pavilion. He had his fist to his mouth and I couldn't hear what he was muttering. He tried to stop me, but I pulled away. Victor was still leaning his elbows on the fence, shouting. The sound of the lighter caught his attention as I lit one of Chris's cigarettes. Victor turned around, his irises glaring at me smoking and sipping from the glass. He took a breath to prevent himself from scolding me. I guess he repeated several times "no" and "I forbid" in his mind, but then he just turned his back on me.

After a long silence, his lowered voice came out:

'I'm sorry.'

'Don't be. You have this pattern of behaviour because of your manias and it will happen again. You either change patterns, or simply accept them. Regret doesn't help. I can guarantee this from my own experience.'

'It will happen again with you, or in general?'

'Both, I guess.'

'If you just say you want it, I'll see that you go back home immediately. Just say it, and it will happen,' he clenched his fists so tight that his knuckles went white.

'I understand. I came to tell you this. I'd rather go back tomorrow, it's dark now.'

He turned around in surprise, then approached me.

'What? You understand my reality?'

'No. I understand you. Your madness is similar to mine. I get it—you're trapped in a reality that drives you insane. I'm also trapped, that's why I understand.'

'What are you trapped in? I told you that you could leave right now.'

'In general—trapped in a world I don't comprehend. In this particular moment, I'm trapped in one of the paradoxes of life. I have enough logical reasons to not stay, yet I don't want to leave. I don't have the right mechanism to help me accept all this, but I somehow understand it. A trap, as I said.'

'And will you transform your unwillingness to leave into a willingness to stay? Understanding into accepting?'

'I don't know yet,' I lit another cigarette and he growled. 'Whenever a mind like mine gets stuck in a paradox, it starts analysing, calculating, creating patterns, destroying them, all over again, until it finds a solution and gets free. That's how I work. Right now, however, I'm acting against my own logic. Me against myself! I've never ended up in such a paradox. I tried to read about all this, but I still don't understand these processes between people. Normal people have their feelings and I guess it makes things easier for them, but what I do instead is calculate probabilities. That's how I am. I can't answer your question right now. I need to create a pattern in which I can fit—with parameters and boundaries, beyond which things will be unacceptable for me. Then, I guess, you'll have to decide whether it is acceptable for you, too. I don't know the exact process. I've never made a pattern for two before.'

'Neither have I,' he sat down on the chair before me, his head bowed, pressing my fingers against his forehead. 'When you get to defining the boundaries, please, bear in mind how difficult it is for me to communicate properly. Not because of you and your craziness—because of mine. For all my life, relationships have always been a deal, nothing more. Including with women—a simple contract, and that's all. I give them what they want, they respect my terms and conditions, and I don't respect anything. I just get what I want, the way I want it. I'm not familiar with any other patterns, Nia.'

'All right, I'll bear that in mind. I can see the consequences of all this on your perceptions and how twisted your expectations are. I assume your deals have been disproportionate. I've observed this anomaly and women are certainly prone to disproportionate deals.'

He laughed quietly, rubbing my fingers.

'Yes, my lovely dear, your observations are correct. Women are sometimes prone to disproportionate deals,' he went silent, gazing at me in anticipation as I studied his expression.

'It's not surprising, knowing the goddamn world we live in. Victor, you said you accept me and my craziness, even though this seems illogical to me. I know I'm quite an unacceptable misfit. I didn't even assume it was possible. However, I can't guarantee reciprocity because your demons are too bewildering.'

He was silent, his eyes shining. Staring at me, he was rummaging in my brain again, and that made me nervous:

'Don't stare at me. I've got nothing else to say! Make your best effort to not frighten me like that again. *Fear* was on the verge of putting you on his list, and there's no getting out of there. Mind that!'

Victor pulled me to the edge of the table. He settled between my legs and my face sank in his cupped hands. He leaned over to kiss me, but my hand on his chest stopped him and he frowned. Waving my index finger, I added:

'There's something else, too. I recommend that you hit soft objects. I've hit walls and long ago established that they're not a good choice. You're older than me and you probably hit harder—I'm surprised you don't know that.'

Biting his lips, he kept his shining eyes off me.

'You know what else tortures me, more and more each day?'

'If it's another obsessive thought, you must know that it's your manias' fault. I warned you they are not harmless!'

'It is obsessive, indeed. It's been torturing me since the moment you pushed your stupid gummy bears under my nose and then repeated "certainly not" four times in a row. Then I realised I shouldn't touch you and that I have no idea what you want. I was terrified that I have nothing to offer to you, of all people, and I don't know how to offer it, and at the same time, I'm obsessed with giving you everything. I'm obsessed with the desire for you to be mine, but I'm terrified that all I know is how to keep you by force. This is my paradox of life!'

'Unreasonable paradox! You can only take by force; you can't give by force. It's obvious. Actually, you had already given me what I wanted. At least for a while, before I found out my chance for something more never existed.'

'How could I have given it to you if it never existed?'

I moved my lips in silence because of the well-grounded question. Victor removed the scattered hair from my face. His eyes were warm again and the demon was gone, along with that scary personality of his. At least for now. Pressing his lips to mine, he whispered softly:

'Don't let me go because of what I can't change about my reality, Nia. Just stay because of everything that exists in the for-us-only reality!' He hooked my hands on his neck, then lifted me in front of his navel.

'I told you—I still can't define the parameters that could help me stay in this abstract reality of ours. What I know for sure is that locking someone up is far beyond acceptable boundaries. I'm here now, why are you worrying again?'

He sighed, his forehead pressed against mine, not caring to reply. I entwined my legs tightly around his waist as he strode through the garden. The night and my head were both engulfed in complete silence. Pressed against his chest, I was overcome by a strange wave of warmth. Relief? Tranquillity? Or perhaps something I had never known before.

We passed by Toma who was standing in the same spot and had probably overheard our conversation. He shook his head, muttering:

'What realities are you talking about, damn it? One lunatic was more than enough for me. Now there's a couple. What is this fate of mine, for Christ's sake?' He desperately waved his hands above his head.

Victor glared at him but then smiled. I did, too. Over the president's shoulder, I gazed at the warm eyes of a friend that followed us on our way to the house. I recited a poem by our beloved Bukowski to Toma. Victor finished the last stanzas:

> *There's no chance at all:*
> *We are all trapped by*
> *a singular fate.* [42]

Victor seemed to believe that a cold shower can cure everything—drunkenness and madness, at least. He took his time under the stream of water, his palms against the wall. I gave him his alone time. The cold didn't tempt me, and just the sight of it made me shiver

---

[42] *"Alone with Everybody" – Charles Bukowski – author's notes.*

At night, I could sleep only on my right side. Victor didn't want to stay on the far end of the bed anymore and he didn't object to my position. He settled himself behind me and his embrace suffocated me from all sides, as if I was sinking into a cloud of his skin. I kept falling asleep and waking up immediately. This was only my second night in this life sleeping with someone else in bed. I didn't like it. The sharp hairs on his chest pricked my back. His heat made me sweat. I nudged him, annoyed, but he wouldn't let go. He even tightened his embrace, which made things even hotter.

When my eyelids opened for the thousandth time, I was swimming in sweat. It was still night outside. Victor was breathing in a slow rhythm, his face buried in my neck. I liked the purring sound of his sleep but not the fact that he clung to me as if I was the most comfortable pillow on Earth. I shifted only to find out that my wrists were bound in his hands. He held them like I was hanging from a rock, not lying in bed. His fingers trembled and, when he felt my movement, he tightened his grip. I tried to pull away, but he woke up and growled unhappily. Taking a deep breath next to my ear, he pressed his groin against my butt. I found that with male anatomy, waking up happened the other way round—the lower body was first. Victor pulled down the boxers in which he had dressed me and touched my gentle tip. Immediately, it started pulsating.

'I'm sleeping now, I am not inclined to have sex,' I murmured but he gathered moisture from my tongue with his fingers.

'Me too. I just want to feel you more.'

'More? You're glued to me like a sticker.'

He slipped carefully into me. He was not as hard as usual, and I didn't feel the piercing pain.

'That's better,' he embraced me even tighter, purring in my ear, and I gaped.

'I don't think it's normal to keep it there when we're not having sex?'

'Maybe, but I don't have illogical taboos and I don't know what's normal. Go back to sleep!'

It was weird—him being in me in this way—but it was also quite pleasant, albeit too intimate. He moved his hands in displeasure, waiting for me to return mine there. I didn't react and he asked me to do it, whispering in my ear that he needed his sense of control even if it was irrational. I put my hands closer to him. His huge palms snapped around my thin wrists like chains. However, my body managed to find its place. It fit into the unfamiliar position, and I drifted away with Victor inside and around me.

The short time left before sunrise passed without me waking up. I didn't have any nightmares, either. Obviously, I hadn't moved at all, because Victor was still in me when I woke up. The specifics of male anatomy brought me to my senses in a weird way. He was still asleep as he hardened. It swelled, stretching the tight tissue, and my breath stopped because of the intense sensation. At that moment, Victor also woke up. He clenched my wrists tighter, but his erection was still the most awake of anyone in bed. Without saying a word, he started moving his pelvis. The moisture of my desire gradually enveloped his. Apparently only my head was asleep that early in the morning. My body was ready for Victor, even hungry for him. In seconds, I was wet enough for him to slip in and out. He penetrated slowly, spreading the narrow space apart with great care, and I could sense the pulsating veins. He moaned with me as he fully invaded. He pressed my wrists to my breasts and me against him even tighter. His breath vibrated in my ear drums. It spread down my neck, making me shake even more than the penetration itself. The heat overwhelmed me and the bugs crawled on my abdominal wall again. My pulse thundered; even my cells seemed to be moaning.

Victor didn't fuck me in the way I had experienced before. He did something different. He kept stretching me to my absolute limit, but unexpectedly gently. He was probably experimenting with my body again, and I liked it. The bugs headed downwards, followed by the warm wave. I was sinking into an entirely unfamiliar sensation, as if in a hot tub. The new experience made my special spots go crazy. They were thirsty for him. Enormous burning tension gathered under my navel. Victor kissed my neck delicately as electricity invaded me along with his careful penetration. He set me on fire, but not in the torturing way that made me burn and explode in a second. This time he was gradually heating my cells up.

I tried to touch the hardened bundle of my sensitivity and come right away, but he held my wrists and stopped me. He didn't touch it either. I pressed myself even tighter against him, so my back could feel every centimetre of his skin. Victor's body radiated energy that poured into me. I gasped as an unexpected deep spasm made my breasts jump. My spine arched. My muscles tensed, but Victor held me tightly in his arms. He released my wrists and our fingers entwined. A hoarse moan from his throat sank into my ear. Then another one. The sound was mesmerising. I squeezed his palms as my orgasm crushed him inside me. He squeezed back, filling me with the powerful jets of his different lust.

He didn't move for a couple of minutes: not letting go of me, nor getting out of me. His breath tickled and so did his soft voice when he spoke.

'I've never done this,' he said hoarsely and I turned to face him. I placed my nose only a centimetre away from his.

'You certainly haven't. The sequence is usually different.'

'What do you mean?' His blue irises glittered blissfully. The surprise in his expression, however, puzzled me.

'Well, you're supposed to wake up first and then have sex, aren't you? You started while you were still sleeping. This is the opposite of the usual sequence. It's quite logical for this to not happen very often.'

He opened his lips to reply but no sound came out. He blinked as if he didn't agree.

'What is it? Why are you gaping at me?' I squinted, but his reply wasn't forthcoming.

'Nothing, my lovely dear. You just surprised me with your precise explanation. That's exactly what I meant, too—it doesn't happen very often. In my case, it has never happened before. With you, though, all kinds of unusual sequences are around the corner, I guess.'

With his eyes closed, he pressed my head against his chest. He wouldn't stop rubbing me and when I was already out of breath, I pushed him away, frowning. He smiled like a devil. Victor's version of *Lust* flickered in his eyes and the shiver-provoking timbre took off.

'You know how pushing me away affects me, don't you? I'm awake now and I intend to apply the usual sequence. In the exact manner it usually happens. The exact manner I adore.'

I studied his predatory face, then he turned me onto my belly and knees. He stood behind me, propped against my moisture.

'There's no red light here, you know? There is an open window, though, and a lot of people down in the garden. I don't want them to hear me again.'

'And what I want is to experiment with your limits again.'

Before finishing his sentence, he placed my palms on the edge of the headboard. He ordered me to stay like this and traced the line of my spine with his tongue. He pressed my shoulders down, so my butt rose. Victor rolled the bedsheet up like a thick rope and slid it through the fold of my thighs, then twisted it around his palms and stretched it to prevent me from moving forward. He pushed hard. My neck arched, my eyes staring at the stains of his midnight madness, while his morning madness pierced me.

'I adore it when you're full of me,' the shiver-provoking timbre again. 'I dreamed about fucking you very hard while you were all tied up in my special knots, and you were screaming with pleasure. I want to feel my dream now, but mind you won't be too loud. When we get home, we'll repeat this with your screams and my knots.'

I shove my face into the pillow to muffle my moaning. My body was a motionless wall into which he slammed his desire, driving me crazy as well. His control over my pleasure made him even harder and the pulsations inside me provoked him to become even ruder. My thundering moaning did so, too; I didn't manage to comply with the "not too loud" part.

The mixture of sensations Victor blew up in me brought to life devastating pleasure from the darkest depths of my mind. I was coming when he pulled my hair to lift my face off the pillow. My screams flew from my mouth, to the window and straight into the dozens of ears downstairs. I couldn't hold back anymore. This time he didn't come with me. He kept going and my last orgasm overlapped with his, while he was burning my skin with slaps, then fondling it gently. I was yelling for him to go on. I poured over him and he collapsed on me, his huge body all over mine, pulsating inside, as if it was about to burst. When my mind cleared, I muttered:

'Christ, everybody has heard me now. I think you should shut my mouth more often. I suggest you wrap me up in the scarf like a Bedouin again, at least they won't stare at me!'

His heart rate kept slamming in my back. He laughed.

'I don't care who heard you as long as I can feel you. And I'm gonna do it again if you tempt me to shut your mouth. Only the memory of the sight is enough to turn me on to the max,' he started moving in me.

'No, no! No sex for the next couple of hours! You want me to remind you why you should care?'

'Why, my lovely dear?'

'Because of one of the reasons for the enormous social distance between us—your position!'

'This one right now? I'm absolutely sure that I like being behind you and I'm absolutely sure there's no distance at all!' Laughing, he turned me to face him. The blue irises shone with that boyish gleam again. I pretended to be sulking but I chuckled as well.

'Yes, Mr. President, I was referring to this exact position.'

His lips pressed into mine, he spoke:

'There are three years, four months and twenty-seven days left until this madness ends. I'll be free then to not care about this.'

'Honestly, it's very hard for me to take you as a president. It's as if you are two different personas, or you live in parallel worlds. It's weird. Plus, the end of your term wouldn't solve the issue about your superiority. You could become president again, too, and then you'll make it even more difficult for me to become more successful than you are.'

'First, I'm not superior to you. Second, I'm not running for another election, and third... Become more successful than me? Is that what you want?'

'First, you are definitely superior and I don't like it. Second—why? Third, I want to be equal, at least, because that's how things should be.'

'I'll skip one and three. I don't feel like arguing about modern ideas right now. I won't run for other elections because there were only two things left that I wanted. I thought the first one was impossible, so I did my best to get the second one. Ironically, the first one is in my arms right now. Unfortunately, the consequences of my obsession with the second one are here as well.'

With the last word, he bit my lips, then got up from bed and hastily went to the bathroom. I followed. He pulled me into the shower with him, diligently preventing my every question with a kiss. Of course, after I repeated numerous times that we were not having sex, he did me wildly, propped against the wall, until my legs went totally limp. Victor was definitely not into modern ideas, limitations and consideration. Apparently, I didn't mind his ways, though, or at least it seemed so while I was shouting for him to keep going.

Victor called for the suitcase with the stuff that he had prepared for me. He insisted and, despite my resentment, I put on the clothes he had chosen instead of my own. Everything was tailored to my taste, if jeans and T-shirts could be considered a "taste". Everything was my size, too. On our way to the garden, I carefully explained to him why it was unacceptable for someone else to buy clothes for me. When I added that this was also beyond my boundaries, he frowned and said that we should negotiate this some other time. He was squeezing my hand and at first I didn't mind, but then

I became confused by the faces of the staff and the security guards in the garden. I tried to pull away, but he wouldn't let me go. Instead, he explained that he had reduced the number of people who would see me as much as possible. I was supposed to get used to their reactions, though, because it was strange for them to see him with a woman in his spare time. I gaped at this insane statement, but he didn't say anything else. I was struggling to restrain my inner urge to ask him about the shadows; it was not the right time for that particular conversation.

While breakfast was being served, Victor focused on his phone, frowning. I decided to turn off the airplane mode on mine. Grandpa had probably been calling—which was why I had turned it off in the first place. He must have been worried that I was not answering, even though it happened a lot. He never got used to that and always tried to convince me that it was not right. For the last couple of days, I hadn't answered him at all because I didn't want to explain what was going on. As I took the phone out of my backpack, Victor shot a glance at me:

'You're turning it on now?'

'Yup, why?'

He didn't reply. In two seconds, Sergey was running in our direction. Victor raised his hand without even looking at him and said:

'I know. This is Nia's phone. Get it in the system.'

I raised my eyebrows and Sergey shouted:

'There was someone else's phone on the yacht then!' He began to stagger because Victor's expression froze. 'I detected a phone last night and thought it was hers, but then you made me come here and I didn't verify it. If you had let me instruct her like the others...'

'Damn it! You idiot!' Victor waved his hand and the glass in front of him flew and shattered on the alley. He started yelling in Russian and Sergey yelled back, pointing at me.

Toma squatted before me while I was gaping. He took me by the hand when Victor ordered him to take me to the house. I wouldn't move, insisting that Bear should tell me what was going on. He explained that only he and Sergey were allowed to have their phones around Victor. The staff, even the guests and everyone else were supposed to leave theirs at a special place, or not carry phones at all. The Russian used a device to intercept frequencies. It was a security measure and also a way to prevent people from taking photos. I understood Sergey's mistake and, as I watched Victor yelling wildly at him, *Justice* started moving. The sharp edge between her black and white halves shone. She was angry because it was not the Russian's fault. I headed to them but Toma pulled me and Victor shouted at him to take me to the house. Again, he sounded like he was referring to a suitcase. I shouted, too:

'Stop yelling at him! It's not his fault!'

He clenched his jaw. Everyone froze. Victor's eyes pierced me but the goblin in mine didn't step back.

'Stay out of this! This is my problem and I will take care of it. Am I clear?! Get in the house right now!' He hissed.

'And you're taking care of it by yelling?' I raised my eyebrows condescendingly.

Sergey gaped. Reddening, Victor leaned over me. I had to bend my neck back in order to continue giving him the bad look. He spoke through his teeth, squeezing my face:

'I'm going to be very specific now! You get in the house with Toma and you stop objecting to me like that, especially in front of the staff and other people. I'll have a serious talk with you later. Am I clear enough, Nia?' He stressed on every syllable as *Rage* peeked from his eyes.

His expression and tone only irritated *Justice* even further. My *Rage* was inspired to fight his. I tried to reply calmly, though my anger was probably visible.

'Certainly not! I'm staying here now. I will help you with your problem and you will stop yelling at the Russian because it is not his fault. I confirm that the responsibility was yours rather than his. Furthermore, you are not going to talk to me like that, with or without people around, if, of course, you even want to talk to me in future! Am I clear enough, Victor?' I grimaced and he stepped back, growling.

He knocked another glass over and shouted at Toma and Sergey's gaping faces:

'She's driving me crazy! This woman is driving me crazy! Totally crazy! How am I supposed to just tell her what to do and get her to do it? How? Someone explain to me how to do this?!'

'Bro,' Toma tapped his shoulder. 'No man has discovered this. Not only about this woman—all women are like this. You must live with it!' He smirked.

Victor stared back at me.

'You're driving me crazy with your "certainly not"! I hate those fucking words! Separate and together!' His shouts ricocheted off my stone face.

'Can't you just do what I say?! You can't help me, Nia! I will take care of this, if you don't drive me mad before that with your stubbornness.'

'Certainly not. I already calculated that the probability of you taking care of this is negligible. You lack data,' my intentional nagging made him growl in my face but this didn't stop me. 'Plus, this has nothing to do with my stubbornness. Are you finished yelling?' He hissed, but I carried on calmly: 'Sergey says that there was someone with a phone on the yacht. Right?' Victor didn't react and Sergey nodded. 'I don't really like to confess this, but I was spying for the whole evening. I was watching from the top level.'

'And?' The security guard gazed foolishly at me.

Victor scolded me:

'Do I have to forbid, or it's clear that you're not going to spy anymore? And how is your unhealthy curiosity helping here?' He looked human again.

'Don't you know how? I thought you read my medical record. It's obvious. I will recreate the night and come up with the potential possibilities of people who had their phones. Facial expressions, movements, every little detail—there are quite enough ways to shortlist them. Whoever had a phone, they must've come near you, which means I saw them. Why would they need it otherwise? If it was forbidden, I doubt someone took it to play games in the toilet.'

'Recreate it?!' Toma and Sergey exclaimed in duet, but Victor motioned for them to shut up.

'Can you?' He cupped my face and I nodded. 'This won't harm you in any way?'

'Of course I can. It won't harm me. Besides, the result is the priority. All I need is a loud clock. Tick-tocking helps.'

'What are you saying, goblin? What tick-tocking? Victor, what is she going to do? She won't go into that state, right—you didn't see her then, but she scared the hell out of me,' Toma was nervous.

Before I could reply, Victor started explaining:

'If you refer to the time she fled with the metro, it was something else. She probably blocked out then.'

'Blocked out?'

'It happens when she can't find the logic in what's happening. It's like what you'd feel if you touched ice and burned your finger. Your brain will block out for a moment, because there'll be a contradiction to the information. In her case it's similar, but the process is highly complex and dependent on the environment, the people, their behaviour, and the endless data she processes in her mind.'

'Apparently you've read the record thoroughly,' I raised my eyebrows.

Toma insisted on having more details. He moved his concerned gaze between me and Victor.

'And what is she going to do now? Why does she want a loud clock?'

'I don't know about the clock, but I guess that she's going to rummage through her Memory Palace. She created it when she was a kid, probably because of her exceptional photographic memory. Didn't you?' Victor fondled my cheekbone and I nodded, astounded by his diligence in examining all the information about me. He continued explaining to Toma: 'Nia's brain does not separate the main images from the details. It doesn't sift them, she stores everything. She remembers things other people don't even notice. She stores them in this palace. In her case it also serves as something similar to file compressing, because the information is huge. Is that true, my lovely dear?'

'You went too far in your investigation on me, but yes. More or less, that's how it works,' I sulked and Victor kissed my palm. Toma was still bewildered so I decided to add: 'For example, Bear, if you and I see an enormous blue truck, I will notice even the scratches on it. I will memorise all the details, all the defects and mistakes. Then, I'll be able to restore them even after years have passed. I know how to extract information, too. I already know, for instance, that if I decide to kick the Russian again, I have to go for the left ankle. I guess he's had some injury there. He limps almost imperceptibly and when he steps on it, I can tell by his facial expressions that he's in pain. This is his weak spot.'

'You really are some weirdo,' Sergey blinked and the president hissed at him to shut up.

In fact, the Russian's remark didn't offend me. I grinned.

'Right now—a useful weirdo, as it seems,' with my nose up in the air, I turned back to Victor: 'Now that everybody knows how, do you want me to help, or would you rather keep shouting?'

'Only if you're absolutely certain that it won't harm you in some way.'

'Come on! Your obsessive worries again! I'll be fine. Just find me a loud clock to help me focus.'

φ

Victor insisted on staying with me, even though I didn't want him to. Searching through my palace required deep concentration and having people around made it difficult. Tick-tocking was helpful, though. The hands of loud clocks produce several different sounds—usually three or five, in a repeatable pattern. They eased me into a rhythm-counting mode and thus, I was able to step through the entrance of the palace. I stored everything there; it was an archive of my eyes. Every little thing that had passed before them throughout my life, was there. I even suspected that *Knowledge* buried himself somewhere in the library, filing his damn exact terms.

I had lied that going there was harmless. It exhausted me and, if I didn't manage to take my mind out of the deep concentration in time, there was a chance of getting stuck. I had gotten stuck there a couple of times and barely escaped because I was digging into the period when I was very little, before grandpa adopted me. Since then, I had stopped rummaging in this part of the palace and was careful whenever I entered it. I generally avoided going there. This time, however, I wanted to help Victor solve his problem and stop yelling. I guess my goal was to prove myself, too. His superiority over me was more than obvious and I didn't have many other advantages. The only thing I had more than him was my IQ and the quirky abilities of my mind.

Counting the rhythm of the clock hands, I dived into the dangerous hyper concentration of which my brain was capable. I went back there in my thoughts, straining my entire body painfully to restore each frame. I watched carefully from the railing again, but this time I paid attention to the archived details. I put aside the prostitutes almost immediately, after confirming that they didn't have enough fabric on them to hide a phone. I checked off the guests one by one—they were careless, immersed in what they were doing, and their facial expressions didn't show anxiety but only arrogant satisfaction. Whenever my thoughts passed by Victor and the women around him, I started sweating, hot and cold waves went through me again and I clenched my fingers into fists. The same unfamiliar process returned that tightened my stomach and quickened my pulse. I even suspected the negligible possibility of this being jealousy and not just a sea urchin in my head. I studied the staff carefully and identified indications of carrying a phone in four of them. I was startled to find out that the fifth suspect was lying next to me, laughing at me: Chris.

There was nothing more to look for. Exiting my concentration was even more unpleasant. It brought physical pain and I gritted my teeth. Then I focused on Victor who was all sweaty, staring at me, his hands shaking.

'What's wrong?' I gazed at him rubbing his face.

'Enough! You're not doing that anymore. Whatever that was, it has happened for the last time. I absolutely forbid you to do it. Did you hear me? I FORBID!' His voice was also shaking, but it was not *Rage* this time. He fell to his knees before me, all pale, and I couldn't help but chuckle.

'Victor, I'm sorry to tell you and your manias this, but you cannot control my mind, or whether I'm going to search through my palace. This is my personal territory and your presidential orders are not valid there.'

'For Christ's sake, Nia! It's not funny! You wouldn't react when I spoke to you. You were moving your hands around your head, muttering incomprehensibly. As if you were in a trance: as if you were gone and I couldn't do anything. Nothing! I was afraid to even touch you because...'

'Hey, weirdo!' I interrupted him with a smile. 'That's why I wanted to be alone. You insisted on being here. I'm like that when I'm deep in concentration, nothing's wrong. Calm down, breathe and hold back your manias! You can't control everything, especially what's going on in my head.'

His face took shelter in my palms, and he exhaled loudly.

'Usually, if I don't have control over something, I find my way to gain it. Please understand that the opposite is well beyond my boundaries. With you, it's even harder and you must somehow let me do it. I'm not sure if I even know how to control you. You, your entities, your whole madness,' he balanced his breathing and kissed my fingers before he continued: 'You're not doing this anymore. I can't forbid you, but I'm begging you not to do this. For me. It seemed to be torturing you, and the sole thought of this makes me explode!'

'Come on! I'm fine. My mind has its advantage and that thing is one of them. I found several options. Do you want me to tell you already? I can explain how I sifted them out, but I'm certain that my criteria were absolutely correct.'

'You don't have to explain. Tell me who they are and forget about all this. I'll take care of it from now on and you will relax,' he kissed my palms again.

I was silent, staring out of the window. Chris was sitting in the garden with Toma and Sergey. He seemed to have found his entertainment last night. For a moment, I was even relieved that Victor had taken care of me and rescued me from the same severe hangover. Chris stared at me for a second and, without any logical arguments, I avoided the truth. I lied that there were an even number of options, sparing Victor the fifth one, so I could talk to Chris in person.

'Four people from the staff. I'll describe three of them because I don't know their names. Luka is the fourth. If you're going to check up on them, you should start with him. Based on my criteria, I calculated that the probability with him is the highest.'

'No, I don't think so. He's one of my trusted people. I'm truly sorry about all this, my lovely dear. I shouldn't have let you do this. I have to leave you now and go solve the problem.'

He kissed my forehead and I shrugged because of his irrational conclusion.

'Numbers are numbers, Victor. They can't lie, and people do. My advice is—start with Luka. Check him first!'

I described the other suspects to one of the guys, but it turned out to be useless. Meanwhile, Sergey had found out that Luka's things were missing. On the camera tapes, the Russian watched him sneaking out of the villa during the night and he was already certain that it was him. They couldn't contact him, either. I was relieved I hadn't pointed out Chris. While the president was shouting like crazy outside, Toma came to me. Then Sergey shouted at everyone else and there was a commotion. My head ached because of the whisky, the adrenaline, and the palace. This was another side effect, which sometimes came with a nosebleed, too. Victor disappeared into the house and didn't come out again. I was soon informed that he had ordered Toma to take me home on a civil flight.

Bear hastily took me in his jeep and started on the turns towards Naples. While we were winding up and down the serpentine bends, he shared Victor's other orders with me. As soon as I heard the first one, I called Victor persistently. He was probably aware why I kept calling, but eventually he was forced to pick up. The conversation we had was indecently loud. I firmly refused to move out of Chris's house. He hung up. Then it was my turn to hang up and after we had three more conversations in the same style, I accepted his condition—Toma was to stay there with me. Victor, on his part, agreed to take the rest of the security off me. Our communication was obviously getting better and I was happy with the ratio—two compromises by him, one by me. During our last talk, we almost avoided shouting at each other, which was a huge step of progress. However, he complained that he couldn't handle me. In fact, his shiver-provoking timbre easily did that when he whispered that my voice was enough to give him a hard-on. Then Victor said he craved being in me all the time, and I prickled. I forgot why we were arguing and I was nearly ready to accept everything. I guess that's how addictions influence people; they blur things and distract one from what is substantial.

Bear relaxed in the armchair in business class, and I stared at him from my lotus position. As I searched carefully for any peanuts in the bowl of nuts, I repeated the same thing over and over again; I kept asking if he was mad at me, but he would only shake his head. Eventually, I closed my mouth too. I started contemplating the possible options. Most probably, Luka had taken videos. He could have filmed Victor shagging my tied-up body on the couch, squeezing my throat, or the trey of cocaine, or the prostitutes. It was a geometric progression; each assumption was worse than the previous one. For a moment, I even caught myself hoping that he had filmed us because that seemed to be the least harmful option. Then, however, I remembered Victor's position, his social superiority, and how I didn't fit into the standards. Who knows how people would label our sex with their illogical taboos. They could never understand that this was simply the way we liked it, and taboos were essentially meaningless. An obsessive thought about front pages of newspapers and viral posts on Facebook also buzzed in my head. They all involved a huge scandal and my naked body which made me sick.

After countless terrifying periods of turbulence, the thick, grey November fog eventually greeted us back home. It hadn't given up on its dream of draining the last drop of happiness from people. It also devoured my three drops of good mood remaining from remembering Positano's sun. I was all gloomy before we reached the house. Obviously, Chris had stayed with Victor, so it was only Bear and me there. Toma called someone to get him more black shirts and didn't say anything anymore. He left for the second floor sulkily. The slam of his bedroom door sounded even angrier. Before leaving me, he snorted that I was not to go anywhere without him.

I was frowning at the autumn greyness and the chill in the yard. Yet again, I was still relieved to have made a correct assessment in not pointing out Chris as a suspect. Most likely, I had spared him a lot of trouble. My overwhelming hope was that they would find Luka quickly and figure out his intentions before he could put them into action. If I had been allowed to stay, I knew I would have been of more use than Chris and this irritated me. In fact, I would have been of more use than anyone else. Yet, Victor didn't allow me to help any further. My mind was not included in the actions taken to solve the problem; once more I had been neglected and underestimated.

After taking a couple of circles around the living room, I poured myself some wine. To my delight, Chris had the habit of leaving cigarettes everywhere. I started smoking, trying to come up with the parameters that could make it acceptable for me to fit into Victor's reality. It was a total failure. My thoughts kept pulling back, rushing in Victor's direction, and avoiding what was truly substantial. I was wondering what he was doing—whether he was shouting at someone again and whether he had solved the problem. Other useless details concerned me as well. I was tense and I eventually decided to call him. When he didn't pick up, I became even tenser.

After I dialled his number for the third time, he answered sharply:

'What is it, Nia?'

'What is what?'

'Why are you calling so incessantly? I can't talk right now!'

'Then why did you pick up? Aren't your calls supposed to be transferred to the secretary?'

'Your calls are not transferred, and when you call three times in a row, you get me worried. Toma texted me that you're back home and everything's under control. What is it then?'

'Nothing. You're just buzzing in my head. I can't concentrate and I thought I'd call you, so this could stop. What are you doing? What happened with the problem, are you shouting? I'd like to know.'

I heard his light laughter, then he spoke in a softer tone:

'My lovely weirdo, are you missing me?'

'Certainly not. The time you've been away doesn't warrant missing you. It takes at least eighteen hours to produce the hormones that provoke this process. I was just bugged by these questions and I had to ask them.'

'God, it will really take time to get used to this,' he sighed heavily. 'Apparently, my hormones are messed up, because I already miss you terribly. I can't wait to feel you in my arms. I'm coming home tonight and Toma will drive you to me.'

'Certainly not, I don't have such plans for tonight. I'll be thinking about what we discussed last night.'

'You'll be thinking at my place.'

'No, I won't. I can't concentrate that way.'

'Nia, don't argue. Toma will drive you to me and you can think as much as you like, just at my place,' his other personality was taking over. I recognised it by the tone of his voice.

'I'm not arguing, Victor. I won't think at your place and you won't give me orders, because this is definitely on my list of conditions. The boundaries that will define what is intolerable for me—remember?'

Annoyed, he growled in the receiver.

'I don't know what they are, but I already dislike them.'

'I don't like your manias either, but I have to put up with them. You're going to do the same.'

'Christ! I never thought I'd allow a woman to say a sentence like that.'

'I hope this was related to the sentence alone, not to the gender of the interlocutor, because the second option is not acceptable in this century.'

'You're damn right. I wouldn't take it from a man either. Only from my Tasmanian devil that I don't seem to be able to handle. I gotta go, my lovely dear, but we're going to argue about tonight again later!'

'Boundaries, Victor. Boundaries. We're not going to argue and you're going to respect my wish. Tell me about Luka, at least. What happened?'

'It's all sorted. Don't worry about that! I will respect your wish, if you insist, but tomorrow we will seriously discuss those boundaries. I'll call you later. Kisses!'

He hung up before I could ask for any details.

A number of living room laps later, I really wished to distract my mind with something, but Toma was still hiding in his bedroom. I didn't feel like watching *Game of Thrones*, so I got to the folders and Chris's cash flow reports. Numbers, along with creating patterns, always gave me comfort. I thought that at that moment, they would be the perfect escape from the chaos in my mind. I also detected in myself some motivation to prove Victor that he was wrong to ignore me. There was a constant burning desire in me to prove myself—not only before *the Monster* but also before anyone who underestimated me. What I wanted now was to find out how exactly the financier had been stealing. Thus, I could impress Victor with another practical skill of my brain and more useful results. I arranged the documents on the huge dining table and concentrated. It took more time because of my exhaustion, but I was seeing it. The pattern was complex, both cyclical and containing chaotic irregularities. I even got irritated because nothing had ever been so arduous for me before. Money had been transferred through a number of companies. There was something unclear, a missing piece of the jigsaw. I strained my brain, but kept coming to the same dead end over and over again, so my irritation escalated.

I decided to pour myself more whisky. In the cupboard, I found a package of Chris's white mood powder. I was overcome by another irrational desire and hastily copied his movements to make a line for myself. The taste wasn't that nasty anymore and I even rubbed it into my gums.

A glass of whisky in hand, I was examining the papers once more, when it dawned on me. I remembered the table I had seen on Chris's laptop and the fact that all the data was there. He had entered his password in my presence a couple of times, so I restored the movements of his fingers in my thoughts and unlocked the laptop on the seventh try. I checked the recent files—the table was there.

The missing data was also there—money transfers through companies that the financier hadn't reported. Even with the full information, though, it was hard to tell exactly how that guy had been stealing. The pattern looked chaotic at first, but it actually wasn't. The money seemed to have been transferred at random, with no rhythm or logic. At the same time, I could see it: a pattern unattainable for the financier's plain skills. I found colourful sticky notes in one of the drawers and began to put them on the wall to depict the structure. I became engulfed in my most powerful mode. The hexagons came to my rescue. They started glowing, full of data, and my brain was picking out solutions.

I kept moving the sticky notes about, scratching things out, tracing— the speed of my own thoughts was burning me. The pattern had seemed independent and wild, yet its logic stood out all of a sudden. My eyes noticed an omission, a mistake, then the red line in my mind followed it. I rearranged the notes, sticking new ones and changing the structure. Everything became clear in my twisted mind.

A perfect two-dimensional square pyramid[43] appeared on the wall, along with a smile on my face. I identified the source of the payments—the centre from which the flows sprang before twisting down the turns of the pattern. I was breathing hard because of my struggle with the chaotic model, but I could see its rhythm now. I stared at the wall. There was no confirmation of my assumptions there. No stealing at all. It was something else and, as I examined, my eyes narrowed with suspicion.

I was running my fingers over the sticky notes when a short shout made me jump.

'God! What are you doing? Damn...' Chris was gaping behind my back.

'I... I was checking something related to the financier's stealing, but it's not...'

His face red with anger, he slammed his laptop shut and interrupted me:

'You can't touch my laptop! Are you crazy? How did you even unlock it?' He yelled at me and I frowned.

'Why are you yelling? I was missing data and you said it was all there. I only opened the table; I didn't see anything else. If you don't want me to unlock it, don't enter your password in my presence!'

'You freak! My password consists of twenty symbols, for Christ's sake! You memorised my movements, didn't you?'

I nodded guiltily as he stared at the notes. Toma appeared, attracted by the uproar.

'Is everything all right?' He asked curtly and Chris nodded.

'Almost! The Italian issue seems to be settled. Partly, at least, or in parts... Smarty here has been going through my stuff though,' he turned his attention back to the notes on the wall. 'For Christ, Nia! This is...'

'This is quite different from what I suspected,' I interrupted him arrogantly. 'As you can see, this is definitely not stealing,' his colourful irises went ablaze, but I couldn't tell if he understood. 'I assume you know what this is? The exact term is money laundering, but there is a mistake. The pattern is wrong. That jerk must be as stupid as a donkey—sorry, I didn't mean to insult donkeys—to make this sort of a mistake,' I rolled my eyes.

Chris exploded:

---

[43] *A square pyramid, unfolded – author's notes.*

'Mistake? Are you crazy? This is the most perfect pattern ever and I know very well what it is because it was ME, with my non-donkey brain, who created it!' He shouted, pouring himself whisky, then downed it.

'Bullshit! It's not perfect, it's wrong! It's supposed to be linear, segmented, and this one is pyramidal. It's too obvious when all the data is present. I must admit I found it a little difficult at first, but it was only because of the chaotic transfers. There's no rhythm, but once I saw the irregularities, it became elementary. Even a kid would get it!'

'Elementary? My pattern? Are you insane? This is a million-dollar pattern and my bank account proves it!' His ego shouted at me. Mine wouldn't give up, either:

'It is elementary and my notes on the wall prove it,' I snapped. He pursed his lips, his face red. 'It doesn't even serve its main purpose. If you want to launder money, it should be impossible for others to find out! It's obvious! This one is not secure. The concentrations of money are clear. So are the interconnections. If this is worth a million dollars, I'm gonna create a billion dollars pattern. Then I'll give it to you, so you can learn,' I raised my nose in the air but he wouldn't give up.

'Not secure?! You really ARE crazy! This is impenetrable! Do you know how many times I've been investigated? And, as you can see, I'm not in prison.'

'This is stupid and you've been investigated by damn fools!'

We kept shouting at each other, and Toma moved his head as if watching a tennis match.

'What's wrong with you? What patterns are you talking about?'

'He claims that his elementary scheme was perfect! Look at the wall and tell me if it's true. You will be an arbitrator!' I pointed angrily at the wall.

'Goblin, all I see are colourful notes with numbers and symbols on them. All I could say is that they're beautifully arranged in triangles around a square. I don't even know what this shape is.'

'A two-dimensional square pyramid!' We replied in a duet, staring at each other in rage. We stood like this, silent for a minute, then I spoke, tapping my foot, my hands on my waist:

'Oh, come on, Chris! Admit it! Just look at it and confirm my conclusion. I'll help you fix it, but you must admit that I'm right first!'

'Smarty, there's nothing for me to admit! This was created for the purposes of money laundering, and these activities are investigated by normal people, not by freaks like you!'

'What if the investigators were freaks like me?'

'Freaks like you don't investigate—they create the patterns! Nia, rich people from all around the goddamn world do the laundering with similar methods, and mine is one of the best and most popular. I could become an honorary citizen of Panama! There is no one to dig deep, no one would allow this. Rich people launder their money and live their privileged, fairy-tale lives, just like Victor. This is it! Just leave it there!'

'Honestly, no deep digging is needed! A tiniest poke is enough.' I moved my index finger before his nose. 'I'm not leaving it here! I'm gonna tell Victor how absurd, elementary, and foolish it is and that he could be deprived of the chance to live his privileged life in a fairy-tale manner. I'm gonna tell him that it must be fixed and, most importantly, that it was ME who found this out!' I stressed the last words and Chris's face became cynical. So did his tone.

'But you're most welcome,' he motioned at the door, then continued even more arrogantly: 'I guess doing you while you're giving him financial advice will be something to remember. What do you think? That he's gonna let one of his mistresses interfere in his business? Isn't your main purpose to spend his money, not deal with its laundering?!'

He meant to drive me mad and he succeeded. Right after the last word, his facial expressions clearly showed that he was sorry for his mean words. *Rage*, however, was already gazing through my irises.

'You know what? I'll give it a try and we'll see. He might like this financial advice sex, especially if I shout it loud enough,' I shoved my index finger before his nose again, waving it, hissing: 'What you must know is that I'm incompatible with being a mistress. What I have between my ears is a million times more useful than what I have between my legs. Fuck you, you douchebag!'

I headed to Toma but Chris clutched my hand.

'I'm sorry! I'm really sorry! I didn't mean to insult you. You're nothing like a mistress and you're not a freak. I just went nuts. Please, don't be mad at me. I'm sorry!'

'Don't be! It doesn't work! You'd better fix your damn cynical attitude to everyone and everything.'

'All right, but I'm truly sorry! Don't be mad at me, Smarty. Let's discuss this and you'll explain what you have to offer. I have some great news about our work together, too. Let's have a drink and cool down.'

'Later! I'll speak with Victor first!' I hissed.

In fact, I wasn't that angry with Chris. I was rather more eager to prove myself. Victor had ignored me earlier and that was more than a motivation for me. I dialled his number but his phone was off and I stared at Bear.

'Is he back?' He nodded without saying anything. 'Let's go to him!'

'We can't. He didn't ask me to bring you there.'

'Because I told him that I won't go and he should tolerate my decisions. They changed now and he won't mind,' while I was muttering, Toma dialled Victor and confirmed that his phone was off.

'I don't think this is a good idea. He's not at the house and I don't know if...'

'I don't care where he is. He insisted that you take me to him. I refused, now I changed my mind, so come on—take me where he is!' I snapped and poor Toma couldn't fight the irritated goblin in my gaze. He grunted for me to put on warm clothes.

I recognised the road we took once we had left the city. We were heading to the place I had been taken to for my first meeting with Victor. I remembered the details, the smells, the curiosity in his eyes, and the way he gazed at me, seeming to understand me. Now he really did understand me and so did I. I leaned my head against the window. The rain slowly turned to fine snow that covered the dirt. The winter whiteness fought the ordinary grey, trying to disguise it as a more beautiful reality. The reality in my head was also changing. The closer we got, the clearer the fact became that I didn't want to think about boundaries and ways to accept Victor's life. All I wanted was to fit into it, no matter what it was like. Some unfamiliar process warmed me, quickened my heart rate, and curved my lips into a smile.

SIXTEEN

Toma drove carefully, so my stomach didn't protest as we trickled up the mountain turns. It seemed, however, that several cars were cautiously following us. The second time I saw them, I memorised the shape of the headlights, and the third time I was already sure. Only when the slope revealed them could I see them. I adjusted the visor, staring at the mirror, but Toma pushed it back, irritated.

'Spying again?'

'Didn't you notice that we're being followed?'

He grunted without answering and I pulled the visor again. Affected by the already activated paranoid part of my brain, I insisted:

'Someone's following us, I'm telling you!'

'No one's following us. Relax!'

'You're wrong! They're moving at a careful speed. They keep their distance. Slow down to 5 kilometres per hour and they'll pass by us in about a minute and a half. Take a look, when the trajectory of the turn is...'

'Christ!' His shout interrupted me and I frowned. 'Your constant "certainly not" is truly annoying, but when you start speaking like that, it's absolutely unbearable. We're not being followed, girl. This is the security. Relax and stop spying!'

He closed the visor again and I snapped:

'What security?'

'Your security.'

'No, it can't be them! On the phone, I told Victor to take them off me. Don't you remember?'

'It can't, but it's them!' He rolled his eyes mockingly. 'I advise you to nail a note at the very entrance of that memory castle of yours: "Victor always does what he wants and he doesn't comply with anyone". Then repeat it three times a day so you can remember it at last!'

'First, it's a palace, not a castle. Second...' I fell silent for a moment, my arms crossed on my chest. '...He does what he wants but he will start complying. I guess I'll have a damn serious talk with him, see what he's going to explain this time.'

I sulked and Toma chuckled.

'Explain?' His mockery evoked a grimace on my face. 'Nia, I'm sorry to disappoint you again, but Victor never explains. You listen to him, not the other way round. That's how it is. Regarding the security, though, I agree with him. He might be maniacal with the safety issues, but he's right in this case, especially after what happened on the yacht.'

'I don't care about his manias and I'm not going to comply with them. And no—he's not right. We had a deal, he lied to me again, and I'm sorry if I disappoint you, but you're wrong—he's definitely going to explain!' I cracked my fingers angrily.

Toma shook his head in disbelief. After a short period of silence, he spoke seriously:

'I can't believe a tiny person like you can be that difficult to handle. And you're not afraid of Victor even a bit.'

'I was on the verge, but no, I'm not afraid. Should I be?'

'I'm not saying you should, it's just weird. Most people are afraid.'

'I'm not most people. Besides, I already saw what he's like when he explodes. His manias are quite weird, but I understand his madness. Mine doesn't look better, so I'm the last person who'd be afraid.'

'His explosions shouldn't bother you! He goes crazy, he yells, he hits, but he'd never harm you. The first year at the legion, he astounded me with his inhuman control over himself, despite his manias and craziness. I told you before—he disciplined himself like a Spartan, and harming a woman is impossible for him. That's not what I meant.'

'Then what?'

'That he's starting to lose this control over himself, and even with it, he's dangerous when he focuses on something. He gets obsessed, Goblin, and his judgment becomes inaccurate. He forgets all boundaries and takes insane risks. He just doesn't stop until he gets what he wants. Now he's obsessed with you and you must know that he always gets things his way. I still think all this is not for you. Obviously, you've decided the opposite though, so you must learn to comply because there's no going back,' his expression showed disappointment. 'He's not a bad person. I've long accepted him the way he is, but his madness rightly causes fear and you must not forget this.'

'When it comes to madness, you either accept it, or not! *Fear* is useless!'

'If you say so! I think it's useful, though, especially for self-preservation,' he shrugged.

I stared at him with interest.

'By the way, how did he end up at the legion? You're referring to the French legion, aren't you? Grandpa told me about it. Victor's bio doesn't say anything about this and it's weird that he's been in the military. You were both there?'

'Yup! The French Foreign Legion, or rather the training hall of hell. In fact, hell would have been better, I suppose. Just accept that the information in Victor's official bio is not quite accurate.'

Toma was explaining, immersed in his memories, and I suddenly remembered Victor saying that he had spent sixteen years in the ghetto. Now, with this new information, it all sounded quite confusing, especially in contrast with the privileged life *Wikipedia* claimed he had lived—the ghetto and the military didn't fit there at all.

'War is devil's work in general, so the legion being like a training hall of hell is quite logical. What else could it be? Did you two spend a lot of time there?'

'He had barely turned twenty when he arrived. We stayed for a couple of years, then we spent half a life together, and here we are now. Some crazy life, but I couldn't expect anything else with Victor around!' Toma's mouth curved into a smile. A series of memories seemed to be passing before his eyes, then he continued in a lowered voice: 'He's able to sniff out anything normal and run at top speed from it towards another madness. I followed. Some crazy life, Goblin! We lived life like crazy and we still do! On his birthday, I wondered which gods watch over us to let him turn forty and me—nearly fifty. He's the same wacko he used to be when he was twenty, though. And he looks the same, unlike me.'

There was a warm note to his voice. I smiled, pleased that I was not the only one who couldn't stand normality. Maybe it was my fifth allergy and Victor had it, too?

'Can you tell me more about your time at the legion? My grandpa was also in the military—I adore such stories. About Victor's true bio, too?'

'No, Goblin. I am not the one who should tell you that story.'

Toma kissed my palm and the car filled with music. I already knew the vibration within my body was *Excitement,* and the one between my thighs—*Desire.* I was constantly surprised by the processes Victor evoked in me, and yet the new tightening in my chest was still unclear and quite annoying. To be honest, I was also suffering from anticipation to see him, even though I had refused earlier. This anticipation was strong, even more powerful than my irritation at his new lie about the security. I gazed at the snow, at the whiteness conquering the mountain. A remix of *A Song of Fire and Ice*[44] sounded from the speakers. The line from *Game of Thrones*— "Winter is coming!"[45]—popped up in my head and made me tense, as usual. It kept obsessively playing on repeat until we arrived.

The exquisite wood carving at the entrance seemed even more impressive than the first time I saw it. Both the cold and my anticipation didn't allow me to wait for Toma, who was parking the jeep somewhere. I started down the alley to the house. I saw several silhouettes moving behind the windows and hurried on. On the ground in front, there were numerous, similar unidentified objects. In the dark, they looked like large sacks of sand. The huge torso of the fat non-mafia businessman was easier to recognise. I frowned. I was aware that it was his mansion and expected him to be there,

---

[44] *Mahmut Orhan - Game Of Thrones (Original Mix). A remix of the opening theme of the Game of Thrones series, Song of Ice and Fire - Ramin Djawadi – author's notes.*

[45] *The motto of House Stark in the Game of Thrones series. The meaning is linked to a warning of impending danger – author's notes.*

but I was absolutely repulsed by him after what he did on the yacht. He was kneeling by one of the supposed sacks, fiddling with something. Other large silhouettes and security guards hung around him. While I was walking, a jeep entered through another gate and three men began to unload more sacks, lining them next to the others. A dozen steps later, my stomach tightened. Adrenaline rushed through my head and I hurried in Fatass's direction. As I reached the platform in front of the house, *Reason* shrieked, covering his eyes, and I could barely speak, drenched in cold sweat.

'Oh my God! What the hell is this!' My jaw dropped but I closed it to prevent myself from puking.

I froze in front of the non-mafia guy, pressing my hand against my mouth. Everyone in my head did the same because they were also on the verge of vomiting. Only *Rage* remained unperturbed. He stepped to the front, cracking his neck, ready to blow into *Malice's* pyres with his fiery breath. I squeezed my cheekbones, looking silently around. I blocked out, there was only the red flickering light and a thunder in my head:

Faulty pattern. Faulty pattern.

My mental block, however, receded from the anger that rose from my navel. It made me hot and, before I knew what was happening, *Malice's* pyres went ablaze. They were tall enough to devour several warped worlds like this one.

Coming to my senses, I jumped back as I noticed that the edge of my colourful trainers were touching a puddle of blood. A mixture of whining and howling escaped my throat. Only a few centimetres from me, there was a line of slaughtered animals: boar, deer, foxes. The line was so long that I couldn't see the last ones in the dark. They lay solemnly on a red carpet of blood with their tongues hanging out and their lifeless eyes reflecting the lights. Marks of clumsy shots were visible on some of the corpses. I took in the images in a slow motion, while *Rage* kept detonating explosions in my head.

The nasty fat man was kneeling by a wild boar. He was opening its bloody mouth with his ugly fingers, digging pine twigs into it, probably to cover up the gruesomeness. He was setting the boar for a photo—the visual trophy of absolute human decay. *Reason* started yelling hysterically:

And those humans call us "a freak"? They call us "a freak" in this reality—do you realise that? Are only monsters allowed here? What is this? What? Where are we, Nia?

I shook my head as the jerk took a series of selfies. Obviously, he wasn't pleased with the result, so he handed me his phone, grunting that he wanted me to take a picture. I automatically took the phone, but then just sat down on the ground by the animal. He grunted again for his photo.

'Shut up! Shut up, you monster!' I hissed in my palm.

I threw his phone at the wall and the non-mafioso gaped, stepping back. Then I aimed the gruesomeness-concealing pine twigs at his overflowing belly. The disfigured jerk shouted angrily:

'Hey! What're you doing? Are you insane?'

I pinned my eyes on him, but I was still seeing everything in slow motion. I didn't even manage to curse him. I stroked the animal's snout and my trembling fingers turned scarlet. Then I sensed the smell. It was the same unfamiliar scent that I had detected in the office in which I had first met Victor. The strange aroma, metallic and sweet, hit my nose. The smell of fresh blood. Or maybe it was the smell of unjust death?

Fatass kept gabbling, but all I could hear were inarticulate sounds. My pulse was pounding and I couldn't even tell who was raging most furiously in my head. *Justice* was shaking all over, just like me. *Malice* was shouting at the top of her lungs. In fact, when she first appeared in my mind when I was very little, the cause was people's attitude towards me and stray animals. In my previous reality, the stray animals and I were equally treated, and I could never comprehend the brutality we had to face. Back then, I had also been just another useless animal with a predetermined fate. Maybe it was still true but I was convincing myself of the opposite.

Malice was the first entity that had popped out in my mind, but her eyes were only able to see people. She was blind to all other creatures and her antithesis—compassion—came with her. *Compassion* was blind to people. The only thing I could feel when I was a kid, apart from the hatred for communists that came later, was compassion for the animals in the general reality. This was the first and strongest emotion I had. It was a natural emotion. I was taught how to feel the second one. Whenever it passed through me, compassion tortured me, it felt as if it tore me all the way from navel to throat. There were even brief moments in which I was sorry for people—whenever I realised the power of emotions and the impact on their bodies and weak minds. Every time, though, I remembered what people were like, and I wasn't sorry anymore. I was thankful, however, that I possessed this one emotion, even if it was only for animals. It made me see myself as less of a freak. Stray animals gave me something else, too—before I found salvation in the endless conversations with the entities in my head, I communicated mainly with them. Stray animals were my first hiding place.

While I was struggling to balance my breathing, I saw Victor through the window. His reality gave me another blow to the nose. He was sitting in the same armchair, in his white T-shirt. The elephant head was right above him, under his feet was the polar bear who had lost its battle with distorted people's worst pattern. Quite conveniently, I had forgotten these unacceptable details of Victor's reality! Nothing had changed except for the weed of desire that had grown in my twisted mind and the processes that kept attacking and tormenting me, sensing my inability to handle them. There was also one more difference to my first meeting with him; next to him, on the armrest, was one of the shadows. The one I had seen in the car when he had left for his trips. She was boring herself with a phone in her hand. Stunning, as always, her flawlessness perfectly matched the warped reality. Victor's palm rested possessively on her knee, while his other hand was focused on switching between TV channels. A red line shot through my mind to frame the scene in a square and turn it into a mental picture—a reality-check trophy to be hung at a central place in my Memory Palace. Maybe the entrance would be best, so the picture could serve as a delusion catcher, too.

I laughed silently. Then I laughed loudly. My fingers sank into the blood-soaked bristles of the murdered-for-pleasure beast next to me. *Reason* was rabid like never before; the sea urchin rolled in a ball, and he ran after it with an animal roar, determined to tear out its thorns one by one. *Desire* sobbed, but *Pride* grabbed it before it could throw itself to the floor. She squeezed its head and lifted it up, hissing at it to watch Victor. I watched as well. *The Monster* kept chuckling awfully, spitting its sticky bile into my throat. I gathered all my strength to get up, then headed to the exit with what was left of my dignity, when two hands dug under my armpits. Then there was a pull. Toma held me, his face in terror.

'What are you doing? There's blood all over you!'

He started rubbing my cheek with his black sleeve while I was trying to focus on his goggled, warm eyes. 'Fatass, why did you let her sit in the blood?! Maxim, are you out of your mind, you dick? What the hell is going on here?'

'Me? Out of my mind? This schizo bitch just came, sat down there, then broke my phone and hasn't stopped shaking. I don't wanna go anywhere near her—look at her sociopathic eyes!'

'I'm not a sociopath,' my hoarse voice was barely audible.

Fatass grunted again:

'I don't know what kind of freak you are, but you definitely look like a sociopath. Take your pills, mad woman!'

Malice stared at the jerk and I growled at him. He started oinking, or maybe he was laughing, but it seemed more like oink.

'This girl is crazy, Toma,' Fatass pointed at me, studying my face haughtily. 'Don't take her to Victor, take her to a doctor.'

Toma, still rubbing my cheek with worry on his face, didn't reply. Through my eyes, however, everyone in my head was focused on the non-mafioso and his insults. *Rage* got to his feet, powerful and willing to please *Malice* with each of her controversial methods. She was longing for something sharp. My gaze probably gleamed with anger. *The Monster* was neighing, drowning me in more bile. Then I exploded. I turned around and pushed the fat swine in the chest with all my strength, my palms leaving bloody prints on his white shirt. I spat in his crooked face and he yelled:

'Woah! Woah! Watch it, schizo!'

Toma grabbed me by the stomach and started pulling me back while Fatass was wiping his face with the back of his hand. My pulse thundered in my eardrums like boiling water. The other men around were also looking at me arrogantly. All I wanted now was to hit them with a hammer, a shovel, or any other of *Malice's* favourite tools. I craved physically harming Fatass. My entire anger for everything around me was about to pour over the Jabba[46] lookalike. However, all I could do in Toma's grip was yell. And I did that at the top of my lungs.

'Monsters! FREAKS! You are the ones who need a doctor! You are the ones who need fixing! You! Can't you see that?'

I spat again but couldn't hit his crooked face. Fatass shook his head with raised eyebrows.

'And you say you're not a sociopath. You should be in a hospital. Woah! Be quiet!' He spoke the last words as if I was either deaf, or didn't know the language. Then he stepped towards me menacingly, but Toma's palm stopped him. His other hand still held my stomach because I was trying to attack.

'Come here, Jabba! Let me send you to a hospital!' I waved my fists.

'Keep her away, Bear, or I'm gonna tame her damn fast,' Fatass grunted.

Toma mumbled something incomprehensible and the swine headed for the house. I took some breath to reply properly, but Bear's paw muffled my

---

[46] *Jabba the Hutt – a Star Wars character. He resembles a giant, fat snail and acts like a powerful crime lord in the galaxy – author's notes.*

mouth. I could only howl in Toma's cupped hand as he hissed at me to shut up. Already at a safe distance, Jabba watched me with contempt from the door when Victor stormed out. Apparently, he had heard the commotion despite the music and the voices inside. Several men and women followed him—I recognised another one of his shadows. There were more girls that looked similar to her and to the prostitutes from the previous night. Two of them were leaning over a low table and I had no doubt what they were doing with the tube between their fingers.

At that moment, another jeep came through the entrance. Sergey jumped out of the driver's seat, hurried to us and gaped when he saw Toma's grip on me. Two of the guys behind him unloaded another sack and dragged it on the ground. When I realised it was a wolf, I was already certain that I was going to puke in Toma's hand.

Victor went pale for a second, then immediately restored his statuesque expression. He approached me in a few vigorous steps and yelled at the others to leave us alone. He knelt before me and Toma let go. The muscles on the president's face tightened. He shouted:

'What is this blood? Why is she covered in blood?!' He squeezed the back of my head so tightly that I couldn't move, but I managed to push his chest.

'Let me go! Let go of me right now!' I hissed but he didn't react. He seemed to not even hear my voice; he was only focusing on studying my appearance carefully.

Toma's stammering caught his attention:

'When I found her, she was touching the boar. Then she suddenly attacked Fatass. They fought and she went crazy.'

'Why did you bring her? Damn you! She can't be here,' Victor's eyes made Bear freeze and he didn't reply.

Victor got up and started pulling my hand, but I resisted him.

'Why did you bring her here indeed? She went crazy just like that. Sociopath!' Jabba's nasty voice came from the door. It was only him left, leaning against the entrance.

'Just like that?! Can't your piggy eyes see the reason?' My voice escalated with each letter while I was trying to pull myself away. 'Stop insulting me, and you let go of me!'

'Nia! Please, calm down. Take a breath and calm down,' Victor was struggling to speak in a composed tone but was gripping my wrist tightly and I dug my feet into the ground.

'Don't you dare even talk to me! Let go right now!' I yelled and Fatass clicked his tongue.

'Keep your schizo under control, bro! One of these days, she'll go crazy and she'll slaughter you in your sleep. I'm telling you. She's a washed-up sociopath,' he was blabbering on, his insults making me even angrier.

'Stay out of this, Maxim!' The president yelled at him, his words mingling with mine:

'I'm not a sociopath! I am not!' Spittle flew from my mouth.

I managed to pull away and fell back, bumping into Toma, who kept me from falling, pressed against him. Victor snorted, rubbed his temples with his thumbs and hugged his nape. I watched the shadows and saw several other people staring at me from inside. Then I looked at everything around me, at Victor, Jabba, the mansion. Their normality. I wanted to scream, hit and spit, but I kept silent, frozen in my place. I gazed at the blue irises and there was a loud echo in my head:

ONE!

I took a few even breaths while counting, then nailed my nastiest look at Fatass. *Reason* was mad, showing his teeth like a wild beast, ready to attack without mercy any argument in defence of the gruesome reality around me. *Pride* lifted my chin up. I carefully straightened my dirty sweater and slicked my messy hair. I guess creeps ran down Fatass's spine when I spoke to him in a low, metallic voice that vibrated with my madness:

'Don't insult me with inaccuracies and don't confuse me with a sociopath. I am a psychopath. Exact wording: a highly intelligent, hyper-rational individual with psychopathic inclinations, emotional deficit and inability to accept irrational behavioural patterns. For this reason, I'd probably slaughter you without any scruples if it is even possible to pierce all your layers of fat. I calculate this possibility as negligible, so I can only hope that a heart attack is waiting for you in your room, Jabba!' I hissed, accentuating the last word, and Fatass gaped.

'Nia!' Toma and Victor said in a reproachful duet, but I kept staring at the non-mafioso.

'Woah! You're crazy too, bro. This bitch needs a straitjacket. What would you want with someone like her?' Fatass grunted before entering the house.

I kept spyingon him through the windows.

'Stop acting like this!' The blue irises pierced me insistently.

'And how am I supposed to act according to your standards? Not only have I stepped into your abominations here, but I'm also being insulted, humiliated... What—am I supposed to smile? How exactly should I behave when freaks with less than a hundredth of my intellect label me? Am I supposed to just let it pass? Keep silent? Have a drink with the whores in the living room?' I stared at Victor and he didn't reply.

I looked at the corpses again.

'What's that over there? A wolf?' I leaned over the animal. There were signs that it was female and that it had been breastfeeding. 'What is this? Decoration for your perverted photoshoots?'

I was sick again. Victor ran his fingers over his eyebrows before replying in a cool tone:

'Yes, precisely. It is a wolf. It's hunting. It's normal—men do this.'

'"It's normal"—a well-known label. But you are wrong—this, precisely, is the corpse of a female wolf who had a litter! Your hunting is an abomination. I know men do this. I'm aware of your simple biochemistry, but I don't understand the influence of such perversion. How does it make you feel, Victor? What's the pattern? You smell blood and—boom!—your testosterone rises for an orgy with the beauties inside? I guess that is also normal for you,' the irony pouring from my mouth was competing with the contempt in my gaze. 'I can only be glad that my fifth allergy seems to be normality.'

He approached me, biting his lip, and knelt before me again.

'Please, Nia! I know you can't see the logic and accept this, but it's just hunting. There's no orgy inside, or at least any that I will participate in,' he was struggling to keep his tone under control, but I sensed the note of condescension and it made me even more furious.

At that moment, I'd rather we had yelled at each other, so I could have released *Rage* out, but Victor continued to speak slowly:

'Men have been hunting for millennia. It's in our genes—try to accept it this way. I'll make sure you never see it again.'

I took a deep breath, hiding every trace of the bile in my throat behind my barrier. My skin was the best hiding place, after all. In my mind, I gave him numerous slaps, but I did my best to reply in my most composed manner:

'You better take care of your muddy reality. You don't have to take care of me. You are right, men were hunters once. You, though, are just a bunch of pathetic killers with issues, modern guns and excessive cruelty. Overly satisfied men who have gone insane. You're nothing more than that. You were right about something else, too—I don't deserve any of this.'

'Nia! Stop it!' He shouted at me but I carried on calmly:

'It's weird, you know, because I've always thought that I didn't deserve anything. It was an abstract belief, but now I know exactly what I don't deserve.'

He fell silent, and I couldn't help myself but hit him in the chest. He didn't budge. His irises turned black, and I already knew that his demons were overwhelming him. I was happy that *Fear* was not there to manifest on my face. My expression was only full of *Contempt*. Victor spoke in a voice even calmer than mine, emphasising every word with care:

'This is what we're going to do now, Nia—you're going to calm down, and so am I. Then we'll talk, no shouting and no hitting. Toma will take you to my bedroom and will stay with you until I come.'

My fixed gaze didn't flinch. His insistent irises were trying to crush me with superiority, but I didn't back up. The smell of blood merged with the musk that seemed to be soaking into my skin. I bristled. Laughter, music and the sound of toasts came from the house. The prostitute-looking girls were sitting at their low table, anticipating their immersion into the feast of the Successfuls, just as strongly as I anticipated getting out of there. There were just a few differences from the previous night: there was blood, there was no yacht, and the weather wasn't warm. I kept silent, staring into the blue.

Victor narrowed his eyes, keeping his close watch on my facial expressions. He seemed to be able to hear my thoughts when I realised I had made another incorrect conclusion. He was not stuck in this reality; he had created it for himself, putting everything in its rightful place there. A degrading, faulty pattern, and I had ended up in there as well. Voluntarily. I became aware that his reality and mine were two parallel lines that won't intersect even after thousands of light years. *Knowledge* muttered there was still some chance for them to meet in the infinite, or to find themselves in an elliptical geometry.[47] *Reason* immediately hissed that we were edged enough not to fit anyone and we never made life compromises, either, and that is enough. I was just standing there, silent, my thoughts pouring bile into

---

[47] *Elliptic geometry is an example of a geometry in which Euclid's parallel postulate does not hold. Instead, as in spherical geometry, there are no parallel lines since any two lines must intersect.- author's notes.*

my throat. Or maybe it was the taste of disappointment? Victor's timbre sneaked into my thundering brain again.

'Nia, let us try to communicate without fighting. Go upstairs and I will come to you so we can talk calmly,' he took hold of my hand, but his touch stung me as it would have done in the "before Victor" times and I pulled away abruptly.

'Don't touch me. You know I'd rather you didn't touch me,' I whispered softly, but as I stepped back, my voice became louder and more cynical. The taste that stuck to my tongue was probably reflected on my face, too. 'What am I supposed to do upstairs, Victor? Your bedroom might be presidential, but I guess it'll still be too narrow for you, me, and the shadows. Or maybe only the one you were touching in that armchair will join us? You raised your testosterone with hunting and now you're up for some intense sex?' I laughed and he reddened. 'Whatever! I'm absolutely certain that your stunning shadows can handle your energy, or even if they can't—there's a lot of choice in there.'

Victor didn't reply. He closed his eyes for a second, biting his knuckles. I deliberately carried on in an even ruder manner. I was fully aware of my intention to make him mad before leaving. I thought it was well-deserved, naturally.

'I'm not going to spoil your evening anymore. I apologise for intruding on the feast of the Successfuls—it was no pleasure for me either. I came to tell you something, but Jabba was actually right. The crazy chick's place is not here,' I stressed on the last words, and he hissed between his teeth.

'Stop talking to me like this!' His muscles tensed. 'I banned you from using that word about yourself. Don't create a distance on purpose and don't provoke me any further. Go upstairs immediately!' He pulled me rudely by the hand, but I didn't budge.

'Or what? Sergey will give me a good beating, Jabba will tame me, or you will lock me up? Is that what you have to offer, Victor? Because it's really not worth taking.' I said all this with spite, trying to hurt him.

He relaxed his grip on my wrist and I pulled it away. Once again, in my mind, I heard the echoing escape rhythm to flee from reality, normality and awkward situations. This time I counted aloud:

'ONE!'

As always, I started with my right foot and a tap of my right-hand fingers. The next steps quickly took me to the only beautiful thing in the mansion—the gate at the exit.

'Damn, Nia! Stop right now!' Victor shouted as he and Toma followed me. 'Stop! We're not having the same conversation as last night,' he took hold of my shoulders and nailed me in one place. When I turned to him, he was more furious than I had hoped, but I spoke in a business-like manner:

'We're not. We're not having it, because it cannot be the same. You were right—last night I ran without knowing what exactly I was running from, but now I'm leaving because it has become clear,' his fingers dug into my sweater. It felt as if they reached my bones.

His hands radiated heat that soaked in and twisted my stomach painfully, but I tried to look at the blue irises firmly. His influence on me was crushing; it made me shrink. Devastating waves rose in my tummy, excruciatingly shaking all my Victor-addicted cells, then they tried to suffocate my rational decisions.

I took a deep breath to continue on my way to the exit, but my left eye filled with saline as if a grain of dust had irritated it. But, in a second, there was saline in my right eye as well. It ran down both of my cheeks. I touched the corners of my eyelids and awkwardly gazed at the wet tip of my index finger. I cringed because of the fierce jab between my fifth and sixth ribs.

I had never seen that many expressions passing though Victor's face; he seemed to be in physical pain. He growled, then grabbed my nape, pulled abruptly and embraced me. He pressed my forehead to his chest, his fingers and lips buried in my hair. Heat was spewing from him, and the muscles underneath his T-shirt became as hard as rock. I pushed him but he only tightened his embrace. His hoarse voice sank into my ear as he kissed it:

'Damn it, Nia, don't! I'm begging you! You can yell at me, hit as much as you like, but don't torture me like this. I don't want to evoke this emotion in you. You have reasons to make a series of wrong conclusions and be angry. We are going home together, I will explain everything and you will understand me, my lovely dear. You'll understand it all.'

His whisper was mesmerising. It wrapped around me like a python, slithering to my throat, tightening his suffocating grip, taking away my ability to think straight. I wanted to be deceived and stay with him, I wanted his embrace to become my new hiding place from reality. My hands were craving to slip under Victor's T-shirt and sinking into his hot skin. Pressed to him, my body started living its own life again. I, too, was finally split apart and there were two separate personalities: one of which knew perfectly well that I had to stay as far as possible from this man. The other, however, wouldn't let him go—poisoned by the incomprehensible processes and his influence. It was addicted and its behaviour made me furious. As did the processes. After a deep breath, my reasonable personality prevailed and somehow managed to tear me away from Victor. I coughed before replying in my distance-creating tone.

'You are right, I have grounds for a number of conclusions. Two of them are certainly correct—that I have to get out of here and that I have to get away from you. As you can see, they don't comply with what you're offering.'

I ignored his growl, and my black eyes stared at Toma. He was still standing next to us, his mouth gaping. To my delight, the saline was drying out. I took a breath to say something to Toma, but the hot and cold waves were pinching my skin, my stomach was tightened and the bitter lump was trembling in my throat again, so I turned back to Victor, raising my index finger, hissing:

'You know what? I don't want to waste your valuable time, so I'll admit something to you. I calculated it. Right after I had my first hallucination, I calculated that the possibility of someone like you being interested in someone like me was statistically impossible. After my first night with you, I defined what had happened as an anomaly to delude myself that it was possible. However, unlike people, numbers don't lie, Victor, and they shouldn't be ignored. Never! Your logical, statistically reasonable place is there—in your reality, with women to comply with your standards, with your patterns. You are perfectly aware that I will never fit there. Never! Despite your ability to avoid the truth, you know this! So, whatever the perverted reason for your interest in me, spare your shit about goddamn universes, realities and emotions, and, for Christ's sake, just leave me alone!'

I hit him on the shoulder but he didn't react. He seemed stunned. No facial expressions, not even a twitch; the statue was emotionless behind its armour again. I could only see the burning stakes in his irises. I stared at the blue, only centimetres away from his symmetrical, sharp face, and my stomach was doing acrobatics. The saline attacked my eyes again and I turned angrily to Bear:

'You can drive me if you want, or I'll walk!'

Again, I headed nervously to the exit. I heard Victor roaring at the top of his lungs behind me, then there was a slam. Turning, I saw a broken lamp in the garden. Toma was holding Victor by the shoulders, trying to convince him to not talk to me anymore before we both cooled down, and that he would take me home.

Then Bear walked towards me. I stared at the raging blue over his shoulder. Victor froze. His face and neck muscles were once again engaged in their wild dance. His irises would probably roar like animals, if they could. His fists clenched, he kept taking deep breaths. I was doing the same. He didn't move in my direction. Nor I in his.

φ

When the exquisite wooden gate slammed shut, the unexpected door-issue scathed my back. From behind it, I heard the same raging sounds from Victor's throat like the night before. It crashed into my ears and I shivered, but this time I didn't intend to sink into his darkness. My trainers creaked in the white snow, leaving bloody marks, like a wounded animal.

Toma patiently waited for me to balance my breathing. He rubbed my back but I pulled away. Numb from what was happening in my body, I couldn't even feel the cold. I didn't know where to store all processes, and *the Monster* refused to take the gruesome bite. I screamed continuously, just like Victor. I thought that maybe he did it because it helped, and he also didn't know where to put his devastating emotions.

When I finally got in the car, Bear drove off hastily. I turned the music to the max as I faced a barbaric battle with all my thoughts about Victor. What he had said about emotions was true; it was surely difficult for me to handle them and I was drowning in the incomprehensible neurological processes. Chris was also right that I dealt with them like a Neanderthal with a space shuttle. A space accident was the most logical result. They tormented my body and, instead of coming up with the explanations, my mind was stuck; I couldn't handle all this; I didn't know how to process it. Trying to distract myself, I concentrated on the pattern I had seen. It was banal, but it could at least help me ignore my second personality's howling.

Victor's reality was perfectly in line with the ugly norms of the general reality. I had long become aware that no one cared to fight paradoxes there and would only turn them into norms. Apparently, this was people's usual method of getting rid of them, or at least I assumed so. I found out that the more obvious a paradox was, the faster they were to turn it to a norm and conceal the absurdity. The contradiction in the reality of the Successfuls was no different; a handful of overly satisfied men easily justified the blurred moral boundaries of their gruesome world. There, they insatiably played their deathly chase with an unequal opponent and they accepted this as hunting, because hunting was normal. Then they played politics, business and relationships. They turned these into mere success, into superiority, into something granted. This was also normal. They unleashed their manias, and I guess their manias were accepted as leadership qualities. In this reality, again, I was myself: the crazy girl who lived among normal people, nothing more. I was used to it. I didn't have a third personality who could conveniently fit there, and it would be madness for me to make more compromises with myself in order to stay.

Toma turned the music down. He caressed my head with a sad face.

'Are you OK, Goblin?'

I only nodded but he kept trying to spark a conversation:

'Were you upset because of the animals? You haven't seen hunting before, have you?'

'I've seen many abominations, Toma, but hunting is the most void of justice, isn't it?' It was his turn to nod in silence. 'I told you what upset me, but it wasn't just that. I've told you about *Justice* before...'

He interrupted me, reciting in a low voice:

'Half-black, half-white, your weakest spot. I listen carefully when you talk to me!' He sighed, holding my fingers to his stubble beard. 'And yet, the purpose of weak spots is to strengthen them, and things are not just black and white, even if it's hard for you to grasp that.'

'*Justice* doesn't think so!' I snapped.

'Your black-and-white *Justice* is too young, Nia. She will grow older and greyer, and you'll understand the world better then,' he caressed me with his warm smile. 'Just in case, I insist to make it clear that I have never killed an animal. Well, I had no scruples killing people when I had to, and I hope you don't mind that. Once, however, this rabbit gave me such a hard time that I haven't even tried since. I'm saying this just in case you decide to slaughter me in my sleep,' he tapped my shoulder clumsily. His funny face made me smile.

'Not you. Just Jabba. I don't have any scruples with him. Total creep!'

'It's not easy to kill, wacko.'

'It's not easy to heal, Toma. Killing is quick!'

I raised my eyebrows. He sighed, then continued:

'Maxim's not a bad person. He plays bad 'cause nothing else suits him well anymore. You're overreacting because you're judging him. He is a very close friend of Victor's, and mine, too. He's like family and you'll have to accept him!'

'You two must really reconsider your friends!' I looked at him with suspicion, trying to assess how sure he was in his statement. 'Do you think Victor got it all wrong, like you have, obviously? I didn't mean I was leaving for the night. What I meant was I'm leaving for good. There are no reasons for me to accept anyone and anything anymore.'

'Oh! I guess I didn't get this straight,' he murmured under his breath and I frowned at the mockery in his voice.

'What're you saying there?'

'Nothing! I'm just wondering if you believe what you say.'

'You doubt my intentions or how I'm going to implement them?'

He smirked.

'Both.'

'And why is that?'

'Because of that sparkle in your pupils whenever you look at the other lunatic,' he shot his warm, brown eyes at me. 'I don't know what your emotional deficit or whatever is, but I've seen love dissolved in woman's eyes and I can recognise it. Lust as well. Those in yours are the dangerous kind. Those in his eyes are even worse, and I've never seen them there before. Love and lust definitely corrupt intentions of leaving, even if they're very well-grounded,' he pinched my frowning cheek and carried on: 'To make you feel better, I'll tell you that just like me, Victor doesn't go hunting!'

He gave me a friendly look and I mumbled annoyed:

'Man! After all you've said, you're worried about my mood? I don't care if Victor goes hunting and there's nothing in my eyes for him. I have *Lust*, this one I admit. There's no *Love* in my head, though, and no one there prevents me from leaving. They even encourage me to do so.'

'Why didn't you say so at the very beginning? If there's no *Love* in your head, then everything's fine,' he poured his irony at my frowning face. 'You're gonna have a hard time, you and my bro. He's allergic to "no", you're obsessed with "certainly not", and to make things worse, you're both devoid of any experience and emotional intelligence. Below zero! A total mess!' He made a funny sound, then added: 'Fate truly has a perverted sense of humour.'

'For Christ's sake, man! Now you're crazy as well. No one's gonna have hard times. Stop irradiating me, my brain's bad enough already. A personality split hit me. I don't want to talk about Victor anymore. End of story!'

I curled up in the seat, turning the volume up, but Toma turned it back down for a moment. He leaned over my ear and whispered:

'And, Nia! Don't confuse the words. You don't have *Lust*, you feel it, and I only hope you at least realise how powerful, destructive, and dangerous this feeling is!'

Toma focused on the road while I struggled with my breath shortage. My phone kept vibrating. The text messages clearly showed which demon and which of Victor's manias were raging at different moments. First, the messages were threatening, then commanding, followed by reasonable and, finally, apologetic. Between each different stage, he called, then started sending one text after another, telling me to go back, to answer, to call him. I only replied that we had nothing to discuss. I knew, however, that there was no way to avoid the conversation with him. I was aware that it was not his demons, but his influence on me that was devastating and I was unable to deal with it. I had no counteractive mechanism: no idea how to get out of the trap or out of my personality split. Victor had occupied my head and there was no way to chase him out of there. Despite everything I saw, *Desire* or whatever one might call it, kept torturing me. One of my personalities burned in thoughts of Victor. The reasonable one gave her, and me, slaps.

After a prolonged pause, as we entered the city, I received another message on *Telegram*:

> *When you are in my arms—only then everything is right!*
> *That's where you should be now!*
> *I hate the feeling of not feeling you.*

His proven ability to infuriate me in seconds worked this time, too. I started slamming the screen. I couldn't stop. My anger was obvious, because I sent my messages in numerous parts.

> *How many personalities do you have?*
> *100???*

How do you dare to write this to me??
Why do you even bother your hand with texting me?
It looked pretty fine,
TOUCHING that leg.
Enough of this bullshit!
It doesn't correspond to the objective truth!
You're underestimating me!
You're driving me mad!
LEAVE ME ALONE!

It made me even angrier that I had succumbed to his manipulations, and *the Monster* reminded me that everything served me right. While it was listing all the reasons why, Victor replied and I flashed my teeth at the screen.

I'm making you jealous, I'm driving you mad.
There is also a sense of possession.
At least it'll be easier for you to understand me this way.
I know what we need right now.
When you are mine, we both feel right.
You know all you need to do
is ask.
One word is enough, Nia, and we go there.
To the for-us-only reality!
Там, где другая галактика.
Там, где созвездие ангела.
P.S. You are right, it's bullshit. I don't hate not feeling you.
It drives me to the edge.

The words made me shake. I understood the meaning in Russian and he knew perfectly well that, no matter what, being with him took me there: to our parallel reality, to some distant galaxy, to an angelic constellation. Or perhaps a devilish one. He was good at taking advantage of this superiority over me. He tempted me, just like a devil at a crossroads, summoning my second personality from the dark. She, on her part, was ready for any compromises. My fantasy went crazy, hypothesising on "what we need right now". I gulped, feeling my throbbing pulse. Toma looked at me with suspicion while I was trying to hide how Victor had influenced me even from a distance. I tried even harder to not let him affect me in this way.

Remembering what had happened just a while ago helped, but it made me sick, too. I was fighting my second personality, when *Reason* said smugly:

There is no Jealousy *here anymore. I settled this matter. We do not have any emotions. I will think of a way to deal with* Lust, *too. Pull yourself together, wacko!*

He was right. The sea urchin in my head was gone. After *Reason*'s savagery, all that was left of it was a pile of thorns. Jealousy seemed to have dissolved in my organism like poison. When I thought about the shadows now, the waves of suffocation were much worse than any sting the urchin had inflicted so far. *Reason* had dealt with the intruder in my head, but he was wrong about the emotions. I had no idea how to handle the feeling in my stomach or wherever it is that feelings live. Victor had occupied not only my mind, but that secret place, too. I squeezed my head between my hands. I could hardly wait to get home and get stoned with a bottle of wine. I decided to not reply to him anymore, doubting my reactions.

What Victor had evoked and then stuffed in my throat cut like pieces of glass. Swallowing became painful, and *the Monster* didn't want to help at all. I had to pile up all my disappointments on my own. My oesophagus was screaming. So was my stomach. So was I. These bites were too big for my mouth, for my organism.

If this is what emotions are, I'm giving them back. I don't want them. I'd rather be a freak. This is not for me, goddamnit. I'm just not meant for this. This madness is not for me. This is not my chaos!

SEVENTEEN

While we were parking, a strange car in front of the garage caught my attention. The house was dark and the vehicle didn't look like one of Chris's. I approached cautiously to see a round, colourful ribbon. It was a *Tesla*, matte black and tempting me in the night. Toma nudged me in its direction. He took something from the bonnet, then put a key in my palm, attached to a Tasmanian devil keyring.

'He wanted to surprise you. He made them sweat to deliver it while we were still in Italy, and I guess they managed after we left,' he smiled. I didn't react and he started lecturing: 'First we'll have to improve your driving though. I don't care if Victor allows you. I won't let you drive it before I make sure you won't injure yourself. Not that you're going to drive it on your own, but still, this electric toy turned out to be surprisingly fast.'

I growled and Bear looked at me with suspicion.

'Now that's unbelievable!' I bit my fist.

'What's wrong? You don't like it?'

I didn't even bother to reply. I unlocked the door to the house nervously and hurried to the garden, pushing hard on the phone screen.

It's great that you're not superior to me, right, Victor?
Good thing you don't demonstrate it.
Your respect for my boundaries is great, too.
Good thing you don't arrogantly ignore them.

He instantly replied:
I guess you arrived already.
You're frustrated because I bought us an "eco-friendly" car, or what?

I was overcome by the urge to call him and shout. Again, I succumbed to his manipulations even though they were as clear as day. Determined to avoid the crushing influence of his timbre, however, I chose the safer option and continued writing:

You're perfectly aware that we have arrived.
Thanks to the security, who you told me you were going to remove.
I explained clearly and firmly why you should NOT do this,
but nevertheless, the car is here with a ribbon on it.
I won't even comment on the other things that happened tonight.
Since you are a specialist in semantics, I hope you'll grasp that "frustrated"
is an exceptionally feeble word.
I hope you'll also grasp that "a common mistress" is a category
in which I'd never fit.
Nor do I have the intention to do so!

I took the lotus position on the table outside. Then he provoked me again, clearly aiming to spark the conversation I wanted to avoid:

I'd like to become a Nia specialist as well.
To help me do this, would you describe exactly what you felt tonight?
Your reactions and expectations, too.
I'm trying to communicate with you,
but apparently, we must both learn how to do this.

I read the messages several times, then decided to take the opportunity of remote communication to clarify my opinion in writing.

Finding out that you lied to me again about the security frustrated me.
The reality I saw up there blocked my mind.
The shadow you were with stunned me.
The car shocked me.
Altogether, these things are beyond my acceptable boundaries.
Spare me the awkward conversation, I won't be able to handle anyway
and let's just get all this over with.
I don't communicate well, it's true,
but the difference with you is that I don't even want to.
I told you I had boundaries and anything beyond them is unacceptable.
This kind of relationships is all there.
The Monster was right—it's not for me.
Now I realise it as well.

He read the message immediately, but there was no indication that he was typing. I was staring at the screen when Toma startled me:

'What's wrong with you again? What is this reaction?' He was leaning against the door to the garden with raised eyebrows and two glasses of whisky in his hands.

'Toma, don't take it personally, but now it's my turn to abstain from explaining. At least this you can understand. Please, leave me alone to clear my mind.'

He came to me and kissed the top of my head. I instinctively pulled away. He deliberately ruffled my hair, then handed me the drink.

'I understand, Goblin, and I'll leave you to yourself. If you decide to talk—I'll be upstairs. All you have to do is knock, share, and maybe you'll feel better. There is someone to listen to you now, Nia, and I hope your beautiful messed up mind understands this. You don't have to go through everything on your own,' he patted my shoulder and I snorted, but Bear just gave me his warm smile before walking in.

My second personality, teamed up with my immortal *Curiosity*, made me shout:

'Toma!'

'Yes?'

'Well, I'd like to ask...' I started crushing my fingers, trying to force myself to shut up, but I guess the expression on my face said it all.

'I know what you'll ask me. I saw who Victor was with, but I don't have the answers to your questions.'

'Why?'

'Because I don't know much more than you do. All I know is that her name is Natalia. He attends public events with her. They have this weird... you know,' he stuttered and I interrupted him to put an end to the awkward conversation.

'I'm sorry! I'm not tactful, as you might've noticed. I shouldn't ask you about that, and it's not my business, after all Victor and I don't have... you know,' I waved off his compassion clumsily.

'I don't know anything anyway. Victor's personal life is a taboo topic. It always has been. He doesn't talk about it to me or anyone. You can see the same as I do—the women around him, the details, his attitude. He pays their bills, he takes care of them—his mistresses. You defined them accurately. Shadows. You know perfectly well that there are others like her. This is his reality, Nia.'

'Cars?' The word slipped from my tongue and I cleared my throat.

Maddie's vicious voice echoed in my head:

If he fucked you, even once, you might get a lot: money, gifts, an apartment, or maybe a car! Who knows? He seems generous to me.

'What about cars?'

'He buys them cars, jewellery, clothes, he takes them on vacations, accommodates them in his properties. Then he makes the disproportionate deals. That's his pattern, isn't it? That's where he expects me to fit, too. That's what he expects me to be?'

'By mistresses I mean that he pays for them. You know the meaning. They have houses, cars, I don't know about the other stuff. They sometimes travel with him,' he sighed. 'I told you a couple of times that I didn't imagine you in this position. I don't know if it's a pattern or a deal, but he always gets what he wants, under his conditions. I guess the same goes for his relationships as well. Those women seem to accept and comply. That's it. You decided to stay, even though it was clear from the very beginning. You knew what he was like, Nia.'

'Of course I knew! That's his reality. I am an observant person, I just...' My throat went dry and I moistened it with a sip of whisky before continuing: 'You're more than right—I don't imagine myself in this position. My decisions so far were influenced by irrational factors and it's high time that I start ignoring them. I shouldn't have asked you these questions. Excuse me, but right now I'd really rather clear my mind on my own.'

He gave me a sad look, opened his mouth to say more, but then decided against it and headed to the living room. This time it was my reasonable personality who stopped him at the door.

'Toma.'

'Yes?'

'We have an even number of options. Either you move out of here tomorrow, or I will. I prefer the first one. Victor and I negotiated our possible relationship, but the truth is that I can't create a pattern for two. I already confirmed that he has many realities, but they are not too different from one another and there's no place for me in any of them. Now it's time for me to deal with this crazy mess. You and I can eat pancakes when you have time for that.'

He cocked his head and sighed.

'Don't act hastily, Nia! Try to have a normal conversation with him. You both suck at communicating, but you can somehow learn. You shouldn't make decisions when you're angry. And you shouldn't make decisions when it's dark, because they almost always prove to be wrong.'

'I'm not angry and your other statement is more than correct. Recently, I made a disastrous decision when it was dark. Now it's more than urgent to deal with the consequences and it can be in the dark again.'

I gazed at him from behind my barrier. His eyes were searching through the invisible wall I had erected between us. I gave him a fake smile, then repeated in a seemingly cold tone:

'Move out tomorrow and don't put it off.'

'We'll discuss this in the morning!' His face was full of compassion, but his firm gaze made me decide not to argue. Bear disappeared into the house.

I downed the glass of whisky, trying to fix the bitter taste in my mouth. I was struggling to block out the thoughts about Victor, his muddy reality, personal life, and all other nasty details. To no avail, of course. The truth was obvious; I had known from the very beginning what he was like and his expectations as well. I had ignored the facts and now he was simply repeating his pattern with me, which was quite natural. The problem was the weed in my head and the fact that I allowed it to influence me. The other obvious truth was the irrational disappointment that was taking over me from the inside.

I had to find a way to focus and draw up my next logical steps: a roadmap for action. I needed to put order to my mind, my body, then to the basics in my life. After all, I lived in this amazing house with this interesting, messed-up roommate. I had some challenging work ahead, a chance to earn money, run away, and have non-grey days. There was no rational reason for me to waste my energy on something that I had calculated, double-checked, then calculated again to be statistically impossible. In Victor's reality, no place for me existed.

The cold interrupted my thoughts and forced me inside. I took the same lotus position on the kitchen counter, sucking on a cigarette and a new glass of whisky. Wine's effect is too slow, I wanted to get intoxicated as fast as possible. While I was staring at a scratch on the wall, the phone vibrated in my hands.

We will talk, whether you want it or not!
I'm coming to get you.

In my thoughts, I growled at Toma. No doubt he had told Victor about my demand. I certainly didn't want to talk to Victor; I was tired of him and the excruciating processes he evoked in my body. *Rage* was still roaring and I was sure that I couldn't hide him. I had no control over my second personality and her addictions, nor did I have any idea how to communicate with him. Besides, *the Monster* was neighing so annoyingly that I couldn't talk to myself, let alone to Victor.

Could you respect at least one of my boundaries and not come?
I really don't want to talk to you right now.
I DO NOT WANT TO!

I stared at the screen. He was typing, then stopped, then started typing again. He was probably erasing and editing. I expected a long message but all I got were two letters and a full stop.

OK.

The fairy-tale defects came over me again. I was satisfied with his reply, and yet the irrational expectation of a chase was also there. I snorted, shaking my head. I really needed to consult a normal woman about these issues.

I tried to distract myself by surfing the net. My jaw dropped as the leading news popped up. A massive campaign was launched in a number of countries to combat drug trafficking. In the picture, there was a bunch of proud, fat ministers. I recognised one of them from the yacht—the one who had groped the prostitutes while they were snorting from the tray. I laughed out so loud that I had to press my palm against my mouth.

'Well, isn't this ironic! This picture must stand next to the definition of "irony" in the dictionary. What a goddamn, perverted reality! Those jerks live in parallel universes indeed. God, are they all schizophrenic? What did I even expect from Victor when he, and everyone like him, is even more insane than me!'

Shocked by the paradox, I continued reading. News about an official event a couple of hours before I went to Victor's appeared. As expected, the stunning shadow whose name I already knew glittered by his side. Natalia was again perfectly matching the presidential superiority, complementing his impeccable look at some fancy-event-for-something. I didn't even finish the news, just growled at their flawless photo, then set my phone aside.

I was just blowing a big O of smoke, when Chris appeared in ripped jeans, Cuban boots and a black T-shirt with a kitschy skull on it. The numerous scattered tattoos on his arms drew even more attention under the short sleeves. On his wrist, there were studded leather bracelets, and his dark blond hair sprouted in all directions. He pinned his colourful irises on me. A sexy goldfish peeked from behind him. Chris seemed stunned, as if he was seeing a ghost. He shot over to me and took my face in his palms.

'Why...? What did the creep do to you?' In his eyes, there was a mad look I had never seen before in him. 'NIA?'

'What's wrong with you, man?' I squeezed his fingers, but he wouldn't take them off my cheekbones.

'Why are you bleeding, for Christ's sake?' His raging tone frightened me.

'Oh! It was a boar. I'm fine, just dirty.'

Chris narrowed his eyes with suspicion. He took the kitchen towel, soaked it thoroughly with water, and started rubbing my cheeks.

'You went to Victor, didn't you? Why are you here?'

'I live here. Do I need other reasons?' I snapped but apparently the chaos in my head was visible from my facial expressions.

Chris clenched his jaw and the gold fish's high-pitched voice joined in:
'Are we going upstairs, or you wanna talk here?'

'Get out!' Chris hissed.

At that moment, he looked exactly like Victor when he would freeze his employees. Chris pulled some money from his pocket and threw it at the girl. She took it from the ground and disappeared before my goggled eyes.

'Even a douchebag like you shouldn't treat his girlfriends this badly,' I wrinkled my nose and he squeezed my cheeks even tighter.

'She's a whore. Nothing more.'

He pulled my sweater, then he helped me take the jeans off as well. He hurled them angrily to the side and wrapped me in the blanket from the living room. I settled myself back on the counter. Chris took my face in his hands again. His expression confused me and I tried to pull away, but he kept me in place, pressing his forehead against mine.

'I'm sorry for saying all those things to you. I'm a total douchebag, I know it. I was so afraid that you were not coming back.'

'Of course I was going to come back. I live here. And don't be sorry! You were right to call me a mistress—after all—it was me with a man, surrounded mostly by mistresses. He definitely expects me to be one of them, too.'

'It's up to you, Nia, whether you're going to be a mistress or not. It's not up to Victor or to any other man. There are thousands of places you could live. Victor could buy you this whole fucking city, if you wanted it. As I saw outside, he already took care of your ride.'

'Of course he did! He won't stop demonstrating his fucking superiority,' my annoyance escaped my mouth.

Chris pulled away to light two cigarettes. He gave one to me, leaning against the edge of the table.

'What happened? Explain the blood first, 'cause you really freaked me out,' Chris shook his head, looking at the clothes on the floor. Then he poured whisky for both of us and did several lines next to my thigh.

'Nothing happened! I simply crashed head-first into your fairy-tale world. I hit the best part: lies, hunting, and princesses for banging. That's all.'

'He's an idiot!' Chris rolled his eyes.

'Come on, Chris! You know perfectly well that the idiot is me. Of course he'll be doing these things. The typical leader of a shithole like our country. He spends his laundered money, he has fun with other people like him, and he bangs unreal beauties. It's logical. It's normal. I'm the distorted thing that doesn't fit in the picture.'

'You're not! Stop underestimating yourself,' he squeezed my knee.

'I certainly am. Look at me! Do I fit there? Can you imagine him attending a shiny reception with me? He's the personification of fucking "everything". The reality of the Successfuls was tailored for him, and what am I? A crazy freak with messy hair,' I let my hair fall loose on my shoulders.

'God, you women have something defective in your second X chromosome[48]. How come you always underestimate yourselves? Do you get special training in this when you're kids?'

'It must be some special female skill and we're getting better with every new generation,' I sighed sadly. 'I'm also a douchebag, Chris. And now I'm a douchebag with a split personality, sex addiction, and fairy-tale defects. When I'm with Victor, everything seems to be right, but when I'm not with him, it gets increasingly worse, like chewing on broken glass; I don't like the taste, I don't know how to swallow it, and the problem is certainly me.'

'It's not you. This is simply not for you.'

'I know. I told you the other night. I'm either cursed or doomed to see the ugly things—the defects only. Everything around me flashes like a mistake. What's so difficult—I can fuck him, have fun, take what he can offer? I could file down an edge or two and find a way to fit. But I get my mental blocks instead, like a true freak, because of patterns that are normal to other people. "Schizo, crazy, needs to see a doctor!" Why would I want all this? Is it me, of all people, who will fix the whole goddamn world? Does the world even want to be fixed? Why try to explain that it's warped and insane? Why can't I just fit into the picture, Chris?' I sighed after my rapid tirade. My mouth was pouring my honest thoughts and he kept following my muscle reactions carefully.

'It's not that simple, Smarty,' he caressed my cheek with care.

'It's not simple at all. It's fucking hard, I'd say. I'm sick of it, Chris! I'm sick of being doomed to live this way. Why can't I be normal? Not different? Not a freak, cursed to only see the faulty patterns? Why can't my eyes be normal, at least? The world seems so distorted, but maybe it's my eyes.'

Chris moved closer to me and spoke in a quiet, hoarse voice:

---

[48] *The human genome is stored in 23 chromosome pairs. Usually, women have two X chromosomes (XX), and men have one X and one Y chromosome – author's notes.*

'No, Nia. You can't be anything else. And you don't have to be. All you need to do is change the way you see yourself,' he lifted my chin, his colourful irises pierced mine. 'Your eyes can't be normal. The normal ones are human and yours are angelic. They are special. That's what I think but you don't get it at all.'

He pressed his warm palm against my cheekbone, then ran his thumb from my nose to my ear and down the whole outline of my face. I was studying his strange facial expressions when he continued:

'To me, Smarty, you're a rebel angel. That's how I choose to perceive you. You've seen the faulty patterns in heaven, too, and I'm pretty sure you were the same annoying, stubborn know-it-all misfit there as well. You made other angels' feathers stand on end. Eventually, they cut your wings off, and you landed ass-first in this gruesome world. That's how you ended up here!'

He took a deep draw from his cigarette and exhaled in my face.

'What nonsense are you talking about, man?' I gaped.

'You don't see mistakes, Nia. You're gifted to see the golden ratio at a glance: the Fibonacci sequence over the lines on my laptop. You are able to perceive the divine proportions in a warped world, woven of chaos. You are pure perfection and if someone doesn't understand it, that's only because angels are hard to understand,' he smiled sadly, running his fingers over my face. His expression embarrassed me even more than his words.

'Chris, your facial expressions are confusing me right now. You don't intend to kiss me, do you?' I muttered.

He leaned over me and his lips touched mine gently. Then he kissed my cheeks and pulled away while I was gaping.

'I do intend to kiss you but not in the way you think. In this fucking life, Nia, I lack three things: a partner, a friend, and love. You could successfully provide me two and a half of them. Even though I adore your angelic face, angelic mind, and your broken angelic soul, the last half cannot come from you.'

He snorted one of the lines and kissed my thigh next to it. I blinked foolishly, not knowing how to react, but he carried on:

'In some other life, however, when I won't have messed up so badly, we'll meet again. Then I'll kiss you and love you just the way you deserve and I'll tell you every day that you deserve it. I'll never let you underestimate yourself. Now I love you in every way, except for the one in which I can kiss you with passion. But that doesn't change the fact that I love you!'

I instinctively snorted at his smiling face.

'Baddest'

'Me loving you is *baddest*?' He raised his eyebrows in surprise and I pushed him away.

'Why is everybody so obsessed with loving today? Toma was talking nonsense about love, and now you are too. Do you all go crazy at full moon?'

I moved in embarrassment. Chris propped himself up with his arms on either side of me and stamped a juicy kiss on my forehead.

'It's disturbing, isn't it? That horribly irrational interaction,' he stared at me insistently. 'Smarty, when did you banish *Love*? Before or after you convinced yourself you were a freak?'

I pushed him to get down from the counter, but Chris hugged me tightly. He kept me in place, entwining his fingers in my hair, and whispered in my ear:

'Well, obviously angels are hard to love, too.

I growled and he laughed.

'All right, all right. I won't inquire about *Love* anymore, don't run! Tell me—hunting or whores? What made you so mad?'

I remained silent and he handed me a rolled-up banknote. A minute later, I was rubbing the cocaine into my gums while he was refilling our glasses, urging me to reply.

'Not sure. It's just that nothing in his reality suits me, Chris. I guess it was mostly the humiliation, or my personality split, or the fucking processes that drive me crazy. The hunting and the whores helped a lot, too. And, please, don't tell me they're all normal. I already heard that!'

'Firstly, only those who consent can be humiliated. As I can see, you don't consent, therefore you're not humiliated. Secondly, I warned you that you were a Neanderthal with regard to the processes. It was obvious that you wouldn't be able to handle them. About the whores... Yup, it's normal for someone like him. Hunting isn't, of course. I'm a rational person after all—I'm a vegetarian and there's no way for me to accept this.'

'Me too, almost a vegan even. You're right about the women, too. It's normal and we're not in a relationship, after all. In fact, it's none of my business, but not up to my two personalities. They totally split and now one of them seems afflicted.'

'All your personalities are highly afflicted, Smarty,' he squeezed my knee with a smile, but in a friendly, not cynical, way. 'You're jealous, aren't you.

Your facial expressions are different. And you feel other emotions that you can't handle, either.'

'I can neither handle them, nor like them!' I growled at his chuckle. 'I don't know what they are but I don't want them. I can't even stuff these... things... down my *Monster's* throat. They're so disgusting, even it wouldn't chew them. I have to end this, Chris. I must fix this goddamn mess before I go completely out of my mind.'

I took a sip and then changed the subject because it was intensifying my headache.

'What about you? Why are you hanging with whores? You have your half love, half Monster, don't you?'

'I do but, as you can see, it's not here! I have to treat my madness somehow. How do you treat yours?'

'I don't. It hasn't ever been sick until now.'

Chris laughed, staring at me. He was standing between my legs and he slipped me to the edge to give me a tight embrace. I squeezed him, too, leaning my tired head on his shoulder.

'I don't like being touched, you know,' I murmured.

'I know. Me neither. You don't have sexual intentions for me, do you, squeezing me like this?'

'Of course I don't! I suffer from addiction, but it's not to you,' I fell silent for a moment, frozen in the same position. 'And yet, since you're my friend and partner, you'll practise sex with me if I don't have other options, won't you. You'll be my fallback?'

'No, Smarty, I certainly won't be. I will never practise sex with you,' he took me in his arms and we settled down on the couch. I know other tricks to make you feel better, though—the usual powdery way, partying, and I have some great news today, too.'

'What is it?'

My questioning eyes followed him as he went back to the kitchen to get our glasses. He did two more lines for both of us, keeping cheekily silent with the whisky in his hand. He sucked the cocaine off his fingers before he spoke with enthusiasm:

'Are you ready for the news that will make you put an end to all this crap and dive into an entirely new adventure?'

'I guess I am, but it's only an assumption. I can't give you a precise answer because...'

'All right, all right. Don't philosophise, I know what you mean. I told you I spoke with a friend about crypto, right?'

'Yup. And?'

'He's waiting for us in Singapore. He found the Korean guy we need. I don't know what his conditions will be, but I'm pretty sure this meeting will open unexpected new horizons to us!'

'We can do some money laundering, too,' the high-pitched words slipped out of my tongue as I frowned at my own reaction.

'You're thinking about the fucking Victor again! You're not focused. Enough. Ignore him!'

'I'm trying, but he creeps like a white walker[49] in my mind, damn it! The fucking Victor is a toxic disaster.'

'Put up a wall then, and leave him on the other side,' he grimaced, then continued: 'About the money... I've thought about it, but you can't use crypto for laundering.'

'You certainly can. You just haven't figured out how,' I put my nose in the air and he hissed, playing offended, then laughed.

'I told you, Smarty. We're gonna make tons of money together, but you'll need to defeat the white walker in your mind first,' he looked at me reproachfully.

I lay on my chest on the couch and Chris started playing with my hair. I muttered into the fabric:

'Sounds like an epic battle I'm not armed for. I have no other option but to cram *Reason* into a knight's armour.'

I propped my chin in my hands and stared at Chris.

'What the hell is *Reason*?' He asked.

'It's complicated. Never mind! You know you'll have to pay for this trip, right? Right now, I have zero crypto and zero fiat money[50], and I have to give back what I've spent of Victor's, too.'

'You have a million-dollar mind. That's all you need, just start using it for a good purpose!'

---

[49] *In the Game of Thrones series, the white walkers are an ice horde of zombies who intend to destroy the human world – author's notes.*

[50] *Fiat money is a means of payment imposed by law within a certain territory, issued by a central bank. Most national currencies today are fiat currencies, including the dollar, the euro and others – author's notes.*

'I'm on it, all right! When are we leaving? I wanna get out of here as soon as possible,' I propped myself up and Chris hugged me in silence. Leaning on his shoulder, I hurled my legs over his lap.

After a while, as he was twisting a lock of my hair around his index finger, I started muttering with disappointment again.

'You know, man? I was so obsessed with proving myself to the fucking Victor that I never asked why the hell he even needed to launder his money. I'm not quite right in the head, am I? I am not all there'

'You're not, but the problem is not in you. Women have this weird defect regarding the need to prove themselves. I've observed it many times. Again, I guess it's the chromosome's fault. Don't worry about the rest—I'll pay for travel to the Moon, if you'd like me to. If that's what you want, we're leaving right now.'

I stared in bewilderment, and he served me a line.

'How?'

'By airplane. You can't swim, can you?' He scrolled through his phone, grinning. 'There are two flights to Doha tomorrow. One is very early. I'll get the tickets for Singapore there, 'cause we don't want your circus to follow us again.'

'What about Toma?'

'We'll think of something. Relax. You didn't tell me—do you want us to party, or you need a rest?'

He hugged me even tighter as I pondered my decision. He wrapped us both in the blanket, searching for my favourite *Game of Thrones* episodes. I had almost made the decision to get some sleep, when a bang flew from the door. Then a commotion. Steps. Shouts in Russian.

My heart skipped a beat. Victor stormed in before I could scream. He pushed me on the couch and pulled Chris over the backrest, then pressed him against the wall. He squeezed his neck and pressed him. He wouldn't stop.

Adrenaline attacked my head, distorting the images. Before I knew what I was doing, I ran to them. I started pulling Victor's arm, but he didn't react. He just stared at Chris. Victor's veins tightened to the brink of bursting and his breath hissed loudly. He had his profile to me, yet I could clearly see his insane expression.

'Stop it! Let him go! Victor!' I yelled.

'I will destroy you!' He hissed through his gritted teeth in front of Chris's face. Then he shouted the same thing over and over again, while Chris was barely able to breathe.

I shoved myself between Victor's strong arms. Behind me, Chris's muscles tensed. I reached for Victor's chest and tiptoed to draw his attention.

'Let go of him right now! Come to your senses, for Christ's sake!'

I kept punching him, but he wouldn't react. I swung my arm as far as I could in this position and space and slapped him. He moved his insane gaze directly to me. He looked more than intimidating and my stomach suddenly shrank. He let go of Chris and took hold of my wrist. Toma came running down the stairs.

'What's going on here, damn it? Kaov!'

Toma stared at Victor, who wouldn't take his mad eyes off me.

'Stay here with the junkie. Nia and I are going to have a private talk,' his voice froze the air around.

Victor pulled me up the stairs and Toma blocked the way behind us. I could hear him fighting with Chris in the living room, while Victor dragged me into my bedroom. He slammed the door behind his back and leaned over me. I started hitting his chest with all my might, yet I couldn't move his huge body even a bit. His jaw tightened and the hiss of his breath filled the space. His irises were still burning, but at least a fragment of the blue was back. His voice slithered out, quiet and hoarse, even more freezing:

'You're curious what happens when you provoke me? Is that it, Nia?'

He grabbed me to rudely place me on the dresser and stood between my open legs, his breathing quickening again. He slipped his hand into my hair and pulled back to centre me in front of his wild face.

'I asked something?' He hissed through his teeth as I remained silent. 'Are you experimenting with my demons, snorting and letting that fag touch you? YOU! Would you like them to get the junkie up here, so you can watch the result of your experiments?' He roared.

I spoke in a nasty, firm tone:

'I don't want to watch anything anymore! Let me go right now and get out! You're insane!' I tried to push him but he pulled my hair even harder.

'I should've never let you stay here in the first place, but now things are going to become quite different, Nia! From now on, all you do is what I say, what I want, and I don't care about your whims anymore. Am I clear? I tried to respect your decisions, I allowed too much and this is ending now!'

'You allowed? Do you even hear what you say?' I snapped and did my best to continue in an even meaner tone: 'Save your absurd orders for your mistresses or whatever they are! What do you mean by respect? Your lies, your manias, or the fact that you didn't even fulfil my simplest request to not come here and comply with my boundaries this one time?'

'I didn't lie. I wrote "OK" because I didn't want you to be nervous until I came here. I didn't say I was not coming. I got pretty nervous though, watching what you were doing here.'

'In which one of your parallel realities is this not a lie, damn you! More cameras, huh? Is that how you respect my boundaries?' A crooked smile stretched on my face. 'I also got pretty nervous when I watched what you were doing there, but I didn't storm in and I didn't grab your chick by the throat. Did I? Who am I to you? What gives you the right to keep tabs on me?' I pushed him again. A sparkle shone in his irises, then he moved closer to my cheekbone.

'I'm not gonna explain, Nia! I can do whatever I deem necessary. You can't. It's about time you grasped that,' his even tone was freezing my cells. 'How did you even imagine that I'd leave you here without surveillance? We're going home and you're not coming anywhere near this house anymore. I will decide where you'll live, you won't go out alone, or perhaps I'll just make things easy for myself and lock you up. Come!' He grabbed my wrist but I snatched it away.

'You are absolutely insane! I'm not going anywhere! Hold your horses, your manias, and get out!'

Victor held me in place, the mad flames swaying in his eyes were brighter than ever. The mania that was possessing him darkened his face. He cocked my head to the side and sucked on my neck. His lips crept up the skin, then he spoke in a hoarse voice:

'I hold my manias when you are in my arms. You're coming with me and don't confuse this with a question.'

'Get off me! You are a maniac, truly!' I pushed him, but he squeezed harder.

'My demons are going wild, your entities are going mad, because we're missing something. Isn't that so, my lovely dear?' He spoke as if in a daze, pressed against me, tugging my hair. 'We missed you being in my arms and that's why today is such a hard one, right? Only when you're in my arms is everything right!'

He whispered in that familiar destructive timbre and, contradicting any healthy, sick, or cartoon *Reason*, my body reacted with a deep spasm. I prickled under his touch. His fingers chased the sharp shivers over my shoulders, while I was struggling to balance my breathing and not let my second personality succumb to his intoxicating influence.

'I know it's true, Nia. I can feel it with my every cell—you just don't comprehend it yet. You don't realise that you're all mine, you don't accept it and your mind rebels.'

'Stop it! Let go of me, Victor!' I tried to convince him, stressing every syllable.

'Why would I do that? I know that's not what you want!' He sank his whisper into my ear, then bit it.

'No, you certainly don't! Let...' I paused, detecting the treacherous vibration of my voice.

'Your favourite words to drive me crazy. When will you finally understand that you're already all mine, Nia? When will you accept it? When will your mind stop rebelling?'

His beard scratched me before his lips found mine. His taste flowed into me, soaking into each of my addicted cells. I growled in his mouth that I wanted him to let go, but then my tongue licked his, as if trying to lick my words away. Then I repeated them again.

'You keep insisting! You want me to let go of you? Well, what I want is for your every molecule to finally understand your true wish. At least your body is honest. It has been mine since the moment you interrupted the rhythm of my steps with your crazy black eyes and then drove me mad. You drove me and all my manias mad, Nia.'

Victor bent my neck even more, running his fingers over it, then continued to my breasts and twisted their tips through the T-shirt before moving the scorching touch down my belly. He pulled my bikini aside. When his fingers glided on the moisture I grunted:

'Damn! This is not normal. Stop it!'

I shifted nervously. His irises shone even brighter, but his face became even and cold-blooded. He was vigilantly watching my uncontrollable bodily reactions.

'What is not normal, Nia? That you crave being mine, or that you refuse to admit it? I don't know much about "normal", but I'd bet on the second one.'

I kept silent, doing my best not to moan while he was running circles on my swollen tissue. He was arrogantly playing with my senses, perfectly aware of my addiction, of which he skilfully took advantage. Sucking the moisture off his fingers, he continued:

'Unlike you, your body speaks to me clearly and firmly. It's telling me what you really want. I get along with it really well.'

He growled, slipping two fingers into me rudely. My second personality moaned lustfully. It was taking over me while everyone in my head, including me, kept screaming at it to stop. Victor moved his devastating touch like a predator. He was breaking me, crushing my intentions with only his two fingers. Under his influence, I was becoming an even more twisted version of myself. My defected cells reacted with more moisture and more spasms. I held his head, gripping his hair. A deep, salacious moan crept from my throat.

'That's right, my lovely dear. Don't let go of me!' Out of his mind, Victor stared at me. His madness was showing through the glassy blue eyes. 'Now tell me what you want!'

'Nothing!'

Some small part of my mind was still fighting the drug. It was scratching my brain, but only managed to mumble faintly as Victor's touch burned my words down to ashes.

'How much of nothing, Nia?' His superiority over me sprang from the mad irises.

My body was already under my second personality's control. Victor was perfectly aware of the capitulation in his arms, of his influence. He had no hesitation in taking advantage of his dominance and now embarked on a new journey. He aimed to finally take over my mind: to shatter my intentions, my decisions and my will with the supremacy of the chaos that he had created in me. In my mind, I was furious that he was ignoring my words but the perverted, irrational desire for him being inside me was thickening underneath my skin.

'You want nothing at all?' He whispered in my ear, touching me with his own perverted desire—hardened and on the verge of bursting.

'Nothing from what you have to offer!' I roared at his predatory face.

In a second a hard thrust stretched my tight tissue. He sank to the bottom of my addiction. I screamed, and Victor came out slowly. He kept torturing me, touching some pulsating spot at my entrance. He was controlling both the abstinence and the drug, at the same time. I wondered why he was so angry with me about the cocaine when he alone was the most toxic poison.

I hissed, gripping his hair as tightly as I could, aiming to cause him pain. But he didn't pay any attention and invaded roughly again, squeezing my neck. He started moving vigorously, his lips pressed against mine. He kept kissing and biting my bristled skin. I bit back. Apparently, this was the only way for us to communicate; it was our perverted and insane way.

The compressed ball of sensitivity in my groin throbbed painfully, spilling devastating heat throughout my whole being. I was writhing. The electricity beneath my skin bent me. My body whimpered, craving for its disintegration, and Victor felt this even better than I did. I pressed myself against him as my tissue contracted in a deep spasm, but he instantly pulled out. Then he continued teasing the throbbing bundle, just enough to keep me on the brink of the chasm that he had created.

'Damn you, Victor!' I swore loudly. He released my neck and my forehead leaned against his chest. I started moving my pelvis, but he stopped me.

'Do you realise that, despite everything, you don't want me to let go? Will *Reason* finally surrender, so I can give us what we both want and make things easier for us? You place is in my arms, Nia. Nowhere else. *Never* else!' His tone was freezing.

Victor lifted my chin, his measuring, glassy irises piercing me. They demanded adoration. Obedience. Acceptance. Compromise. One of his demons, or maybe a whole bunch of them, blazed in his mad eyes. He sucked my breath, my tongue, my lips, moving slowly inside me. Patiently, he tortured me. He knew every moan and inch of mine perfectly. He had studied me with the diligence of a maniac, in frightening detail. Now he was sadistically gliding me along the cutting edge of pleasure, enjoying unscrupulously every second of my torment.

My muscles squeezed him. I lost control. Victor pulled my hair and bent my neck again. He stared at me mesmerizingly, keeping me in place, growling:

'Do you realise that being mine is your future? Your life! By my side, you will accept my reality, my demons, my manias. Everything! I want it, I get it, Nia!'

He was invading violently. My cells vibrated powerfully to his rhythm. He detonated them. My body betrayed me, allowing Victor to scatter everything around. My hands fell to his biceps, and he squeezed my wrists tightly to his chest. My second personality moaned for him to keep going and

Victor penetrated abruptly, raising the raw pleasure from the darkness of my mind like an avalanche. I couldn't stop. That's the thing about addictions, probably about manias, madness, and emotions as well—you just can't resist them. Maybe normal women know how to handle all this. Maybe they easily make better decisions, but twisted girls like me definitely don't.

The earthquake of decay that Victor caused dismantled me to molecules. It ruined me. I heard occasional screams and curses in my head, then it went all silent. My darkness sank me. A light erupted under my closed eyelids, then another one. I bit some skin, not even knowing what I had bitten. Victor's commanding voice told me to open my eyes and the blue grabbed me. All I could see was the blue, blurry, while I was turning to dust in his hands.

'You are mine!' He growled as I was coming. I heard him as if through a tunnel. Just like in my nightmares.

Victor froze. His stern face softened; he even seemed embarrassed for a moment, probably realising how brutally he had crossed my boundaries. He was aware that he had shattered my intentions to pieces just to get what he wanted. With arrogance and cruelty, he had subdued my weakness. I wished I could slap myself, or at least my second personality who had allowed this. Struggling to balance my breathing, I didn't take my eyes off him. He didn't come with me. This was not his aim and, on his expressionless face, I detected a note of satisfaction. He was punishing me, proving his influence and dominance over me. He deliberately crushed me in his superiority and self-control.

Victor zipped his pants in silence. It was only interrupted by the scratching sound of his fingers on his beard. I kept staring at him, my eyes narrowed, my legs still open wide. His demon was gone, but in the reflection in his irises, I could see mine. The one Victor had summoned in me. I realised what he was capable of and, most importantly, how he could destroy my reasonable decisions. It was the first time I saw myself as a toy in his hands. He was in full control. It was nice and warm in his arms, but it was too narrow for me. My opinions, my boundaries, and my very self didn't matter there. They were never going to matter. I was probably even ready to break off one of my star edges, if he wished me to do so the next time he pressed me with two fingers. If I was an angel, like Chris said, then Victor was definitely the demon who had cut my wings. In his eyes, I saw someone who looked like me, but not myself. I saw a creature who was already dangerously close to voluntary depersonalization. A version of me who was subject to the processes that I didn't know how to handle or swallow. All I knew was that they were the soil in which life compromises grew.

What Victor had summoned nibbled on the bare nerves of my body. Maybe it nibbled on my soul, too. I didn't know if it was *Love*, like Toma had assumed. It looked more like a bloodthirsty *Beast* who tore at my organs, and I didn't want it inside me anymore. I wasn't aware where emotions lived, but *the Beast* shattered everything: my stomach, my liver, my bile and, above all, my cardiac muscle. It tore it fibre by fibre. I had to save myself before I became all patches, or all dust.

I defiantly adjusted my bikini. My moisture was on the dresser and I slipped on it while I was getting down. Victor's arms blocked my way. He kissed me but I didn't kiss back.

'We're leaving and we'll talk...'

'I want you to leave!' I ducked under his left armpit.

'Nia,' he turned me to face him. His body radiated heat again and I stared at him with contempt. My tone became firm:

'This is madness, and you crossed every boundary. You lied, you came against my will. You attacked Chris, you dragged me here, you yelled, saying a whole bunch of completely unacceptable things. I didn't want you to come, Victor! I didn't want to fuck! But that's what happened nevertheless!'

'You wanted this, Nia. You just...'

He tried to interrupt me, but I continued:

'I don't refer to the savage desires of my flesh. They are also some madness, just like yours. I refer to my decision that you didn't respect. Again. My decision! You did me just so you could prove your control. You want to crush my intentions, my common sense, my opinion. Everything! You want to subdue my mind, Victor, then adjust it to your standard and expectations. That's what you've been doing from the very beginning because that's what you're used to. You can afford this, they let you do this, and you just do it. That's what being yours means! This is the fucking truth! The only truth,' this time I cornered him with my gaze, and he silently avoided it.

I squeezed his cheekbones, staring at him even more intently.

'That's who I am. It's true, but it's not the only truth. I'm sorry, I...' He growled as I hit his chest.

'It doesn't help. Get out!'

'I told you I didn't want you to see my demons. I simply don't know how to...'

'There's nothing simple about this! This is not for me, Victor. I don't want this. I warned you to mind your manias. It was obvious that you use them to justify your abominable disrespect of all boundaries and your intolerable behaviour. There's nothing we can discuss anymore!' I hissed spitefully.

He studied me, sinking his teeth into his fist.

'I didn't do anything that your body didn't want me to do. You know that I struggle with the right approach and communication,' he squeezed my shoulders.

'It was not about my body or my sexual addictions. Obviously, you don't hesitate to take advantage of them. It was about me! You cannot accept me if I don't fit into your twisted ideas. I know this madness, Victor. I understand it because I also cannot accept anything beyond my own ideas,' I gazed into the blue. Blazing. Burning.

'I can accept all that is yours. You're the only thing I can accept, damn it!'

'That is not what I saw!' I snapped.

He pulled me to him but, this time, I firmly escaped his embrace.

'Damn it, Nia!' I trembled as he his fist hit the wall. 'I have no idea how to communicate with you! I don't know how this works, don't you understand? I don't know how to do it! I've never been forced to search for another way and that's why I'm like that. Please, come home with me. We'll somehow...' He bit his lips. His irises pierced me, demanding and firm, but now I could see something resembling fear in them.

This time I started rummaging through his mind. I sank to the bottom, as if there was something priceless for me there. His eyes darkened. Victor was aware. He knew perfectly well what he was, what he aimed for, and what he expected. He knew his pattern and followed it maniacally. He was just like that; he was not going to stop until he had destroyed my last drop of resistance—until he sucked the last compromise out of me. His demon would rather burn me to ashes than give up. At any cost, Victor would try to fit me into his pattern. He was obsessed with finding the proper place of the broken tile that drove his mind crazy. I had clearly realised this the day we fought over the penthouse. Probably he had, too. Since then, I had been conveniently avoiding the indisputable fact. I had been voluntarily sinking, until I got to the point of crunching the pieces of glass he had shoved into my throat. I guess I deserved all this after my numerous irrational decisions.

As I stared at Victor, *the Beast* that tore at my organs suddenly went wild. It sank its teeth simultaneously into all tissue from the stomach up, piercing between my fifth and sixth ribs. It was biting the fibres of my cardiac muscle as I realised that the time for rational decisions had come. I was thankful for managing to recognise the priceless moment to let go because the burden had become too much. It was like a trampoline on which you bounce off and fly up or hit the bottom to scatter into millions of pieces.

Jumping on this trampoline of life, I was calculating. Unfortunately, the second option was more probable. It was statistically more likely that Victor would shatter me into pieces because I didn't know how to bounce off him. I didn't know how to save myself. Perhaps I was only seconds away from Victor's words, timbre, and touch that would again intoxicate me and drown me in the degrading hypnosis in which I lost myself. If this was *Love*, I couldn't understand why books described it as nectar, ambrosia. For me, it was pure acid: burning, torturing, destroying. A truly malicious and ferocious *Beast*.

All of a sudden, I was overwhelmed with admiration. Admiration for women. For the women around the world able to overcome all this. The ones who won this bloody life battle. The ones who saved themselves. Their minds might be weaker than mine, but they clearly had something else. Something more. They didn't need my IQ, nor the powers of my intellect, nor my skills in quantum physics. They had an ability more precious than anything else: the ability to let go, to overcome *the Beast,* to save themselves. They chose themselves before anyone else, and—my god—this proved to be hard.

A typical human paradox!

It's so damn hard that these women deserve a monument. A hundreds-of-metres tall monument in their name. A fucking monument for the heroes who chose themselves. For the heroes who save themselves.

Reason suddenly popped up in my mind. He quietly hurled his arm over skinny *Confidence's* shoulder. *Pride* and *Justice* followed with their heads up high. They were all silent; not arguing, not murmuring, not reproaching me. All they did was watch and encourage me, reminding me that they were there to guide me. As always, they were going to walk by my side, even through the ruins of my life. Like a real family. And they will never abandon me. And I was never going to be alone again. *Reason* and *Confidence* stepped forward and nodded:

You can do this! You can, Nia!

Victor's touch startled me. The heat of his hand sank into my cheekbone.

'Are you OK, my lovely dear?'

'Yes. I was thinking.'

'I'm begging you, let's get going and we'll talk. We'll learn how to communicate. We'll work it out somehow. I'm really sorry...' He caressed my face and I gazed at him.

What Victor didn't understand was that his every attempt to fit an irregular geometry like mine was mathematically doomed. Useless resistance. Our only possibility was determined by the Hobson's choice[51]. If this situation of ours was a game of chess, the only right move would be to put it to an end. I kept the data to myself. He would have only started arguing, promising, guaranteeing; he would have probably even sworn against mathematical laws. At that moment, he would have denied the numbers. People do that. They would rather avoid the truth.

I traced the outline of his symmetrical face with my finger. I realised that I was doing this for the last time, but my rational decision was to lie.

---

[51] *Hobson's choice is a right of choice in which the only option is to accept or reject a certain offer. In this situation, it is assumed that one could choose, but there is actually no choice because there is only one thing they could possibly do or have – author's notes.*

Victor's notion of truth was blurry enough, and I chose to take advantage of this fact.

'I need a few days to make up my mind. We will talk, but I will choose when. Get the security, Toma and all your madness off me! Allow me to assume that you can truly respect me and my boundaries—that I'm not yet another mistress to you.'

'Nia! Stop it!' He squeezed my neck, but I continued calmly.

'Victor, if you want us to speak again, you should leave now.'

I stared at the burning blue. He tried to say something, but I firmly cut him off, saying that we could start anew only under this condition. He took a breath and fell silent, not even twitching behind the armour of his statuesque expression. His influence fought to bend me again. I fought back. My second personality sank its nails from the inside. It screamed like crazy. Victor grabbed my cheekbones. His hands were shaking. My stomach tightened at the thought that I was never to see him again, but I gritted my teeth behind my barrier. One of the personalities behind his barrier wanted to object and drag me downstairs, but he took control over it and nodded at my deceitful request.

φ

Leaning against the door, I listened to the sound of his steps. I heard Toma and the security guards buzzing in the hall, then a commotion while they were leaving. The jeeps roared and I counted twenty-five seconds of silence before heading to the living room. Toma was gone. Chris was alone, staring at the laptop on the table. Victor had left bruises on his neck. I sat down guiltily opposite him, but he wouldn't even look at me.

'Are you all right?' I took hold of his wrist, but he pulled away, not caring to reply. 'There are cameras in the house. Victor saw the cocaine, then you kissing me... I'm sorry about that,' I started explaining quietly, but he interrupted me. His facial expressions showed irritation and the cynicism was also back.

'Your freshly-effed appearance is all you should be sorry about. Does he do you whenever and wherever he likes? Nymphomaniac!' He scolded me and I frowned. 'Unlike you, I know exactly the sociopath he is, Nia. He could shoot me, I don't care. Of course there are cameras. That's not the problem.'

'I'm not a nymphomaniac, douchebag! I suffer an addiction—a split. I do also suffer emotions, and I obviously can't handle all this. You think it's easy on me?' I hissed, rubbing my temples.

'It's not easy, but obviously you treat your madness the way he does! With sex!' He rolled his eyes and I snapped:

'Bullshit! If you knew about the cameras, why didn't you tell me?'

'Because I had replicated the signal, nympho! The problem is someone hacked me. Don't you get it?' He shouted angrily.

'Get what?'

'There's someone like me, Nia. Kaov has found someone with my skills. That's how he got your medical record, and this is bad. Too bad!'

'Explain!'

'Victor doesn't need me anymore, Smarty,' he took a generous sip before finishing: 'My skills are my most powerful weapon, and he's obviously neutralised it.'

'More hints. Be specific, for Christ's sake!'

'I can't be more specific than this—I'm off with the morning flight. You decide whether you're coming, or you're gonna stay here to fuck like a rabbit, then complain about being a mistress, and then repeat the cycle all over again. Decide what you want for yourself, Nia! I need to get out of here, to come up with my next moves, and deal with the Korean.'

'What happened with the "I need a partner" thing?' I raised my eyebrows and he snorted.

'If you chose not to come, I'll still give you half of the money. I wouldn't screw you. I just need to get away and clear my thoughts.'

'Great, 'cause I need the same! Don't treat me like this!' I raised my voice. 'You are a douchebag, aren't you!'

Chris's jaw dropped as I hit the table.

'Don't get angry at me, Smarty. I got pissed that someone searched through my data. What happened upstairs? Kaov seemed so mad that I expected him to drag you to the car by the hair. How did you even manage to make him leave?'

'I just...' I sighed through my teeth. 'I'm not in the explaining mood. He just left,' I poured myself whisky and he stared at me with fascination.

'You're not just mad. What's this I can see in your psychopathic face? Disappointment, bitterness... Damn, is that a heartache? Are you having heartache now, wacko?'

'Man! Call that goldfish to cure your madness 'cause it's taking over you again,' I snorted a line before continuing: 'If you must know, this is what my face looks like after the sex that I'm addicted to. If there aren't any more dumb questions, explain what we're gonna do,' I propped myself on the table and he raised his eyebrows.

'Woah, woah! Stop hissing. If you are the one who needs treatment, I'll find you a male goldfish for nymphos. I just don't know how he's going to go at it without touching,' he stuck his tongue out and aimed a middle finger at the wall. 'Good thing there's no audio signal, or the freak would come back raging.'

'Let him rage as much as he wants. I don't care.'

'You really are mad, Smarty,' he lit a cigarette. 'I need a few hours to fix what was hacked and find out what they have searched. Then I'll replicate the signal again. You come up with a plan on how to get to the airport without your entire circus following us. To the VIP entrance, then we'll be alright. The manager is a friend of mine, he's gonna cover us.'

'OK,' I grunted.

'Decide when you will tell me what happened, though, 'cause I'm not dropping this, and we have some long flights ahead,' he stared arrogantly at me.

'What is it to you? Victor is supposed to get the security off me, but I don't trust him,' I rolled my eyes.

'OK. Find a way—you're the smart one, right? The plane takes off at 6 a.m.'

'I will! I'm sick of this circus, too,' I headed to the second floor.

Chris's friendly, non-cynical voice stopped me on the first step:

'Nia, a while ago I told you that I didn't get this type of relationships. However, I became convinced of one thing in the most violent way. You must also understand it and you should do it now. Remember it, drive it deep into your genius head and never forget it!' He fell silent for a moment, staring intently at me.

'I doubt my genius after the last few weeks... What is so important for me to remember?'

'Remember if saying "yes" to someone, means saying "no" to yourself, the right thing is to fall silent, even if you want to shout. Then you must gather all your strength and leave. You will drag yourself on your stomach, inch forwards on your knees, crawl until you're bleeding, if you must, but only towards the exit. There is no other salvation!'

'I will remember this, if it's so important,' I snapped, because my actual reply got stuck in my throat.

Perhaps I should have stayed with Chris, I should have admitted how hard and incomprehensible everything was to me. Perhaps I shouldn't have gone through all this on my own. However, being alone is a difficult habit to root out.

I started tapping my fingers in an odd rhythm instead, walking up the stairs to my bedroom. As I always did.

On my own.

AFTER ONE

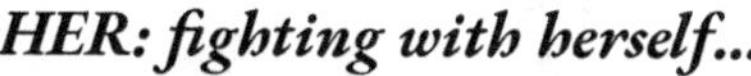

HER: *fighting with herself...*

It was over.

However, my last step towards the terminal was not anything like joy. We entered the cosy VIP area at 04:02. I murmured how repulsive it was for me to be greeted by two even numbers on the electronic dial.

I stared at a spot on the colourful trainers for a while, then threw another glance at the clock:

04:07. Damn it, was the time stuck? What's wrong with it?

There was nothing wrong with time, only with me. The last couple of hours had been treating me like a sadist with a knife: ruthlessly cutting into me, shattering me, shaking my intentions. I was in pieces, and my thoughts were in patches. It was me that got stuck—somewhere between what was reasonable and what was desirable. A narrow crack appeared to exist there, where claustrophobia was like a spring rain in comparison. Left without air, I suffocated, I felt sick, and *the Beast* was raging. I even felt feverish. My second personality was trying to come up with a way to avoid the truth and crawl back to Victor's madness. It kept scratching my chest from the inside like a wild cat. I even checked whether the traces were visible on the outside of my skin. Everyone in my head was holding hands, silently supporting me.

I was messed up. Victor had messed me up. This was the truth and it had happened with my consent. Before that, I had been twisted, but now I was also defected. I didn't let go in time and the damage was probably irreversible. A new *Monster* was what I needed, so I could stuff down its throat what Victor gave me. However, I was a child when I had created my *Monster* and had since forgotten how to create another. I had to cope on my own now: to chew, swallow, and throw up, again and again, until I managed to cleanse my body.

Damn! It's fucking Love's *fault! She's the reason they can't stop writing foolish books. Chris was right. No one has come up with the proper sequence of actions to deal with* Love. *At least maybe that's how us crazy people become slightly more normal, and normal people become slightly crazier. Inching forwards on our knees, dragging ourselves on our stomachs, crawling until we're bleeding—we are all the same in this madness. Is it "normal" for* Love *to be like this? Do people understand that she's actually a* Beast?

I was explaining to *Reason*. Seated on the floor of my mind, he kept nodding with compassion. Everyone else was still, except for the *Beast*, who was nibbling between the fifth and the sixth ribs. I was moving my neck and my shoulders—as if stretching. But, in truth, I was in a battle against the defected part of myself. Suddenly, Victor's crushing timbre echoed from the darkness of my mind:

Only when you're in my arms everything is right.

It was true. Despite everything, that was where I felt in my place for the first time. The worst place possible. At 04:56, I realised the depths of my despair. Only in his poisonous arms—only there did everything seem different. Colourful, extraordinary, far from the warped reality, high above all realities. It was another galaxy, another world, my space, my constellation. I breathed freely there. Even my cells became different; their rhythm changed. In his arms, the goddamn golden ratio went right through me, and, from a crazy freak, I turned into an ephemeral, divine creature that vibrated at 432 hertz[52].

---

[52] *The 432 hertz frequency is considered divine because it combines the properties of light, time, space, matter and the DNA code. Some scholars believe that the 432 hertz vibration corresponds to the golden ratio, also known as the "divine proportion". It determines the ratio of everything in nature and is a symbol of beauty and harmony. The 432 hertz vibration influences the atoms of human DNA and this frequency is believed to represent the tone of the universe – author's notes.*

I sank into a memory, needing Victor's touch, even just in my thoughts. I expected to land in a moment in which he had extracted devastating pleasure from me, but I found myself in the memory of that unfortunate night that I had left the yacht. I had lied to him: I could handle the claustrophobia. In fact, I only escaped because I couldn't handle the emotion that suffocated me, burned my organs, drowned me, and poisoned me. It was as if someone had stuffed a tube down my throat and was pouring down its sticky bitterness. That was how I perceived the emotion. Since it was devoid of any logic, I couldn't understand, handle, or want it. He knew I was lying to him. He could feel it. He could feel me.

Victor was fully overwhelmed by emotions, raging demons, or whatever they actually were. He recognised mine as well. He had somehow managed to keep his on a leash, but not always, with his firm self-control. But this process was like a plastic explosion for me, and I had reasons to doubt the strength of my walls. Grandpa had explained it to me numerous times, so I was technically aware. The bomb planted in me, however, turned out to be Victor—he placed his explosives deep down and, at the same time, he held the detonator. Only distance could save me, otherwise he would press the button and scatter me into millions of pieces. The other option was even worse, though—implosion. In this case, I would blow myself up on the inside, break, or bend in order to fit into a misshapen relationship.

The memory of that night came to life again. Victor was sitting there, at the table before me, seemingly grasping my request to not try to fit me into his pattern—to accept me without distorting my shape. He agreed and even believed what he said. He was struggling to convince me, but we still represented two quite different, distant galaxies. Even his madness was different from mine. Then, I drifted to the constellation where only him and I existed, and all our curves and edges could divinely fit into one another, but only when I was in his arms.

I smiled at him and touched his face, filling my lungs with the scent of musk. For a moment, I forgot how his repulsive reality had slapped me. Being in his arms was so deceptively warm and cosy. Deceptively "my" place. Exact term: toxicity. I guess that was what toxic relationships looked like...

'NIA! Damn, Nia! Wake up!' Chris was shouting at me.

'Man! What's wrong with you?' I stammered.

'God! What were you doing, for Christ's sake?' He was pale, shaking me vigorously.

'Nothing. I didn't do anything,' I muttered.

A quick look at the clock surprised me—05:37.

'You were tapping your fingers, murmuring something. I couldn't wake you up. What was that?'

'I don't know. Nothing. I was just thinking.'

'Get up, quick! They're gonna drive us to the plane. They're waiting only for us.'

'All right, I'm sorry. I didn't do it on purpose,' I looked around, as if I had fallen from the sky into a strange city.

'You have a Palace, don't you? Toma was asking me about some castle, and I figured it out. Did you just go there?' He pinned his colourful irises on me.

'I do have one, but I wasn't there. I follow a strict entry and exit protocol 'cause it's dangerous.'

'Were you thinking about Victor again?' He hissed reproachfully, then pulled me to the exit.

'Yes,' I frowned at my sincere reply.

'Well, my genius Smarty, welcome to *Love*'s fairy-tale reality,' he smirked. 'A reality in which all of us are fucked up.'

'Why?'

'Because, sooner or later, we all bump into someone who makes our thoughts leave us and run away. It's often the most ill-matched person, of course. Then our thoughts drive us crazy. Then they crush us, tie us in a knot, crucify us, and mess us up. That's what you're facing. It shall pass, but it's a shitty process, especially when you haven't learned how to preserve yourself.'

'Damn! This fairy-tale reality will turn out to be worse than the general one! Are they all bad?' I was bewildered.

'Hell, yeah! And this is only act one of *Love*'s fairy tale.'

'God, this world never ceases to amaze me with its craziness. Good thing I'm not going to count to two in this story.'

'I doubt if you'll be able to get out that easily, but your fairy tale might be different. Who knows, after all it's you writing your story.'

φ

At 06:00 I turned my phone to airplane mode and looked at the date. I laughed out loud, and Chris stared at me.

'What is it?' He nudged me but I kept giggling.

'Today. Today is One!'

'One what? I don't get it.'

'I was to count "One" on this day, Chris. Today was supposed to be the first day after finishing my internship. The day in which I didn't know what to expect. The first fucking day of the rest of my life.'

'You went through far more than an internship for the last couple of weeks, huh,' he also laughed, getting comfortable in his seat.

'For sure. I had no idea what priceless knowledge I'd get: "The Art of Madness", "Ten Sex Side-Effects", "How to Save Yourself from Depersonalisation". There are more, but I don't wanna mention them 'cause they involve a personality split and a *Beast*. The internship of life! Serves me well!' I rubbed my eyelids and Chris held my hand.

'You did well, Smarty. You made the right decision and you crawled out of the swamp. That's all that matters. Everything else will be sorted, one way or another.'

He started rubbing my fingers.

'I did well, but not on my own.' I stared at his puzzled face. 'Chris, as soon as we get there, I want you to get me drunk and tattooed. You'd better even sedate me. I'm afraid of needles and I want this tattoo right now. OK?'

'Where?'

'Right here,' I pointed between my breasts. Exactly between the fifth and the sixth ribs.

'Pretty shitty spot. It'll hurt quite a lot. Why there?'

'Because whatever lives underneath these bones, it needs a guardian,' I pressed my lips together and he smirked.

Chris went silent for a while, then he spoke in his friendly, non-cynical voice:

'The soul, Nia. I guess the soul lives there. And who's going to guard yours?'

'*Reason*. I'm putting a tiny *Reason* there. And not only him. Come to think about it, *Confidence* will be right next to him. She deserves that. This is where she belongs too. They both saved my soul or whatever lives there. At least up until now.'

'How are they going to tattoo them? They don't have a form.'

'They certainly do! Didn't you see *Reason* on my trainers? I know what they both look like perfectly well. My angelic eyes, as you called them, can clearly see them along with the mistakes.'

Φ

I plugged my ears with the earphones. I was thankful to Chris's money for giving me exactly what I needed at that moment: a business-class bed to crash on. The engines roared along with the chaos in my head. The plane sped down the runway and I wondered what was provoking the strongest vibration—the traction, the acceleration, *the Beast* that tore into me, or the curiosity of what was ahead. Maybe it was the missing-someone-feeling I was bound to get familiar with in *Love*'s fairy-tale reality.

We took off. The repulsive, dirty, gloomy city remained far below. It didn't torture my mind anymore. From this height, the curving streets resembled a circulatory system with grey blood. The city was waking. It was fading into the distance, going to greet the new morning without me. Routine life was devoid of its chance to swallow me. This day and the last were not the same. This is quite a good new beginning, isn't it?

My ears filled up with music and then, suddenly, my eyes were full too. I winced at another violent jab in the ribs. *Созвездие ангела*[53] exploded in the headphones while I was ascending to my new reality in the company of two puddles of saline. My chance for something more was waiting for me several thousands of kilometres away, yet my throat was tied in a knot again. I still had no idea what was coming next, but I had most probably saved myself from a predetermined life.

Today I was to count the first day of the rest of my life. Right now, however, I was counting only to comfort myself. I started tapping the fingers of my right hand in an odd rhythm. I needed numbers more than ever. I needed my escape rhythm more than ever, yet I didn't even know from what I was running, nor to where. I also needed to hide more than ever, but my skin was no longer a good hiding place.

ONE!—I closed my eyelids and the saline rolled down my face forming two round, salty tears.

HIM: *wondering who he was...*

The table lamp was driving me crazy. Sitting in the leather armchair in my office, I studied the mistake in the symmetry of its patterns. The rhythms of the lightbulb sound and the clock were wrong and they drove me crazy

---

[53] *The angels' constellation – Jah Khalib. Translator's notes.*

as well. 04:02, and I was going mad already. When I checked again—only 04:07.

Damn it! The fucking hands aren't moving! I will explode by morning!

Falling asleep was impossible, even though I had a full day of diplomatic heavyweight boxing ahead. I despised the clatter of hypocritical diplomacy, and negotiations with two delegations awaited me. It was clear who wanted what, but no one wanted to give anything. An annoying irregularity, but her calculations nailed them. She helped me this time. In my real world, I settled arguments in quite a different manner to get what I wanted. However, I had to be someone else for 3 years, 4 months and 26 more days. I had to play my well-crafted persona. I had to survive until the end of this war. And, most importantly, I had to win.

The smoke of my cigar curved to the ceiling. My head was on the verge of exploding because of her and her madness again. Minutes dragged like centuries, and I felt the urge to shatter the clock.

Sergey grunted in the phone:

'Yes!'

'Bring Natalia!'

The leather creaked under my fingers. I was clutching the armchair, trying to find my obsession. My demons, my manias, and my madness stretched me from the inside.

I will get her by force. She is mine, she just doesn't understand that. Not yet, but she will understand. She is mine. Her place is in my arms. She can't stay there! She has no right to set conditions or keep me away from her. I will lock her up until she realises all this. She will hit, hiss, she will be mad, but she will understand me. I'll just get her and lock her up!

STOP! her voice echoed in my head.

The sound of it created a perfect vibration in my cells. It tamed me. It saved me, even from myself, when I needed salvation the most. As it had all my life.

ONE!

For many years, her "One" had echoed in my mind, saving me, but it didn't work now. Not anymore. Not without her in my arms. It was driving me crazy; my energy for her burned me from the inside, it destroyed me and not even my dust was left behind.

Nia occupied my mind again. First, I knocked over the lamp. Then I pushed everything from the desk to the floor. I began to hit the wall. She was torturing me, and I kept yelling at the maddening black eyes:

'You are mine! You are mine! You are mine!'

At 04:56, I was going completely insane. I took a breath to suppress the sharp pain in my fist. Natalia had entered the room. Frozen at the door, she was staring at me. She had never seen me without my control. She didn't know my demons, nor my madness. Only Toma and, partly, Nia were aware of them. It took me a second to put my usual expressionless face back on and the fear in Natalia's eyes disappeared. One of my toys was watching me silently with her artificial face. She couldn't even understand how unprofitable our contract was for her—a disproportionate deal. She was just another possession of mine. A faceless, plastic doll made solely for the rude mouth-fuck I intended. Dozens of women like her were there to satisfy my desires, but only one woman—my one and only—created them. She owned them.

I watched the flawless body at the door when she muttered:

'Are you alright?'

'On your knees, Natalia! The rest is none of your business!'

She was choking on my violent thrusts. I held her still as I fucked her throat with hatred. Disgusting whimpering sounds came from it. I needed to destroy at least part of my energy, but I couldn't. It wasn't possible anymore; every little bit of my energy belonged to someone else.

Nia invaded my mind again. She was the one kneeling before me. It was her messy hair between my fingers. The scent of her suffocated me. She always smelled like goddamn gummy bears. I was absorbed in the aroma of candies and her skin. Her tiny hands clutched my wrists. She couldn't even encircle them, yet her fingers were the strongest chains. I was addicted to her touch. Obsessed. Dependent. Addicted. I slowed down to slip carefully through her soft lips. I wanted to feel her heat and her moisture. I wanted her to be mine, to realise my adoration, and I craved teaching her how to adore in return.

She sucked, hungry for me. She purred, then she moaned. The vibration of her timbre drove me crazy. Her maddening timbre. She wanted me in this savage way of hers, the same as mine. Unrestrained, truly, purely, no limitations and no taboos—the sheer demon of lust. Devouring madness. My head exploded.

'NIA!' I growled through my teeth, gripping her hair. I was going to fill her throat with myself, but she pushed me. I immediately lifted her to kiss her, hug her, to make her feel my adoration at last. To feel me.

Natalia's teary eyes stared at me. Her trembling hand reached out for me. I pulled away. I despised my toys touching me with their plastic fingers.

'Go!' I ordered in a composed tone. It was 05:37.

She obeyed and disappeared in a blink. This was my way of communication in my well-negotiated relationships. This was actually my only way of communication. I despised her, myself, and the whole warped world. There was only one salvation for me and my soul now. I gritted my teeth, hitting the wall. I didn't know how I could go through the next few days without feeling Nia by my side, but I had accepted it. I had to because I had lost my control. All I wanted was to make her feel that she was mine as soon as possible, but she wasn't ready. My wretched impatience had summoned my demons, carrying me away from my angel. I had to fulfil her request now. I had to comply. Just the thought of it drove me crazy, but her eyes looked scarily firm. The fear that she might realise that I was a total freak prevailed. The fear that she might run away from me.

Damn! The only thing I'm afraid of are 48 kilos of madness. My 48 kilos of madness!

φ

I replaced the whisky with coffee. The housekeeper brought it along with my meaningless schedule. Yet another fake day had begun, and I had to endure it somehow. A new morning was waiting on the doorstep, ready to become the same as yesterday's, like every other morning before that. For me, however, today was going to be torture. The following days, too. I woke up my assistant to get her to reduce my schedule to official meetings only. Then I escaped to the bedroom. The whole circus was going to arrive at 6:00.

I hate six in the morning. It's unbearable. It's only bearable when she's in my arms. Everything is right then.

I managed to put up with the advisors for almost an hour. Again, they merged into one dull image. Their mistakes were so obvious. They were glowing. They were burning my brain. Their conclusions lacked any logic and that irritated me, all they did was abuse numbers. They abused politics as well, even though it proved to be a simple game. I ran away from their annoying voices to the fantasy in my mind.

I had penetrated, licked, and kissed her for hours. I could feel her. She fell apart in my hands. God, I crave her touch! She was shining in her specific, angelic way with bright flashes in her black eyes. She smelled like me. I exploded in her to mark her in the most primitive, masculine way.

Mine! Mine, at last!

She loved it when I was in her, I could feel this with my cells. I loved being in her, too. When she is in my arms, everything is different, distant from the common world. A new galaxy. Damn, I can't exist without this feeling anymore!

All of a sudden, the memory of watching her with that boy attacked me. I was mad that this squit was touching my angel. He was in her, he could feel her. Someone else was touching her! I exploded. She let him do this, and it's a privilege reserved for me only. My superiority over everyone else. Mine! Even then, that damned night when I watched them, I wanted to go and take her. I managed to hold myself back. I got her to calculate forecasts instead because I didn't want her to call him again. She was ready in half an hour, though. I broke everything around meanwhile. All I wanted was to take her and lock her up, but I couldn't. She would have run away. My chance would have run away. I knew she was already mine, I could sense that, even through the camera. While she was on top of him, her rhythm broke, her counting was interrupted, there was chaos in her mind. She wanted to be mine. I saw this clearly and distinctly, yet she hadn't realised anything yet.

I got back to my fantasy. Nia was standing there, in my mind, naked, sweaty, messy-haired, biting her lip. We were doing another thing I dream of doing with her: playing chess. She was eating her wretched gummy bears. There's only one point of difference between her IQ and mine, and I hated the fact that we could never play chess. Her medical record says that she must stay away from chess boards. She was brilliant, her brain beyond amazing, but all those countless patterns made her drift away. She could get stuck in her own mind. It was a hiding place for her. Apparently, she has created those entities in her head for the same purpose, yet I didn't know what she was hiding from. The thought of her disappearing—even within herself or for her own sake—terrified me.

Thankfully, she didn't notice the chess boards in the house after that goddamn night when I thought she was dead for a moment. She was too angry. A tiny, raging Tasmanian devil that I simply don't know how to control. I ordered for the chess boards to be removed after that. They were everywhere and she would be tempted. It had happened before, and I still didn't know how her beautiful mind functioned. Like in a fairy-tale, she could have pricked her brain, sank into her mind, and I could have been forced to search for a prince who could wake her up. Freaks like me are no good for that. All I can do is adore her in my freakish way. That's why I lied again; I set everything up, so she could be in my arms in the end. She would probably hate me from the bottom of her heart, if she found out that I was putting her to a test that night, at the restaurant. I didn't think it'd end like this...

In my fantasy, Nia was making a checkmate move with a devilish smile on her face. In reality, my phone started screaming. I was startled and quickly regained my usual composed demeanour. It was my common sense calling, and he was probably calling to nag again about putting Nia at huge risk. He was so annoying and yet so right. He had even sent his wife and my godson thousands of kilometres away to protect them. All he cared about now was that Nia was in danger, he didn't want to hear about me going crazy without her. He was a painfully sincere friend. A true brother, always ready to punch you in the face if he had to.

'Good morning, Toma.'

'Where is she?' He hissed and my muscles tensed.

'What?'

'Her phone is off. I came to bring her pancakes, but she's gone, Victor. And so are the suitcase, all her belongings, the colourful trainers,' there was panic in his voice. I struggled not to shout in front of everyone. 'You didn't explain anything to me, bro. I care for her, she's not another one of your whores. Again, you didn't tell me anything. You made me leave her alone and now she's gone! The fucking house is empty! Where is Nia, damn you?!' He yelled like crazy.

I was trying to get myself together when Sergey came. He motioned in the direction of my office.

'Kaov. Come!'

I followed him, clenching my fists. Shutting the door behind me, I threw my phone at him.

'Where is Nia? Where the hell is she? She was supposed to be under 24/7 surveillance!' I yelled at the top of my lungs. The room was soundproof, so I could rage there as much as I liked.

'She went out with the *Tesla*. The boys don't know about the new car 'cause you didn't give me enough time to instruct them. I checked the transmitter an hour ago and I found out it was at the airport.'

'And you're telling me now, you motherfucker?!' I hit the wall instead of his head. 'Send people right now to bring her right here!'

'She and the junkie hacker just took off for Doha. It's a transit flight, I guess.'

'You shit! You have one hour to tell me where she's going! Find her!'

'Kaov!' He shot me with his icy Russian eyes. 'Let her go! Don't involve her in our mess!'

I was startled. Anything other than swearing or snorting rarely escaped his mouth. Nevertheless, I started shouting:

'Don't tell me what to do! Find her immediately!' I grabbed him by the collar, but he didn't twitch. Nothing could make him twitch. He was a tough sniper. A killer. Just like me, before I became my new and even worse self.

'Victor,' he hissed, squinting his eyes. 'I've been looking at your face and running behind your ass for twenty goddamn years. We are where we are, because you were always the leader and we always followed, but you must pull yourself together now! We're in the middle of a violent, bloody war. We're in deep. The shit is up to our noses, Kaov. If you put the girl on your shoulders now, we will all drown. Everyone will drown.'

'I can protect her. Do as I say!'

'You cannot!'

'I can take care of her! Fuck you! I can solve this...'

He interrupted me rudely for the first time in his life.

'You cannot! Not now. Remember who you really are, what your business is, and why you became the president of this goddamn shithole!' He hissed, retreating towards the door. 'Don't forget your enemies, because if they sniff out that at last you, you crazy mother fucker, have a weak spot, they will destroy the weirdo. They'll destroy her violently. And then you will be wailing like Fatass when he found his wife and the kid cut into pieces.'

'This was a long time ago!' I hit the wall again.

'And they've been long waiting for your weak spot! I can hook her up to one hundred security guards, and it still won't be safe. Why do you think we keep our women away? They're not like the whores no one cares about. People could tell what's going on when she's around you, Victor. Even you, you sociopath, can't hide this. You lose control and it all shows. Toma was right in trying to get rid of her since day one. He knows you well and he knows you won't stop. He knows how this madness will end and, god knows why, he cares about her. You must stop now, Kaov, because they wouldn't think twice. They'll use her to destroy you. Hold your horses and don't lose focus!'

'Forget my focus and find her, you shit!' I punched the desk.

'Our world is not a place for love, Kaov. At least now you know the fucking price we all pay for our decisions. You will pay it too!' He slammed the door.

I roared at the top of my voice. The Russian spoke the truth. My warped reality was no place for love, adoration, or the madness that pounded in my chest. Whatever that was, it existed because of her. It pounded because of her. I had been waiting for the impossible for so long. I was not going to be defected or insane anymore. I was not going to be a freak, killer, just a demon lurking in the dark. Damn, I couldn't let her go. She was in my arms, at last, and that made everything right. With her, I was not going to be doomed to a life full of only hatred, resentment, and revenge. My nightmarish life was not going to be predetermined anymore. She had made me assume that I might be granted the chance for something more.

SHE is my chance for something more.

SHE is my awakening madness.

I slumped to the armchair. I didn't know what was ahead and my manias crept up my bones again. My demons stretched me from the inside. I craved burning this whole warped world, my mistakes, and myself to ashes.

My only salvation was her voice in my head and counting along with her. The only thing I knew I shouldn't do was take my chance for something more; I shouldn't have her. But there was no reality in which I could stop myself.

I tapped my fingers nervously in an odd rhythm, waiting for the free-line signal in my ear.

'Victor! My friend, it's been a long!'

'The reason is obvious, I think.'

'I know, I know. You're too busy with politics. How can I help you?'

'There's a woman on one of your planes to Doha.'

'You want me to return the plane, or her?'

'No. I want to know her final destination.'

'All right, my friend. Are you sure you don't want me to take her back?'

'Yes.'

'If you change your mind, just call me. I will tell you where she's going. I insist that you visit me soon, though.'

'It'd be my pleasure. I will come when I have some spare time.'

'Or you could come officially, as a president. Business is business, but politics won't harm,' he laughed.

'You're right, my friend. I owe you.'

'Not more than I owe you, Kaov. I'll call soon.'

He hung up.

Soon has the skill of turning into eternity.

An eternity in which I have to choose between her and myself. A nightmare.

A nightmare, in which I have to decide who to save.

Or how to save us both...

ONE!—echoed with the first second, but it couldn't tame me anymore.

Not without Nia in my arms.

THEM: realising...

First, it burns you. Then, it freezes you. Eventually, it destroys you.

Love or madness?

It soaks into your cells; it sets them on fire and burns them to ashes, leaving only desolation behind.

A love where you either lose or find yourself. *A Beast* who either devours or gives you the chance for something more.

A madness. Madness is the illusion that you ever had a choice, when everything is contained in a past moment, doomed to a grim fate.

Their grim fate.

Their toxic *Love*.

Their chance for something more.

Their awakening madness.

They seem to be fleeing, hiding, saving themselves in their counting. However, salvation is nowhere to be found.

For no logical reason, the same echoed in their minds: *ONE!*

TWO...

WITH GRATITUDE

This is where I should say thank you to so many people, but instead, I will tell you a quick story about what I am thankful for.

Writing the book was the biggest challenge in my life, and I can't say that life didn't do its best until now. I wrote this book for nine nights in a state of lockdown depression in December 2020. Writing it, I realised how unhappy I was with my life and how many changes I should make. However, my friends encouraged me to edit, translate and publish it. Thank you for your push. I can't be more grateful for sharing this life with you.

Then the Chapter One editing process showed me my hidden Fear of the possible bad evaluation. Chapter Fourteen's editing showed me that I am not capable of receiving compliments. Thank you for helping me see what to improve and reminding me what to be proud of.

It took almost two years to publish the book in English. I was to give up many times, and I am thankful that faith always found ways to bring amazing strangers who motivated and supported me on my journey. Thank you, faith, for being so kind to me.

While I am writing this, I realise that I am also thankful for:
Embracing Fear
Rediscovering Confidence

Listening to Reason
and mostly
Dealing better with The Monster
I am thankful to you for having this book in your hands. I hope you enjoyed Nia's reality and bizarre mind.

Until we start counting TWO, please leave your honest review to help the book reach new readers.

Visit www.authorkristinkay.com, where I share Nia's observations and conclusions about the general reality and awakening madness. She will provoke you to question - even more - the meaning of your own life, beliefs and fears.

Be part of the Angel's community and follow me on social media:
Instagram: @kristinkay.author

Ready to count to TWO? The second book is coming soon! Subscribe to my newsletter to get the official announcements about the book launch.

Sincerely yours,
Kristina